PILLARS OF HEAVEN
Leila Lyons

PUBLISHED BY POCKET BOOKS NEW YORK

A POCKET BOOKS/RICHARD GALLEN *Original* publication

**POCKET BOOKS, a Simon & Schuster division of
GULF & WESTERN CORPORATION
1230 Avenue of the Americas, New York, N.Y. 10020**

ISBN: 0-671-41266-3

First Pocket Books printing August, 1980

10 9 8 7 6 5 4 3 2 1

POCKET and colophon are trademarks of Simon & Schuster.

Printed in the U.S.A.

An Invitation to Heaven

"You needn't sleep on the bar, Luke. You can sleep in my room," said Sophie.

Luke glanced at Maddie's door and was unable to make up his mind. If Maddie found out, she was sure to raise holy hell.

Oh well. Maddie need never know.

Taking long steps, Luke began striding down the hall toward Sophie. She stepped aside to allow him to enter and as he did his body brushed hers. Something like an electricity charge passed through their bodies. They stopped and stared at one another. It was no longer a question of wrong or right. It was a question of compulsion.

To Lee . . .
blarney and all

In peace, Love tunes the shepherd's reed;
In war, he mounts the warrior's steed;
In halls, in gay attire is seen;
In hamlets, dances on the green.
Love rules the court, the camp, the grove,
And men below, and saints above;
For love is heaven, and heaven is love.

Sir Walter Scott

BOOK ONE

In 1848 came the event that forged an industry almost overnight. Gold was discovered in California, and the rush to mine it triggered the greatest mass migration in United States history. Suddenly San Francisco and other boomtowns needed lumber far beyond local woodsmen's capacities. At first, the wood came from far away, mostly from Maine by ship, but the irony of bringing lumber halfway around the globe to a land carpeted with the mightiest trees on earth was not lost on men of vision. Soon a new breed of American entrepreneurs rose up to build empires of wood from the forest of the Far West.

Two such men were Liam O'Sullivan and Rory Fitzpatrick. This is the story of their lives and their loves and of their children who were born in the shade of the pillars of heaven.

Chapter 1

"It's a Christmas card setting," Liam O'Sullivan mused as he gazed through the window of his office. The weather was so crisp that words hung in the air long after they had been spoken. On that day in February 1849, the populace of Belfast, Maine hurried through the biting cold and icy wind blowing in from Penoosco Bay. Huddled in wool greatcoats, massive fur caps pulled over their heads, they were unrecognizable. A mist of snowflakes swirled about the yard. Whether they were falling fresh from the dark gray sky or were being blown from their various resting places, Liam could not tell.

He sighed heavily. It was a melancholy sound. This was the last time he would be watching life as it passed by his office window. A group of small children played near the log run of the Belfast Lumber Company. They were so bundled up that Liam could not distinguish the boys from the girls. They were attempting to make

3

snow people from the very dry snow. One enterprising young lad had brought a bucket filled with icy water from the Bay and was employing it to sculpt his particular project—a muscular snowman patterned after the robust men of the lumber company. He was a darkly handsome child, sturdily built and exuberant. A patch of black hair protruded from his cap, shadowing dark eyes. Liam unconsciously brushed his own black hair aside. Were it not for the fact that Liam was not married, this boy might have been his own.

He recognized the child—the youngest of the Mulvany clan. But Liam could not recall the boy's name. Liam sighed again. Marriage and a family would have to wait. Business, after all, had to take precedence.

Not that Belfast was bereft of young women who were attracted to Liam and would have gladly said yes to a marriage proposal. Liam had dark, brooding good looks attractive to most women. His hair was thick, black and smooth as paint. Dominating his face were eyes so blue that they seemed to reflect nothing but the sky. His mouth, full and generous, kept him from appearing stern. But Liam's manner was taciturn and he had little interest in the frivolities of life. The mere idea of courting a young woman sent him into a cold sweat. Besides, the young women of Belfast did not interest him—save for one. And she was not yet of a marriageable age.

Liam returned to his ledger. A neat profit had been made for himself and his partner, Rory Fitzpatrick, by the sale of the timberland and the mill to the Mulvany family. He smiled with satisfaction as he roughly calculated that the property had garnered nearly five times the amount of the original investment. When a profit was turned, Liam quickly forgot about personal desires. He slammed the ledger shut, got up from his creaky chair and carried the ledger across the room to the wood-burning stove. Using a padded glove, he opened the door and laid the ledger on top of the banked coals. It caught fire immediately. The dancing flames highlighted Liam's face, which looked much older than its twenty-three years.

Liam watched while the entire ledger burned and began to disintegrate. He was a secretive person and had no intention of leaving such records lying about. Suddenly startled by a knock on the door, he closed the stove and strode to the door.

A blast of wind and snow preceding its visitor momentarily blinded him. A young girl stepped inside and quickly shut the door behind her. "Afternoon, Liam," she said and headed directly for the stove to warm herself.

Liam blinked away the snowflakes and smiled. "And how are you, Kathleen Mulvany?"

She shrugged and turned around, surveying the office. "Rory isn't here?" Her voice was soft and breathy as a breeze before a summer rain.

Liam frowned. "I'm the only one here." He had hoped that Kathleen had stopped in to say good-bye to him. He regarded her silently while she took off her tam o'shanter and shook down her hair. At fifteen, Kathleen Mulvany was becoming a beautiful woman. She was a striking colleen with wild Irish coloring. Her hair was so black and glossy that it looked kissed by the moonlight. Her skin was all cream and roses, and her huge blue-gray eyes flecked with green and amber shone like turquoise.

"Will Rory be coming back soon?" asked Kathleen breaking the spell.

Liam turned away and pretended to busy himself at his desk. "He's gone to the tavern," he replied offhandedly. "To have a farewell drink with some of the men."

"Oh!" Kathleen sat down in a chair, her face forlorn. "Then I don't imagine he'll be coming back here. I did so want to see him before . . ." Her voice broke. "Before the sailing."

"We're not leaving now till tomorrow morning. The weather is supposed to clear," remarked Liam tersely.

"A sensible decision," announced Kathleen in her not-quite-convincing worldly manner, which never failed to intrigue Liam. "Why do you have to go at all?" Suddenly she was a little girl again, held-back tears colored her voice.

"We must," said Liam gently. "We've exhausted the trees on our acreage."

"And now my father's bought your land and the mill," Kathleen bitterly continued, "leaving you and Rory free to go."

"It's the second time your pa has changed our lives. He allowed us to come and now he's allowing us to go. I even made a good profit. We have a seaworthy ship jammed with the final lengths of lumber. And, God willing, we'll do all right for ourselves in San Francisco."

"But it's such a dangerous trip!" Katherine was near to pleading.

"I have faith in Captain Fallon. He's rounded the Cape before. He'll get us there in one piece."

"This was your idea, wasn't it, Liam?" accused Kathleen. "I mean, Rory would have stayed. He couldn't want to go—to leave Belfast."

"There's nothing holding Rory here," replied Liam sharply, immediately regretting his words.

Kathleen jumped up from her chair. A wounded sound escaped from her lips as she dashed from the office.

"Kathleen, don't go!" Liam called out the door, but already she had disappeared into the fast falling snow.

Liam slammed the door shut and cursed his petty jealousy. Then he returned to his desk to continue his lonely task of sorting papers, thus ending his and Rory's life in Belfast, Maine.

Kathleen stood outside the Limerick Tavern trying to make herself inconspicuous. It was almost impossible to see through the amber panes of leaded glass.

Squinting, she searched the blurred forms for Rory's familiar figure. She did not see him, but that did not mean that he was not there. Gloveless—she had left them in the office, Kathleen thrust her hands into the pockets of her coat. Her left hand toyed with the small tissue-wrapped package—her farewell gift for Rory.

Kathleen was cold and had to come to a decision. She had never been inside the tavern; it was not a place for a young woman of morals. She shivered as the sharp wind penetrated her greatcoat. Morals or not, she would enter!

She pushed open the heavy oak door. Her nostrils were assaulted by a pungent odor—a mixture of beer, roasting meat and sweat. The aroma and the sudden warmth of the room dizzied her. Kathleen felt queasy. Oblivious to the stares of the patrons, she made her way to the bar and asked the bartender for a glass of water.

"Are you all right, Miss Mulvany?" the bartender asked with concern.

Kathleen recognized the man as a member of the church choir to which she belonged. Odd, she never realized he worked at the tavern. "I feel a bit faint, Paddy."

"I'll be givin' you a bit of brandy." Kathleen started to protest. "No, miss, it's what the good doctor would prescribe, I'm sure." Kathleen accepted the brandy and drank it down. "No, no, miss," said Paddy. "You're supposed to sip it."

The warming liquid rushed through Kathleen's body like a fever. All at once she felt happy and giddy. "I wonder if Rory Fitzpatrick has been here?" she asked boldly.

"Aye, miss, but he's gone home."

"Well, then, that's where I should take myself," said Kathleen sliding off the bar chair. "Thank you, Paddy, for the brandy. I feel much better now."

Paddy knitted his brow, unsure of the meaning of

Kathleen's words. Surely she meant to take herself to her own home and not to Rory's. That would be most unfortunate!

Kathleen dashed across the town square. The maple trees around the square were leafless, their branches stiff with ice and snow. Her footsteps made a soft crunching sound that was somehow comforting. The snow was so thick that Kathleen could barely see much ahead. But that didn't matter. She knew the way by heart.

Rory's small cabin was separated from Liam's two-story house by a growth of elm trees. Rory refused to live with Liam so that he might be free to "entertain" as he wished. Usually his cabin was filled with hard-drinking cronies. But that night Rory had only one guest—his mistress, Mary McGrath.

Kathleen reached the edge of the grove. She stopped to catch her breath, pulled her hands out of her pockets to blow on them and, in doing so, the present fell into the snow. She quickly knelt down to retrieve the article, digging into the snow with bare hands. The dye from the ribbon had stained the tissue paper, which was now wet. Kathleen tore off the wrapping and cast it aside. Her farewell present was a delicate wooden cross she had carved from a piece of oak. It was fastened to a thin chain of gold, which had been her mother's. She clutched the cross tightly in her hands for fear of losing it. Near tears and breathless, she reached Rory's cabin.

She stepped under the eaves to compose herself and heard laughter coming from within. Standing on the tips of her toes, Kathleen peered through the frost flowers on the curtainless window.

In front of the blazing fireplace of the main room was a large copper bathtub. Inside, facing one another, were Rory Fitzpatrick and Mary McGrath. Kathleen, riveted, sucked in her breath and narrowed her eyes. Surely there must be some mistake! It couldn't be her beloved Rory caressing that common Mary. Tears of hurt and anger filled her eyes, but she was unable to pull them away from the awful scene within.

Rory threw back his head and laughed at something Mary had said. He produced a bottle of rum, drank heartily from it and handed it to her. He was a lusty, brawling young man with an expressive, athletic body. His hair was a mass of aggressive auburn curls, and his nose was broad and lightly spattered with freckles. Rory laughed again, crinkling his eyes which were pale blue—the quintessence of an Irish heritage. His mobile sensuous mouth never seemed to rest. Even with other features totally relaxed, his mouth carried on a life of its own, curling upward in sly amusement or in pleasure. Rory was immensely attracted to women and never failed to take advantage of a ripe situation. Women, particularly of Mary's class, liked his rough manners, his gregarious masculinity and the easy way blasphemies rolled off his tongue.

Rory retrieved the bottle from Mary and stood up in the tub. Kathleen was shocked and at the same time thrilled. He waved the bottle about and bellowed so loudly that even Kathleen could hear him despite the howling wind.

"Here's to the best little piece in Belfast!"

Mary's broad, ruddy face broke into a wicked grin. She began laughing, her huge breasts bobbing on top of the water like summer melons.

Kathleen could watch no more. Her feelings crushed, she ran blindly through the elm grove. She threw herself against a snow bank and lay there sobbing.

Liam, deep in melancholy after his long evening of closing out the books, trudged homeward through the snow. The sight of a body huddled against a snowbank bordering his grove shook him from reverie. "My God!" he muttered to himself, stumbling and hurrying through the drifts to the still figure. "Just on the eve of our sailing! What kind of bad luck—"

Liam stopped in his tracks, dazed when he recognized the blue greatcoat, the orange tam o'shanter barely covering the black locks, now sodden from melting snow. "Kathleen!" Liam cried and stumbled forward, reaching her on his knees. He touched Kathleen's shoulders and through the cold and wet cloth he felt her shudder and sob and pull close to him. Liam gathered her up in his arms.

"Liam," she said softly in a faraway voice and pressed her face against his broad shoulder.

He carried her directly to his house. "Mrs. Flanagan . . . Mrs. Flanagan!" Liam called as he entered.

The housekeeper, a gentle woman of middle age, came bustling out of the kitchen. "Saints preserve us, Mr. Liam! I've been keeping supper hot for sometime. What—what have you got there?"

"It's Kathleen Mulvany. I'm afraid she's fallen in the snow. Please fetch some warm blankets and make her a pot of strong tea."

Mrs. Flanagan hurried out of the room as Liam set Kathleen in a high-backed chair next to the fireplace in the parlor. He pulled the chair closer to the fire and removed her wet boots. Mrs. Flanagan returned with the blankets and a tray of tea things. After helping Kathleen out of her wet coat, they wrapped her in the blankets and Liam fed her the tea while Mrs. Flanagan hung her coat up to dry.

"I can do it, Liam," said Kathleen, taking the tea cup from him. "I'm all right, really I am."

Liam didn't query the young girl about the situation. He sensed that she had found his younger partner and that something had happened to upset her. Perhaps Rory had been drunk, or even worse, had ignored her. Kathleen wouldn't be the first female to have her heart broken by Rory Fitzpatrick.

While Kathleen had several more cups of the bracing tea, the blazing fire had dried her greatcoat and her boots.

"I'm going to walk you home," said Liam, putting on his own coat.

"No, really," protested Kathleen. "You've already been so kind."

"I insist," replied Liam bruskly. "There have been reports of timber wolves."

Kathleen smiled enigmatically but said nothing.

The snow had stopped falling and the wind had died down. A quarter moon hung in the starless sky like a thin slice of lemon. The bushes lining the path bowed low under the heavy snow as if in supplication to Kathleen and Liam. They walked at an easy pace, each lost in their own thoughts.

When they reached the Mulvany home, Kathleen wanted Liam to come inside, but he protested. "I don't like long good-byes, Kathleen."

"Will I ever see you again, Liam?"

Her words cut through him. "I don't know."

"Here's a cross I made," she said, and pressed it into his hands. "I want you to have it to remember me by." Then she quickly kissed him on the lips.

Liam knew the gift had been meant for Rory. "It's beautiful, Kathleen—like yourself."

Her eyes filled with tears, but before they could overflow, she slipped inside the house. Liam stood on the porch for a long time turning the cross over in his hand. He was profoundly touched.

At six thirty the next morning Rory appeared at Liam's house with Mary on his arm. "Mornin', Miz F.!", Rory swayed and gestured his greeting.

Mrs. Flanagan was scandalized and speechless. This is the first time he's brought one of them "loose women" here, she thought. And both of them drunk, too! She turned away with a silent prayer in her heart. It would be the last morning she would be making breakfast for "her boys."

Liam heard the commotion downstairs, punctuated

by Mary's raucous voice. Who besides Rory could be calling at such an early hour? Just before putting on his cambric shirt, crisply ironed by Mrs. Flanagan, he hung Kathleen's cross around his neck. The delicate piece nestled in the profuse black hair of his chest. Liam crossed himself and continued dressing.

When he had finished he carried several canvas bags packed with clothes and personal articles down the stairs.

"Mornin', Liam," greeted Rory, his face flushed with liquor.

"Mornin'," echoed Mary timidly. Her large cow eyes stared at the floor.

"Good morning," replied Liam gruffly. Unlike Mrs. Flanagan he was not going to conceal his displeasure at Mary's presence.

Mrs. Flanagan wept intermittently as she prepared a huge breakfast of coffee, corn bread, smoked halibut, bacon and eggs plus an assortment of her own jellies and preserves. She had quickly added a place setting in the small dining room to accommodate Mary. She prayed to her favorite saint, St. Anthony, that Liam would not "get his Irish up" over the girl.

Breakfast was a strained affair marked by Liam's icy disapproval, Mrs. Flanagan's flights to the kitchen to weep and Mary's maudlin wails of losing "the best goddamn man a girl ever had!" Rory, oblivious to the combustible atmosphere he had created, ate heartily and joked about the imminent voyage. "I hope Captain Fallon has got the *Connemara* in shipshape. Sure wouldn't want to swim all the way to San Francisco."

"San Francisco," wailed Mary, "that's the other side of the world! What am I going to do without you, Rory?"

He plucked her under her ample chin and replied, "Just keep doin' what you're doin', Mary, till I get back. Believe me, you'll make a lot of men very happy." He turned to Mrs. Flanagan who was leaning against the wall biting her lip. "Any more eggs, Mrs. Flanagan? I could eat me two or three more."

The housekeeper sniffed in a great linen handkerchief and shambled into the kitchen.

By seven thirty both Liam and Rory were ready to leave. Rory hitched the gelding to a two-seater sleigh. He, Liam, Mrs. Flanagan and Mary, sitting on and around a variety of luggage, left for the Belfast harbor. The morning air was crisp and the sky as clear as a sheet of blue paper. Many of the townspeople yelled wishes of good luck from porches and windows.

The harbor was shrouded in fog, which was rapidly burned away by the bright morning sun. The *Connemara,* a hundred and forty ton brig, sat majestically in the Bay awaiting their arrival. Captain Fallon stood on the forecastle puffing impatiently on his clay pipe. He was a crusty old man of the sea who firmly believed that one was never too old for adventure. Troll-like, he had a full flowing beard white and foamy as a wave cap. He ordered two crewmen to help Liam and Rory with their luggage and then spouted orders to prepare the *Connemara* for sailing. Captain Fallon would not dillydally when the sea beckoned.

The women cried profusely. Mrs. Flanagan, forgetting her prejudices, held Mary tightly as they comforted one another. Liam and Rory, anxious to get underway, hurried up the gangplank. The sails were unfurled and billowed like the bellies of pregnant brides. Liam and Rory stood side by side on the deck and watched the shoreline slip away. Hidden in the shadows of the pier, Kathleen's tears flowed in profusion. She watched the *Connemara* sail away from Belfast, cutting neatly through the foamy waves, its nine white sails growing smaller and smaller.

"Odd," Kathleen thought to herself, remembering her own games and play as she became once again the fifteen-year old, "it looks like a toy ship without a bottle."

Chapter 2

Rory leaned against the cabin door, picking an imaginary bit of lint from his elegant sleeve. "Why are we stopping in New York harbor? And why take on thirty-four passengers and freight?"

Liam looked up from his account book. "There's no need to let the cabin space go to waste. Besides, the cost of their passage would pay for what the *Connemara* is costing us. And why do you think I put in such a stock of vittles, Rory? And hired a cook, and all that? Just for you and the crew?"

"To tell you the truth, Liam," Rory grinned, "I didn't think about it at all. Thirty-four, eh? Any women to be aboard?"

"A few." replied Liam quickly. "But I want to warn you Rory I don't want any . . ."

"Same old Liam," Rory interrupted. "Always trying to keep me a virgin, like himself!" Laughing, Rory sauntered away to explore the ship and make friends with the crew.

Liam shook his head, knowing he would never change his young friend. He turned his attention toward the sea. The sound of the waves slapping against the hull was hypnotic. The sunlight dancing on the wave crest blurred Liam's vision. He found himself recalling the passage from Ireland that he and Rory had endured three years earlier.

The passage had been terrible, but not nearly so terrible as what they were leaving.

In 1845 and 1846 the potato crop had failed in Ireland. It was a country of starving, homeless paupers. People were frightful to behold. The skin of the starved ones was rough and dry like parchment. People walked with bloated empty belly thrust out and shoulder blades thrust high and off balance. The hair of adults thinned on their heads, but in children it grew awry. Ofttimes a new growth of downy hair would sprout on the brow, giving them a ghostly or beastly look. Running sores, pustulant and bleeding, grew between fingers and toes. No amount of bandaging could stop the putrid fluids.

Starving folks suddenly became cheerful just before they died. They sat up from their lice-infested bundle of rags, chatted with their nearest companions, cracked jokes and recalled good times. Then abruptly they died. Abruptly they fell dead. The streets were littered with the dying and the dead. People collapsed and lay unattended, a froth of green at their mouths from eating the only food available—soft Irish grass.

Wild dogs roamed the countryside, feeding upon the dead and the near dead. At Dundee the local police shot and killed a pack of marauding canines, and in the mouth of one was a heart and part of a human liver. In the same town a man was seen carrying the body of his child and begging money to buy a coffin. He begged from beggars, and collected only a few pence. He buried his child himself without coffin or shroud.

In the village of Tralee in Munster County, the households of the O'Sullivans and the Fitzpatricks had been hard hit by the famine. Nearly all of the youngest and eldest of both families had died. Both cottages, next door to one another, rang with the unending mournful keening of the survivors.

The death wagon appeared regularly. It escorted the wasted, waxen bodies encased in cheap pine coffins stained with lampblack to the church cemetery. By coincidence the family plots of the O'Sullivans and the Fitzpatricks were side by side. A barrage of tombstones, crudely carved from wooden planks, populated the gravesite. Some of the death dates were only days apart. There were no flowers planted upon the graves, no grass sown. And those who mourned stayed away, not out of contempt but out of fear.

Their cups of weak tea raised in unison, the recently widowed matriarchs of the families, Fiona Fitzpatrick and Molly O'Sullivan, sat in Molly's kitchen and contemplated the situation. Something had to be done to save what was left of the families. Fiona sipped the tea, unconsciously made a face and said in a sad lilting voice, "I miss my husband's hands, Molly, more than his laughter or his body, I miss Kerry's hands."

Molly O'Sullivan, not so outspoken about her marital intimacies, blushed as red as a sugar beet. "Yes, I miss Tomas, too," she admitted. "But after all, Fiona, our men have been put to rest and we've got to make plans for the future."

"What future is there for we Irish?" replied Fiona with a toss of auburn curls. "I don't know which is worse, the English or the famine. Make plans? I'm so cried out I can't even organize the next minute."

Molly, a black-haired beauty whose recent tragedies had etched her lovely face with deep lines of pain, shook her head. "We can't give up so easily, Fiona. I hear there are ships leaving from Liverpool bound for Quebec."

"Canada?" Molly nodded. "I wouldn't have the strength to make the crossing, Molly."

Molly slammed her tea cup on the table with impatience. "I don't mean us, Fiona! I mean our sons. Our lines must continue. We owe that to Kerry and Tomas. And there's nothing here for our boys except despair! Being under the heels of the English will never grant them any peace of mind or a proper vocation."

"Rory? Liam? You mean, send them away, Molly?"

"Aye. It's the best that we can do for them. Liam and Rory are our eldest. Despite everything, they're still sturdy. And only the sturdiest of voyagers will be accepted. There's prejudice against the Irish because of the emigration ships carrying the typhus."

"The tipes," Fiona shuddered, using the slang name for the disease. "There's a case broke out in Killarney."

"Yes, and there'll be more. What are we going to do, Fiona? Sit around, sipping tea, doing nothing—while even our eldest sons continue to be in danger?"

"But why the eldest?"

"They're the strongest. We've got to be practical. Fiona. Little Molly and Kevin, my very own, may not survive this terrible thing. They're both sick and hungry, as I know your youngest are. Liam and Rory still have strength. They could withstand the voyage and then, God willing we survive, the day will come when we will join them."

"And how do we get the money to provide them with the passage, Molly? Are you suggesting we offer ourselves to the English soldiers?"

Molly's face reddened again, but in anger not embarrassment. "Oh, pray God, Fiona! We've both got our valuables. We've talked about them often enough!"

"My silver brooch? Your gold crucifix?"

"Exactly."

"Molly, that silver brooch was a wedding present from Kerry. And that crucifix! Why, that's been in your family for generations! We must hold on to these things. They're all we've got left!"

"They're things, Fiona! *Things!* We've got to hold on to our sons' lives—and our lives." Molly's tone was adamant. "We must sell the articles, Fiona, and use the money wisely."

Fiona looked perplexed. "But where would they go? You say to Quebec?"

"Only because that's the best place for the Irish to enter. I've been in touch with the Mulvanys. You remember the Mulvanys." Fiona nodded. "Well, they've settled in Belfast, Maine. That's near the Canadian border. They're working in a lumber mill— owned by an Irishman!" Molly added with pride. "And the whole settlement is mostly Irish. They'd have friends there. They could get work."

"The Mulvanys would be willing to help them?" asked Fiona dubiously.

"Aye, they would. But first we've got to get them there."

"It's a mad plan you're dreamin', Molly O'Sullivan."

"No madder than death," replied Molly.

The items were sold in secrecy to English soldiers at a great loss. But the money provided the necessary clothing, food and passage across the Atlantic. There was only one problem left: convincing Liam and Rory that they should go. The young men protested violently when they were told of their mothers' plan. Neither of them wanted to leave Ireland. It would be cowardice to do so since they were, as eldest sons, the heads of their respective households. Finally, Liam was able to see the sense of it, bound as he was by his mother's— Molly's—sense of destiny. In turn, he convinced Rory.

After tearful farewells and vows that as soon as they had earned the money their mothers and younger brothers and sisters would follow, the young men started their journey to Liverpool. They had to travel by foot since there was not enough money for a horse and wagon. The highways were crowded with destitute Irish, many of them carrying smallpox and fever. The entire countryside smelled of death. Liam and Rory were suddenly glad to be going—to leave the starvation, the keening, the endless parades to the graveyards behind them. But neither one admitted his thoughts to the other.

That June 1846, deaths by fever increased twentyfold in Liverpool. It had been termed a "City of the Plague." As Liam and Rory approached the city, they encountered many who were fleeing. By cart, horseback and foot, the panicked citizens of Liverpool swarmed across the countryside hoping to avoid death.

On the first day and night of the journey Liam and Rory kept a brisk pace, averting their eyes and thoughts from the surroundings. They stopped silently to renew energies and went on again in unison. The march was broken by Rory who, quickly adjusting to danger and losing all wariness, stopped by the roadside to pump hope into the unfortunate folk stranded there as he passed.

Liam, mindful of his mother's hope—indeed her command for a new life, pulled Rory sharply away from his mission. "What's wrong with you? Don't you know there are highwaymen just waiting for people like us carrying money? Do you want our throats slit? We can't stop and talk to anyone!"

Rory, sensing the truth vaguely but enjoying the adventure of the situation, responded eagerly. "You're right! And we can't rest unguarded. We'll take turns sleeping and standing watch. My fists are ready!"

Liam and Rory arrived in Liverpool twelve days after they started their journey. Liverpool was a city under siege. Fever-crazed victims wandered the streets begging for food or drink or medicine. Homeless children, eyes wide and staring, roved in bands, attacking the weak and elderly, stealing what food or money they possessed. Prostitutes, thin as reeds, drooped in doorways, offering favors for a crust of bread. Shops, taverns, inns were closed. Business was at a standstill, except at the docks where throngs of people gathered hoping to get on ships bound for Canada and America. The immigration officials were stringent. Only the healthiest passengers were taken, and Liam and Rory were among them. They were booked on a vessel named the *Perseverence*. It looked less than seaworthy, but it was nonetheless bound for Quebec.

Liam and Rory were crowded into a section of the hold designated for male passengers. They slept side by side on a berth meant for one. For the first ten days of the voyage they were violently seasick. They were both lucky to be on an upper berth, and their only exchanges were jokes about the unlucky folk in the lower berth bombarded with the retching of those above.

By the eleventh day at sea, Liam and Rory were able to tolerate the vile water and rotting food. Stale bread and cheese kept them alive. By the morning of the thirteenth day they were able to take a shaky stroll around the deck. The vastness of the ocean awed them and also made them somewhat fearful about the ship's ability to get them to Quebec safely. They chatted with one of the sailors who assured them that the *Perseverence* had made the trip many times and would make it many times more. When the sailor was out of earshot, Rory remarked. "I wish I had his confidence."

Liam nodded in agreement. "I, too, shall be most surprised if we survive this voyage."

Halfway across the Atlantic typhus broke out on board the *Perseverence*. Typhus was a disease of the blood vessels, the brain and the skin. Liam and Rory were all too familiar with its symptoms: shivering, headaches, congested face, bloodshot eyes, muscular twitching, and a stupid stare as if the sufferer were drunk. The skin darkened, and on about the fifth day a rash came out and the delirium became a stupor. It was a disease greatly encouraged by starvation, filth and overcrowding.

More than a third of the crowded Irish emigrants on

the *Perseverence* became ill. The first to die was a three-and-a-half-year old child. There were no doctors on board, and the victims were restricted to their stifling quarters by Captain Fallon. The dead were quickly wrapped in canvas and thrown overboard by emigrant volunteers. Liam and Rory helped. No prayers were said over the victims.

The *Perseverence* passed the three-quarter mark in its crossing of the Atlantic and headed toward the St. Lawrence River and Grosse Isle. Everyone who was able watched for sight of land. Liam found Rory staggering about on deck as if he were inebriated. Liam ran across the slippery planks in time to catch Rory before he collapsed.

"I'm not drunk, Liam," Rory grinned. "I swear to God, I'm not."

Gathering Rory up in his strong arms, Liam vowed, "Don't worry, Rory. I'll take care of you."

The destiny of the O'Sullivans and the Fitzpatricks lay heavy on Liam's soul as he cradled the pale, auburn-haired boy who had been his neighbor, playmate and—by their mothers' determination—almost near kin. He carried Rory into their crowded quarters in the hold.

Liam nursed Rory as best he could, keeping him warm when he had the chills, changing his clothes when they became soaked with perspiration and feeding him a salty beef boullion. One experienced passenger explained that the secret to Rory's survival was to get him to live on until the fever broke. It was a game Liam learned to play.

"Rory, Rory," Liam tried to make the youth hold on to happy memories. "Remember when Molly yelled at us when we used the pine branches as a slingshot? She always said it would boomerang on us. But it never did. And Fiona hid her eyes!"

Then, urging Rory to think of the marvelous things America had to offer, Liam talked of the future.

"Rory, we'll make our way in the new land. And we'll have a new self-respect. We will be able to send for the rest of our families. We will all be together again."

Liam forced himself to play the game, and continued to pray fervently to the Holy Father, the Virgin Mary and all the saints in heaven for his friend's recovery.

On Tuesday, August 27, at nine in the morning, the *Perseverence* reached Grosse Isle. It was not the only emigrant ship in the harbor. There were three others and each of them was infected with typhus. The authorities in Montreal and Quebec City stipulated that the ships had to remain in quarantine, but the ill could be admitted into hospitals. Rory was taken to a makeshift hospital in a bell tent filled with beds. Liam stayed at his side, sleeping on the canvas-covered earth next to his friend's bed.

Rory was in a vague mental state quite unaware of his surroundings. His pulse varied from a high of one hundred-thirty to a low of thirty-five.

Liam had become increasingly alarmed. It seemed that little could be done for Rory by the doctors or attendants that he himself could not do. He feared leaving his friend in the stinking tent a day longer, and decided to take matters into his own hands.

Using a bit of the money that was left, Liam bribed a guard and was able to purchase a small wagon and a mule. He loaded Rory into the back of the wagon and hid him under canvas. The guard allowed Liam to leave the island. Liam drove directly to Quebec City and purchased a quantity of limes and other provisions. He continued on to the outskirts of the city until he discovered a secluded spot near a fresh spring. He forced a mixture of spring water and lime juice upon Rory, making him drink as much as a pint an hour. For three days they remained there, and for three days and three nights Liam forced the health-giving mixture on his delirious friend.

Toward dawn of the fourth day Liam awoke to hear

Rory calling his name. Liam crawled out from under the bed of the wagon and went to Rory.

"Liam," Rory asked in a weak voice. "Where are we? Are we back in Ireland?"

Liam placed a hand upon Rory's brow. The fever had broken at last. "No, Rory, we're not in Ireland. We're in Canada. And soon we'll be in America. We've survived the first leg of our journey."

They found a farmer and his wife who put them up and fed them for a small price. Liam wrote a letter to the Mulvanys in Belfast, Maine, and hoped it would reach them before they did. The farmer's wife took a liking to the handsome young men, and her fine cooking soon brought Rory to his feet. By mid-September Rory and Liam were ready to travel. Taking a ship was out of the question. There was a danger of reinfection as well as the growing prejudice against the Irish. Many of the coastal states kept the ships from docking. They would have to travel on the Overland Trail. Liam purchased another mule from the farm couple. Armed with a Bible, a rifle and a strong conviction about their future, the young men set out for Belfast, Maine.

Chapter 3

The veins and the arteries of the morning stretched out against the gray sky, spreading color and life into the day. Seagulls dipped and swooped over the waters, searching for food and calling to one other with harsh cries. The *Connemara* was coming into New York Harbor.

New York was the third largest city in the Western world, rivaled only by London and Paris. It was the largest port and most thriving city in the United States of America. Excited as children, Rory and Liam stood on deck and watched with wonder as Captain Fallon rudely commanded his crew and deftly guided the *Connemara* around much grander ships and into an allotted berth at the north end of the wharf.

Liam and Rory were the first to disembark, eager to stretch their legs on solid ground. The waterfront was alive with activity. Scores of ships were being loaded or unloaded by dockhands, and all races seemed to be represented—sloe-eyed Orientals, swarthy Italians, pale blond Scandinavians. The docks were jammed with people sitting on boxes, standing in groups and moving back and forth in a raucous dance of life. A woman's husky voice sang out advertising sweetcakes for sale.

The young men were confused by the movements, the noises and smells. They were accosted by panhandlers, beggars, street sellers, prostitutes. Liam's face froze when a frowzy, rouged woman made obscene overtures to himself and to Rory. Rory laughed heartily, slapped the woman on the backside and promised he would look for her later. Liam merely retreated into the shadows. They walked along the waterfront, marveling at the bustling spirit of the robust people. They passed stalls filled with the first catch of the sea—mussels, shrimp and mackerel. Here and there groups of ragged children hovered about cans of burning trash, fidgeting to keep warm. Liam wondered who they belonged to and thought sadly of his own brothers and sisters.

Even though there was snow on windowsills and roofs, there was none on the streets or the docks; it had been worn away by the surging crowds. The wind was stinging. It swept down the street, carrying loose snowflakes of litter. Rory suggested they go into a waterfront tavern and have a warming drink. Liam agreed without argument, but warned, "We can't stay long. We must check in at the harbor office and see that the goods and passengers are properly taken care of."

"Always diligent Liam." Rory laughed. "Ho, here's a likely spot."

They entered the Mermaid's Tail, and each ordered a hot rum from the bartender. As they sipped the warming drinks, they surveyed the sleazy tavern. Persistent whores were still doing business at that hour of the morning, provocatively wiggling tired hips at bleary-eyed sailors. A sudden fight broke out and was quickly ended. Obscenities punctuated conversations. A sailor pushed through the heavy doors, slumped into a chair and threw up all over a table. A heavily rouged, slack-breasted Oriental tart offered him her wares.

Anxious to get out of the tavern, Liam downed his drink and urged Rory to hurry. Rory wanted to stay and observe the scenery, but Liam did not trust him out of his sight. Reluctantly Rory agreed, and together they went to the harbor office.

For a price the purser from the office assembled the freight and passengers for the *Connemara* and assured Liam he would see that everything would be taken care of in proper fashion. He directed the men to a nearby hotel for the "better class of traveler." Liam inspected the hotel and after being satisfied that it was clean, safe and free of bugs, they checked in and immediately ordered hot baths. After bathing and changing their clothes, they went to the hotel dining room and ate a hearty breakfast, which even Liam had to admit was good.

"I don't know why we can't remain in New York for a few days, Liam." Rory complained. "It may be the only chance we'll get to see the sights."

Liam's face darkened. "I know what kind of sights you want to be seein'," he replied tersely. "But we have a schedule to maintain. Captain Fallon tells me if we delay even a week, he will not answer for the turbulent weather we'll encounter as we round the Cape."

"I don't know how that old man can predict weather thousands of miles away." Rory pouted but, as usual, submitted to his older friend's decision.

The paying passengers were gathered around the gangplank from the *Connemara*. Their suitcases and boxes were strewn about like refuse. For the most part the passengers were as rough and grimy as the harbor itself. Twenty-six of the men were going to California to pan for gold; the remaining one was a preacher intent upon saving souls. There were seven women; five were seeking husbands in the womanless land. Liam and Rory noted that these five were the plainest women they had ever seen.

The other two female passengers were completely different and stood apart like a rare species of flowers in a patch of weeds. The white woman was named Sophie Parmalee. Accompanying Sophie was her maid-servant, a black woman of indeterminate age named Betzy Bedamned—a surname she had given herself.

Sophie Parmalee was twenty and deceptively fragile looking due to her pale skin and light blond hair. Her face was perfectly oval, a frame for two large, luminous green eyes. She was deftly made up and wore a strong fragrance, which caused people to turn their heads and sniff at the air. She was not tall—only five foot three—but her well proportioned figure and sure bearing made her seem taller than she was. Sophie was wearing an emerald green satin dress cinched tightly at the waist and cut much too low for the inclement weather. The dress had a bell-shaped skirt and was decorated on its lower part and bodice with bands of lilac lace. Over the dress she wore a lightweight coat of black wool trimmed with black satin piping. She was hatless and gloveless, but carried a matching parasol.

The black woman was an impressive figure. Nearly six feet tall, she towered over her mistress. She wore a dark gray cotton dress, a black cape and a black felt hat with a wilted flower perched on its brim. Her face was round and jovial, but at the same time showed a quiet determination. Her eyes were bright and inquisitive, and her nose quite broad and flat. When she smiled, her dark red lips revealed brilliant white teeth with a gap between each of them.

Sophie and Betzy stood apart from the others, chatting in low murmuring tones. Their luggage consisted of twelve matching pieces, each a veritable boxed garden of pink and yellow flowers on a dusty rose background.

The crew of the *Connemara* forsook their duties to lean over the railing and gawk at the beautiful young woman and her ominous servant. Male passengers cast furtive glances at Sophie, and whispered wishful thoughts to one another. The preacher, a cadaverous man in his mid-forties, strutted and spouted biblical catch phrases. The five women clustered together like a flock of gray sparrows and made comments in disapproving nods and tones.

Sophie was aware of the commotion she was causing, but she acted blissfully unaware. Twirling her parasol first to the left and then to the right, she allowed herself to glance at the bridge of the ship. The parasol abruptly stopped turning, and she found herself staring directly into the eyes of Liam O'Sullivan.

Sophie, whose taste in men ran toward Liam's physical type, was momentarily stunned. She couldn't remember ever seeing such a handsome man in all her experience. Liam broke the gaze by suddenly looking away, his face, a mask of indifference. Rory joined his friend on deck just in time to see Sophie and Betzy march up the gangplank. "Sweet Jesus in heaven," he whispered to Liam. "I've never seen anything so beautiful in my life!"

As she stepped on board, Sophie looked up, fluttered her painted lashes and flashed a smile at both men. Liam did not return her smile, but Rory, grinning self-consciously, bowed low. Sophie stood still for a moment and once again contemplated Liam's dark good looks. She was surprised to find no reaction. Just as Rory was about to introduce himself, a flirtatious sailor offered to show the women to their quarters. Sophie swept by, trailed by Betzy. The young woman's scent remained in the air long after she had departed.

"What's her name?" Rory asked, his breath coming in little gulps.

Liam scanned the passenger list and replied.

"There's only one woman listed as having a maid. It's Sophie Parmalee."

"Sophie Parmalee," Rory repeated. "It sounds like something sweet you'd spread on bread and eat."

Liam was upset but managed to conceal it. Sophie was obviously a woman of easy virtue. Noting the dazed expression on Rory's face, he foresaw problems.

Chapter 4

The voyage from Cape Horn to San Francisco was an arduous one: eighteen thousand nautical miles in four to eight months. Such a voyage was naturally forbidding. Much had been written about the terrifying rounding of the Cape. The contrary gales, mountainous seas and frigid cold were enough to make the most adventurous of men think twice before venturing forth. Captain Fallon, who had made this journey several times, scoffed at the faint-hearted and assured nervous passengers and the novice crew that guiding the *Connemara* through the treacherous Strait of Magellan was "less an act of god, and more an act of man."

Sophie, upon finding that Liam and Rory were the owners of the ship, decided that Liam was definitely a man worth pursuing. The cabin she shared with Betzy was just down the corridor from those occupied by Liam and Rory. It would be an easy matter to "accidentally" run into the darkly attractive man.

Sophie planned her strategy, staying in her cabin the first few days at sea to make certain she was not going to suffer from seasickness. That would be *so* unattractive! Her absence would give Mr. O'Sullivan, the other male passengers and crew members a chance to wonder about the mysterious Miss Parmalee.

Betzy, outspoken as a parrot, expressed her disapproval of the whole affair while washing out her mistress's "dainties" in a small washtub brought along for just that purpose. She watched Sophie out of the corner of her hooded eyes and frowned. Sophie, wrapped in a pink chiffon dressing gown trimmed in ostrich feathers, was spread out on her bunk like a whipped confection. Her face was screwed up in an intense expression as she carefully enameled her toenails. "I think *he'll* like pink better than the red after all," she said more to herself than to Betzy.

Betzy sniffed loudly, a clear and understood sign of disapproval. Sophie looked up sharply and pursed her lips. "Hah! I say hah to your goddamn opinion!"

Betzy tilted her head to one side. "An' what makes yo' think dat man is ever goin' to see yo' toenails? Why he ain't even looked at de rest of yo'."

Sophie reddened with anger and swung her shapely legs off the bed. She stood up and began pacing the floor of the cabin. "That's all you know. He's interested all right. I can tell." Betzy sighed and went back to the washing.

"He's just a little shy, that's all. He'll come around." Sophie kicked up her leg and pirouetted. "Just think, Betzy, the owner of a ship! Why, one of the sailors, the one who showed us to our cabin, told me that the hold is just crammed full of lumber and that lumber is more precious than gold in San Francisco!"

"We ain't in San Francisco yet," grunted Betzy, who was positive the *Connemara* was doomed.

Sophie decided it was time to appear on deck, particularly since Liam hadn't inquired about her. She opened a trunk and began digging through her flashy clothing trying to decide what would be suitable for her debut. She settled on a lavender frock with a scooped neckline and bell sleeves. As she pulled it out of the trunk, Betzy exclaimed. "Yo' can't wear dat, Miz Sophie. Yo' catch yo' death of cold."

"Nonsense, I'll wear my cape with the hood. I'm not all *that delicate*, Betzy."

"I sure knows dat."

Betzy helped Sophie dress and arrange her hair, parting it in the middle and curling the ends slightly so that it fell seductively around her nearly bare shoulders. Sophie surveyed herself in a length of mirror and pronounced, "He'll notice me today, Betzy."

"I sure hope so, Miz Sophie," replied Betzy and she meant it. When Sophie didn't get her way, she was a terror to live with.

"I'm going up on deck."

"Yo' better put on a scarf, Miz Sophie, or yo' get a sore throat."

"Hells bells, Betzy, I'm hardier than that!"

When Sophie stepped out of the passageway and out onto the deck, a sharp gust of wind hit her nearly turning her around. "Damn," she muttered and grabbed hold of the railing to steady herself. "Damn it!"

"Pardon me, ma'm?" asked a man who was leaning against the railing. Sophie glanced at him. He was one of the male passengers. His beard was unkempt and his clothes smelled of sweat.

"Nothing," replied Sophie quickly with a toss of her head, as she moved away from him. Sophie wasn't about to spend five whole months without a man, but an itinerant laborer wasn't what she had in mind.

Farther down the deck Sophie encountered several passengers leaning over the railing and throwing up. She groaned in disgust and lurched in the opposite direction toward the forecastle. The wind had blown her hood from her head, and she could feel that it was rapidly undoing the curls Betzy had labored over so diligently.

Liam saw her coming. In spite of himself, he smiled and thought, so she has an eye for me, does she? Well, I've seen too many women like her in my life. There's nothing to be gained from knowing them except a brief good time and not always that. He turned away from Sophie and busied himself watching the sailors climb the rigging. He could smell her perfume before he felt her presence.

"Why good afternoon, Mr. O'Sullivan," said Sophie in mock surprise.

Liam slowly turned around, his face expressionless. "May I help you, Miss Parmalee?" he asked in a bland, businesslike tone.

Sophie was flustered. She was not used to men treating her indifferently. "Why—why," she gasped, "I wanted to take a walk around the deck but the wind's so strong I'm afraid I'll just get blown away."

Liam suppressed a smile at Sophie's obvious ploy. "Then I would suggest you stay in your cabin, Miss Parmalee."

Sophie was stunned. She stood there for a few minutes with her mouth slack before she realized that she was staring at Liam's back. The color rose in her cheeks like mercury in a thermometer. "Mr. O'Sullivan," she sputtered, "you are no gentleman."

Liam swung around and, smiling through his teeth, replied. "And you, Miss Parmalee, are no lady."

Betzy looked up as Sophie trounced into the cabin slamming the door behind her. "Help me undress," Sophie snapped.

"How was yo' walk, Miz Sophie?" Betzy ventured.

"That bastard isn't normal."

"Who yo' mean, Miz Sophie?" asked Betzy knowing full well.

"That dark-haired lout. Why he doesn't even have

good manners!'' Sophie lay down on her bed in her petticoats and corset. She tried to fluff up the lumpy mattress as much as possible and said irritably, "I declare, Betzy, I'll be covered with bruises by the time we get to San Francisco.'' She closed her eyes dramatically, "I'm going to rest now, Betzy. It's been a most exhausting day.''

"How about dinner, Miz Sophie?''

"I don't think I'm up to going to the dining room. Perhaps you'd bring me a little something on a tray.''

After hanging up Sophie's clothes, Betzy wrapped a heavy scarf around her head in turban fashion and put on her black cape. As she closed the cabin door behind her, she mimicked, "Maybe yo' could bring me somethin' on a tray.'' The large black woman ambled onto the deck, gazed at the rolling sea with distrust and kept to the opposite side of the railing. She didn't know what she was doing out there. She felt much safer in the cabin. She watched with amazement as the sailors climbed up and down the rigging like monkeys in a tree.

Betzy was hanging on to the looped ropes around the mizzenmast when she heard someone speak to her. "Hello!'' Betzy started and looked over her shoulder. It was the younger of the two shipowners, the one with hair like a brushfire. "I was wondering if your mistress was well?'' asked Rory. "I haven't seen her on deck or in the dining room.''

Betzy closed her eyes and tried to recall what Sophie had told her to say. "Oh, she all right, Mister. She just takin' care not to expose . . . expose her throat to de wind.'' Rory looked puzzled and Betzy continued her recitation. "Miz Sophie's a singer an' singers dey got to be careful with de voice.''

"Is that so?'' replied Rory impressed. "Did she sing in New York?''

"Oh, yes, sir,'' replied Betzy quickly. "In all de best places. Dat why we goin' to San Francisco. Cause she done get an offer dat she couldn't refuse.''

"Now that's really something." remarked Rory. "Is the sun hurting your eyes?"

Betzy snapped her eyes open and, her story complete, began to relax. "No, sir. I guess I just don't like lookin' at de sea."

"And why's that, Betzy?" asked Rory recalling her name.

"It just scares me, dat's all."

"Why there's nothing to be scared of, Betzy. You're safe as a baby in a cradle. Come, let me walk you around the deck."

Rory, who had not learned prejudice against the Negroes, took Betzy's arm. Betzy was shocked, but was in no position to protest. In her experience if a white man touched a Negro woman it was for one of two reasons—either to beat her or to ravish her.

"Come," Rory gently urged. "I want to show you how safe the ship is." Betzy allowed herself to be guided by the handsome young man. Rory took her all around the deck, pointing out the long boats that would be employed in an emergency. Betzy realized he was using her to get to Sophie. Still she liked the brash young man. He was sincere and had an infectious laugh. Betzy always appreciated a sense of humor in a man. By the end of the tour she had decided that if Sophie couldn't muster up some interest in this one, she must certainly be out of her mind.

Sophie sat on the edge of her bed and, using an upturned trunk as a tabletop, was rolling one of her "special" cigarettes. From a chamois bag she sprinkled onto a small square of paper a mixture of tobacco and hashish. She pulled the drawstring of the bag with her teeth and set it aside. Then carefully picking up the paper, she licked the nearer edge and rolled it tightly between her thumbs and forefingers. She twisted one end and put the opposite end between her lips. Using the flame from the whale oil lamp, she lit the cigarette and began inhaling, taking deep, careful breaths.

She lay back against the pillows and welcomed the drowsy euphoria. She became aware of nothing but the sound of her own heartbeats. She savored the delightful feeling of optimism. She would find a new life in San Francisco. With her looks and her talent and the money she had saved, she could go anywhere, do anything. Sophie's eyelids closed; ashes spilled on the floor of the cabin. Yes, things would be different. Her former life was behind her now.

Sophie was born in Bottle Alley near Chatham Square in The Five Points region of the New York City slums. She was the illegitimate child of Madeleine Parmalee who was the daughter of Irish and French emigrants. After her parents died of cholera, "Maddie," a pert girl of twelve, rather than suffer the indignities of the workhouse, took to the streets. Maddie had ambition and became the hardest working and richest whore in The Five Points. She saved her money religiously. At the age of eighteen she purchased a ramshackle boardinghouse near the Fulton Street fish market and catered to the sailors and waterfront worker trade. She kept the house as best she could, substituting garish tastes for actual improvement. She hired herself a bartender and a Negro piano player and called her establishment Miss Maddie's.

The boardinghouse was successful and Maddie gave up her previous work for good. Maddie usually picked one boarder to be her live-in lover, though she often had several lovers at the same time. When Maddie discovered she was pregnant she was delighted, but wasn't sure which of the three men who were sharing her bed had fathered it.

There was one thing that bothered Maddie. How would the child change her life? Maddie couldn't picture herself changing baby clothes or nursing a squalling infant. She frowned, and, sitting at her dressing table, examined herself in the mirror. Despite her life Maddie was still pretty. Her thick blond hair framed a pale but youthful face. Her eyes were clear and blue as a spring morning, and her complexion smooth and unspotted. Still pretty and with a little makeup . . .

Maddie picked up her pot of rouge and began applying it to her face. On her forehead, chin and nose she blended a small amount, just enough to make her complexion glow pink. Her cheeks were another matter. Generously employing the rouge, she painted them until they shone like polished tomatoes. "You're much too young, Miss Maddie," she said, talking to her reflection as she often did. "And I certainly don't intend to give up my good times." She had heard of things that could be taken to induce abortion, but Maddie was more frightened of that than of having a child. Deciding to put aside the dilemma for the moment, Maddie turned back to the rouge pot and darkened the crevice between her heavy breasts.

Maddie's problem was solved less than a week later. She was between lovers at the time and had treated herself to a night out with a few of her "lady friends," former working cronies. After an evening doing the taverns and pleased with herself because she was no longer a prostitute and certainly looked better than her former associates, Maddie made an unsteady trail along Fulton Street. It was a warm July night and the heady aroma of fish hung in the air like a mariner's penance. A giant black woman emerged from behind a pile of discarded crates. Maddie started. Surely the woman meant to do her harm!

"Please, ma'm." The black woman's voice was unsteady, weak and so imploring that Maddie immediately lost her fear. The black woman stepped into the rays of the gaslight. Despite her size, she looked beaten and frightened.

Maddie's natural empathy for the downtrodden was immediately aroused. "What's wrong?" she asked, staring at the woman's unusual face. A strain of Indian blood was evident in the Negress's broad countenance, high cheekbones, dark eyes that shone like polished stones and skin tinted reddish brown like the fertile earth.

The woman opened her mouth to speak and suddenly looked ashamed. "I—I," she lowered her eyes. "I ain't eat fo' a long time now, ma'm."

Maddie's heart went out to the unfortunate woman. She, too, could recall times when she hadn't the price of a meal herself. She fished into her drawstring bag and came up with—nothing. "Oh, damn," said Maddie flustered. "I do believe I've spent all my money." The Negress looked abject. "But wait, I live nearby. Come on. I'll take you home and rustle you up something to eat. There's always a pot of stew on the stove." The woman looked suspicious. "Well, come on," urged Maddie, offering her hand.

The black woman hesitated only a moment and then took it. She would later say that Maddie's heart was, after a long, dark existence, the dawn of her life.

Maddie sipped a brandy and watched with satisfaction as the woman voraciously ate every bit of the stew. Then Maddie offered her a brandy, but the woman explained that she didn't drink spirits. Maddie made her a cup of strong coffee.

"Yo' a kind soul, Miz Maddie."

Maddie smiled, "And what's your name?"

"Betzy, Ma'm. Betzy Bedamned."

"What an unusual name!"

"I give it to myself," replied Betzy proudly. Feeling that she could trust Maddie, Betzy explained further. "I'se a 'scaped slave, Ma'm, from North Carolina. Massa, he was bad to me, so I bide my time an' I 'scapes. Didn't have no last name. Dey never gives yo' last names. So I gives myself one. I say to myself, Betzy, be damned if yo' gonna take anymo' bad treatment!"

Maddie grinned at the woman's sense of humor despite her situation.

"So I comes north, an' Lawd, nobody'll give ol' Betzy a job."

Maddie's face lit up. "How old are you, Betzy?"

"Don't know, Ma'm. Maybe twenty-five, maybe thirty."

"Are you good with children? Babies, I mean?"

"Oh, yes, Ma'm. Babies an' children. I was a house nigger." She cocked her head to one side and looked around. "But dere ain't no babies here."

"Oh, yes, there is," replied Maddie patting her stomach. "And when I have it I want somebody to take care of the little tyke. You see, I have a business to run and, well, I just don't want to give up my personal life. Do you understand?"

Betzy understood, perhaps a good deal more than Maddie realized. Even though Maddie had forsaken the streets, she still looked and dressed like a whore. Betzy didn't approve of Maddie, but she was grateful to her and had liked her immediately.

Betzy became an established fixture at Miss Maddie's. She worked hard for her keep and did a bit of cooking, cleaning, laundry. When Maddie began to go into labor several weeks early, Betzy was there to comfort her. Betzy had experience as a midwife and delivered the baby herself. The labor was a difficult one and Maddie's convulsions lasted nine hours. Maddie, no friend of pain, bellowed loudly with each successive contraction, so much so that her boarders gave up trying to sleep and gathered in the downstairs barroom to drink, play cards and await the birth of Maddie's child.

On a cold, rainy morning in mid-December the baby, a little girl, appeared at last. A light mist of blond hair covered her head. But something was wrong, the baby was not breathing and its skin was turning blue. After quickly tying the umbilical cord, Betzy slapped its bottom several times and still nothing happened.

Maddie raised her head and weakly asked, "What is it, Betzy? What's the matter with my baby?"

Betzy didn't answer. She tucked the naked babe under her arm and rushed toward the window. Using one great arm she raised the window and held the infant outside, letting the freezing rain pelt its scrawny body.

"Betzy!" wailed Maddie. "What are you doing?" She tried to climb out of bed to stop whatever Betzy was doing but was too faint.

The baby coughed, opened its mouth wide and coughed again. Then it began clenching and unclenching its tiny fists. Betzy pulled the child inside and cradled it against the warmth of her voluminous breasts. Then it opened its green eyes and looked up at Betzy.

"Lawd o' mercy!" Betzy exclaimed and rushed to the table to wrap the little girl in a waiting blanket. "She alive, Miz Maddie. She alive!" Betzy's voice was jubilant. There were giant tears in her eyes as she presented the child to its mother.

"I don't understand," murmured Maddie as she cuddled the child close to her.

"It weren't breathin', Miz Maddie. I had to do what I had to do."

"Bless you for it, Betzy," said Maddie gratefully. "Oh, look, look how beautiful she is."

"What yo' gonna call her, Miz Maddie?"

"Well," Maddie smiled weakly, "I hadn't really planned on having a little girl. I was so sure it was going to be a boy. But I think I shall call her Sophie after my mother. She was French, you know."

"Sophie Parmalee," repeated Betzy, rolling the name around on her tongue like a piece of hard candy. "It sound good."

The fact that Maddie now had a child did not interfere with her good times. Betzy was there to care for Sophie and she could not have loved the child more had she been her own. Despite the premature birth, Sophie was a robust infant who was rarely ill and cried only when she wanted feeding.

Sophie progressed without incident into childhood. She loved her mother from afar, which is the only way Maddie would have it. The little girl enjoyed the party atmosphere of the boardinghouse. She loved the music, the flowered wallpaper and the rough men who showered her with random affection and sometimes brought her gifts from faraway places—a porcelain doll from London, a turquoise ring from the West, a tin mask from Mexico, a carved coconut from the Azores, a candlestick from Tangiers. Sophie's favorite gift was the porcelain doll. It didn't matter that its head had been cracked en route. She christened the doll Maude. Sophie carried Maude with her everywhere she went, but she generally found herself drawn to the barroom where Stash, the Negro piano player, held court.

Stash was a great pudding of a man whose heavy buttocks all but hid the piano stool. His head was shaped like a lima bean and his skin was the color of a burnt tree stump. Stash knew all the popular songs and enjoyed an audience. He welcomed the sight of the beautiful little girl. Like Maddie, Sophie usually wore a gaudy party dress and, as always, was dragging Maude behind her. Placing Sophie on the top of the upright piano, Stash asked, "What will it be today, lil' lady? What would yo' an' Maude like to hear?" Sophie's favorite was a plaintive ballad entitled "A Heart That's Been Broken in Two." Sophie, possessed of a clear but wavering soprano, sang along with Stash's mahogany-rich voice. She knew the words to all his selections, even the rowdy ones like "A Sailor at Half Mast."

Setting Maude in the crook of the tarnished wall sconce, Sophie stood up and danced across the top of the piano with all the aplomb of a minstrel man. She would strut and high-kick and do her buck and wing to the delight of Stash and occasional patrons.

Sophie rarely saw her mother in the daytime. Maddie slept late into the afternoon. Then only Betzy was allowed into her room with Maddie's breakfast, which consisted of a raw egg mixed with crushed chili pepper and a pot of strong coffee laced with brandy. Without makeup and her hair undone, Maddie was too vain to let anyone see her, even her own child. Near twilight, bath finished, hair curled, face carefully but heavily made up and after a few straight brandies, Maddie allowed Sophie to enter her bedroom. Wearing a dressing gown of tangerine satin, Maddie arranged herself in bed and welcomed her daughter with open arms. After a few careful kisses bestowed upon Sophie, Maddie would inevitably ask, "How did you spend your day, *ma chéri?*" Because of her mother's French background, Maddie employed as many French words and phrases as possible.

Since Sophie didn't go to school, her days were spent in Betzy's company shopping at the Fulton Street Market and enjoying the sights and sounds of the sordid part of the city. Sophie liked the street entertainers and, bent upon improving her talents, she culled from all she saw. She danced Irish jigs and Negro cakewalks, and learned off-color sea chanties as well as Italian lullabies. Often she performed for her mother while Maddie got dressed for the evening's festivities. Having made her selection from her tawdry finery, Maddie languidly asked her daughter for her opinion.

"You look beautiful, Mama."

"Yes, I do, don't I? The dress becomes me. I do so love poppies." Maddie kissed Sophie lightly on the forehead and scooted her off to bed. Then Maddie would descend the rickety staircase to the barroom below.

Sometimes at night Sophie and Maude would slip out of the window and crawl across the roof until they entered Maddie's room where they played under her large brass bed. If they got bored, Sophie would open the grate and watch the people in the bar on the floor below. Often she fell asleep sprawled upon the musty rose carpet beneath Maddie's bed only to be awakened during the night by bed creakings, laughter and sighs. Sophie was fascinated and enjoyed listening to Maddie and her latest lover having good times. She guessed that all grown-ups had a good time at night.

"Oh, honey," Maddie would coo. "I hope you don't think that just because I let you help me up to my bedroom I will allow you to stay for one more minute! What kind of a *jeune fille* do you think I am? Now, I'll close my eyes and count to ten and you just better disappear!"

Maddie hardly ever made it to ten. Counting wasn't one of her specialties. Her specialty was loving men, and Sophie loved her for it.

By the time Sophie was thirteen her curiosity about sex could not be suppressed. She was too old to hide under her mother's bed. Maude had long since been buried in the backyard beneath a dead oak tree, minus one eye, one arm and with her stuffing falling out.

Sophie was no longer a child. Her body was beginning to blossom and so were her thoughts of sex. She now took to spending part of her evenings in Maddie's room, posing in front of the mirror like her mother. The mirror was cracked and the silver was peeling. Sophie didn't notice the changes that time had made any more than she noticed the difference in her mother's appearance. Maddie's face was becoming worn. Lines, tiny as the webs of spiders, grew around her eyes and from the corners of her mouth. Her hair had lost its luster and her skin had progressed from pale to pallid. But when Maddie was done up for the evening Sophie thought her mother was the most glamorous woman in the world.

Sophie leaned forward and her bony elbows bumped against bottles of perfume. She was definitely not happy with her appearance; her lower lip drooped in a pout. "I wonder if I'll ever be pretty like Mama," she asked her reflection and sighed. Upon impulse, she reached for her mother's pot of rouge and clumsily applied a bright shade of red-orange to her lips and cheeks. "That helps a little. Perhaps some eye color." She put a glob of blue over each eye, managing to smear it both above and below until her eyes looked like two gigantic bruises. Using Maddie's rice powder, she dusted the tip of her nose until the freckles disappeared. "There," Sophie said with satisfaction. "That's just a whole lot better!" As an afterthought she dabbed her neck with a generous amount of strong perfume.

Unexpectedly Maddie entered the room, having forgotten her ivory and lace fan. "Why *beauté!* What have you done to yourself? You look like Fulton Street Flossie!" Flossie was a prostitute whose mind had become muddled with drink and who spent most of her time hanging around the Fulton Street Market hurling fishheads and insults at the men who spurned her. "Now if you're going to use makeup, let me show you how to do it. I'm *très* expert."

Maddie chattered as she deftly repainted her daughter's face. "I guess I haven't been noticing you much, *chéri.* Why you're getting all grown up, beginning to fill out in all the good places. I expect you're getting interested in knowing what goes on between a man and a woman." Sophie blushed because her mother so astutely sensed her feelings. "Well, it's very simple. Let me tell you how things are with Luke and me." Luke, a strapping young Irishman, had a handsome face, a thick shock of black hair and light blue, almost violet, eyes. Sophie worshipped Luke. "You see, Sophie, Luke and me, we got a fever for each other."

"Fever?" questioned Sophie.

"Fever's just a way of saying we make each other feel right—we fit." Sophie looked at her mother without comprehension. Maddie sighed. Using terms as delicate as possible, she explained the sexual act to her daughter.

At that hushed moment there was a knock at the door and Luke sauntered in. "What's holding you up, Maddie? Well hel-lo, Sophie, and what are you all prettied up for?"

Sophie could feel the pulse throbbing in her throat. Every time she looked at Luke she felt dizzy and feverish, and it was difficult not to look at him. "Mama's showing me how to wear makeup," she replied with feigned nonchalance.

Maddie noticed the way her daughter was looking at her lover. "Let's go, Luke, I think I've got a drink waiting."

Luke laughed. It was a rich, hearty sound, which reminded Sophie of apple butter. "You got more than one drink waiting," he replied.

As soon as the door closed, Sophie stood up. Her entire body was trembling. She had a sudden urge to burst into tears. Why did Luke attract her so? He was wild and loose, darkly sensual, a spinner of erotic dreams.

Sophie stomped her foot in aggravation. Then, her mood changing, she danced around the room, slowly divesting herself of her wrapper. She was nude beneath the hand-me-down print. She fluttered her golden lashes, made soft mewing sounds, hugged herself tightly, spun around and cried out in the sheer delight of finding that she was no longer a little girl.

Dizzy with self-love, Sophie fell back on her mother's bed and breathed the name "Luke" to her would-be lover. She kissed the back of her hand and her breath was excruciatingly warm. Bored with her game, she stood up suddenly and went to the dressing table again. Trying to look older she pulled her hair back and told herself, "I'll have a lover, too."

Sophie examined her breasts. They were beginning to swell and seemed even larger than they had the day before. She pinched her nipples until they tingled and turned bright pink. She smiled to herself. She was made of flesh and blood and her body had become a newfound land. She embarked upon a voyage, exploring herself, climbing her own mountain ranges and penetrating the moistness of her secret valleys. Beneath the marvelous structure of her ribcage, her heart fluttered like a caught bird. She flexed her legs, rubbing her upper thighs together, and knew that something very wonderful was going to happen to her soon.

Later that night, a drunken Maddie was carried up the stairs in the strong arms of Luke. After depositing her in her bed, Luke stood in the dim light of the kerosene lamp and contemplated her. Maddie wasn't looking her best. Her makeup was one gigantic smear and distorted even the natural features of her face. Her breasts, once firm, sagged across her chest, and her legs were becoming laced with broken blue veins. It was only a matter of time, Luke thought to himself. But he would be shipping out to California come April anyway.

Luke was closing Maddie's door behind him when he heard another door open. He looked up and at the far end of the hall was Sophie, still wearing one of her mother's hand-me-down robes. "Is Mama all right, Luke?" she asked with concern.

"Oh, sure, she's fine, just a little tired, that's all."

Sophie giggled. "You mean, she drank too much . . . again. Where are you going to spend the night, Luke?"

"I'll stretch out on the bar. Maddie's snoring too loud."

Sophie didn't move; she didn't blink an eyelash. Luke kept staring at her and watched her appearance change before his eyes. Her eyes lost their round innocence. Her hair seemed to grow less fluffy. Her eyebrows, once childish and questioning, puckered in genuine invitation.

Sophie broke the silence. "You needn't sleep on the bar, Luke. You can sleep in my room."

Luke glanced at Maddie's door and was unable to make up his mind whether he should accept Sophie's tempting offer. If Maddie found out, she was sure to raise holy hell, and probably he'd be kicked out on his arse. Where would he stay until it was time to ship out? Luke looked back to Sophie. Her lips were parted and glistened in the gaslight. Her eyes glowed feverishly and their gaze ignited his body.

What the hell! Maddie need never know.

Taking long steps, Luke began striding down the hall toward Sophie. She stepped aside to allow him to enter, and as he did his body brushed hers. Electricity passed through their bodies. They stopped and stared at one another. It was no longer a question of wrong or right. It was a question of compulsion.

Sophie's room was a miniature imitation of her mother's, but scrupulously clean. The walls were covered with a rose-trellised wallpaper. Velvet curtains, hot crimson in color, with thick gold fringes and ropes, framed the windows. Every inch of tabletop was covered with framed daguerreotypes showing popular entertainers. In the center of the room was a single brass bed, somewhat tarnished. Next to it was a dressing table, frilled and flounced, which held a wide three-fold mirror that reflected the bed. Maddie's cheap perfume permeated the air and stifled Luke's breathing. He flung open the windows, and stretched out on the bed.

Sophie stood silent by the open door, as if paralysis had struck her. "Close the door," Luke said in a voice huskier than usual. Then he began to unbutton his shirt.

Sophie responded to his command. She shut the door and walked toward the bed in a trance. By the time her knees brushed against the tattered quilt, Luke was completely nude. Her eyes wandered over his body. It was the first time she had ever seen a man fully nude. Curly black hair covered his massive chest and trailed down his abdomen, almost disappearing in his navel, then sprouted anew over his flat stomach and around his genitals. Luke was growing erect and Sophie was hypnotized by the sight of his expanding flesh. Transfixed, she watched until he grew to his full length. Then she sucked in her breath and frowned. Surely she couldn't . . .

As if reading her mind, Luke said softly, "Don't worry, Sophie, I'll be gentle with you."

He pulled her down onto the bed and snuggled his face against her breasts. "You smell good," he murmured. Then he lifted his head toward Sophie's lips. He kissed her softly at first and then with more urgency.

Sophie was stunned. She had never been kissed in that manner before. She began responding eagerly, wrapped her arms around his thick neck and pulled the black Irishman to her so that their bodies were pressed together in a heated embrace.

"Let me undress you," he whispered in her ear. It was a soft, sensuous sound, and his liquor-warmed breath burned against her cheek. Lowering his head, Luke caught the tie of her wrapper in his teeth and pulled the bow which held it closed. Then he slid his hands up to her shoulders and pulled down the sleeves of the wrapper. Sophie lifted her buttocks and the disrobing was complete.

Over Luke's left shoulder Sophie could see the full moon shining through the window. It was blood red and the sight of it startled her. Could it be an omen? Luke began nuzzling her neck, covering it with tiny bites as his hands fondled her breasts. Sophie felt her nipples spring erect and push against the palms of his hands. Luke knelt over her, and cupped her face in his hands. Her hair splashed across the pillows like spilt champagne. Her eyes were emeralds on fire. Then slowly, easily, he positioned himself between her legs and lowered his body until they were joined as man and woman.

Sophie gritted her teeth and clenched her eyes tightly shut. She saw tiny exploding stars whirling about in the darkness, and in a single instant the pain had vanished as quickly as it had arrived. In its place was an excitement she had never before known.

Luke proceeded with a delicate and unaccustomed slowness so that Sophie could become acquainted with the rhythms of lovemaking. But Sophie's need had gone beyond the slow thrust of a preliminary act of love. Whimpering, she urged him to greater speed. Luke held back until she reached her peak of sensation, then he pursued his.

They searched together, fighting as one to reach their goals. When they did, they held on to one another tightly until they had plummeted back to earth. They were both silent until their breathing returned to normal. Sophie held Luke close with her arms and legs, wanting him to remain there forever. His damp, black hair hung across her eyes blurring her vision. So this was what a man's touch felt like! No wonder Mama craved it so much. Sophie now understood. She understood Maddie and she understood herself. They weren't different at all, but separate parts of the same person.

There was only one problem. Luke was her mother's lover. Now that she had slept with him, what was she going to do about that?

Next morning Sophie slipped out of bed, leaving Luke sleeping with his arms around the bedclothes. She went down to the kitchen and prepared her mother's special breakfast. She was going to deliver it herself in spite of her mother's wishes and Betzy's protestations. If Maddie was surprised to see Sophie carrying in her breakfast tray, she said nothing. As Sophie set the tray on her mother's lap, Sophie was shocked by Maddie's appearance. Traces of makeup were smeared across her pallid face, her hair was matted, and in the morning light, a growth of gray hair was evident near the scalp. Maddie stirred her coffee with her finger and observed her daughter. Sharp pangs of envy shot through her. Sophie was so vibrantly beautiful.

"Mama, I've taken a lover," Sophie said without preamble.

"That's good," replied Maddie, sipping her coffee. "It had to happen."

"Mama, it's Luke."

Without missing a beat, Maddie continued, "That had to happen, too. Luke was getting tired of me, I could tell."

"You talk as if you don't care," said Sophie incredulously.

"It's not that I don't care, *ma petite amie,* it's just that it was nothing that I could stop. I figured it was about time you learned how to make love. I knew that Luke would be a good teacher. Despite his appearance, he's a sweet, simple man. Besides, if you want the honest to goodness *vérité,* I was getting a little tired of him."

"Tired—of Luke?"

"Sure, honey, eventually the fever dies down. And I been looking around. Why, I been attracting men like they were bees and I was a big comb of honey."

"Are you *sure* you don't mind?"

"Of course, I don't mind. I'm happy for you. There's just one thing. Don't get too smitten over Luke. He's not the kind of man who will stay in one place too long."

Of course, he will, Sophie wanted to say. He'll stay for me.

He didn't. Several months later Luke shipped out for California as planned. Sophie was upset for a while. But there were other lovers and now she was performing nightly in the bar. Sophie's fresh appeal and unique delivery made her a favorite. Sophie and her mother became closer than they ever had been. Perhaps it was because they now shared the secret of womanhood— the need for the touch of a man.

In the summer of Sophie's fifteenth year, Maddie became ill. She awakened with the shakes and her body was bathed with perspiration. She called for her daughter.

"It's just the July fever," Maddie insisted. "I've just got to keep myself cool. Betzy, if you'd run down to the fish market and bring me back some ice, and I'll have me a refreshing brandy mist. That'll break the fever."

Before Sophie went to work in the bar that night, she looked in on her mother. Maddie was asleep. Her face looked pale and waxen; beads of perspiration covered her flesh like tiny blisters. Sophie was alarmed and a doctor was summoned.

He examined Maddie and announced that she probably had a touch of malaria. The doctor gave instructions that Maddie was to get complete rest. He wrote out a prescription for quinine and said that she was to have a teaspoon in water every four hours.

Betzy and Sophie attended Maddie, who seemed to be recovering with the quinine. The disease had caused her to age terribly. Her skin was as dry and wrinkled as a pressed leaf. Patches of hair had fallen out, and most of her teeth had become loose. Maddie was devastated by her appearance and wouldn't allow *anyone* to see her except Betzy and Sophie. She drank more heavily than ever and had taken to smoking cigarettes to help relieve her anxieties.

One afternoon while Sophie and Betzy were grocery shopping, Maddie passed out in her bed, a cigarette still smoldering between her fingers. The cigarette fell to the floor and rolled under the bed. The rotting rug began to burn.

Loaded with groceries, Sophie and Betzy made their way back to the boardinghouse. Several horse-drawn fire trucks rushed down the street past them, but they were unconcerned. Fire trucks were a common sight in the tenement section. As they neared Fulton Street, a bright halo of scarlet light and billowing clouds of black smoke appeared. Sophie threw aside the market baskets and broke into a run. Betzy followed. They reached their block. The boardinghouse was a mass of flame.

The entire second story was barely visible through the sheets of flame. Sophie rushed into the crowd and fought her way through the onlookers until she reached Stash, who was standing next to the cordoned-off area. Stash's clothes were streaked with soot and he was crying into his hands.

"Oh, Stash!" shrieked Sophie, "Where's Mama?"

Stash looked up. His eyes were bloodshot and his eyelashes had been burned away. "I tried to reach her, Miz Sophie. Oh, Lawd, I tried to."

"Mama!" Sophie screamed. She clawed at her own cheeks, digging into them as if to tear them off.

Betzy tried to fight her way through the line of firemen holding back the crowds. "Miz Maddie's in there!" she wailed. "I gots to get her out!" It took four firemen to restrain Betzy.

The fire burned for more than five hours before the firemen were finally able to quench it. There was nothing left of the boardinghouse except a blackened chimney surrounded by smoldering rubble.

Maddie had kept a hidden cache of money she had scrupulously saved over the years for her daughter's inheritance. The money had been buried, a jar at a time, beneath the dead oak tree next to Maude, Sophie's childhood companion. And only Betzy knew about it. The amount was just under seven thousand dollars.

Sophie used the money to buy new clothes, luggage and passage to San Francisco on the *Connemara* for herself and Betzy. Her desire to travel had been fired by tales told by her mother's lovers and her own. Unencumbered by her past, San Francisco seemed like a wonderful place for a fresh beginning.

Chapter 5

Sophie had allowed herself to be introduced to Rory Fitzpatrick. Pretending to be a lady, she would let Rory's interest go only so far. But as the weeks passed, Sophie became bored and restless. She made plans to seduce the enthusiastic young man. But as the *Connemara* made its way past the Florida coast, it encountered a ferocious storm that rendered seductions impracticable.

By late afternoon the sky had turned green and was splashed with furry black clouds. There was a calm so complete that everybody on board, including the sailors, were apprehensive. Captain Fallon gathered crew and passengers on deck and gave them his "comfort speech." His words, strident and replete with a Bostonian's broad "A's," hovered above the masts like a ghostly incantation.

After warning the passengers to stay in their cabins and to take care that their lanterns didn't spill, the captain added, ". . . and finally, I assure you good people that I have weathered many a storm and have never lost a ship." Instead of gazing at him in rapt adoration and assured serenity, the passengers were casting furtive glances at the ominous sky.

"Brothers and sisters! Fall to your knees and pray for merciful deliverance!" boomed a voice from the gathering.

All heads turned to the Reverend Poke. His fervent, raspy voice fairly billowed the sails. "Fall down or be destroyed!" The Reverend, a narrow man of considerable height, rolled his milky blue eyes toward heaven. As if on cue, the skies were split by a white zig-zag of lightning. Several people cried out, many dropped to their knees and others ran to their cabins. A light mist of rain dampened the air.

"Kneel down!"

"To hell with kneeling down!" the captain countered with a roar. *"Get to your cabins!"*

A tremendous gust of wind whipped across the deck blowing off hats and plastering clothes to bodies. Despite the preacher's pleas to endure and pray, the remaining passengers scurried below and the crew sprang to their posts. Captain Fallon signaled to Liam and Rory. The two muscular Irishmen picked up the babbling preacher and carried him out of harm's way.

After locking the preacher's door, Liam and Rory started back above deck to see if they could be of any help. The ship suddenly lurched and threw them against the wall of the corridor. Liam was stunned, but Rory had merely bruised his shoulder.

"Are you all right, Liam?" Rory asked with concern.

"Yes, I'm fine. Looks like we're in for what the Captain calls a 'whale of a gale'."

"I'll follow you in a minute," said Rory quickly, seizing the chance to see Sophie and to check on her safety. He hadn't seen the young woman or her maid on deck during the captain's speech. Liam grunted his disapproval and disappeared up the ladder.

Holding onto the railing, Rory, half-stumbling, made his way to Sophie's cabin. The ship pitched. Rory fell against the door and it swung open.

Sophie looked up in alarm. She was kneeling beside the bed. At first, Rory believed that she had heeded the preacher and was praying, then he saw the gigantic Negro woman stretched out on the bed shaking with fear.

"I'm sorry, Miss Parmalee, I fell against the door."

"Sophie," she corrected. "Betzy is deathly afraid of the sea . . ."

"We gonna sink, Lawd God. Betzy's gonna git took by Ol' Man Deep n' Salty!"

Rory approached the bed. "Nonsense, Betzy," he said gently but firmly. "We're just having a 'whale of a gale.' Why I encountered worse than this coming from Ireland."

Betzy's face was the color of burned charcoal. She rambled on, "Oh, I'se sick, Miz Sophie. I'se terrible sick."

Sophie looked at Rory helplessly.

"She's seasick, I imagine," said Rory. "Just keep the chamberpot next to the bed. I'm going above deck now, Miss Sophie, to see if I can help out."

"Do be careful," said Sophie, hoping he would leave quickly so she could retrieve the chamberpot.

As soon as the door closed, Sophie reached under the bed. The chamberpot was sliding about. After several tries, she grasped it and placed it beside Betzy's bobbing head with little time to spare.

Rory reached the deck and was shocked by the terrible tempest. The rain, the gale, the lightning and the thunder all seemed bent upon destroying the *Connemara*. The sea appeared to be all afire, making the small vessel the sport of the wind and waves. The water rushed across the deck and it was impossible to see more than several feet ahead. Rory made his way to the forecastle. As he started up the ladder, the sea

erupted with a roaring force and the helm was seized
beyond control. The pilot of the wheel was thrown
against the foremast. The impact broke several of his
ribs. Crying out in pain, he collapsed on the churning
deck. The ship was then tossed sharply at a forty-five
degree angle. The pilot was washed to the starboard
side, and before Rory could reach him was swallowed
up by the sea. Rory, who knew little of ships, had
common sense. He began turning the wheel toward the
tilt. His muscles strained but could not budge the wheel
more than several inches. He was joined by the first
mate. They managed to right the ship and head it into
the waves.

The storm spanned eighteen hours. Many provisions
had been washed overboard. Most of the passengers
had become ill. The sudden return to calm did not ease
their afflictions.

Betzy remained violently ill and, sure that she was
doomed to be lost at sea, sang a morose slave song:

Oh, Sweet Jesus, my time is come,
I hears dat bugle, I hears dat drum,
I sees dem armies, marchin' along,
I lifts my head an' join dere song.

Betzy sang the song over and over for nearly a week
until her voice was as rough as gravel. She had lost an
alarming amount of weight and her skin was dry to the
touch. She imagined she was being pursued by her
former white master and cowered in the corner screaming, "I kills yo' first, yo' bastard! Betzy be damned if
she takes anymo' abuse!"

She struck out at Sophie, nearly spilling the soup the
young woman was carrying to her.

"Betzy, please. I only want you to eat something."

Sophie knelt down next to her bed. "Now, take some
soup."

Betzy's mouth grew sullen. "Don't wants no soup. It

full of jimson weed." Betzy referred to the seeds of a poisonous plant that brought on a lingering and mysterious death. It was widely used by the slaves in the South, and the poisoners were rarely caught.

"No it isn't," replied Sophie in a soothing one. She began to sip the soup herself. "See, Betzy, I'm eating it. Now come, please, you haven't eaten anything in days. You'll feel better, I promise you."

Betzy, in spite of her delirium, seemed placated and allowed her mistress to spoon-feed her. Just the same her eyes were watchful.

When the soup was finished, Sophie wiped Betzy's chin with her own handkerchief, and for the first time Betzy looked becalmed. "I know yo!" she cried, tears overflowing her eyes. Yo' Miz Maddie."

Sophie burst into tears.

The Caribbean sun shimmering in the waves of heat appeared to be under water. The passengers spent a major portion of their time above deck, sitting or standing in the shadows of the masts and sails and enjoying the caressing breezes as the *Connemara* cut swiftly through the azure waters.

Sophie, parasol in hand and wearing the lightest and briefest of day dresses, appeared on deck. In deference to the heat, Sophie had forsaken her petticoats and only after being nagged by Betzy had she even deigned to wear her pantaloons. The dress was a polished pale blue cotton. The parasol matched her dress, and both were trimmed with crudely embroidered bachelor buttons. It was sleeveless and cut low at the bodice. She wore her hair loosely, so that it fell around bare shoulders.

As she came into view, the coterie of five plain and unmarried women, resembling drab sparrows splitting a handful of crumbs, lowered their eyes and began to whisper in outrage.

"It's a scandal to the jaybirds!" hissed one.

"Appearing like that in front of the crew, not to mention the others!" clucked a second.

"She looks much older in the sunlight," pronounced the third.

"Much older. She's twenty-five if she's a minute," chimed in the fourth.

"I think she looks rather delightful," remarked Armanda Forquette, the lone dissenter. She was a hefty woman with a square jaw and a keen eye. She alone of the five possessed a sense of humor. "And if any of us had her obvious attributes," Armanda continued briskly, "we would dress in much the same manner."

"Armanda, you couldn't mean it!"

"That's simply not true!"

"What a terrible accusation!"

"I, for one, would not want to look like a slattern!"

Armanda favored her friends with a grin. "Ladies, what penance you will get for those lies I can't guess. Shhh! She's nearing." She gave Sophie a broad and generous smile. "Good morning, Sophie."

"Armanda, ladies, what a delightful morning!"

Armanda agreed. The four others grunted in unison. Sophie moved on, completely aware of the hostility. Besides, she wasn't too interested in spending time with women, not with two handsome shipowners aboard.

Sophie sighted Rory on the forecastle deck. She twirled her parasol with anticipated pleasure. Even though she had never cared for rust-colored hair, he really was quite good looking after all. And it had been a long time since she had felt the weight of a man's body on hers. Rory was a hearty specimen! Her inner thighs tingled as she walked toward him, the parasol tipped so that her face would be covered and their meeting would appear to be by chance.

A mischievous gust scampered across the deck, whirled about her skirts and lifted them well above her knees. Three sailors nearly fell from the rigging. The cook threw his slops onto the lower deck. The five women clucked and cackled. Rory walked into the foremast.

Sophie squealed. It was impossible to hold onto the parasol and her skirts at the same time. The parasol blew inside out with a loud whump and Sophie uttered an expletive, which the wind conveniently carried out to sea. Rory rushed to Sophie's rescue. With his broad hands he helped her hold down the billowing skirts. When the prankish wind had suddenly departed, Sophie acknowledged Rory. "You really are a friend in need, Rory Fitzpatrick."

"I'm sorry about your umbrella," Rory stammered. "Perhaps I can fix it."

"*Ca ne fait rien*—It is of no consequence," said Sophie grandly and tossed the parasol overboard. Several gulls, skimming the surface of the sea, squawked in protest.

"And how is your maid?"

"Completely recovered, *merci*. To allay the boredom of the trip, she's made friends with your cook. Perhaps you've noticed a bit more dash to the dish?"

"I beg your pardon?"

"The food, ain't it tastier?"

"Why, yes, now that you mention it."

"Betzy was one of the finest gourmets in the whole of New York City." Sophie pronounced proudly but not truthfully.

"You speak French?" said Rory with amazement.

"*Un petit*," replied Sophie with a self-assured smile. "My mother was French, you know."

"That explains it," said Rory, half to himself.

Sophie quick to take offense, snapped, "Explains what?"

"Your being an entertainer."

Sophie sighed, "Oh, yes, I've inherited all of my talents from *mama*." She fluttered her eyelashes coquettishly. "And how did you discover my secret?"

Rory lowered his head and tried not to blush, but within seconds his freckles bled into the rest of his red face. "I'm afraid I questioned your maid."

"I see."

He's *most* appealing and polite, Sophie told herself. He respects me. *And he's so well-built!* She shifted her weight, uncomfortably aware of her sexual needs.

"And what are you doing to allay the boredom of the trip?" asked Rory as delicately as possible.

He's got the fever just as much as I do! She lifted her face to his and smiled seductively. Rory stared into Sophie's eyes. They were as green as a slice of fresh lime. For the first time he noticed the tiny mole on her cheek caught between her left eye and her hair line. It was a delightful discovery, and he had the strongest desire to bend his head forward and kiss it.

"You haven't answered my question, Sophie."

"Oh, I study my music and practice my songs. I've had an offer of employment . . . a very exclusive club. It's on the Barbary Coast, you know, which I just couldn't refuse."

"What's the name of the place, Sophie?"

Sophie looked up flustered. "How silly of me! It completely flew out of my head. Betzy will remember it, if she ain't forgot."

Liam was strolling along the deck, talking to passengers. He saw the couple approaching and tried to avoid their attention. Rory saw his friend and waved him over.

"Liam, you've met Miss Sophie Parmalee, of course."

"Why yes, of course," replied Liam coldly.

"She's an entertainer and she's on her way to San Francisco to work in an important club."

Liam nodded in Sophie's direction. The expression on his face infuriated her. He was not fooled by her story. "I'll bid you good-day, Miss Parmalee, and I hope you continue to enjoy your voyage." Liam said and quickly made his getaway.

After he was out of sight Sophie remarked, "I don't believe Mr. O'Sullivan likes me."

"You're mistaken. Why, Liam likes everyone. He's just quiet, that's all," explained Rory. "He thinks a lot."

"And tell me, Rory," asked Sophie, turning her charm on the man at hand, "do you think a lot? And if so, about what?"

"I wouldn't be telling you, Sophie." he grinned brashly.

His blue eyes burned with the fever. Sophie stared deep into them for a moment and thought she was falling. She quickly regained her composure. It's silly. I'm tired of playing games. "Would you like to walk me back to my cabin, Rory?" she asked, anxiety sharpening her voice.

Rory swallowed hard and managed to reply, "That would please me, Sophie."

Sophie slipped her arm through his and Rory felt a sudden warmth rush through his body. He could hardly believe his good fortune and was quite aware of the envious glances he was getting from the sailors and male passengers. When they reached Sophie's cabin, Betzy was sitting near the porthole repairing a torn hem. "Betzy," said Sophie in her grand pose, "I wonder if you would go to the galley and see if you can talk that cook into preparing us some tea?"

Betzy departed and decided that after serving the tea, she would be wise to make herself scarce for the rest of the afternoon.

Rory looked around the room. Bright filmy scarves had been draped here and there—over the table, the backs of the chairs, about the portholes, like curtains. A bright pink feather boa hung from the nail on the back of the closet door. And pinned about the wall were pages torn from Godey's *Lady's Book*, which illustrated the latest fashions.

"You've made the cabin quite attractive, Sophie."

"I did what I could, Rory, to recreate the atmosphere of my room in the townhouse."

"Townhouse?"

"Yes, my family owns a lovely four-story home on Gramercy Park. That's where I was brought up."

"Are your parents still alive?"

"Unfortunately not," Sophie replied, lowering her eyes. "I've had to make my own way in this world and let me tell you it hasn't been easy. But I thank the *bon Dieu* that I've been blessed with a certain amount of talent."

"How did you get into the field of—uh—entertainment?" asked Rory earnestly.

Sophie, eager to embellish her make-believe life, sat down on a chair and acted out her story. "You see, Rory, I was a very gifted child. Mama recognized it very early in my life and I was given singing lessons. Father, of course, was opposed to all of this, but Mama, as usual, got around him. I improved by leaps and bounds and I knew that my life could have but one course. I was too talented to be confined to singing at teas and small family gatherings, so with Betzy's help I plotted to steal out of the house at night and seek work before the public where I would be appreciated. I got me a job singin' at a very high class music hall. Of course, I was immediately adored by the public." She paused for full effect. "Some *précieux* critics even compared me to Jenny Lind."

"Really?"

Sophie shrugged her shoulders. *"Zut alors,* I had no choice in the matter really. I had to do what I was destined to do. I had to use my God-given talents. I had to give myself to the world!"

Betzy arrived with the tea tray and quickly made her exit. She recognized that look in Sophie's eyes.

Sophie continued spinning tall tales about her background and singing experience. Finally bored with her own voice and fantasies, she stopped and appraised Rory. He looked more attractive than ever. It had been weeks since she had been with a man, and she craved that close companionship.

Sophie got up, went to the door and bolted it. "In case of a storm," she smiled. "It wouldn't do to have the door swinging open, don't you agree, Rory?" She drew out the young man's name, giving it an extra syllable so that it slid off her tongue like butter. Still smiling, she sat on the edge of the bed and carefully arranged the folds of her dress.

Rory was flustered. He didn't know how to react. It seemed such a bold move for a lady.

Sophie waited patiently. When he didn't move from his chair, she patted the mattress beside her. *"Mon cher,* you look uncomfortable in that hard chair," she wiggled on the bed. "Why don't you come over and sit by me? The mattress is padded."

Rory shot out of the chair and sat down beside Sophie, breathing hard. He had never felt clumsy or awkward before, but in Sophie's presence he felt like a complete novice. Sophie turned her head and stared at his profile. A fine mist of perspiration had broken out on his upper lip. She threw back her head and laughed. "Why Rory, I do believe you're afraid of me." Before Rory could answer, Sophie traced the top of his upper lip with the tip of her finger, wiping away the droplets of sweat.

Surprised, he turned to her. Their faces were inches apart. Sophie moved her face closer and lightly kissed him on the lips. He took her in his arms and returned her soft kiss with a rough passionate one. Sophie then let her hand come to rest on Rory's thigh and began moving it until finally her palm rested directly on his groin. Rory's reaction was immediate; he began to get an erection. He held her tighter and his nervous hands cupped her breasts and began to knead them through the thin fabric of her dress. Their breathing became more labored as passionate feelings were unleashed.

Rory felt Sophie's nimble fingers unbuttoning his trousers, and he thought he was going to faint. Still kissing her, he began fumbling with the buttons on the back of her dress.

"Let me," she said softly.

Sophie stood up and began removing her clothes. Rory watched with fascination as she stepped out of her dress and blithely kicked it to one side. She placed her hands on her ample hips and said, "Am I to undress alone?"

Rory jumped to his feet and began ripping off his clothes. He was completely undressed before Sophie had even finished removing her pantaloons. Panting, Rory stood before her. "Let me," he gasped. He plunged his thumbs into the waistband of her lacy pantalettes and pulled them down as he knelt in front of her. Sophie stared down at him, looking directly into his eyes, making him feel terribly self-conscious. There was a sudden pain in his chest and his mouth became dry.

The sunlight drifting through the portholes burnished her body and tinted her hair crimson. Looking up at her, Rory knew that he had never, would never, know a woman so completely beautiful. He opened his trembling lips to speak but nothing came out. Sighing with ecstacy he wrapped his arms around Sophie's hips and pressed his cheek against the soft mound of her stomach. Sophie, whose needs were insistent, did not want to take time with an abundance of foreplay. She, too, knelt down and grabbed Rory's thick manhood. Rory sucked in his breath and began kissing the resilient mounds of her breasts. Her nipples swelled in anticipation, turned bright pink and stood erect. Sophie stretched out on the rough planks of the cabin floor and invited Rory to take her. Their initial coupling was so swift that Rory could not remember the catharsis of their lovemaking. He could only remember that it felt like nothing he had ever before experienced. He was refreshed, satisfied, totally fulfilled.

They made love several more times. There was time for caressing and casual exploration of each other's bodies and particular wants. By the end of the afternoon Rory knew that he was in love with Sophie. To him their lovemaking had been a revelation. To Sophie it had been a pleasant way to pass the time.

The *Connemara* plowed the seas with unaccustomed grace and was rapidly approaching the equator. Captain Fallon, a true believer in celebrating the Crossing, made plans with his mates for entertainment. The Crossing was a seaman's supreme holiday. Captain Fallon would become King Neptune. His deeply wrinkled face broke into a self-conscious grin as he recalled his impersonations of the mythical king. How many times had it been? Thirty? Forty? The celebrations blended together into one kaleidoscope of hazy memory.

The captain leaned back in his chair placed his hands behind his head and remembered. He took a long swallow of rum and stroked the bottle before putting it to rest. Memories stirred. He closed his eyes and saw the green tropical islands. The Pacific? The Caribbean? They were all the same. A stray tune tickled his memory. The captain moved his lips and tried to find the words to fit it. A young woman with unruly blond hair smiled at him. "Josh," she whispered.

His wrinkled lips formed the words, "Yes, Marie."

"Come to me, Josh. Come to my cabin tonight." She ran her tongue seductively over her plum-colored lips.

"Marie," he said out loud and opened his eyes, but Marie was gone. The captain sighed sadly. "Marie," he murmured and then frowned. Had her name been Marie? There had been so many—moist, willing women all eager to please the captain of the ship.

"Old fool!" the captain grunted. "Marie, Mary, Marianne—what in the hell difference does it make. She's gone."

He went to his trunk, unlocked it and began digging through an accumulation of possessions. A jade figurine from the Orient, a shrunken head from South

America, ivory from Africa. None of it meant anything anymore. He threw some things on the floor, pushed others aside, until he found what he was looking for—the canvas sack with his King Neptune costume. He laid the sack gently on his tabletop and opened it. From it he withdrew a trident, ornately carved of wood and painted gold, a metal crown studded with semiprecious blue and green jewels, which he always wore rakishly tilted over his left eyebrow, and finally the robe, a flowing mass of aquamarine, embroidered with starfish, seahorses and shells.

The captain removed the jacket of his uniform and slipped on the robe. He added the crown, tilting it just so, and went to examine himself in the large brass plaque hanging on the wall. His reflection, blurred by the wavy surface of the brass, was pleasing. The lines of age disappeared and his snow white hair was once again blond and golden. He was young, he was desired, he had the power to please women. He was Neptune, King of the Sea.

The day of the crossing was filled with elaborate pranks, elaborate costumes and a considerable amount of rum. The sailors and passengers, all ludicrously dressed, mixed freely. The crew wore their uniforms backward or switched breeches and shirts so that their bare buttocks hung out for everyone to see. Many decorated themselves with tropical flowers picked at an island before the crossing. The male passengers dressed in female clothing supplied by the five unmarried women. Led by Armanda, even the five women got into the spirit of things. They, too, decorated themselves with flowers, seashells and garish items dredged up from their wardrobes. Armanda wore her undergarments over her outer clothing. Corsets and petticoats were stretched to their limits. The drunken, highspirited sailors teased two of the spinsters. And, with benefit of rum, banjo and song, the women freely gave themselves over to the festivities.

Liam and Rory dressed as pirates, patches over their eyes and bright sashes at their waists.

Only Betzy refused to get involved in what she called "white folks' foolishness." "I like to know who's takin' care of de ship. Why, we liable to run into one of dem storms again. An' den where we be? Down at de bottom of Ol' Man Deep An' Salty feedin' de fish!"

Sophie had not appeared on deck the entire day, saving herself for the evening festivities and a late party on deck. Sophie had rehearsed with musicians she rounded up from the passengers and crew. She intended to entertain, accompanied by a violin, guitar, flute, clarinet and banjo. Despite the raucous noise and rowdy laughter from above deck, Sophie remained prone on her bed for most of the day. She intended to make the most of her appearance. She would dispel rumors that she couldn't sing! And she was intent upon impressing Liam who, since her affair with Rory had begun, ignored her more than ever.

Using an iron heated upon a brazier of hot coals, both cajoled from the cook, Betzy patiently pressed each and every ruffle on Sophie's costume until they stood out like curled strips of folded paper. Betzy placed the iron back on the coals and grumbled, "Seem to me like a lot o' trouble fo' dis here low-class trash. Don't know why yo' extendin' yo'self. Ain't gonna get yo' no'where!"

"Oh, do be quiet, Betzy," muttered Sophie, peeking from under her eyepads. The pads were pockets of muslin which had been stuffed with damp tea leaves and were an excellent remedy for puffy eyes. Not that Sophie's eyes were puffy, but she imagined they were since she had been up late entertaining Rory in her cabin. Betzy had been sent to sit on deck and count the stars.

"Dey gonna be so drunk by de time yo' come flouncin' on, dat dey won't know what yo' singin' anyways." Betzy was still smarting from being barred from the cabin.

"You think they don't drink on the Barbary Coast?" Sophie snapped. "From what I hear, I'll be lucky to get through a song there. The miners come right up on stage and try to carry you off."

Betzy grunted, meaning one of two things. Either "Dat don't sound so bad to me," or "Since when did yo' raise any objections!"

"God dammit!" cried Sophie sitting up. "It won't happen again. I had no idea Rory was here so long. Next time we'll go to his cabin."

"Dat would seem like de ladylike thing to do," replied Betzy somewhat placated.

There was a rap at the door. "Get rid of whoever it is," hissed Sophie.

Betzy ambled to the door, opened it a few inches. It was Rory. He was so flushed from rum that his face blended into his hair.

"Is Miss Sophie all right, Betzy?" he slurred.

"She all right, Mister Rory. She jes restin' fo' tonight." Betzy glanced back at Sophie who shook her head. "She asleep now an' I don't dare to wake her."

"I understand," replied Rory, attempting to hide his disappointment. "I'll go now. But you tell her I called for her."

Betzy closed the door and looked at her mistress with disapproval.

"Damn it, Betzy. I've got to get some rest. I can't be bedeviled every minute by that Irish lout!"

Betzy went back to her ironing. "Dat man in love with yo', Miz Sophie."

"So what?" replied Sophie tartly. "A lot of men have been in love with me."

"But dis one different. He think yo' a lady."

Sophie angrily threw aside her eyepads and sat up. "And who says I ain't? I'm just as much a lady as any of those pussies on board." She paced back and forth, grinding her teeth together and raging helplessly. "And so what if I ain't?" she turned on Betzy. "I'm gonna be a lady in San Francisco. You just wait and see!"

Betzy lowered her eyes and concentrated on the ruffles. "Maybe yes, maybe no," she muttered.

"*What?*" cried Sophie.

"I says, maybe yo' be a lady after all. It take a gentleman to make a lady. An' from what I hears, dere ain't no gentlemen in San Fran-cis-co."

The decks were crowded with passengers and crew. Many of the sailors hung precariously from the rigging. Everybody was a bit drunk. Each was expectant. Sophie Parmalee was going to perform. The five women sat together near the steps of the forecastle. That part of the ship had been designated as the stage. Every lantern, every lamp had been brought up on deck until the *Connemara* looked like a floating pleasure ship. A sail had been loosened from the foremast to serve as backdrop to the entertainment. And a row of kerosene lamps, their chimneys black with soot, were arranged in a semicircle to act as footlights.

The crew had never been critical of Sophie and were excited about her appearance. The male passengers were of two minds: one group believed she was nothing but a showy tart, the other group argued that she probably did have talent. None of them denied her appeal. Reverend Poke had protested loudly to the captain concerning the festivities and the appearance of Sophie Parmalee in particular. "The woman is an instrument of the devil! You have no right to inflict her sinister being upon the easily impressed members of this ship!" Captain Fallon ignored the maniacal ravings of the reverend and silently wished that keel-hauling could still be employed.

Liam and Rory stood to the rear of the women. Liam secretly hoped that Sophie would make a sorry spectacle of herself and, indeed, expected it. Rory had difficulty containing his enthusiasm. "She's been rehearsing and rehearsing, Liam," he bubbled. "She's a real professional. And she knows French. Did I tell you she knows French?"

"So did Madame DuBarry," replied Liam tersely.

At the appointed time Captain Fallon gave orders to drop anchor, thus avoiding the possibility of a sudden list by the ship. He was in Sophie's corner, and did not want to see her trip doing a dance. The good captain, bleary-eyed with rum and attired in his ridiculous Neptune outfit, stared out to sea and suddenly realized why he was so attracted to Sophie. She reminded him of Marie. Prettier, of course, and pounds lighter. But still a fun-loving, moist woman, and to his way of thinking that was all that counted.

The first mate rang the galley bell signaling the start of the entertainment. Sophie was not to appear until the other acts were finished. She was, as she put it, "the grand finale."

Armanda began the applause and it grew until the entire ship shook. First on the program was a male passenger who considered himself an amateur magician; the audience good-naturedly agreed. Then a trio of sailors crooned flatly in unison. The bawdy lyrics of "A Sailor at Half Mast" came tumbling down the ladder to Sophie's cabin. She smiled to herself. It was a good sign. She was going to be better than she had ever been. Even Liam would be impressed.

Sophie examined herself in the mirror. Deftly made up and coiffed, she resembled a porcelain doll not unlike Maude, her first and only doll. She tilted her head to one side and the other, and was pleased with her appearance. The sailors had finished their song. Two male passengers, one in blackface, were now doing a minstrel turn.

Captain Fallon had given Sophie permission to reach the stage through his own cabin. Outside his cabin window lay the cruise head and the marine catwalk. A ladder had been erected so that Sophie could reach the forecastle deck without being seen by any of her audience. As the first notes of her song were struck she would appear from behind the backdrop.

The minstrel team was tiresome, and everyone had

heard the jokes many times before. The audience sighed with relief as the minstrel men stumbled off stage. Then Captain Fallon himself took center stage. Everybody applauded enthusiastically. The sailors and the passengers alike had grown very fond of the crusty sea captain. They whistled, stomped their feet and yelled. The captain held up his hands and signaled for quiet.

"Ladies and gentlemen," the captain began. "I have the supreme pleasure of presenting you the toast of New York City who will soon . . ."

Sophie heard the captain's words and hurried out of her cabin. She encountered Betzy in the corridor. "Everythin' is ready. De music mens is all upstairs an' I got yo' costumes hidden behind dat sail an' I be dere to help yo'."

Sophie felt a rush of affection for her beloved Betzy. She hugged her tightly and kissed her cheek. "God damn it to hell, Betzy. What ever would I do without you?"

"I 'spects yo' never find out," Betzy replied with a broad grin.

A sailor, reeking of rum, awaited Sophie and helped her up the ladder. So many hands were touching her arms, back and bottom, that Sophie could have sworn that there had been at least three sailors, not one. She climbed onto the forecastle deck and positioned herself behind the drop just as the captain finished the speech.

". . . and so I give you—Miss Sophie Parmalee!"

The musicians began an insistent rhythm. At the appropriate moment Sophie strutted onstage. She was dressed in a vibrant pink gown with matching accessories. The mob cheered Sophie merely for being there. Everyone except the four women who were adamantly trying to get Armanda to stop clapping. Sophie marched to center stage, and acknowledged her audience's fervor with several deep bows. The band vamped while Sophie waited for the spectators to become quiet.

Then Sophie walked toward her audience. Her easy manner made them comfortable. The sailors nudged one another with delight, and an air of expectancy raced from person to person. She was still Sophie, still beautiful and certainly still flashy, but there was something *different* about her. Sophie waved to the musicians. Then she started to sing. She started easily, gently, gathering up the folds of her skirt and showing off just a bit of leg. It was a raucous song of the period entitled "Heaven Help the Working Girl and the Working Girl Helps Herself."

Captain Fallon's eyes became moist. He turned away from the stage and wiped away his tears. Even the four disapproving ladies were stunned by Sophie's theatrical expertise. She was born for the stage, she belonged there. As the number progressed, Sophie grinned at her audience and began strutting across the forecastle in a high-stepping cakewalk, shifting the song into double time.

When the song ended, there was complete silence. Betzy, afraid that her mistress had somehow offended the audience, stuck her head out from behind the sail. Suddenly the applause began and for what seemed like hours the audience cheered and stamped and screamed for more. They simply would not let it end. They would not let Sophie get away. Sophie gracefully acknowledged their approval, bowing deeply and blowing kisses. And as their clapping hands and shouting voices reached a crescendo, she disappeared behind the lowered sail and, with Betzy's help, began changing her costume for the next number. This was a striped gown of red, white and blue satin. The skirt was caught on either hip by a tiny bouquet of red satin roses, revealing Sophie's shapely legs. A matching hat with red, white and blue ostrich plumes decorated her head. Betzy was an expert dresser, and Sophie was ready for her second number before the applause began to fade.

The banjo plinked and plunked. Sophie strutted onstage.

Rory jumped up and down and slapped Liam on the back. "You had your doubts, didn't you, Liam? Where are those doubts now?"

Liam didn't reply, he couldn't. Despite anything else he thought about Sophie Parmalee, he couldn't deny her talent as a performer.

The audience was baffled, awed and rendered helpless by Sophie. She finished her act and disappeared behind the sail, but they would not let her leave. They screamed until their voices were hoarse and clapped until their hands felt as if they had caught fire. Liam's mouth tightened as he watched Sophie take curtain call after curtain call.

"They love her," yelled Rory. "They just love her!" Liam had not reckoned on Sophie possessing anything but the obvious. He looked at his partner. Rory's eyes were shining with pride—and something more.

Sophie, who hadn't prepared an encore, marched out on stage, sat down on a barrel and to the plaintive accompaniment of her orchestra began an almost gospel-like version of the theme song of the migration:

Oh, Susannah, don't you cry for me,
I'm off to California, with a wash-bowl on my
knee . . .

Chapter 6

"*La-and! Ho-o-h!*" the young sailor cried from aloft, jarring the silence of the early morning. The crew, who had been sleeping in hammocks on deck, tumbled to their feet. Passengers, who had been sleeping fitfully in oppressively hot cabins, swung open their doors and shuffled onto the deck.

The *Connemara* was approaching Brazil and Rio de Janeiro Harbor. They would dock for several days so that supplies could be replenished and travelers could stretch their legs, see the sights, and revel in the delights that the fabulous city afforded.

"I'm going to stay drunk for three days and three nights in the arms of a big-titted whore," announced a sailor who was swabbing the deck.

"Be careful you don't bring back the pox!" heeded an older and more experienced deckhand.

Reverend Poke, Bible in hand, stood on deck searching out the coastline. He planned to make a pilgrimage of the "low places of the heathen city." If he could just save one soul, then for him the trip would be a success. He squinted against the sun and held up his worn Bible to shield his eyes. Pursing his liver-colored lips, he fought back a feeling of despair. He had done poorly thus far. The sailors laughed at him, and the passengers treated him as if he were a fanatic. But, no, he mustn't falter. He was just being tested. And he would abide.

A peal of laughter caught his attention and he turned his head toward the disturbance. Sophie and Rory, arms linked, had come on deck. The reverend could feel bile rising in his throat. He could barely hold back his outrage. The two of them, standing there, flaunting their lasciviousness for all to see. The young man hadn't seemed such a bad sort at the start of the voyage, but now that she had cast her spell upon him . . . that Jezebel!

Sophie and Rory nodded in the reverend's direction and swept by him, still laughing at some private joke. The reverend clenched his Bible so tightly that the tips of his fingers made indentations in the black leather.

"Let's go to the forecastle, Rory," urged Sophie. "I want to see, I want to watch." They scrambled up the ladder to the forecastle deck where many of the passengers had gathered to watch as the ship came into harbor.

Armanda and her four companions, shielding themselves with drab parasols, staunchly gathered around the foremast.

Rory nudged Sophie. "There's Armanda and her armada!" Sophie collapsed in a fit of giggles.

Captain Fallon came forward to greet the twosome. "Do you know," he began, "I'm looking forward to a stretch on dry land as much as anybody. You must see the sights. Rio is a beautiful city and the Brazilians are a wonderful people."

"Oh, look!" cried Sophie.

The *Connemara* was nearing the coastline. The ship
sailed past a ridge of mountains that resembled a
dinosaur's back. The water turned from deep green to a
vibrantly bright blue. Natives in canoes carved from
logs paddled out to greet the ship. The catchy rhythms
of a native band floated over the waters.

The passengers were awestruck by the lush green
vegetation spattered with bright tropical flowers. Giant
ferns dipped into the waters and, in their shadows,
alligators, resembling half-submerged logs, lay in wait.

The pilot guided the *Connamara* into Guanabara Bay,
which was strewn with countless islands and huge
rocks. Rio harbor lay within the rocky remains of
shoreline mountains, a coastal plain of beaches and
inland mountains supporting rich tropical forests. The
natives of Rio, called the Cariocas, were justly proud of
their city, declaring that "God made the world in seven
days, but two days were devoted to creating Rio."

The ship passed pristine beaches of white sand edged
with coconut palms. They sailed through a sheet of
delicate rain no wider than the ship itself. The rain
lightly dampened the passengers and continued on its
furtive way toward the magnificent Sugar Loaf Mountain, creating a rainbow over the scene.

Sophie clutched Rory's arm and whispered, "I don't
think I've ever seen anything so beautiful in my life."

"Neither have I," agreed Rory.

The harbor was filled with large ships—brigantines,
frigates, schooners, windjammers—and many smaller
vessels from sailing ships to yachts. It was midafternoon by the time the *Connemara* was safely at dock. As
soon as the gangplank was lowered, the passengers
eagerly lined up. Rory invited Liam to explore the city
with Sophie and himself, but Liam made excuses.
Armanda, leading her brigade, announced that they
were off to find themselves each a rubber baron. The
four ladies shrieked and giggled in protest. Armanda,
pleased with her outrageous remark, grinned broadly.

Betzy joined her mistress on deck. Since the *Connemara* was to remain in Rio for three days, Rory and Sophie were to take a room at a hotel and secure a smaller one for Betzy. They were looking forward to luxurious drawn baths and being completely alone. Betzy was concerned only with getting her feet on dry land.

The Rio waterfront was like every waterfront in the world. Peddlers ruthlessly hawked their wares and engaged in pickpocketing when business was slack. Beggars swarmed over the passengers like the flies and the mosquitoes. Each was missing an organ—an eye, a nose, a limb. Negroes and mulattos loaded and unloaded cargo, from ships' holds to warehouses and from warehouses to holds. Eager porters in white jackets jumped up and down and yelled for trade. They called out the names of hotels, each promising the lowest rates available. Captain Fallon had recommended the Imperio. Rory, being taller than most of the waterfront denizens, spotted a hotel porter and waved him over. He was short and thick, with skin the color of molasses.

"Si, Senhor," he grinned and approached Rory.

Rory looked helplessly at Sophie. "Can you speak Portuguese as well as French?" Sophie looked blank. The porter bowed deeply and said in a heavily accented voice, "No trouble, Senhor. I speek Onglash."

"Good," replied Rory with relief. "Then get us a carriage and take us to your hotel."

The porter glanced at Betzy. "The black one, too?"

"Of course, you idiot!" snapped Rory. "Now find us a carriage and be quick about it!"

Betzy threw back her head and laughed. "Yo' know, Mister Rory, wid all dese colored people about, I should feel right at home here, but somehow I jes' don't."

The trio waited patiently for the porter to return with the carriage. The smells of the waterfront accentuated by the heat of the day were potent—decaying flowers, rotting fruit, spoiled fish and the pervading odor of unwashed human flesh.

The porter arrived with a small two-seater driven by a man who was nearly nude and covered with flies. Rory and Sophie were to take the passenger seats, and the porter and Betzy would stand on the railing in the back. Rory insisted that Betzy sit next to her mistress, and that he and the porter ride behind.

As they were driven away from the waterfront, the city became more beautiful and the air became sweeter. The hotel was located on the side of a sloping hill. It was three stories high and made of adobe brick and plaster. It had been whitewashed, but in the glow of the afternoon sun it appeared golden pink. There were wrought iron balconies on every floor, and the building was framed by majestic palms and clumps of red and white poinsettias.

"This can't be the right place," Sophie whispered to Rory. "The captain said it was inexpensive."

Rory smiled and hoped that the captain knew what he was talking about. Liam had not been overly generous. When they entered the lobby, they were even more intimidated. The floor and walls of the lobby were covered with light pink marble. Chandeliers, railings and sconces were fashioned from brass. But Captain Fallon was right—the rates were very reasonable. Rory booked a room for himself and Sophie, and was pleased to find that accommodations for maids could be had on the same floor.

The porter, after showing the trio to their respective rooms, stood expectantly before Rory, his smile frozen on his face.

"He wants a tip," Sophie loudly whispered. Rory blushed in embarrassment and gave the man two American dollars. The porter was delighted and bowed his way out of the room. "You tipped him too much," said Sophie. "A dollar would have been more than sufficient."

Rory scowled. It hurt him to be criticized by Sophie, but he said nothing.

Sophie danced around the room. "Oh, Rory," she sang. "Come look at the view of the harbor. This is the way to live," she bubbled. "Oh, I'm going to have lots and lots of money!"

"What about your family's money?" Rory asked.

Sophie's smile slid from her face. "Oh, that—er, well, you see. Naturally everything was left to me but . . ." Sophie screwed up her face in concentrated thought. "But you see I wasn't of age, that is, to collect the money. I won't be eighteen for some time yet." Sophie, pleased with her ingenuity, went on. "Oh, yes, there'll be lots of money coming to me when I'm eighteen. But of course I shan't need it by then. I'll probably be wealthy in my own right. Entertainers become very wealthy, you know."

Rory frowned. All this talk of money and career depressed him. He took her hand and changed the subject. "Come," he said, guiding her back into the bedroom toward the bed. "Let's make love."

Sophie held back. "Oh, Rory, not now. Let's go explore the city. We may never get a chance to see Rio again and we can always make love. Now, I'll just get Betzy to come unpack me." Before Rory could answer, Sophie darted out of the room.

Captain Fallon pushed through the hoards of beggars and motioned Liam to follow him. "Come on, Liam. Let's have a 'dry-land drink' before we explore Rio's possibilities."

They took a table in a small brand of a waterfront tavern, and were greeted by a burnished young female. The captain said, "They carry a good supply of Scotch and Irish whiskies here."

"What?" asked Liam who was staring openly at the waitress's heavy breasts. The captain laughed and repeated himself.

"I'll have an Irish whiskey," said Liam quickly.

The captain spoke to the girl in Portuguese and gave her the order. As the girl shimmied away he remarked to Liam, "Quite a bundle, eh Liam?"

The Irishman grinned. "Now how do you suppose that girl got such big breasts? Why she couldn't be more than fifteen."

"Fourteen more likely, and she probably has three kids at home in a variety of colors."

"You mean she's been married more than once?" asked Liam shocked.

The captain grinned. "She probably hasn't been married at all, my lad. Ah, here we are. Now drink up."

After four more Irish whiskies Liam was drunk. The captain suggested that they "stop by a place I know" and Liam complied. They walked up a narrow street littered with shops.

"I want to buy a present," Liam said suddenly.

"What kind of present?"

"A present for a young lady."

"Then, come with me. I know a place, or at least it used to be there. It's run by an old Chinaman. He's a dope fiend, but he's honest."

The shop was dark and the smell of opium hung in the air like a lost dream. The old man, his face as yellow as ancient parchment, appeared through a beaded curtain. He remembered Captain Fallon and greeted him in pidgin English. Fallon explained what was wanted and the old man began showing his wares. Liam's eyes fell upon a pewter cross that had been set with cabochon emeralds. "This is what I want," said Liam thickly.

The captain bargained with the Chinaman for a suitable price that would include postage on the first ship going to the States. Liam handed a wad of money to the captain and asked him to count out what he needed. Then he sat down at a bamboo writing table and penned a short note to Kathleen.

Dear Kathleen,

Rory and I are in Rio de Janeiro, Brazil. I saw this cross in a shop and decided that since you gave me such a lovely one, I should return the compliment. We are both well and hope you and your family are the same.

Best regards,
Liam O'Sullivan

After writing the address on a piece of brown paper for the proprietor, they left the shop. "I hope it gets there, Captain."

"It'll take some time, but he'll see that it's put on the right ship. It'll probably be sent to New York first, then onto Maine." The captain contemplated his red-faced friend. "I didn't know there was a girl you left behind."

"There isn't," replied Liam quickly. "She's just a family friend."

The captain accepted Liam's explanation but didn't believe him. One didn't send crosses encrusted with emeralds to a family friend.

"Where are we going?" asked Liam, pausing to catch his breath on the steep street.

"It's just a little place of entertainment. I stop here every time I'm in Rio. Satisfaction is guaranteed."

The house was painted pink. Lounging across the veranda were half a dozen young women in all shades of yellow, red and black.

"This is a whorehouse," whispered Liam.

The captain grinned. "Some call it that. Come on, we'll have a drink and a plate of rice and beans. And after that? Who knows?"

The madame, a short, thick woman with light creamy brown skin, hurried out to meet them. "This is Concepción," said the captain as he genially introduced the madame to Liam.

"Sega benvindo," said the woman as she offered a deep curtsey.

Concepción waved them inside. As he passed, Liam noticed that she smelled strongly of vanilla and something more. It was the same aroma he had encountered in the Chinaman's shop. Opium? They were shown into a main room where there was a bar. The walls of the room were covered with a dark red wallpaper and there was an Oriental carpet in shades of red and purple covering the floor. The bar was a long mahogany affair with cupids and fruit ornately carved on it. The bartender was a white man named Ned. It was rumored that he was a British sailor who had jumped ship.

"Good afternoon, gents. What will be your pleasure?"

"Two Irish whiskies. The best you've got," replied the captain.

The girls sauntered into the barroom. Captain Fallon called them all over to the bar and ordered a round of drinks. Most of them seemed to drink gin flavored with sugar and gingerroot. The whiskey made Liam feel more comfortable. He looked over the girls, and decided that although they were gaudy, they were attractive.

The girls clustered around. Liam unloosened his tie and ordered another round of drinks for himself, the captain and the six women. It was then he realized that two of the girls were twins. They introduced themselves as Flora and Fauna. Liam grinned drunkenly and wondered what sailor had given them such ridiculous names. Flora, the more forward of the two, climbed up on Liam's lap. She was small, less than five feet, light but compact. She turned to him and smiled, her breath smelled like honey. Fauna, not to be outdone, pressed her small breasts against Liam's arm and tickled his earlobe with her carmine-colored lips.

"It looks as if you've made friends," the captain laughed.

Out of the corner of his mouth Liam replied, "How do I get out of this?"

"Don't you mean that the other way around?"

replied the captain and broke into a gale of laughter.
"They want you to go upstairs with them."

"Me? Why?" asked Liam not comprehending.

"Come on, man," urged the captain. "If I could
manage two I'd take two myself. I'll be doing well to
get one up." The captain slapped Liam on the back and
began laughing again. Then he turned his attentions to
a rotund whore with a great mane of shiny black hair
and melonlike breasts. "Is your name Marie?" he asked
drunkenly.

The girl nodded. *"Si,* Marie."

"Then let's go," muttered the captain and, with the
girl's help, climbed off the barstool.

"Where are you going?" cried Liam in alarm.

"Upstairs. Where do you think I'm going, laddie?
Come on, put one of them pretty little things under
each arm and let them hoist you up."

Before Liam knew what was happening, Flora and
Fauna had managed to steer his unsteady legs toward
the rickety staircase.

"I really don't think—now, girls—I—"

The girls ignored Liam's protestations and pushed
him up the steps. A few minutes later Liam found
himself lying in the middle of a giant bed. Flora and
Fauna had divested themselves of their clothing and
were removing his clothes. Liam started to protest once
again, but he was too drunk. He lay back on the bed
and while the chandelier whirled in circles above his
head, Flora and Fauna quickly stripped him naked.

Suddenly his body felt as if it had been covered by a
hundred ravenous mouths. The girls were biting and
kissing his flesh in every place imaginable. He could
feel something deep inside of him move like a coil
unwinding. He lifted his head and watched the girls at
work. Reaching out his hands he touched their satin
smooth bodies and sighed heavily. It had been a long
time since he had touched a woman so intimately. The
girls rolled him over on his stomach and began licking
his shoulders, his back, his legs, his buttocks, even his

feet. Liam groaned with ecstacy. Never in his life had he experienced such erotic treatment. He dug his fingers into the bedcovers and gave himself up to the two voluptuaries.

Sophie, her skirts tucked into the waistband of her dress, raced ahead of Rory crying, "Catch me, Rory, catch me!"

They had climbed the side of the mountain directly behind the hotel and reached a plateau. Rory was out of breath and paused beneath a eucalyptus tree. Sophie had kissed him and had run away. He could see her in the distance standing before a thicket of bamboo. She had taken off her shoes and was waving them at him.

"Wait for me, Sophie!"

"You'll have to catch me!" Sophie shouted. Digging her feet into the soft carpet of moss, she ran into the thicket. She hid behind a tree and waited for Rory to overtake her. She was filled with the excitement that comes from putting off something pleasurable just a little while longer. Standing on her tiptoes, not daring to breathe, she pressed herself against a tree and let Rory pass. Then she ran in the opposite direction, hung her shoes on a limb where he would be bound to see them and shouted. "I'm over here!"

Rory turned quickly. A flash of green parakeets exploded from a flowering bush, causing him to jump. He caught sight of Sophie's pink dress as she dashed behind a banyan tree dripping with orchids. "Damn!" he mumbled and bent down to take off his own shoes. Tingling with excitement, he searched until his eyes fell upon Sophie's shoes. He plucked them from the tree and tucked them into the back pockets of his trousers. Which direction had Sophie taken? Despite his eagerness, he was impressed by the startling vegetation. Everything was outsized, overlarge. Plants and trees crowded each other in a kind of insane harmony. There didn't seem to be enough space for healthy growth, yet the lush green vegetation was everywhere. It went on forever.

Rory spotted a path snowy with honeysuckle. Pressed in the damp ground he saw Sophie's footprint. He smiled and ventured on, savoring the tingling sensation that was growing in his groin.

Rory entered a rain forest. The pungent aroma of tropical flowers caused him to sneeze. And he heard a distant voice call out "Bless you." Rory turned to the right. Draped over a large hibiscus and blowing gently in the breeze was Sophie's dress. He gathered it up, tucked it under his arm and continued on. The forest became dark and eerie, lit by an iridescent moss that glistened like dragonflies' wings. Brazilian sparrows, tanagers, parrots, manakins and flycatchers darted about his head protesting his intrusion. There were orchids everywhere in colors Rory never knew existed—bright reds, butter yellows, virginal whites and marvelous soft harmonies of white, mauve and pink.

He caught sight of one grouping of yellow orchids. The blossoms were broken. Rory found a half-hidden footprint in their shadows. As he looked up he saw a flash that did not seem to belong to the rain forest. Through the undergrowth a patch of color, pinkish white and opalescent, appeared. His heart thundered as he raced toward it, pushing the vines out of his way. Hanging from a low slung tree were the last vestiges of Sophie's clothing.

Then he saw her, poised in the frozen position of an angelic statue. Rory let her clothes fall from his hands and walked toward her, shedding his own. By the time he reached her he, too, was naked.

Sophie looked at him. "You caught me," she said softly.

He wrapped his arms around her and felt her heart beating as rapidly as his own. Then slowly he pulled her down to the ground.

Later when the sun was a mere scattering of pale yellow flecks shining weakly through the treetops, Sophie got up and retrieved her undergarments. "We'd better be getting back to the hotel before dark. Besides, I'm starving. Let's get dressed up and go to a nice restaurant."

Rory looked up. His face was serious. "Once we reach San Francisco, what's going to happen, Sophie?"

"What do you mean?"

"Well, I mean what's going to happen to *us?*"

"I don't rightly know, Rory. I have to make a living, of course, and I do have a commitment to fulfill."

It wasn't what Rory wanted to hear. He wanted to hear words of undying love and eternal bliss. Suddenly he was on his feet. He seized Sophie in his arms and began kissing her with all the fervor of his love. Sophie, gently but firmly, pushed him away. "Rory, we've got to get back to the hotel. What if we should become lost?"

He took her face in his hands and looked at her as if he were searching for something. "Sophie, you *do* love me, don't you?"

She lowered her lashes and replied. "Of course, I love you, Rory. What a silly question!"

Rory's hopes soared. She had said that she loved him. With that on his side, he knew that once they reached San Francisco he could change her mind about being an entertainer.

And they would be married!

On their way back down the mountainside, Rory whistled a jaunty Irish tune. It was a happy sound and something that reminded him of his childhood in Ireland before the famine. Sophie was quiet and thoughtful, but he didn't notice it.

Chapter 7

The three days in port passed all too quickly. Crew and passengers of the *Connemara* reluctantly straggled to the dock where Captain Fallon awaited them. Sailors, disheveled and still drunk, many carrying bamboo cages containing tropical birds, staggered toward the ship. Reverend Poke, his face sucked into an expression of eternal disapproval and clutching his Bible, walked swiftly across the dock. He hadn't found a single person in Rio who wanted to be saved. Armanda and the other ladies struggled with their souvenirs. Straw hats were perched rakishly, and strings of flashy beads were draped everywhere their bodies could hold them. Beads, bundles and brightly colored shawls vied for attention.

Liam joined the captain. "It looks as though everybody had a good time," he remarked wryly.

"Afternoon, Liam. Well, Rio's the place to do it," he winked and added, "as you well know."

Liam colored. "Captain—uh—I would prefer you

didn't say anything about—well, you know—
about . . ."

"Of course not, Liam."

The third mate hurried over. "Captain, everybody's
on board except Mr. Fitzpatrick, Miss Parmalee and
her maid."

"Now where the hell could they be?" grunted the
captain. He irritably glanced at the sun. "We can't be
lettin' 'em hold us up too long."

"Perhaps I should go ashore and look for them,"
suggested Liam.

"Wait!" cried the third mate. "Here they come. Here
they are now."

Holding hands and strolling casually across the dock
were Sophie and Rory. Betzy trailed behind. Liam
could see that Rory was in love with the brash young
woman. He bit down on his lower lip. It was time—past
time—to have a talk with his young friend.

Sophie went directly to her cabin. Liam saw a chance
to speak to his partner. Rory was in his cabin,
unpacking his clothes, when there was a sharp knock on
the door. "Come in," he called, hoping it was Sophie
who had changed her mind about resting.

The door opened and Rory looked up expectantly.
"Oh, Liam, come on in."

"I hope you had a good time in Rio," said Liam with
an edge to his voice.

"We had a wonderful time," boomed Rory.

"I thought I might be seeing you."

"Well, we got ourselves sort of busy," replied Rory
and continued unpacking.

"I want to talk to you, Rory."

Liam's tone caused Rory to stop what he was doing
and turn around to face his friend. "Yes, what is it,
Liam?"

Liam looked at Rory sharply. "Your behavior with
the young woman has been highly irregular. No, don't
say anything. Let me finish first. It's been the subject of

much banter among the crew members and has offended several passengers."

"To hell with all of them!" exploded Rory.

"It has also offended me, Rory. Why, why she's not even Catholic!"

"Then, to hell with you, too," Rory said bitterly through clenched teeth.

"I'm sorry you're taking this attitude. I tried to warn you about this woman. She's no good, can't you see that?"

"She's good for me, Liam, that's all I can see. Besides, we're in love. We're going to be married when we get to San Francisco."

"Married!" Liam was incredulous. "I won't allow it!"

"You're forgetting, Liam, that you're not my father."

"No, I'm not, Rory, but there have been times when I've had to be. If you marry this trollop, I'll cut you out of the business. I can do it, you know. I'm in total control of our assets." Rory was stunned. He couldn't believe that Liam was serious.

When Rory didn't respond, Liam asked hopefully, "Then you'll give her up?"

Rory let the shirt he had been holding drop to the floor. He lowered his head and replied quietly, "No, I can't, Liam." His voice broke. "Don't ask that of me. I'm of age and I—love her."

"Bah! Then go to her and be done with it!" Liam stalked out of the cabin, slamming the door behind him.

Rory lowered himself onto his bunk, picked up the shirt and automatically began to fold it. He couldn't believe that Liam had threatened him. He wouldn't go through with it, of course. They had come too far together to let a childish argument destroy their partnership.

Liam leaned against the wall of the corridor waiting for his anger to pass. He wiped his perspiring brow and fingered the cross around his neck. He knew he shouldn't have threatened Rory, but he had been pushed into a corner. The girl was a tramp, couldn't Rory see that? A shipboard affair was one thing. But marriage! Liam prayed that something would impede the marriage plans. He never realized that it would be Sophie herself.

The *Connemara* proceeded southward and the captain had to choose between rounding the Horn or sailing through the Straits of Magellan. The strait route was shorter and with perfect luck it would mean quicker passage. However, the channel was torturous and narrow and there were strong currents. The shores were rough and inhospitable and sudden storms were characteristic. Pervading winds came in treacherous gusts. Anchorages were few and unsatisfactory, Gloomy skies, snow squalls and the persistent headwinds made most captains regret having chosen that course.

Captain Fallon stomped into his cabin. Yellow oilskins protected two suits of heavy clothing. He spied the welcome pot of coffee, which the cook had just delivered. He sat down and poured, savoring the warming mug against his calloused hands. After taking a gulp, he dipped the tip of a pencil into the coffee to wet it and began writing in his journal.

April 1st, 1849, 1200 hours, aboard the *Connemara*.

73 days out, bearing S.S.W.—latitude 54°1′, longitude 64°12′—the temperature has dropped sharply. This morning we saw the mountains of Tierra del Fuego. We are perhaps only five or six leagues from the Cape. Judging from the thickened weather, I felt it would be better to avoid the long and dangerous passage of the Straits of Magellan, But Mr. O'Sullivan has ordered me to go by that shorter route

and we'll take our chances. Although I've taken the straits before, it seems to me an unwise decision . . ."

There was a knock at the door. The captain quickly closed his journal and gave the knocker permission to enter.

Liam, also in yellow oilskins, stepped into the captain's cabin. His face was ruddy and beaded with frozen raindrops. "There's a gale blowing up, Captain."

"I'm not surprised. It'll be the first of many, you can count on that."

"You're still planning on going through the straits?"

"I am following your orders, Liam, but I still think . . ."

"Captain," Liam interrupted, "I want to get to San Francisco as quickly as possible!"

Captain Fallon picked up his mug of coffee, sipped and contemplated the young man over the rim. He realized that Liam's change of temperament was due to his estrangement with Rory. But that was their business. The captain made it a rule never to interfere with his employers' personal lives.

"You're a hard man, Liam," he remarked as dispassionately as possible.

The ship abruptly jolted to the starboard side and Liam was thrown to the floor. The mug of coffee flew out of the captain's hands and spilled across his desk. He quickly moved his journal out of the way and began mopping up. Then there was a sound as if a giant were knocking on a great hollow door.

"What's that?" cried Liam.

"It came from the hold. Some of your lumber must have come loose!"

"I'll see to it," said Liam sharply. "I'll take some men down and we'll use more rope. You stay above deck and get us through this damned alleyway!"

The captain shrugged his shoulders. He had had no

intention of dealing with the lumber. Just the same, he didn't like taking orders on his own ship. As the cabin door slammed, the captain muttered to himself, "The April fool is the devil's tool."

Liam, Rory and a score of sailors worked feverishly restacking the lumber and securing it. Patches of ice had formed in the hold and made footing difficult for the men. While they labored through the night, the temperature dropped to thirty degrees below zero. The men worked in shifts, warming themselves intermittently with hot coffee and the glow of kerosene lamps, while the contrary winds continued to buffet the ship. Dawn arrived before the men realized it, for the nights had become nearly as bright as the days. A cold wet snow clouded the sky.

By midmorning the planks of lumber had been secured. There were still crates and kegs to be righted. Rory offered to stay below until the work was finished. Liam nodded coolly, glad to relinquish the damp bowels of the ship for whatever comfort his cabin could offer.

The snow was blowing in thick frozen sheets. Liam, exhausted, made his way back across the deck. The high winds carried the snow down the corridor, making visibility impossible. By mistake Liam entered Rory's cabin instead of his own. His only thought was to get out of his wet clothes and be comforted by the dry covers of the bunk. He stripped himself nude and climbed into bed. Soon the heavy wool blankets warmed him and he fell into an exhausted sleep.

Sophie nervously paced back and forth in front of the porthole. She could see nothing except the swirling snow. If she couldn't see, then how could the captain possibly guide the ship? Sophie smoked one of her special cigarettes, but no such relief came. Betzy, fully dressed, huddled under the covers of her bunk, moaning in terror.

"Oh, shut up, Betzy!" said Sophie sharply. "Nothing's going to happen." But her own fears were almost as great as her companion's. Frightened, cold and bored, Sophie decided to defy the captain's orders. She put on her cape and started to tie a scarf around her head, but thought better of it. Rory liked her hair windblown.

"Where yo' goin'?" Betzy cried.

"I won't be long," replied Sophie and slipped through the cabin door.

She bunched her cape around her shoulders and hurried down the corridor, the corners of which were filled with glistening white drifts. Her thin carpet slippers became soaked, but no matter, she would be warm soon.

She opened the door to Rory's cabin and, shivering, stepped inside. She shook the snow from her cape, hung it on a wall hook and turned expectantly toward the bunk. In the obscure light coming through the porthole, she could see the sleeping form. She locked the door automatically and hurriedly began to get undressed, muttering to herself, "The goddamn ship is probably going to hit an iceberg, so I might as well be happy about it . . . Je-sus, it's cold." In her haste Sophie tore several buttons on her pantalettes. She angrily kicked them off, then lifted the covers and slipped into bed.

The combination of the opium cigarette and the warmth of a man's body made Sophie feel all the more sensual. She pressed herself against his back and buttocks and moved her arm around his waist. She walked her fingertips down his flat stomach and across his downy pubic hair. Sophie was confused. Rory's pubic hair was coarse. She explored further. And there were other differences! Sophie lifted her head and stared at the face that belonged to the body she had touched. Her eyes saw Liam in the pale light. She blinked and looked again. Was she really in bed with Liam O'Sullivan or was it all an opium dream?

Liam stirred, moaned softly and wiggled his buttocks against her soft crescent moon of belly. Sophie's body began to tingle with a delicious thought. Could it be that he was awake—had been all the time? Sophie lay quiet. She was still shivering, not from the cold but from the intense heat generated between them. Her first impulse was to slip out of the bed and hurry out of the cabin. But no, if he were playing possum, then she would wait for his next move.

Sophie waited and waited. Impatient with the game, she threw her leg over his and began lightly biting the flesh of his back. It was salty with the sea. Liam sighed deeply and wiggled his body. Sophie continued her oral ministrations.

Suddenly Liam turned over so quickly he caught Sophie in the jaw with his elbow. She cried out in pain, and the noise further awakened him.

"Miss Parmalee, what do you think you're doing?"

Sophie rubbed her jaw and glared at him. "How did you get in my room! In my cabin!"

"Your cabin?" shrieked Sophie in outrage. "You're not in *your* cabin! This is Rory's cabin and this is Rory's bed and that's who I thought you were—" she screamed into his face. "*Rory!*"

"*Rory's cabin?*" Liam shouted back. He jerked his head around and noticed his younger friend's clothing and possessions lying about. "*Son of a bitch!*" Liam scrambled out of bed, tripping over the bedclothes and fell face first on the floor.

Sophie threw back her head and howled. Liam was stunned, stunned and angry and embarrassed. He vented his emotions on Sophie. "Don't you laugh at me you—you—harlot!" He grabbed his wet and chilly trousers, stepped into them and winced audibly.

Sophie continued laughing. It had become a hysterical whoop. Liam grabbed his clothes and holding them in front of him, rushed toward the door. He turned the handle and nothing happened. "*Jesus Christ, she's locked me in!*"

Sophie began laughing anew until streams of tears poured down her cheeks. Liam managed to get the door open and stumbled out into the passageway. Sophie ran after him. She stuck her head into the corridor and shouted, "And don't tell me you didn't like it, you hypocrite bastard!"

Liam disappeared into a swirl of snow and Sophie heard the door to his cabin slam.

"Whore of Babylon! Jezebel!"

Sophie, startled, turned her head. Standing in a veil of sleet was the Reverend Poke. One hand shielded his eyes from her nakedness and the other pointed a long and accusing finger at her.

"Satan's slut!"

Even through the swirling snow Sophie could see the preacher's red eyes glowing like live coals. She opened her mouth to tell him off, but the cold choking air stopped her. She pushed the cabin door shut, ran to her abandoned clothes and began to get dressed.

The preacher began pounding on the door. Sophie hurriedly got into her clothes, not bothering with her torn pantalettes.

Reverend Poke continued beating the door and calling her vile names. Suddenly the door burst open. Like a creature from the depths of Sophie's childhood nightmares, he stood glowering in the doorway, a dark silhouette against a moving white background.

"It wasn't enough that you had to corrupt one fine young man, you had to poison two!"

"What are you talking about?" yelled Sophie. "You're crazy, you're a . . ."

Reverend Poke stepped into the cabin. *"Jezebel!"*

Sophie's anger overrode her fear of the maniacal preacher. She put her hands on her hips, threw back her head and said, through clenched teeth, "You sneaky *cochon* . . . that's French for pig . . . how dare you spy on me? What makes you think you have the Lord's blessing?"

"Don't speak *His* name, strumpet!" the preacher

screeched in outrage. Spittle as white as sea foam
formed on his lips. He thrust forward his Bible and
commanded, "Kiss it! *Kiss it* and beg *His* forgiveness!"

Sophie sucked in her breath and, as she lifted her
skirt, she spat out the words, "Kiss this, you freaky
bastard!"

The reverend stiffened as if suddenly struck by
lightning. His mouth gaping, he stared at her sex.
Sophie seized her chance, and ran past him into the
corridor. She pounded on Liam's door.

"Let me in, God damn it! Let me in!"

Liam pulled the covers over his head to blot out the
sound of her voice.

The preacher made a grab for Sophie, but she
quickly sidestepped and ran. She was on the deck now.
Her slippers slid over the icy boards like glass on glass.
The ship was rolling violently, and the snowstorm was
so dense that Sophie couldn't see anything. She
reached out blindly for a railing, for a mast, anything.
A numbing wind struck her body and turned her
completely around. Unaware of her direction, Sophie
rushed directly into the preacher's outstretched arms.

"*Kiss it!*" he roared and grabbed her arm and held
her fast. "*Kiss it!*" he repeated in a thick, rasping voice.
His breath was sour. Snatching Sophie's hair, he
managed to pull her down to her knees on the deck. He
lowered himself and pushed her back, then using his
staunch legs, pinioned her to the floor. He let go of her
hair and held onto one of her arms and began thrusting
the Bible toward her face. Sophie dug her fingernails
into the soft flesh beneath his eyes. The reverend cried
out and fell back on his haunches. Clawing at the icy
planks, Sophie crawled away. She got to her feet and
ran from him. Her shoulder slammed into the main
mast and she nearly collapsed from the pain. Glancing
over her shoulder, she saw his approaching dark form
stain the whiteness of the snow. She continued on. Her
shins struck against something and she clamped her
hand over her mouth to keep from crying out. It was

the ladder leading to the forecastle deck. She tried taking the stairs two at a time, but slipped and fell on one knee. Then she turned and saw him coming at her, his cheeks streaming blood and his arms grasping the air. With all her might Sophie pushed her fists against his chest and the reverend fell backward. His arms flailed in space, and the Bible went flying as he tried to grab something to hold onto. There was nothing. He landed on the deck with resounding force.

"Jesus, God!" Sophie cried. She paused on the top step a moment to look at him. He didn't move. Thinking that he was dead or mortally injured, Sophie climbed back down the ladder. "Preacher! Preacher!"

The reverend's eyes snapped open and he growled, coming at her on all fours. She turned to run but his bony fingers wrapped around her ankle. She held onto the railing and kicked. The heel of her foot slammed against his forehead. She felt his fingers slip from her ankle, and she continued running up the steps. "Jesus, God, help me!" she screamed. From out of the swirling mass of snow a pair of hands grabbed her shoulders. Sophie gasped and collapsed on the deck.

"Sophie, what in God's name?" Rory swept her up into his arms. Covering her as best he could with his oil skins, he hurried toward the cabin.

Rory kicked open the door to Sophie's cabin. Betzy sat up in bed and screamed, "Lawd o' mercy!"

"I don't have time for any foolishness, Betzy!" Rory snapped. "Now get out of bed and go to the galley. Bring some hot water, some hot tea and if you can find it, some brandy."

"What happen?"

"How the hell do I know? I found her wandering around on deck with hardly anything on. Now move!"

Betzy, who was already dressed, hurriedly stepped into a pair of shoes and threw on her cape, then disappeared through the cabin door. Rory put Sophie down, quickly tore off the soaking clothes and wrapped her in every blanket he could find. He held her fast,

warming her with his own body heat and rocked her
back and forth, saying her name over and over.

Sophie didn't even sustain a head cold from her
exposure to the elements. Reverend Poke, who wasn't
discovered until some time later, contracted a severe
case of pneumonia from which he did not recover.

Twenty-three days later, as the *Connemara* successfully passed through the Straits of Magellan, the good
reverend expired. As the ship neared the islands of
Diego Ramires, he was buried without pomp and
circumstance and without tears. Then he was quickly
forgotten.

Chapter 8

Beneath the shadows of the sails, Betzy and Armanda sat side by side on a grouping of packing crates. Over the months they had become friends. As they gossiped, they furiously fluttered hand-held fans against the incredible heat off the Peruvian coast.

Armanda dabbed her perspiring face and neck with a damp hankerchief. "How's Mr. O'Sullivan faring, Betzy?" Liam had become ill with dysentery from pickled meat that nevertheless became spoiled because of the heat.

Betzy shifted her considerable weight and sighed. "Don't know, Miz Armanda. Seem like Mr. Liam a lot sicker dan de others."

Armanda clucked her tongue against her sagging cheeks. "If only this terrible heat would let up."

"It a misery, dat fo' sure," agreed Betzy. "Right now Miz Sophie is layin' stark naked on de floor of de cabin. She claim it cooler down dere."

"Let's hope she doesn't decide to do the same on deck," quipped Armanda.

"Well, dere no one to stop her now. Since Mr. Liam laid up an' dat crazy rev'und done got dumped in Ol' Man Deep An' Salty."

"Oops! There's a breeze. Quickly, Betzy, turn your crate to the left. Ahhhhhhhh!" Armanda groaned, holding her hair high so that the furtive gust could caress the back of her neck. "Doesn't that feel sweet?"

The two women quickly moved their crates so that they were facing the small wind.

Armanda leaned her head back and frowned. "The sails are still droopy. Nasty little breeze wasn't even enough to give them a billow."

The *Connemara* moved slowly, imperceptibly through the blue Pacific waters. The crew, bereft of every article of clothing save a pair of cut-off trousers and an occasional straw hat, worked as slowly as somnambulists. They sporadically licked a few grains of salt.

"Lawd, dis here a bad situation," Betzy pronounced.

"The captain told me he's heading directly for the Galapagos Islands so that we can obtain fresh food and water," responded Armanda, who draped her wet handkerchief over the sunlit edge of a crate. It would dry in moments. "Course that's a long way off."

"I mean de situation here on de ship," confessed Betzy. "Mr. Liam. He an' Mr. Rory, dey still don't talk much. An' Miz Sophie, she jus' leadin' one on when she really want de other."

"Well, it won't last after we reach San Francisco," Armanda observed. "I suppose it's obvious to everyone that Sophie does prefer Liam, obvious to everyone except Rory, that is. But, I'd do the same thing in her place. If I couldn't have one, I'd have the other. They're both fine looking men. Hmmm . . . wonder what I'm going to find for myself in San Francisco?"

"Yo' countin' on gettin' married, Miz Armanda?"

"That's right. First come, first served! I hear tell there's a hundred men to one woman out there. Even a middle-aged lump like me can get a man and make him happy. That's all I really ever wanted to do, Betzy. Just make some man happy." She patted Betzy's hand. "Course it would be a lot easier if I was beautiful like Sophie."

"Yo' beautiful inside, Miz Armanda. An' in de long run dat's what count."

"So they tell me. But no man ever stayed around for the long run, and *that's* what counts."

Betzy threw back her head and laughed. She cut herself short in the middle of a guffaw. "Whew! It too hot even to laugh."

Rory glanced at the porthole hoping for a moving cloud. If only it would rain! That would bring some relief. Liam moaned. Rory turned back to the bed where his friend was fitfully sleeping. Liam's flesh had a greenish cast. He was perspiring so heavily that his nightshirt was sticking to his body. Liam's illness went against the grain of his methodical life. Rory checked a second nightshirt that he had stripped from Liam's fever-wracked body not an hour earlier. The heat had dried it.

"Come on, Liam, old friend. Time for another change." He slid his arms under Liam's and hoisted him to a sitting position. With effort he stripped the soggy material from Liam's body. He threw it across the chair and proceeded to put the dry one on.

Liam opened his eyes. They were fever-glazed and glowed like blue embers. His dried lips parted and he croaked, "Rory, I must make peace with you in case I should die."

"Nothing's going to happen to you, Liam," replied Rory gently, his eyes misting with tears.

"No," Liam weakly protested, "let's be practical. I have signed papers stating that if anything does happen to me you'll get everything."

A lump rose in Rory's throat. He turned away and pressed his fist against his lips.

"And, one more thing, Rory. I—I—I'm sorry about the woman."

"Sophie?"

"Yes. I'd forgotten her name. Why should I forget her name?" His breathing became more strained. "I'm sorry about our disagreement, but I'm still not giving you my approval."

Rory smiled. That was Liam through and through. Unbending to the end.

"Rory, I regret my quarrel with you. And you are of age. Whatever mistakes you make must be your own!" Liam made a hoarse whisper.

"Thank you, Liam. I appreciate that. Now take a cup of tea?"

"I'll try," Liam managed a smile. "And let's pray that it stays down."

The words spoken, Liam sank into a coma. Rory made him as comfortable as possible, then knelt at his friend's side and began to pray. "Dear God in heaven. I wish to make a covenant with you. If you spare Liam I promise that I will adhere to his wishes and give up Sophie Parmalee."

Several days later the torrid weather dissipated. The tradewinds came up, and the *Connemara* sailed across the sea as smooth as a raindrop sliding down a pane of glass. Captain Fallon headed the ship toward the Galapagos Islands off the coast of Ecuador.

The Galapagos Islands were the peaks of a volcanic complex that centuries before emerged from the depths of the Pacific. They were located where warm and cold currents met without mixing. The two different currents accounted for both the desert clime and the lush tropical forests that covered the Galapagos. There were six main islands. The nearest one to the course charted by Captain Fallon was San Cristobal. As it came into view, passengers and crew watched the strange and forbidding island with trepidation. A black line of dark cliffs and rocky beaches, brightened here and there by sandy patches, stood in stark contrast against an ink blue sky. In the distance steep mountains were enveloped in constantly shifting mists. The early Spanish navigators called them *Las Islas Encantadas,* because the mountains appeared and disappeared at the whim of the veil-like mists.

Captain Fallon decided to drop anchor some distance away to avoid the coral reefs and underwater plateaus. Many of the superstitious sailors refused to go ashore. Captain Fallon ranted and railed until he managed to get eight of his men to agree. Rory, ever the adventurer, insisted upon going, too.

"*Mon Dieu,* Rory," beseeched Sophie. "You can't go on that island! It looks haunted!"

"Miz Sophie right," agreed Betzy. "De Lawd never made dat chunk o' land, uh huh!"

Rory grinned broadly. "That's nonsense. We need to get fresh food and water. With me along to help, we'll get it done that much faster." He frowned, "Sophie, didn't you say you were going to sit with Liam while I'm ashore?"

Sophie knitted her brow and chewed on her inner lip. "He's asleep, Rory. I don't see why . . ."

"I goes an' sits wid him, Mr. Rory," Betzy interrupted. "Don't yo' worry, I's takes good care o' him."

"Thanks Betzy, you're heaven sent!" With that Rory joined the men in the longboat, and they began rowing toward shore.

Captain Fallon stood at the helm of the longboat, staring down into the waters. There lay the sleeping coral ready to strike and rend the wood of the hull. As the longboat neared the shore, the horrified sailors spotted a sort of prehistoric monster—dragons that were three-feet in length. Several wanted to turn back. The captain laughed. "Those are just iguanas. We'll catch a few. They make good eating."

The longboat abruptly scraped bottom. Captain

Fallon jumped out of the ship and was waist high in water. Rory followed, but the men remained motionless.

"Get out of that ship, you sissy sons of bitches!" roared the captain. The men doggedly complied, jumping in the water as if it was molten lava.

The longboat was duly pulled onto the shore. The water kegs were picked out. Not knowing which direction to take, the captain pointed sharply to the land ahead. The coast sloped down to a sandy white beach swept by the surf. A fringelike mass of dark green surrounded the rocky shore. Mangroves guarded the entrance to a tropical forest. The ground was black mud dotted by the droppings of the birds—white egrets, blue-feathered herons and brown pelicans.

As the men noisily made their way through the underbrush, the birds forsook the trees and took flight. Every plant seemed edged with thorns, tearing at the clothing and exposed flesh of the men. Later they were surprised by what they first believed to be a rock, but was a giant tortoise. The tortoise awoke and began to move away from them with surpassing ease.

"We'll get some of them on the way back," announced the captain. "Tortoises can be taken alive and can provide food for weeks to come."

Rory groaned. "You mean you've eaten those ugly things?"

"Certainly," replied the captain. "Tortoise flesh is delectable. Better than chicken. And when the fat is melted down it tastes just like fresh butter."

They followed the trail led by the captain and passed a forty-foot long petrified tree trunk. There the forest suddenly ended and a desert of lava began. The landscape was stern and dreary but nevertheless gave an impression of wild grandeur. The expanses of cracked lava were strewn with cacti and oddly shaped rocks. Occasionally a rock would move, giving testimony to the captain's remark about the tortoises.

"There's no water in this direction," grumbled the captain. "Let's head toward the mountain."

As they trudged on, the earth beneath their feet became damp and soft. Toward the base of the largest mountain they encountered a grassy pasture. The men pushed through the tall grass, which brushed against their bare skin and made their flesh itch.

"There's no fresh water on this God forsaken island," complained one sailor.

"Shut up, Harry," snapped the captain. "The birds and tortoises don't live on salt water. There's a pond around here somewhere."

The tall grass ended where marshland began. The rain-soaked earth squished around the boots and bare feet of the sailors. The captain cocked his head to one side, held up his hands for silence. "Listen," he cried excitedly. "Listen! Do you hear it?"

"Hear what, Captain?" entreated one elderly crew-member.

"Pipe down, Silas!" shouted the captain. "Everyone knows you're half deaf! Everybody be quiet! Shhh . . . *Now* do you hear it?"

"I hear it," piped Rory jumping in the air. "It's the sweet sound of rushing water!"

The men cheered and broke into a run. They reached a pond fed from a spout of gushing water coming through a crevice at the base of the mountain. The men threw themselves into the pond and drank greedily, then began splashing and playing like schoolchildren.

The water casks were filled. Tortoises, iguanas, cormorants, pelicans and albatross were captured or slaughtered to provide food for the hungry passengers and crew. When the longboat returned, it was laden with provisions.

Rory was disappointed to find that Sophie wasn't waiting for him on deck. But his main concern was for Liam. He went directly to his friend's cabin. He found Betzy patiently mopping Liam's brow. And he was awake. His eyes looked clear and a hint of pink crept into his complexion.

"He all better, Mr. Rory," Betzy announced.

Rory's heart leapt with joy. "Are you, Liam? Are you better? Are you really better?"

"I think so," Liam replied softly. "Had a bit of a shock a while back. I thought I'd died and gone to hell."

"Well, now I doubt that, Liam," Rory responded brightly. "Why you're much too good and honest a soul to give the devil his due."

"I wonder," Liam asked himself. He looked at Rory. "I'm sorry I was such a bother."

"You were no trouble," Rory replied with sweet understatement.

"Did I say anything . . . anything important while I was sick?"

"No, nothing," Rory grinned. "At least nothing that made any sense."

Chapter 9

One hundred and eighty-four days after setting out from Maine, the *Connemara* reached the harbor of San Francisco. A wilderness of masts jammed the harbor—clippers, sloops, frigates, prison hulks, galleys, brigantines and bilanders as well as reconditioned hulks and even coastal freighters. Many vessels, abandoned by passengers and crews rushing off to dig for gold, lay rotting at anchor. Some were still laden with cargo. Some had been dismantled for their canvas and cordage, but most of the Round-the-Horn fleet had simply settled into the mud. A few of the deserted ships had been converted into hotels, warehouses, taverns and restaurants to suit the needs of the expanding population.

After a near collision with a large frigate, Captain Fallon was able to bring the *Connemara* into dock. The waterfront was encrusted with barrels, boxes and crates. There was a surplus of tobacco, beef, flour and stoves. But lumber was in short supply and was bringing record prices.

The docks were crowded with men from all walks of life and major countries of the world. Most of them were young, but there was a startling number still in their teens. They all had one thing in common . . . they all had the dream. It showed in their eyes. It was the fevered look of those who had been tempted, drawn and seduced by the lorelei of gold.

"Oh, Susannah!" had slipped in popularity and was put to rest along with wishful thinking and journeys past. A new song exemplified the greedy dream!

Oh, the gold! They say,
'Tis brighter than the day,
And now 'tis mine, I'm bound to shine,
And drive all care away!

It was a song destined to end in an anguished cry, for most of the dreams of gold would lead only to dry waterholes and death.

Sophie and Betzy were in their cabin packing. Betzy slammed shut the lid to a small trunk and said, "Well, we here, Miz Sophie. Now what yo' gonna do 'bout Mr. Rory?"

Sophie looked up. Her mouth grew egg-shaped with indignation. "I made no promises, Betzy."

"No?" replied Betzy in a disapproving tone of voice. "But he still all hot-eyed over yo'. He want to marry yo'."

"One simply can't travel without a man. Believe me, Betzy. And as for marriage—piffle. I've got bigger fish to fry."

"Seem to me like Mr. Rory done got stuck to de pan."

Sophie ignored her companion and continued to pack. When she had finished, she smoothed the folds of her emerald green satin gown. Sophie checked her makeup in the mirror and, using a bit of spit, tightened a curl at her temple.

"We'll just wait a while down here until the riffraff leaves the ship, Betzy."

Betzy shook her head, sighed and settled her weight on a large trunk.

The passengers crowded around the closed-off gangplank. For many of them it would mean new beginnings; for others it would mean quick defeat. Armanda gathered her entourage of homely but erstwhile homemakers. "Tits high, ladies! There's men awaiting!"

The gangplank was lowered. Armanda led her brigade onto the wharf where they were greeted by stares, whistles and several shouted proposals of marraige from the eager and lonely men. The male passengers quickly followed, their faces unable to mask anxiety about the future.

Sophie flounced on deck twirling a parasol and carrying a hatbox. Betzy struggled behind her with two heavy suitcases. Sophie was carefully made up, and her hair had been curled into tight little sausages. She stopped short at the sight of Rory, nearly causing Betzy to drop the suitcases. She flashed him a dazzling smile and strode forward extending her hand as she approached.

"Rory, why, are you waiting for me?"

"You know I am," the young man replied.

"How sweet! Perhaps you'd be good enough to help Betzy with our luggage."

She turned and waved to Liam. "*Au revoir*, Mr. O'Sullivan," she called out brightly. "I do hope you're successful in your business ventures."

"But, but I don't understand," said Rory. "Where are you going? I thought . . ."

Sophie pursed her lips and said as evenly as possible. "You thought what, Rory? I told you I was coming to San Francisco to work and work I will!"

Rory looked stricken. He ran his fingers through his

hair in a gesture of despair and stammered, "Ah, ah, where will you be working?"

Sophie looked flustered, twirled her parasol and quickly said, "I—I—just can't remember the name of the place." She turned to Betzy, placing the burden on her. "Do you, Betzy?"

The Negress shook her head. "No, Miz Sophie. I can't think of it fo' nothin'."

Numb with disappointment, Rory followed Sophie's orders and helped carry her luggage onto the dock.

"Now be a dear and get us a carriage," smiled Sophie. Rory did as she asked. When the two women and the luggage were loaded onto a wagon, Sophie blew him a poorly aimed kiss and said brightly, "Goodbye, Rory. You've been a dear. You must come and see me where I'm performing." Then she nudged the driver sharply in the ribs with her parasol to drive on.

Rory, stunned, stood on the dock staring after them. Liam, who had witnessed the parting, walked down the gangplank and went to his friend. He put his arm around the young man's shoulder and searched for words of comfort he did not feel. Rory looked up at him, tears welling up in his eyes, his voice breaking. "Not even a good-bye kiss."

Sophie noted that most of the people milling about the streets were young men. At the sight of her, the miners whooped and hollered and shouted their names. Sophie demurely lowered her parasol and decided that San Francisco was going to be the place for her. Somewhere in the city of San Francisco there were men who would appreciate a beautiful and talented woman. And Sophie wanted a lot of appreciation.

The driver, a ferret of a man, sneaked a look at Sophie and asked timidly. "Where to, Miss?"

"What's the best hotel in town?" demanded Sophie. "The very, *very* best?"

Without hesitation the driver replied, "The United States Hotel, ma'am. But it's mighty expensive."

"Never mind that!" snapped Sophie. "You take us there!"

"Yes, ma'am," replied the driver and accompanied his reply with a snap of the whip. The horses trudged forward through the muck and mire that was designated a street.

San Francisco was the ultimate boomtown. Spontaneous, unplanned and overflowing with people, it teemed with vigor and untamed emotions. On every side stood buildings of every sort, either just begun or half-finished. Most were canvas sheds, open in the front and covered with signs in all languages. People hurried to and fro, keeping themselves busy until their dreams came true. They were as diverse and bizarre as the buildings.

Word that a beautiful woman was arriving brought the miners, the gamblers, the up-and-comers and the down-and-outers out of the tents and buildings. Out they came, holding mugs of beer or cups of lather and razor, in all stages of dress and undress. They began clapping, slowly at first, in a stark beat. Then the pace quickened and the applause built to a crescendo.

Sophie was obliged to smile, nod her head occasionally and blow a few kisses in the air. Several adventurous men attempted to climb upon the carriage, but Betzy quickly dispatched them with a few jabs of Sophie's parasol.

"Tell me, driver," Sophie asked, "what exactly is the population of San Francisco?"

"About twenty-five thousand," the driver punctuated his answer with a spat of tobacco. Sophie shuddered as she watched the brown glob hit the backside of one of the ragged horses.

"I never seen so many hornytoad critters in all my life," Betzy grumbled.

"Don't complain, Betzy," Sophie admonished. "They're going to make us rich."

They stopped to allow a cattle drive to pass. Sophie

held a silk handkerchief to her face to hide the odor of the dung-bespattered beasts.

"They seem to be mostly men," Sophie commented to the driver.

"What, miss?"

"I said they seem to be mostly men!"

"Yes, miss, and they ain't used to seein' a white woman out here."

"And they all look *so* young," Sophie added with relish.

They continued on, passing row upon row of campers' tents and board shanties where bunks without mattresses were rented for fifteen dollars a night. They drove past liquor stores, Chinese laundries and whorehouses. Slatternly women the miners called soiled doves peered at Sophie enviously. Their faces were disfigured by thick makeup. She watched in horror as huge gray rats the size of terriers rushed from the buildings and tried to bite the horses.

The driver whipped out a Colt 45 and buried a handful of bullets in the mud. The rats scurried away.

"Goodness, driver," exclaimed Sophie. "Is it always this muddy?"

"It's been worse, miss. Many a mule or horse or sometimes a drunk has gotten sucked right into the mud an' perished."

"How dreadful."

"Yeah! You got to be careful crossin' them streets."

When they reached Clay and Kearny Streets, the heart of the city, the driver had to get out of the wagon and shove brushwood under the sunken wheels to get them moving again. A sign nailed against a tree caught Sophie's eye:

THIS STREET IS UNPASSABLE,
NOT EVEN JACK-ASSABLE!

Betzy tugged at Sophie's sleeve. "Did yo' see dat sign? How we gonna get to de hotel?"

"We'll manage, Betzy. We'll manage," replied Sophie confidently. "How much further is it to the hotel?" Sophie asked the driver.

"Not far now, miss."

At that moment three villanous looking men jumped the wagon. One of them tried to snatch the reins from the driver, another attempted to carry off Sophie and a third went after the luggage. Sophie began stabbing her assailant with her parasol and screaming loudly. Betzy picked up a heavy suitcase and lambasted the thief across the chest, knocking him off the back of the wagon and into the mud-filled street. The driver was struggling with his attacker. Sophie's screams attracted the men in the street, and they hurried to her rescue. The vigilantes descended upon the wagon. They subdued the three attackers, beat them into the ground and kicked them senseless.

Sophie was beaming over such a display of male courage. "Now everybody step up here," she ordered. "I'm going to give you my personal thank you." The men lined up, and Sophie rewarded each one with a kiss upon the cheek and made them promise to watch for her when she was performing on the Barbary Coast.

"How come yo' sure yo' goin' to be workin' on de Barbary Coast, Miz Sophie?"

"Hush, Betzy. Why, of course I am."

"Yes. But jus' how?"

"I'll figure that out later."

After two more mud-filled streets, the driver pulled the wagon up to the United States Hotel. It was a rambling three-story building with a pretense of luxury. It was white, one of the few buildings in San Francisco that had been painted, and properly ornate. The driver carried the luggage to the front desk. Sophie paid him for his services and tipped him handsomely.

Sophie and Betzy surveyed the lobby. It was expensively furnished with overstuffed velvet-covered furniture, oriental carpets, crystal chandeliers and potted palms. The desk clerk, a toothpick of a man with an effete manner, smiled at Sophie.

"May I be of some assistance?" he asked in a high fawning voice.

"Yes," replied Sophie as charmingly as possible. "I'd like a suite of rooms for myself and my maid."

The clerk uncomfortably shifted his gaze to Betzy, lowered his voice and said, "We don't usually allow coloreds to reside at the United States Hotel, miss."

"Then you'll have to make an exception. I just can't get along without my personal maid. If there's any problem I'd be glad to speak to the manager."

"Well—uh—that won't be necessary, miss," replied the clerk, obviously anxious to avoid problems. "I can let you have a suite of rooms on the second floor."

"What are your rates?" asked Sophie, steeling herself for the worst.

"Five hundred dollars a month . . . in advance," the clerk replied blithely.

Betzy's skin turned ashen and she shook her head sharply as if testing her hearing.

Sophie, who was just as shocked as Betzy, concealed it with aplomb. She forced her mouth into a tight smile and even managed to control her eyebrows from arching in shock. "I'd like to see the rooms first, please."

"Of course!" The desk clerk rang for his replacement, took the keys from the board and escorted the two women up the winding mahogany staircase to the second floor. The suite consisted of a sitting room, a bedroom and a bath. The rooms were small, but Sophie reasoned that if this was the best that San Francisco had to offer, then she would have to make do.

"Where will my maid sleep?" she asked.

"We can have a single bed brought up, miss."

"You do that and have it placed in the front room. And while you're at it, send up a bottle of well-iced champagne and . . ." she smiled at Betzy, "two glasses."

The clerk shifted his feet on the flowered carpet and lowered his head. "And the . . . money?"

"I shall have it ready for you when you return."

After the door had closed, Betzy collapsed on the sofa in a heap. Her words came whistling through her widely spaced teeth like wind through a thistle. "Miz Sophie, how we gonna 'ford dis place? Five hundred dollar a month—we could build our own house fo' dat."

Sophie strode about the rooms. "I agree, Betzy. Mighty tiny rooms for the money. But we can't live in a tent, can we? Now help me unbutton my dress and loosen my corset so I can get out the money and pay that wretched man."

A half hour later Sophie and Betzy, happy to have the arduous voyage behind them, had allowed themselves to become a bit drunk. Sophie, her sausage curls unfurled, picked up the bottle of champagne and held it up to the light. "There's just enough for another glass each."

"Goodness, Miz Sophie," Betzy slurred, "I couldn't drink no mo' of dat stuff. It might go to my head."

Sophie gazed affectionately at her friend and began giggling. "Not if it has a choice, Betzy." She cried. "Not—if—it—has—a—choice!"

Captain Fallon had given the crew leave save for a few men who would guard the lumber on board. The crew streamed off the ship, eager to release pent-up emotions. They wore their most tattered clothes and carried a change of duds under their arms. First they planned to head for a communal bathhouse and get themselves bathed, shaved and spruced up. Then after committing their ragged garments to the trash, they would don fresh clothing and head for the saloons in search of liquor and women.

Liam had bathed in his cabin and was dressed in a black suit more suitable for a wake than the brawling city of San Francisco. He went to Rory's cabin and knocked on the door.

"Aye, it's open."

Liam frowned. Rory's voice still had that hollow sound, sustained ever since Sophie's departure. Sighing, Liam pushed open the door and stepped inside, wondering which of Rory's moods he would encounter—dark sorrow, cloying self-pity or smoldering rage.

Rory was sitting in a tub, staring dully at the sponge in his hand and shivering in the cold water.

"Why aren't you ready?" asked Liam, trying to ignore his friend's somber mood.

"I don't think I . . ."

"You're coming ashore with me," Liam took the sponge from Rory's hand. "The water's cold, man. You'll catch pneumonia." He roughly began scrubbing Rory's back. "Hell, what am I doing? You're not a child." He handed Rory the sponge. "Now finish bathing and get dressed. Your life hasn't ended simply because some tart . . ."

"Don't speak like that!" Rory exploded.

"I'm sorry," Liam said gently. "I'm sorry for the hurt you feel, but you'll get over it in time."

"How do you know I will, Liam?" Rory retorted. "You've never felt anything for anybody."

"Perhaps not," Liam replied quietly, "but I'm not entirely insensitive to the feelings of others."

"I'm sorry. I had no right saying that. I'll be ready in a few minutes. I'll meet you on deck."

Liam nodded and left his friend.

The sun had set and the boisterous town began kicking up its heels. Thousands of kerosene lamps had set the hillsides ablaze with light. The combined sounds of fighting and shouting, buying and selling made a dull roar.

Captain Fallon standing on deck next to Liam remarked, "Just listen to that, Liam, that's the sound of a city being born. And old mother earth is getting the worst of it. Oh, well, her labor will be short if mighty painful."

Liam contemplated the sprawling town, which grew up from the foot of the bay. So much humanity made him feel ill at ease. He was anxious to get the lumber sold and leave San Francisco as quickly as possible. But for where? His plans had taken him no further than the Golden Gate.

The captain asked, "And what have you made up your mind to do, Liam? Are you going to travel north after all?"

Liam pursed his lips. It irritated him to be without a ready answer. "I've heard tales of trees as tall as the masts of a ship, and if they're true, there's a fortune to be made. Why, the need of lumber is so bad here that I can probably get any price I ask."

"Aye, that's true enough. By this time tomorrow you'll be a rich man. You could set up any kind of business you want right here in San Francisco."

"Lumber is my business," said Liam tersely. "I think that San Francisco is a bit . . . boisterous for my tastes."

"But not for Rory's?" parried the captain.

"Rory will do what I wish," said Liam bluntly. "And a lot could be said for putting some distance between Liam and that woman."

The captain refrained from commenting on Sophie Parmalee, for he had truly liked her. "Well, I'm inclined to agree with you about San Francisco, Liam. I've seen too many cities that cater to the darker side of man's desires." He grinned. "Of course, you know I haven't suddenly turned moral—just old. So if you're thinking of exploring the coast and you could use a slightly worn sea captain, I'd be more than willing."

Liam turned to Captain Fallon. He was touched by the genial old man's offer. "I was hoping you would say that, Josh. I'd sure as hell miss your company."

Rory joined them on deck. Despite his hangdog expression, he appeared as bright and shiny as a brass button. The captain patted him on the back. "Well, son, you look ready for the best kind of trouble."

"Don't you want to come with us, Captain?" Rory asked.

"Oh, no, son. I'm determined to keep the thieves at bay." He patted the pistol tucked into his waistband. "They'll get nary a knothole with Joshua Fallon at the helm."

Liam took Rory's arm. "Come on, Rory. Let's see what San Francisco has to offer."

At the foot of the gangplank, two of the captain's crew stood guard. They, too, carried pistols.

"Sweet Jesus," Rory muttered. "You'd think they were guarding a pirate's treasure."

"It's going to be worth a lot more that that, Rory. Everybody's clamoring for lumber."

They pushed their way through the denizens of the waterfront. Rory spotted a nameless bar. "Now there's a likely place, Liam. Shall we start there?"

"Whatever you say," replied Liam, determined to keep Rory in an even humor.

The bar was a mud-spattered canvas tent. Next to it was an open yard, and tacked upon a tree was a crude sign: CLOTHING REFRESHED. Several laundresses were slaving over steaming pots of boiling clothes. They were Mexican women, rudely called *greaseritas* by the San Franciscans. Liam shuddered as he eyed the swarthy women at work.

The tent was smoke filled and dimly lit by kerosene lanterns. Riding over the raucous voices of the clientele was a two-piece band—a violin and an accordian played by a Mexican and a Negro. The miners and dock workers at the bar made space for the two "gentlemen." The bartender, a burly man who sported the handle of a pick ax tucked into his trousers, ambled over to them. "What will it be, gents?"

"Two Irish whiskies," replied Liam.

"Make mine a double," added Rory.

When the whiskies arrived, Rory downed his and

immediately ordered another double. Liam, frowning, said, "Look, Rory. I know you're upset over that young woman. But you've got to put aside your disappointment."

"I want to go back to Maine," Rory replied sullenly.

"That's impossible!"

"Why? We have the ship."

"I plan to explore the coast, Rory. Why, I hear there are trees that reach the very sky and are as big around as a house."

"All you ever think about," said Rory bitterly, "is timber, timber and more timber!"

Liam, embarrassed by his friend's outburst, looked around the bar. He grabbed Rory's arm and said, "Come on, we'll get a table."

They seated themselves at a small, shaky table and were immediately surrounded by three women whose occupations were apparent. Two were Mexican and the third Chinese. Matching gowns, low cut and cinched at the waist, exposed their nipples. The ballooning skirts ended at the knees, revealing striped hose. They circled the table, making wet noises with their red lips and whispering their specialties. The Chinese girl reached out and grabbed Liam's crotch. He blushed and angrily pushed her hand away. "What's the matter, sweet thing? Don't you like girls?" The men sitting nearby laughed.

Liam turned to Rory. "Come on, let's get out of here. Let's get ourselves some supper."

One of the Mexican women lifted her skirt and shouted. "You can get your supper here, *amigos!*" The entire bar broke into uproarious laughter. Liam pulled Rory to his feet and spirited him out the door. Liam stopped a passerby and asked where they might find a decent supper.

"The only decent dining room in town is at the United States Hotel, but the prices are dear."

"Where's it located?" asked Liam. The man gave him directions, and Liam and Rory hurried through the bustling streets dodging drunks, thrown bottles and mudholes.

Despite the condescending host, Liam felt at ease in the hotel dining room. Rory ordered another whiskey and Liam remarked as lightly as possible. "You'd better get some good food in your belly before you drink anymore, Rory."

Rory scowled in rebuttal. The menu was printed in French. Liam waved it aside and ordered a hearty dinner of steak and eggs for both of them, hoping it would slow down Rory's state of inebriation. When the food arrived, Rory stared at his plate and ordered yet another whiskey.

Liam began eating ravenously. "Your food's going to get cold."

"I'm not hungry," growled Rory. He looked around the dining room. "Nice place! Why don't we stay here?"

"You know it's too expensive. We'll stay on the *Connemara* until we get the lumber sold and then we'll explore the coast. Get outselves some acreage and . . ."

"I know. Start a mill," replied Rory sarcastically.

"Rory, there's a fortune waiting for us up there. Don't throw it away just because you're upset over that tart."

"Don't call her a tart!" shouted Rory and pounded his fist on the table. People turned to stare at the noisy young man.

"Shhh!" admonished Liam. "People are looking at us."

"So what the hell do I care?" replied Rory defiantly. "We're going to be *timber barons!*" he announced to the shocked patrons. They looked away or stared uncomfortably at their food. The host appeared and spoke to Liam, "Your friend is going to have to control himself, or we'll have to ask him to leave."

"He'll be quiet," Liam assured the worried man.

"Will he?" Rory grinned menacingly at the frightened host. "Bring me another whiskey!"

Liam shot a warning glance at his young friend. "Shut up, Rory!"

Rory stood up, knocking over his empty glass. He was ready for a scene and was about to start one. Just then he saw Sophie enter the dining room. She was wearing a gown of orange so brilliant that it hurt his eyes. Around her bare shoulders she clutched a rust-colored feather boa.

Liam turned his head to see what Rory was staring at. When he saw Sophie, he inwardly groaned. "Rory, don't . . ."

Rory ignored Liam and strode across the dining room to Sophie, who was waiting to be seated. Waiters halted, forks stopped in midair. Everyone turned to watch the spectacle about to take place.

"Sophie!"

Upon hearing Rory's voice, Sophie immediately scowled. But as she spun around, she put on a charming smile. "Why, Rory, how delightful to run into you, *n'est pas?*"

Rory scanned her face for encouragement, but saw none. "Sophie, what are you doing here?"

"Why, I'm eating here, of course. It's the only decent dining room in San Francisco."

"Are you with anybody?"

"Can't you see that I'm not? I decided to partake of the French cuisine."

Rory grabbed her arm. "Sophie, I've got to talk to you."

She stared at his hand. "You've been drinking."

"Sophie, what's happened to you? You weren't cold like this on the *Connemara.*"

"Please," Sophie whispered, "people are staring at us."

"Let them stare!" Rory said angrily. "I want some answers."

Sophie glanced irritably about the room. It was not

the kind of audience she had hoped for. Now it was her turn to become angry. "You want some answers? Then you shall have them, Rory Fitzpatrick. It was a shipboard affair. That was all. But now it's over. Do you understand?"

"Sophie, don't!" Rory's voice was anguished.

"Take your hands off me, Rory. Let me be. Let go!" Rory released his grip on her arm. Sophie rubbed the bruised spot.

"I'm sorry, Sophie. I didn't mean to hurt you."

"Well, you did. Just look at that mark. I'll have to go change gowns. It looks like I've been beaten up. Now just stay away from me." Sophie backed away from him. "Do you hear? *Just stay away!*" Sophie turned and fled from the dining room. Rory stared after her a long time, watching her walk out of his life once again.

He felt a hand touch his shoulder. It was Liam's. "Come on, Rory. Come and eat."

"Give me some money, Liam," said Rory intensely.

"For what—more liquor?"

"I want some money now. I'm tired of you always carrying the cash. I've worked hard and the lumber's going to fetch a pretty penny. I'd like to see some of it . . . now."

Liam knew better than to argue with his headstrong friend. He opened up his wallet and withdrew a handful of bills. Rory snatched the money and tucked it into his boot.

"When will you be coming back to the ship, Rory?" Liam asked.

"You'll see me when you see me," Rory whirled and left the dining room.

Liam returned to his table and tried to finish his supper, but he had no appetite. He called for the check. Not knowing where to go, he returned to the ship.

Captain Fallon was still standing watch on deck.

Liam told him what had happened. The captain shook his head and replied, "Well, he'll need a good drunk to help flush it out of his system. But he'll be back, don't you worry. Where else has he got to go?"

"Where else has any of us to go?" replied Liam sadly.

Early the next morning the lumber went on sale. The *Connemara* was jammed with eager buyers. The bidding was opened, and the lumber brought a record-breaking price of one dollar per board foot. By noon every board, straight or warped, had been sold for cash. Only the persistent odor of timber and a few shavings were left. Liam was greatly pleased with the profit, and wished Rory had been there to share his triumph.

The money safely stored in the ship's safe and guarded by two of the captain's most trusted men, Liam and Captain Fallon toured the waterfront saloons hoping to garner knowledge about lands to the north of San Francisco. In the saloon Liam had visited only a day earlier with Rory, the men met two shipowners who had fantastic tales to tell.

A German named Goetz and an Irishman named Hartnett had been sent North by "Fast Jack" Baxter, notorious owner of the Alhambra, Barbary Coast's most successful saloon. Their mission had been to bring back a cargo of ice chipped from icebergs. Baxter and the shipowners reasoned that the northern waters, at the same high latitude as Newfoundland, held great floating islands of glacial ice. Goetz and Hartnett set sail from San Francisco and traveled up the coast to Puget Sound. The gateway to the sound was the Strait of Juan de Fuca, the middle of which was the newly drawn boundary between the United States and Canada. The men discovered that the sound was ice free because of the warming Japanese current year around. Instead of ice, their ship returned with a load of pilings cut at the water's edge, and these were sold at a tidy profit.

The men were enthusiastic about logging in the Northwest, but neither of them wanted to do it, for they were both homesick for their families in Texas. Their descriptions of the giant forests, the easy possibilities for transporting the timber and the availability of land—there were less than one-hundred white people settled on the sound—fully convinced Liam that his and Rory's destinies lay in the great Pacific Northwest.

After leaving the bar, Liam told the captain, "I've heard enough, Josh, to convince me that we should travel North immediately. We'll take a skeleton crew and when we get back to the ship, we'll make up a list of supplies."

"But what about Rory?"

Liam in his enthusiasm had forgotten about his absent friend. "We'll have to wait for him, of course. But there's every possibility he's waiting for us at the ship this very moment."

"I doubt it, Liam. A man doesn't get a woman like Sophie Parmalee out of his system in such a short time."

Rory did not return to the *Connemara* until three days later. He'd done a tour of the dives of Telegraph Hill, those elaborate establishments around Portsmouth Square where anything could be had for the proper amount of money. He continued drinking at various bordellos, and after being ejected from several of better class, he began working his way through the notorious "cribs."

A crib was exactly what its name implied. It was a small, narrow, one-storey shack, divided in two by heavy curtains. Inside, Rory would find two or three Chinese girls. Each girl wore the traditional costume of her trade—a black silk blouse with a narrow band of tortoise on which flowers had been embroidered across the front and back. In cold weather the girls wore black silk trousers.

The back room of the crib was meagerly furnished with a washbowl, a bamboo chair and hardboard shelves covered with matting. The front room was usually carpeted and contained a rickety bureau, chairs and perhaps a wall mirror. The entrance to the crib was a narrow door set with a small barred window. The girls took turns standing behind the bars and calling to passing men. When an interested male stopped, the whore displayed the upper part of her body and cajoled with seductive cries and obscene motions. "Chinee girl nice! Come inside please?"

Even though the Chinese prostitute was clean with her own person, washing her entire body daily and taking frequent baths, most of the Oriental whores in San Francisco were diseased. The girl's master always compelled her to entertain every man who applied, regardless of his condition. A San Francisco law stated that parlor houses could refuse to admit boys under sixteen years of age, but the cribs made no such distinctions. White boys as young as ten and twelve found their way there regularly. At the cribs a man could have his choice of girls for twenty-five or fifty cents. Special rates as low as fifteen cents were offered to boys under sixteen.

The sight of the cribs sobered Rory. He was outraged and disgusted by the forced prostitution. Many of the girls were obviously diseased. Most of them were no older than twelve or thirteen. Sickened with himself and feeling contempt for his fellow men in general, he decided it was finally time to find his way back to the *Connemara*. Dirty and unshaven, but dressed in his once Sunday best, he wove an unsteady path through the narrow mudlined streets.

On his way back Rory was set upon by a motley group of thieves. Taken by surprise, he was beaten into unconsciousness and robbed of his jacket, boots and money. Ignored by the passersby, he awoke in a muddy ditch filled with rain water and horse urine. His exposed flesh was covered with blow flies. Feeling like he had seen hell firsthand, Rory managed to right himself and ask directions for the waterfront. He had no idea how long he had been gone from the ship and fervently prayed that Liam had not left without him.

Liam was standing on deck supervising the loading of the cargo for the journey and for settlement. Despite his anxiety about Rory's disappearance, he was determined to go ahead with his plan. About midafternoon of the third day that Rory had been missing, he looked up to see an appalling apparition stumbling up the gangplank. Rory was so covered with dried blood, mud and grime that Liam did not recognize his friend. He was about to order the terrible straggler from the premises when he saw Rory's pale blue eyes shining plaintively through the filth.

"Rory!" Liam cried and ran to his friend to help him on board. "What the hell happened to you?"

"I got rolled."

"And the money?"

"They took every cent. I didn't know where else to go. But if I'm not welcome here . . ."

"No, no. You were right to come back here. I'm sorry we quarreled. But now you're back and that's all that counts." He threw his arms around Rory's shoulders and embraced him. "Come on," urged Liam. "I'll see you have a bath. Then I'll take you to the galley. You'll have a good meal and then I have something to discuss with you."

An hour later Liam and Rory were sitting in the galley sharing coffee and a bite of stew. Liam told Rory that he had sold the lumber at a dollar per foot. Rory exclaimed, "Jesus Christ! The damned boards *were* more valuable than gold!"

"I bought the supplies, and Captain Fallon and a small crew are going to take us exploring up the coast. Rory, I tell you I've heard stories of trees—pines, hemlocks, cedars, anywhere from 60 to 120 feet high—and nobody's up there claiming the land except for a handful of settlers who only think a tree's something to piss against!"

Rory threw back his head and laughed. It was an artificial sound.

Liam was aware of Rory's forced enthusiasm. "She's still on your mind, isn't she?"

"No, damn it! She's out of my system, I tell you."

Liam regarded his young friend thoughtfully and wondered if Rory were telling the truth or only thought he was.

Loaded with enough machinery, tools, trapping supplies and men to get started in the timber business, the *Connemara* set sail that very evening. The weather was mild and the seas were friendly and they made good time.

On September 12, 1849, the *Connemara* dropped anchor in Discovery Bay, seventy miles inland from the rocks of Cape Flattery that guarded the Strait of Juan de Fuca. Following the advice of Goetz and Harnett, Liam had brought along a small sailboat. Liam, Rory and Captain Fallon boarded the sailboat and began exploring the inlets. They were astounded by the magnificent forests that rose beneath the sky. Giant hemlocks, white pines, cedars, spruces and firs were in abundance. Some of the trees grew at least 250 feet straight up in the air, quite unlike the squat gnarled trees the young men had used for lumber in Maine.

Liam's hands twitched. He could hardly wait to level an ax. He could fairly hear the sound of a sawmill buzzing in the background, blotting out the squawks and whispers of the forest creatures. For a long time the men dared not speak, they were so in awe of the land and its bounty. They left the sailboat and, standing on the needle-strewn ground, they removed their hats in deference to this great work of nature. Then they slapped each other in high spirits, and Captain Fallon began whistling a long-forgotten tune. They leaned back, their eyes straining to see the tops of the great trees.

"Look at them, Liam!" exclaimed Rory. "They go right up to the sky. Why, it looks like they're holding up the clouds."

Liam solemnly replied. "They do indeed. They're the very pillars of heaven themselves!"

BOOK TWO

Chapter 10

Puget Sound was part of the Oregon Territory.
Under the Oregon Donation Land Law, a single man
could lay claim to a quarter section or 160 acres of free
land. Liam and Rory claimed theirs, founding their mill
site on the east bank of Hood Canal, a natural channel
that George Vancouver had discovered in 1792. In
sheltered Gamble Bay the water was deep enough for
ocean-going ships, and there was a flat sandy spit of
land large enough to accommodate the mill buildings.
The *Connemara* was brought to the site and unloaded.
Liam, Rory, the captain and a crew of twelve men
began building a bunkhouse, a cookhouse and the
framework for the Connemara Mill Company's first
sawmill.

Liam was pleased when the captain and his men
offered to claim their land and then turn it over to the
newly formed enterprise for a percent of the profits.
That meant that the company was starting with 2,400
acres of land. It was a considerable source of irritation

to Liam, however, that he could have claimed twice as
much land had he been married. His thoughts turned
back to Maine and to Kathleen Mulvany. Touching the
wooden cross she had given him, he sat down to write a
letter.

"My Dear Kathleen,

Rory and I are finally settled, and if you wish to
write, as I hope you do, you may address your
missive to Port Gamble, Oregon Territory. And I
shall hope to receive it. We managed to round the
Cape and, despite the usual shipboard calamities
and illnesses, we all survived. After selling our
lumber at a goodly profit in San Francisco, we
then traveled up the Coast and decided to settle
here. If you could only see the land you would
know why.

Oh, what timber! You cannot imagine. Forests
so thick you could not possibly ride a horse
through them. Forests into which you cannot see
and which are almost dark under the bright
midday sun. It is nature in her most wonderful
state. Primeval, some would call it, but I prefer to
think of it as a veritable Garden of Eden, an Eden
which will certainly pave the way to the success of
our newly formed Connemara Mill Company.
Rory and I and our men have laid claim to a vast
amount of land. And if my plans do not go awry,
more lands and more trees will be forthcoming.

Oh, the trees! They thrust themselves through
the clouds and are as mighty as anything on earth.
A true wonderment displaying God's good grace
to man. Why there must be hundreds and hundreds of square miles of timber here.

I'm smiling to myself for you are probably
thinking how I do go on about timber. Rory
ofttimes tells me the same thing. I hope you
received the present I sent you from Rio de

Janeiro and that your parents were not displeased
by perhaps the too personal selection of my gift. I
hope that they are all in good health. Likewise
your brothers.

I remain your sincere friend,

Liam O'Sullivan"

Liam underestimated the woodlands of the great
Pacific Northwest. They covered, not hundreds and
hundreds of square miles, but thousands and thousands
of square miles. It was the greatest concentration of the
greatest trees known to man. They were a treasure that
would surpass all the gold and silver strikes that had
already inflamed the American imagination.

Sophie was beginning to worry about the money she
was spending on living expenses. The small suite at the
United States Hotel was costing her five hundred
dollars per month, and the price for meals was astro-
nomical. Like her mother, Sophie respected the value
of a dollar, and valued financial independence above all
else.

At first she had been delighted by the attention of the
women-hungry men of San Francisco, but the novelty
quickly wore off. Now she rarely ventured outside the
hotel, for wherever she went the miners rioted to see
her. Several times she felt panic as the unruly mob
swarmed about her. And the constant threat of fire
unsettled her even more. Almost daily flash fires swept
through the hastily assembled buildings and tents of the
mining boomtown. Fire protection was crude and
scanty. After the flames were put out, the debris was
simply cleared away and new buildings swiftly erected.
Sophie had never gotten over the horror of her
mother's death. The unnerving sound of fire bells sent
her into a depression that only her opium cigarettes
could ease. And she was running out of them.

She *had* to seek and find employment.

Sophie sat on the flowered rug in the middle of the bedroom floor counting her money for the third time. "Three thousand two hundred and nine, three thousand two hundred and ten, three thousand two hundred and eleven. God damn it! It comes out different each time."

Betzy came into the room. "What de matter, Miz Sophie?"

Sophie blew a curl out of her eye. "Each time I count our money, it comes out to something different."

Betzy chuckled. "I guess yo' need a protector an' a bizness man. Now dat nice Mr. Rory, he would take care of dat."

Sophie grunted in exasperation. "Well, we've got either three thousand two hundred and eleven dollars, three thousand two hundred and three dollars or two thousand one hundred and eighty dollars left."

"Dat money sho' is flyin' fast, Miz Sophie. We ought to move to a cheaper place."

"No! I won't live in a sty. I've already done that."

"Miz Maddie's weren't no sty, honey. I seen sties an' I know. Yo' should try livin' in a nigger shack on a tobacco farm in Carolina."

"I know," admitted Sophie. "I'm sorry. Mama always did the best she could for both of us."

"She sho' did, honey. Now, I can get me a job doin' laundry or maybe even cookin' in de hotel kitchen."

"No! I won't have you working like a common woman," Sophie smiled. "Besides you've got enough to do to take care of me. No, I've put this off long enough. Betzy, we're going out tonight and I'm going to get me a job." Sophie crooked her little finger and added in an elegant fashion. "Now Betzy, you just go fetch me a bath."

Betzy cocked her head to one side. "Gets yo' a what?"

"That's ladylike talk—go fill the tub!"

After a luxurious bath, one of Betzy's elaborate hairdos and her own deft makeup, Sophie was ready to dress and conquer San Francisco's famous Barbary Coast. She selected her red satin gown, which Betzy had meticulously trimmed with shiny red beads she had discovered in an Oriental market. It had been a long laborious effort, but Betzy contended that it kept her from going crazy while being cooped up in the hotel room. Betzy helped Sophie into the gown. Standing in front of the mirror, Sophie was highly pleased with the effect.

Betzy stood back and cheered. "Oooo-whee! Dat dress is goin' to start de biggest fire dat dis here town ever seed."

Sophie, exhilarated by her own appearance, gaily cried, "Bring me my boa, Betzy. Bring me my red feather boa!"

They left the hotel by the back entrance to avoid the scruffy men. Sophie, partly hidden beneath a sweeping black cloak, stood near the kitchen pantries waiting for Betzy to return with an enclosed carriage. The Chinese scullery workers stood watching her with startled expressions, chattering among themselves. Finally a beefy man wielding a copper saucepan chased them back to their posts, but only after pausing to savor Sophie himself.

A large, black carriage rolled up to the back entrance. Betzy pulled open the drapes and called to Sophie. The driver, a shy young man, nearly fell off his perch when he saw Sophie emerge from the back door of the hotel. When Sophie was seated, Betzy rapped on the roof and commanded, "Now get dis thing movin' to de Alhambra! An' we don't want no stops, no jerks an' no collisions!"

The carriage began to roll. Sophie asked Betzy, "How do I look?"

"Like de only pretty woman in dis here mudhole," replied Betzy. "Now don't yo' be nervous. Yo' gonna be de main talk by dis time tomorrow."

The carriage came to an abrupt stop. Betzy thumped on the paneling and shouted, "What de hold up?"

The young driver flipped open the trapdoor and replied casually. "There's a hangin' at Davis Street. Everybody's rushin' to see it."

"Well *I* don't want to see it," snapped Sophie. "Try to get us past as quickly as possible. We're late as it is."

The carriage inched along, for the driver had no intention of missing the hanging. He drove straight down Davis Street where the militia and the mob gathered around the gallows.

The entire sky was lit up with a red glow, almost as if there were a fire burning somewhere. The driver's dark brown hair was tinged red by the sunset. "Sailor's delight," he muttered as he urged his horses forward. The clip-clop of their hooves alerted the mob, and they parted to let the carriage pass. But being a drunken and unruly throng, they began beating on the sides of the carriage with fists and bottles. The men peered through the drapes and, seeing Sophie, began grabbing at her. Sophie drew back, Betzy slammed shut the left window, but the right one would only close halfway. "Give me dat parasol," snorted Betzy. "I poke out a few eyes!"

The mob surged against the vehicle, threatening to overturn it. Sophie and Betzy held onto the hand straps. Betzy pushed open the trapdoor and poked the driver in the buttocks with the parasol. He cried out in pain. "Now yo' gets us through dis jam or I shoves dis all de way up yo' ass!"

Cursing, the driver headed toward a clear space. The carriage passed the scaffold, and the two women had a clear view of the proceedings. The evening air came through the window, pungent with the smell of the crowd. It was a cruel odor, brutal and fearful.

Sophie and Betzy gasped for breath at the same time, and allowed their eyes to focus upon the scene. Two despairing men, silhouetted against the scarlet sky, were standing in the center of the gallows. Waiting nearby was the executioner robed in black.

"Don't look, Miz Sophie," whispered Betzy.

Sophie tried to tear her gaze away but could not. The expressions on the faces of the two condemned men was something she would never forget. They looked like haunted souls lost and completely without hope. The taller man began crying, and the other one cursed him for it. The executioner stepped forward and placed black hoods over each of the men's heads, then guided them into position over the trapdoors. He placed a new rope around each of their necks. The man who had been crying stained his trousers with urine. The executioner pulled the handle and the trapdoors were released. A roar shot up from the crowd as the men's bodies jerked and dangled like puppets on a string.

Sophie covered her ears with her hands and tried to block out the cheers of the onlookers. The carriage began moving once again. The scene passed from view, but not out of their minds.

The Alhambra was the largest and most successful of the Barbary Coast's saloons, rivaled only by the El Dorado, the Bella Union and the Verandah. The saloons competed by offering live entertainment to their customers. At the El Dorado, a chorus line of Chinese girls performed an act entitled "The Language of the Fan." The Verandah featured a black man who wore pipes tied to his chin, a drum strapped to his back, drumsticks fastened onto his elbows and cymbals attached to his wrists, and played all instruments in unison at approximately the same time. And he also tapped his feet, which were enclosed in large hard-soled shoes that made a tremendous clatter. At the Bella Union an elderly French woman performed upon the violin. There was also a Mexican quintet of two harps, two guitars and a flute. To this they added a male soloist whose most popular number was entitled "You Never Miss Your Sainted Mother Until She's Dead and Gone to Heaven."

In San Francisco a pretty white woman was a rare treat. The Alhambra boasted as its major attraction

"Maggie O'Brien—the Irish Songbird." Maggie was unquestionably the leading attraction on the Barbary Coast. Smitten by her success and the attentions of men, Maggie ignored warnings by the owner of the Alhambra, a handsome forceful man named Jack Baxter, who cautioned Maggie about her drinking. Maggie saw the situation differently. Why not have a bit of champagne when you're indispensable? After all, she was the toast of the Barbary Coast.

Inside the Alhambra Maggie was having a quiet fight with Jack Baxter. She had managed to get herself quite drunk and had already given one shoddy performance noticed by a few discerning members of the audience and Jack. He had dragged her backstage and threatened to fire her. Maggie stared at him out of one eye as he ranted.

"Fast Jack" Baxter was just over five feet, eight inches tall, but his trim build and elevated shoes made him appear just this side of six feet. Thick black hair sprang up from a devilishly handsome head, and his skin, deeply tanned to a rich copper, was as smooth as silk.

"Do you ever shave?" Maggie asked, interrupting his threats. "I don't 'member ever seeing you shave, Jack. Your flesh is as smooth as an Eyetalian's foreskin."

Jack winced at Maggie's crude remark, but continued his tirade.

Maggie easily blotted out his words, for she had heard them so many times before. Besides, Jack was more attractive when he was angry. He lost that boyish appearance. His cobalt blue eyes held her in a tight grip, just as they did when they made love. But it had been a long time since they had made love.

"How long has it been, Jack?"

"How long has what been?" he growled. "It's been about three minutes since you had your last drink, if that's what you're asking me."

"How long has it been since we made love?"

Jack looked at his "Songbird." Late nights and hard

liquor had not been kind to Maggie. She was only twenty-six or twenty-seven but looked a good deal older. Her hair was colored with coffee and hung in lank, greasy curls around her pallid face. Her expression was arrogant. Her dark eyes were puffy, and here and there her face sagged. Despite the dissipation she was still an attractive woman, at least in San Francisco.

"About a year ago," replied Jack tartly, "the last time you were sober."

Maggie moved closer to Jack and pressed her breasts against him. "Well, perhaps later tonight?"

"Later tonight nothing. All I want from you, Maggie, is a decent show. If I can't get that out of you, I swear to Christ you're out."

Maggie doubled over with harsh laughter. "And what would you replace me with, Jack? An Indian squaw doing a wardance or a Chink crib girl singsonging her wares?" She made her way back to the bar for another drink.

Sophie's entrance at the Alhambra was talked about for years to come. She sauntered in first, Betzy following closely behind and holding an open black parasol over Sophie's head so that her face was in shadow. Everything stopped. The bartenders stopped mixing drinks and the customers stopped asking for them. The audience stopped watching the banjo player who stopped playing his banjo. All heads turned toward Sophie.

Sophie stepped forward. Betzy closed the parasol and caught the cape as it slid from her mistress's shoulders. Sophie shimmered in a blaze of red beaded satin. The men sucked in their breath as one and moaned. Jack rushed forward and escorted both Sophie and her black companion to a ringside table. They were served a bottle of the best imported champagne on the house.

Word of the beautiful young woman's appearance had reached backstage. Maggie peeked through the red

velvet curtains and stared wide-eyed at Sophie. She
hurried back to her dressing room and immediately
downed another drink.

The miners were awed by Sophie and kept a respectful distance from her. But soon the more daring ones
walked by her table, politely tipped their hats and
scampered away. Sophie was in her glory. The excellent
champagne had helped soothe her nerves and erase the
memory of the hanging. She was ready, ready to bring
the men cheering to their feet as she had done upon the
deck of the *Connemara*. She leaned across the table
and whispered to Betzy, "Did you bring my music?"

"Oh, yes, Miz Sophie. I gots it right here," Betzy
patted a small black satchel strapped to the waistband
of her dress.

"Good. Now relax, Betzy. I'm going to do *just* fine."

"Oh, I knows yo' is, Miz Sophie. But I's so excited, I
can hardly keep from bustin'."

"Control your enthusiasm," Sophie admonished.
"Or else you will be what the French call gauche."

"Dem French got a word fo' everything," muttered
Betzy under her breath.

The orchestra, which consisted of a piano, banjo,
violin and a military drum, began playing. Maggie
O'Brien, the Irish Songbird, wended her way to the
stage wings. The stage was a half-circle located at the
far end of the saloon. The stage branched out into the
audience by means of a three by twenty-foot runway.
The entire platform was raised so that the performer
was several feet above the eye level of the seated
patrons. A backdrop depicting pink and white clouds
was lowered, and the gas footlights surrounding the
stage and runway were lit by scurrying waiters. A
chaise lounge in the shape of a feather had been moved
to center stage. When the curtain was raised, Maggie
was discovered languidly lying upon it. After belching
delicately, Maggie began singing her major contribu-
tion to the musical arts of the Barbary Coast, a little
ditty entitled "Let Me Make You Cozy."

It was a bouncy number, but Maggie wasn't able to keep up with the music. Fast Jack turned his face away in anger as several of the male patrons began to jeer and stomp on the floor. Maggie got worse as she struggled to her feet and began a wavering progress up the runway, making up new lyrics to fit the ones she had forgotten. The orchestra, used to Maggie's worst performances, was having difficulty following her. Jack was devastated. He wandered over to the bar and ordered a stiff drink from Luke the bartender. "God damned bitch," he muttered. "She's worse than ever. I'm surprised she hasn't fallen off the runway."

"Give her time," replied Luke, without looking up from the bar. A once handsome man, Luke O'Neill now had the ravaged countenance of an opium addict.

Maggie staggered to the edge of the runway and held up her hands for quiet. Then she looked down at Sophie and demanded in a slurred voice, "What are ya lookin' at?"

The house grew hushed. Sophie allowed two beats to pass and then replied crisply and loudly. "A no-talent drunk!"

The laughter began as a ripple and built into a thunderous guffaw. Maggie burst into tears and fled from the stage to her dressing room where she sat down and began drinking gin straight from the bottle.

A gentleman, accompanied by a donkey who had been trained to stamp answers to simple yes or no questions, assumed the stage. Nobody paid any attention to the donkey's antics. They were waiting to see what was going to happen next between Jack and Sophie.

Sophie signaled a waiter who was watching her and inquired, "Is the gentleman who showed us to the table the owner?"

"Yes, ma'am. Fast Jack Baxter. That's him over by the bar. The slim, goodlookin' gent with the black hair."

Sophie flashed Jack a dazzling smile and he responded by hurrying to her table. "Can I be of help?" he asked, bowing low from the waist.

"*Au contraire*," responded Sophie. "I can be of help to you!" Jack looked perplexed. "I see, sir, that you're in dire need of a new entertainer. That Irish baggage is rather pathetic. Don't you agree?"

"Are you . . . an entertainer?" asked Jack incredulously. Surely a woman as beautiful and sensual as Sophie couldn't also be blessed with talent.

"I am and I'm prepared to try out at *absolutely* no cost to you."

Jack glanced nervously around the room. The crowd was in an anxious and angry mood. They needed some diversion. They didn't find it with Maggie, and the donkey hadn't captured their hearts. "All right," he agreed. "But I hope you're good. The boys are a bit disappointed over Maggie's performance."

"I'm good," replied Sophie confidently. The crowd didn't bother her in the least. The situation couldn't have been more perfect. Anyone would look good, Sophie figured, following Maggie O'Brien. She eyed the man and his trained donkey. "How soon will *that* be finished?"

Jack was mesmerized. "Anytime you say, sweetheart. Anytime you say." And automatically he signaled the leader of the small orchestra to cut the performance short. The curtain was lowered.

Sophie got to her feet. "Now if you'll excuse me for a few minutes while I get ready, Mr. Baxter?"

"Of course. But I don't know your name, Miss . . .?"

"Sophie Parmalee," replied the young woman. "My mother was French, you know."

"Dat right!" echoed Betzy as she bounced behind Sophie. "She 'bout as French as dey come!"

The men parted as the two women made their way backstage. While Betzy looked through the prop room for something appropriate for Sophie's song, Sophie cajoled and flirted with the disquieted musicians. She

soon charmed them, even the crochety conductor.
Then she passed out sheet music for her most successful
number, "Heaven Help the Working Girl and the
Working Girl Helps Herself." After humming through
the number with the orchestra for pacing and tempo,
Sophie swept into the wings and encountered a smitten
stagehand who had helped Betzy carry a red velvet
chaise lounge from the prop room. "Why, it's perfect,
Betzy, and it doesn't clash with my gown!" She turned
to the stagehand, a young man with a mouthful of teeth
and a face full of freckles. "When I want the curtain
raised, I'll signal you, that is, if you don't mind
watching me."

"No, ma'am. I don't mind watchin' you at all!" the
boy beamed.

Sophie arranged herself on the red velvet chaise in
her most seductive manner. Then she unbuttoned the
side of her dress so that the tight panels fell apart
revealing just a hint of milky white leg. She signaled the
orchestra. They struck up a blaring fanfare, and then
she blew a kiss to the stagehand, who, with sweating
palms, managed to raise the curtain smoothly.

The patrons of the Alhambra began cheering. They
threw their hats in the air and, despite the house rules,
several miners fired off shots. Sophie waited patiently
for them to calm down. Then she began singing in a
loud, brassy voice. The combined effect of the young
woman's beauty, her vigorous singing and her generous
appeal was immediate. The men rushed forward and
began throwing nuggets of gold at her feet. Sophie
deigned not to notice the glittering lumps as they
bounced across the stage. She moved smoothly into the
next chorus. When she was finished, the mob made her
repeat the song for a second time. At the end she held
up her hands for quiet. They quickly gave it to her.

"I must apologize," she began in a humble, childlike
voice. "But that's all I'm prepared to do. You see, I was
just trying out for Mr. Baxter and I really haven't had a
chance to rehearse with the orchestra." She smiled

demurely and added, "I was hoping that if I entertained you, he might consider hiring me." The crowd broke into a thunderous applause. Sophie beamed with pleasure, kissed several of the men nearest to the runway and bowed low—low enough to expose most of her generous breasts.

"Miz Sophie," Betzy cried in shock from off stage.

As soon as the curtain was dropped, Betzy rushed on stage, began gathering the nuggets and tucking them into her voluminous pockets. Sophie stood still and listened to the pandemonium she had caused. One exuberant miner called out, "Hire her, Jack." And others picked up the chant. Soon the entire congregation including bartenders, waiters and orchestra were chanting, *"Hire her! Hire her!"*

Sophie said to Betzy, "You go back to the table and enjoy the rest of the show, Betzy. And be careful nobody steals those nuggets."

"Yo' don't have to worry about dat, Miz Sophie."

"Good. I'm going to have a little "business" talk with Fast Jack. Let's just see how fast he is."

Luke saw Sophie coming and retreated to the far end of the bar. He was stunned by recognition that even his drugged mind could not shut out. This beautiful singer was the young girl he had known in New York City, the daughter of his aging lover, Miss Maddie. She was the girl he had left behind to go in search of a dream, a dream that quickly soured. Memories crowded his head. Luke recalled that first night.

"Where are you going to spend the night, Luke?"

"I'll stretch out on the bar. Maddie's snoring too loud."

"You needn't sleep on the bar, Luke. You can sleep in my room."

How many times had he tried to remember her fresh . . . young . . . beautiful face. In how many opium parlors, how many cribs? Overwhelmed by self-pity and sorrow, Luke turned to fill drink orders, forcing himself to concentrate, to shut out the memories.

Jack sensed Sophie's presence before she said anything. He swung around and faced her. For a moment they didn't speak, but stared into one another's eyes and sized up one another's strengths and weaknesses.

The chanting began anew as the mob saw Jack and Sophie standing together. *"Hire her! Hire her! Hire her!"*

Sophie licked her lips and asked, "Well, Mr. Baxter. How did I do?"

"What do you think?" replied Jack, acknowledging the miners' hymn of admiration. "How would you like to work here?"

"That's exactly what I had in mind." Sophie seated herself on a barstool. "Now how much were you paying that off-key sot?"

Jack could not keep from grinning. "Three ounces of gold dust per night and, of course, she kept her tips."

"How much is that in hard cash?"

"About forty-eight—fifty dollars. How about it?"

"How about what, Mr. Baxter? I certainly wouldn't accept the same amount that the shanty Irish lush was getting. Besides I have my maid to support. I'll take five ounces of gold dust per night."

"Five ounces! That's eighty dollars—almost double!"

"Well, Mr. Baxter, don't you think I'm worth it?" Sophie leveled a gracious smile at her fans and purred. "Your clientele seems to. And I can assure you that I do not get drunk on the job and that you won't have to hear the same song over and over *and over.*"

"It's been a long time since I've wanted to believe a woman."

The crowd, sensing that Sophie and Jack were discussing business, opened their throats and gave vent to a series of *"Hire hers"* so vehement that the chandeliers began swinging back and forth.

"You're hired," Jack said quickly. And to pacify the

unruly mob, Jack took Sophie's hand in his and held it up over her head as if she were a winning prizefighter. The men grew suddenly quiet and Jack announced, "I give to you, Miss Sophie Parmalee, the Alhambra's new performer. Now everybody, drinks are on the house!" To Sophie he whispered, "I'll go clear out your dressing room."

The men went wild. They rushed over to Sophie, lifted her up on their shoulders and carried her around the full length of the saloon. They returned her to the bar. Sophie decided to treat herself to another glass of champagne. She called to the bartender who was standing halfway down the bar, his back toward her. She noticed his back stiffen but he didn't turn around. "What's the matter with him? Is he deaf or something?" she muttered to herself. "Bartender!" she called in a slightly louder voice. He still didn't move. There was a sleek man nearby staring openly at Sophie. She turned her attention on him. "Oh, sir."

"Yes, miss," the man replied in an oily voice.

"Would you try to get the bartender's attention for me? He must be hard of hearing."

"Be glad to, miss," the man replied with a twisted smile. His teeth were small, even and yellow like kernels of corn. "Hey, Luke! The lady wants a drink!"

Luke turned slightly. His head was bent low, thick graying hair shadowed his eyes and forehead. Keeping his head down he walked toward Sophie. "What is it, miss?" he asked gruffly.

"I'd like a . . ." Sophie stopped. The rest of her words would not come out. Her heartbeat quickened and her pulse gained sudden strength in her throat and temples. Finally, a word escaped her lips. "Luke?"

He lifted his head and the sight of his ravaged good looks made Sophie's eyes water. "Luke, is that you?"

"It's what's left of me, Sophie."

"What's happened to you?"

"A lot. You're looking good and sounding good, too. Maddie would have been proud of you."

"Mama's dead, Luke."

"Yeah, I heard."

"Way out here?"

"Your mother had a lot of . . . friends, Sophie. How long you been in San Francisco?"

"Just a couple of weeks. Betzy's here. She's sitting over by the runway."

"Yeah, I saw her. So you're going to work here?"

"Yes, if you don't mind." Her words were sincere.

"Oh, I don't mind at all," replied Luke. "I like to watch you. I always did." He shifted his gaze away from her face. "Now what kind of drink was it you were wanting?"

"Ah—champagne."

"And champagne it should be," said Luke almost reverently.

Sophie felt a wave of sadness rush through her body. She should be celebrating, but suddenly she didn't feel like it anymore. It seemed wrong.

"No, Luke, don't. I don't think I want a drink after all." She smiled and added. "I don't want Mr. Baxter to think I have a drinking problem like his Irish Songbird."

Luke understood her change of heart. A crescent rim of tears formed on his lashes. "Whatever you say, Sophie," he replied softly, staring at her, memorizing her face. "Whatever you say."

Jack was backstage. The door to Maggie's dressing room was partly open. Jack knew that she had heard Sophie's song and the reaction of the patrons. Without knocking, he entered. Maggie was sprawled in a chair stupidly staring at the open door. Her makeup was smeared and her eyes had an opaque look. Jack roughly pulled her to her feet, knocking over the empty gin bottle. "Get out, Maggie. You're fired."

Maggie looked at him without comprehension. Jack shook her until her curls fell loose. "Don't give me that drunken shit! You must have heard!"

Maggie wet her dry lips. It was not the time for

pretense. "Yes, I heard. I saw. Jack, you can't do this to me."

"You did this to yourself, Maggie," Jack's tone softened. "But hell, you can get another job. You know that."

"But the Alhambra's the best saloon on the Coast, Jack. Anything else would be a comedown."

"You brought yourself down. I warned you about drinking and sloppy performances. Now this little lady's going to take your place and she's going to be a hell of a lot better."

Maggie's face flushed with anger. She spat on the floor. "All right, *Mr.* Baxter. There are plenty of other places that are just dying to have me."

"Sure. I just hope they've got enough liquor. Now get out of here, Maggie. You depress me."

Maggie whirled around and screamed a string of vulgarities that mocked and damned his manhood at the same time. Then she turned and headed for the door.

"Wait a minute!" yelled Jack. "Take off that dress! I paid for it!"

"You take it off! You . . ."

Jack jumped at Maggie. He grabbed the bodice of her dress and yanked so hard it split to the waist. Maggie grabbed a cloak and threw it around her bare shoulders. "You're one hard son of a bitch, Jack Baxter!"

"And don't you ever forget it, Maggie!" said Jack, mollified.

Maggie ran into Sophie who had been waiting in the corridor. "Don't go to bed with him, dearie, unless you like 'em cherub size!"

Sophie entered the dressing room. She was pleased. It was large and now it was hers. "Any problems, Mr. Baxter?" she asked brightly.

"Nothing I couldn't handle. Well, what do you think of your dressing room?"

"It's not bad," replied Sophie blithely. "Of course,

with a fresh coat of paint and some new furniture,"
Sophie looked around pretending not to be impressed.
"Oh, about costumes, Mr. Baxter, I certainly don't
intend to buy my own."

Jack strolled to the large armoire, opened the door
and said, "Look, they're all yours."

Sophie, nose in air, eyed the sweaty alcohol-stained
silk and satin gowns. She made no move to examine
them. "I'm not wearing anybody else's costumes, Mr.
Baxter."

Jack smiled thinly. He tore the gowns from the
armoire and began heaping them in the middle of the
floor. "You don't have to," he replied with a flourish.
"I'll have one of the boys remove them immediately."

Chapter 11

The sun, unnaturally small, seemed in danger of slipping away into the sky. As if to make up for the lack of sunshine, the trees had taken on a red and golden hue and the grass had become a burnished bronze.

Winter was coming to Belfast, Maine. This time of confinement depressed Kathleen Mulvany. She thought of the months that stretched ahead. The canning had already been done; fruits and vegetables were stored in the basement. The hogs had been slaughtered; hams and slabs of bacon were curing in the smokehouse. Winter would be a time for quilt making, reading romantic novels and dealing with various illnesses and injuries sustained by her four brothers.

Kathleen, now sixteen, was the middle child of Delia and Seamus Mulvany, between Tommy, eighteen, Kieran, seventeen, Donal, fifteen and Desmond, fourteen. Delia had never really cared for children and preferred working outside, gardening and caring for the farm animals. The responsibility for looking after

Seamus and his four sons had fallen upon Kathleen's young shoulders. She did the cooking, the washing, the mending. She was always there to "kiss it where it hurts" when one of the boys had an inevitable accident.

Kathleen finished peeling the apples. Soon the entire Mulvany kitchen was fragrant with the rich spicy aroma of applesauce cooking. She mechanically set the huge oak table for the evening meal. As an afterthought, she added a bouquet of yellow mums, picked from Delia's flower garden. The centerpiece would probably be ignored by her parents and jeered by her brothers. No matter, they added a touch of elegance to a plain table. Kathleen kept the kitchen meticulously clean. Whatever color was present—bright flowered curtains, framed pictures of faraway places cut from magazines—had been her doing.

As she stirred the applesause, she contemplated herself in the bottom of a shiny copper pan hanging over the stove. She was pretty, she supposed, for her father told her often enough. And the local young men seemed unduly nervous whenever she made an appearance. Her dark hair was so lustrous that it seemed dusted with moonlight. Her skin was high colored and clear. Her narrow nose had an impudent tilt, and her lips were naturally red, full and sensuous. Only her blue-gray eyes seemed incongruous with the placid countenance. They were the quick, darting eyes of someone very discontent.

"I really am beautiful," she whispered at her image. Then she undid the top buttons of her high-collared gingham dress. A young maiden's dress, she thought with wry bitterness. She unbuttoned the bodice until the tops of her breasts were revealed. Hanging between the small of her neck and her breasts was the pewter and emerald cross that Liam had sent to her. The light glanced off the emeralds, and the stones flashed with vivid intensity. Kathleen smiled sadly and traced the outline of the cross with her fingertips. It was such a lovely present. Surely Rory must have helped Liam pick it out. The cross had scandalized her mother, who felt that a present from a man, even a cross, worn against the flesh was totally inappropriate unless they were bespoken. Kathleen had not dared wear the cross unless it was concealed by a high collar. That afternoon was different. The coming of winter and the depression made Kathleen feel defiant. It was a gift to her and a holy relic. She would wear it openly, proudly, no matter what *anyone* thought.

She tasted the applesauce, added a bit more ground cinnamon. Where were they now? Austere Liam and dashing Rory? San Francisco? It was such an exotic place. In the past year it had become part of everybody's conversation. Kathleen looked at the reflection of the cross once again. She was so happy they had remembered her! Moving gracefully across the kitchen, she checked the dough. Good, it was rising. She put the loaves into the belly of the stove to bake.

Kathleen sat down in a rocker, turned up the kerosene lamp to brighten the gray light of the afternoon and began to read from her father's newspaper. Since the discovery of gold in California, hardly an issue passed without some mention of it. Her quick eyes scanned the first page and fell upon a story entitled *Eureka! The Dancing Elephant.*

The article displayed a comical drawing of an astonished gold miner—mouth open, tools scattered about his feet—staring at a gigantic elephant dancing on toepoints, a bright pink bow around its trunk. The story recounted the miner's experience and feelings at discovering gold and the differences it had made in his life. The unique experience of discovering gold was like "seeing the elephant." That phrase in 1848 and the years following became securely rooted in the American language, synonymous with the lure of California's gold, the excitement of finding it and the hardship and disappointments that usually accompanied it.

Kathleen was charmed by the story. As she studied the picture, she wondered if Liam and Rory had "seen the elephant." Surely they would! They both were adventurous young men whose dreams extended far beyond the kitchens of Belfast! She folded the paper neatly and sighed. Would she ever "see an elephant" or was she doomed to a patterned existence full of activity but no surprises?

The kitchen door slammed open and Kathleen automatically got to her feet. She disliked any of her family to see her relaxing.

It was her mother. At thirty-three Delia Mulvany was a handsome woman with a no-nonsense manner. "Well," Delia grunted, removing her patched chore coat, "the peeps are hatched and, God be praised, healthy."

Kathleen wondered idly why her mother had always shown more interest in the chicks and calves and sows than in her own children. "Well, that's nice," replied Kathleen without interest. She noticed that her mother was staring intently at her and realized that she had left her bodice unbuttoned. She turned and went to the oven to check the bread. She quickly fastened the two lowest buttons as her mother said, "You know my feelings about that cross, Kathleen."

"I do."

"And yet, you're wearin' it."

"Your feelings are not mine, Mama. I think it's a lovely gift. After all, it is a cross. I see no reason why I shouldn't wear it."

"But next to your skin?"

"I find the touch of it soothing."

"Well, it's for naught you'll be wearin' it. For neither of them fine boys is goin' to ask you to marry them, so you might as well settle with that."

Kathleen, her face red with anger, whirled around. "Mama!"

"Well, it's true," Delia went on. "No amount of moonin' around ever did you one stick of good, and that's for sure. The only thing that surprises me is that you heard from them at all."

"The letter was to all of us, Mama. And, of course, we'd hear from Liam and Rory. Why not? You and Papa were very good to them."

"Aye, that's true," Delia conceded and eyed Kathleen. "But there's not many young'uns with a pinch of respect for his elders these days. So if you'll take some advice, daughter of mine, you'll stop waitin' around for someone to sweep down from a cloud and carry you off. You'd be wise to settle for one of the fine young men around here who have been showin' you a bit of attention."

"I'd rather become a nun than marry one of those clods," replied Kathleen tersely. "They all smell of sweat, mule dung and sawdust."

"Bite your tongue! You sound as if you were describin' your father and your brothers."

"Exactly, Mama. I don't want a man like them—all gruff and swagger and bad manners. I want a man who's not afraid to touch me and who'll make me feel warm all over like I was raging with fever. I want someone to love me, not just because I'm a woman, but in spite of it."

Delia stared at her daughter in shock. She had never heard such blunt talk from a woman before. She was about to reproach her daughter when Seamus, followed by the four boys, stomped into the kitchen. Kathleen used the opportunity to escape her mother's tirade. She greeted her father and brothers coolly and began final preparations for dinner.

Later Kathleen, anxious to avoid a confrontation with her mother, quickly finished the dishes while her mother was tending the cows. She put on her dark green wool cloak and left the house to attend evensong at the nearby church. The autumn wind was sharp. Kathleen hurried down the footpath to the churchyard. The hem of her cloak gathered up the damp fallen leaves, and they clung there as if they had been pasted on. Kathleen looked neither to the right or left as the townsfolk gathered. Her disinterest had earned her a reputation as "an aloof miss."

Kathleen dipped her fingers in the font, crossed herself and went directly to the pew designated for her family. She knelt in prayer. Her mind wasn't on God, but on that first time she had seen Liam and Rory.

Young Kathleen had known they were coming. Their mothers had written from Ireland. And they had received yet another letter from Canada. The night Liam and Rory had arrived Kathleen was away from home tending a sickly aunt. On the next day, Sunday, Kathleen decided to join her family at church. Her curiosity concerning the newcomers was considerably more intense than her devotion to her aunt—and to her Savior as well.

On that day Kathleen scanned the faces of those in the churchyard. She saw no one she did not know. Her family was late! The great brass bell signaled that Mass was about to begin. The parishioners filed into the small church and took their allotted places on the hard pews. The interior of the church was comforting to Kathleen. The walls reflected the flickering candles, and the small stained glass window filtered the sunshine and stained it all colors of the rainbow. There were fresh flowers on the altar that morning—roses, peonies, daisies—plucked from household gardens and bordering fields. The altar boys began scurrying about, hair slicked back and scrubbed faces aglow. The priest, an elderly man with china blue eyes, entered from the rectory, and everybody in the church stood. He offered a blessing in a rasping but pleasant voice, and everybody knelt to pray.

The whispering was slight at first, then grew like a summer breeze skittering through tall dry grass. Kathleen looked up from her rosary and saw that she wasn't the only one who had lifted a head. She strained her neck to see what everyone was looking at, and caught her breath. Preceding her family down the aisle was the most handsome young man she had ever seen. Kathleen dropped her rosary. The beads made a sharp sound against the flagstone floor. As she bent lower to retrieve them, she saw that he was filing into the pew in front of her. His hair was as fiery as a sunset and his eyes, even in the dim light of the church, glowed brighter than the candles. He turned slightly and smiled at her. Kathleen, her skin turning as red as a sugar beet, fervently began saying her beads. The rest of the family took their places. Then another stranger joined the young man sitting in front of her. He, too, was handsome and a bit older. But there was something about the younger one, something that made Kathleen forget her prayers.

At last Mass was over. Kathleen scurried out of church, forgetting the final religious amenities. Her one thought was to make herself noticed by this dangerously handsome young man. She positioned herself beneath a maple tree in front of the church, approximately ten feet away from the main walkway. She tried posing several ways to strike something attractive and nonchalant at the same time. She finally settled on clasping her prayer book tightly in both hands and staring dramatically into space as if something very profound were occupying her mind.

The priest ambled to the top of the step so that he could greet his flock on their way out. The parishioners began streaming from the church. Keeping her own face in profile, Kathleen watched out of the corners of her eyes for the handsome young man. When he appeared, Kathleen turned back to her manufactured thoughts and waited. A short time later she heard her mother's urgent voice speak her name. "Kathleen, what in the world are you doing? Don't you feel well? Come over here. I want to introduce you to our new young gentlemen. This is Liam O'Sullivan and Rory Fitzpatrick."

Kathleen, as if in a trance, stepped forward to meet the vital young men from Ireland.

Liam and Rory were lodged in the tack room in the barn. The quarters weren't fancy, but they were clean and the wood-burning stove kept them warm. Each of them claimed a small tract of timberland. Seamus Mulvany, who had been working among the trees since his arrival in America, taught them the rudiments of logging. The young men worked hard and learned quickly. They were determined to earn money for passage to bring their families to America.

All the timber cut in that area had to be processed at one mill. It was owned by the Shannons, Belfast's first and most powerful family. The fee for processing the timber into board lengths was set at fifty percent. Liam and Rory were aghast. What a blow to their profits! They couldn't understand why an Irishman could in all good conscience profit so enormously from the labors of fellow countrymen. They questioned Seamus about the situation.

"That's the way it is, that's the way it's always been and that's the way it always will be," Seamus replied philosophically and drew on his clay pipe.

The young men looked at each other and then at their mentor. Seamus Mulvany was a worn, once-handsome man with a full head of prematurely white hair and mischievous blue eyes. Seamus was content with his life. He had a "fair to middlin'" marriage, "sired enough Mulvanys to give me too many grand-children," and had "enough food for me belly and a warmin' fire for me backside."

"But old man Shannon's profiting from our work just because he owns the only sawmill," argued Liam.

"Right," agreed Rory. "Why can't everybody get together, put in a bit of money and build our own mill? We could run it ourselves and we'd be working for the full one hundred percent."

"Besides," Liam continued, "he cheats us, you know. I estimate that ten to fifteen percent of our lumber is unaccounted for. Hell, Shannon's as bad as the English."

Seamus frowned. "Nobody's as bad as the English and certainly not one of our own kind. Anyway, I don't see how it could be done. The people respect Shannon. They look up to him because he's a success."

"His success is at our expense," grunted Liam.

"No mind. I don't think they'll defy him," replied Seamus. "I, for one, won't."

Liam and Rory realized that the discussion was closed. Seamus rose from the kitchen table, handed the empty teacup to Kathleen for washing and asked the young men. "Do you care for a bit of rabbit hunting?"

"Not us," replied Liam. "The Lord forgive us for working on His day of rest, but Rory and I have a few more trees to fell."

"Then I'll be seein' you at supper," replied the white-haired patriarch.

After her father had left, Kathleen anxiously said, "I'll make you both another cup of tea. There's a chill this morning. It'll help brace you against the cold."

"Another cup of your fine tea would be welcome," responded Liam. Rory merely nodded his head.

Kathleen, happy to have the men with her for a little longer, quickly brewed another pot of tea and heated some freshly baked raisin bread. She served it with a tub of bright yellow butter.

Liam, taking a healthy bite, remarked, "Kathleen, you can cook better than most grown women." Kathleen beamed. "Don't you think so, Rory?" The younger man's reply was muffled by a mouthful of the hot bread.

Kathleen sat down at the table between her two favorite men. They were so unlike her brothers and anyone else in town, for that matter. She fervently expressed her thoughts. "I don't see why you don't open your own mill." They looked at her in surprise.

Kathleen continued and a bitter note crept into her voice. "I mean everybody else is under old man Shannon's thumb. He's made sure of that—loaning them money—at a nice interest rate, of course—extending them credit at his supply store—at fancy prices, of course. The stupid people around here think of him as a benevolent old dear, when in actuality he's no better than a tyrant sucking everyone dry. They may owe him, or think they do. But you don't. And I happen to know that there's a patch of land down by the Bay that nobody wants because it's stripped of timber. It would make a wonderful mill site."

Rory laughed. "Listen to the darlin' girl. She's got it all figured out."

Liam interceded. "No, no. Kathleen's right. The property's perfect. Do you know who owns it?"

"The Killeens, and they'd love to sell it."

"Now, wait a minute, Liam. The money we have saved is going for our families' passage!"

"I know. And I have no intention of touching it. But after that's cared for, we'll save up for the land and the equipment it will take to run a mill."

Rory knitted his brow. "We're asking for trouble, Liam."

"And when did we get anything else?"

About a month later Liam received word that the passages would not be needed. Both Molly O'Sullivan and Fiona Fitzgerald and the few remaining members of their respective households had succumbed to the "tipes."

Rory responded by going on a desperate drunk. Liam reacted differently. He quickly bought the shorefront property from the Killeens and ordered enough equipment to get them started. Liam expected trouble and he was not disappointed. Old Jack Shannon sent for him, sat him down in a chair imported from France and had the butler serve him a snifter of brandy. Then he got down to business. He offered to buy the property at four times the original investment. When Liam refused to sell, Shannon made thinly disguised threats. Liam responded by calling for his coat. He finished the brandy in one gulp and said flatly, "The only thing that surprises me is that you haven't become a Protestant." He left the old man sputtering in rage.

While the mill was being built, Liam and Rory worried about threats of arson. They took alternate twelve-hour shifts. Rifles in hand, they guarded their property against any "well-meaning friends of the Shannons." The mill was completed without incident, but none of the townspeople brought lumber to Liam and Rory for processing. They were afraid.

Liam, unsure how to deal with the situation, consulted the local parish priest, Father Michael McClafferty. He found a sympathetic and helpful friend. The old man's watery eyes twinkled as he added a dollop of whiskey to his tea, explaining, "It keeps an old relic like me from corrodin'." He took a large sip and continued. "Well, now, Liam, I love a good fight. I boxed before I entered the seminary. Did I ever tell you that?"

"No, Father, you didn't."

"Well, there was no reason to. But I'll tell you this now, I've always hated the sight of a big dog pickin' on a little dog. These Shannons and their big dog ways have stuck in my craw for more years than I care to remember. To be sure, they contribute large sums of money to the church, but it's hardly a tithe—not even close. Confound them anyway for drainin' their own, and confound the people for allowin' it!" He punctuated his pronouncement with a repressed belch and continued. "What are you aimin' to charge for processing the timber?"

"Absolutely nothing," Liam exclaimed. "I just want to handle all the lumber under one company. That way we can fetch a better board price and compete with the Shannons. Then Rory and I would only take a fifteen percent profit off the net gross of the sales."

"Fifteen percent? Hell, man, the Shannons steal more than that. You mustn't undersell yourself, Liam. Twenty percent is more to my way of thinkin'."

"Are you sure, Father?"

"You're offerin' these people freedom, freedom from that old son of a bitch!" the priest chuckled. "Let's have a real drink. This damn tea sours my stomach anyway." He poured two generous glasses of fine Irish whiskey, handed one to Liam and winked conspiratorially.

The following Sunday Father McClafferty preached a thunderous sermon concerning the Egyptian pharaohs and the monuments they built on the labors of men in bondage. The parables were obvious and the points well made. On Monday Seamus Mulvany appeared at the mill site and was the first to sign an agreement with Liam and Rory under the newly formed Belfast Lumber Company. Liam slapped Seamus on the back. "Seamus, this is the second time you've come to our aid. And Rory and I appreciate it more than we will ever be able to tell you."

"Don't see what else I could do," stammered Seamus. "After all, your mill has got the church's blessin' and that's good enough for me."

The others followed Mulvany's example. Soon all had forsaken Shannon's mill and were doing business with Liam and Rory. Jack Shannon responded by having a fatal coronary.

Kathleen was a constant visitor to the mill. She brought the young men hot jugs of tea and fresh baked goods. It was obvious to everyone that she was infatuated with Rory. But if anyone had told Rory the news, he would have been surprised. He never thought of Kathleen as anything but Seamus Mulvany's little girl. Kathleen took up woodcarving when she found it was Rory's hobby. She crocheted him a winter scarf. She baked countless loaves of raisin bread, his favorite, but nothing could garner Rory's interest in her as other than an affectionate child who was part of his adopted family.

The young men worked hard. The mill was a success. They were pleased with themselves and led comfortable, albeit completely different, lives. Rory enjoyed his liquor and popularity among Belfast's available women. He thought little about the future. But Liam was worried. The property owned by himself and Rory as well as the other people of Belfast was rapidly being depleted of trees. New saplings had been planted, but enough time had not passed for them to mature into timber. He began looking for an alternate course their lives could take. The answer came to him from the other side of the nation. Gold was discovered in California! The need for lumber was tremendous.

Evensong was over. Kathleen got to her feet and realized her knees were aching. She must have remained in a kneeling position throughout the entire service. She smiled to herself. Everyone must think I'm the most pious girl in Belfast.

While passing through the apse she encountered Father McClafferty. "Evenin', Kathleen, You seemed to be most engrossed in the service tonight." He smiled, not unkindly.

"Why, yes. Most inspiring," Kathleen lied.

"Have you heard from Liam and Rory?"

"As a matter of fact, I received a present from them sent all the way from Rio de Janeiro, Brazil." She opened her cloak and displayed her cross.

"What a lovely bit of work that is," said Father McClafferty. "And how becomin' it is to you, Kathleen."

"Thank you, Father. You don't think it's too . . . well, too flashy?"

"Why, of course not, my dear. You should see some of the elaborate crosses the holy fathers wear. Well, a good evening to you and when you're writin' the boys please give them my fondest regards."

"I will, Father. Good night."

Taking the shortcut home, Kathleen skipped through the graveyard of the church. All was well with the world. She could tell her mother how Father McClafferty had admired her cross and that would be that. Not even Delia Mulvany would dare oppose a priest!

When Kathleen returned home, she made herself a cup of tea, sat down at the kitchen table and began to compose a letter to Liam and Rory.

"My dear friends,

I just returned from evensong where Father McClafferty inquired about your well-being. You see, you are sorely missed in Belfast, by everybody, particularly the Mulvanys. Your wonderful gift arrived and I haven't taken it off since receiving it. I was thrilled by your thoughtfulness and am pleased to be able to wear something that will always remind me of you. I imagine by this time you have reached your destination. San Francisco sounds like it's not even in this country. It's a Spanish name, isn't it? At first I thought it sounded romantic. But I confess I've been doing some reading—practically every newspaper and magazine has an article concerning San Francisco and the gold rush. Life must be hard there, perhaps even harder than here. But the weather sounds delightful. I should like to live in a place that was summer all year around. What delightful flower gardens, what lovely vegetables!

Everything's going nicely at the mill, or so Papa and my brothers tell me. They work very long hours, but at least they are now working for themselves and that is a blessing . . ."

Kathleen paused. She could think of nothing else to say, nothing that she would commit to paper. As far as she was concerned nothing of interest happened in

Belfast. Her own life as well as her family's was completely bereft of excitement. She folded the paper and tucked it away in her diary to be mailed when she had an address.

Kathleen went to bed and dreamed of elephants, flowers and beautiful forests.

Chapter 12

Winter came to Puget Sound. Rory and Liam found it milder than the winters of Maine or Ireland. The men labored eighteen-hour days at the mill. In addition to turning out lumber at an amazing rate, the men had built a bunkhouse, cookhouse, company house and cabin that Liam and Rory shared as both quarters and office. The men were pleased with the extraordinary progress they had made. But Liam was not satisfied. He planned to hire more men under the same arrangement. Better equipment must be purchased, and an experienced highballer—an expert lumberjack who oversaw the other men—was needed.

Liam softened his loneliness by writing to Kathleen and was encouraged when he received her chatty letters. Rory spent most of his spare time playing poker. His good nature and sense of humor made him very popular among his peers. Liam inadvertently assumed the role of the "heavy" and was referred to as "boss" even though Rory had as much to do with running the camp.

The buzz saw reverberated across the Bay. The harsh metallic sound that once scared fish and woodland animals alike was now part of the environment. So great were the demands for lumber that the mill had been kept running twenty-four hours a day, with different men working alternating shifts.

Liam, more muscular and imposing than ever, strode toward the mill. He stopped to admire Rory's handiwork. The younger man was atop a ladder, crudely but boldly painting a newly erected sign that spanned half the mill. "Good work, Rory," he called out.

Rory looked down and grinned at his friend. "I'd much rather be climbing a pine. This ladder's as shaky as hell."

"Wait a minute. I'll hold it for you."

Liam steadied the base of the ladder as Rory continued his sign painting. "How's my spelling?" Rory called out. "Sure as hell hate to misspell our own name."

Liam leaned his head back and moving his lips, spelled out the letters on the sign. "T-H-E C-O-N-N-E-M-A-R-A M-I-L-L C-O-M-P-A-N-Y. That's fine. People should be able to see that miles away."

"What people?" grunted Rory. "There's nobody up here except a handful of ragtag settlers and a bunch of grunting Indians."

"Oh, they'll come. You'll see. Just as soon as we expand a bit, they'll come, all right, and they'll come in droves."

Rory finished with a flourish. Liam relinquished the ladder and entered the sawmill. He bent down to pick up used nails as he habitually did on his rounds. Later he would hammer them straight so they could be used again. The interior of the mill was filled with the steady hum of the buzz saw and the warm fragrant aroma of flying sawdust. Several workers spotted Liam and waved a greeting they did not feel. He nodded as his eyes scanned the floor of the mill. There was a thick layer of sawdust surrounding the mill saw. "Somebody get this dust swept up!" Liam shouted over the harsh sound of the boards being cut.

Rory walked into the mill. "What's the matter, Liam?"

"Damn it, Rory. If I've told you once, I've told you ten thousand times, sawdust has to be swept up every hour on the hour. I don't want any chance of fire. Why the oil lamps could ignite this stuff and burn us out in a blink of an eye."

Rory yelled at the men on duty, and several scurried forward with straw brooms and shovels. Liam was placated. Rory assured him that more care would be taken in the future. The two men walked outside to have another proud look at the sign.

Liam said, "You know, Rory. One of us has to get down to San Francisco and hire more men. Why we haven't even begun to work at full capacity. We could use at least forty more men, another mill saw and a lot of other equipment."

"Where are we going to put them up, Liam?"

"We'll have them build their own bunkhouses when they get here. Of course, we'd better bring along a couple of cooks, as well. I, for one, am getting a little tired of Josh's cooking."

"Same here," agreed Rory.

Liam scanned his partner's face. "Well, Rory. Which one of us will go—you or me?"

Rory hesitated. He ran his tongue over his strong white teeth and thought for a moment. "You go, Liam, and I'll stay here and take care of things."

"If that's what you want. But I had a feeling you might like to have a break from the mill, kick up your heels, and—er—so forth."

"Liam, I've done enough . . . er . . . so forth for a lifetime, and haven't made a very good job of it. You go to San Francisco and kick up *your* heels." He added bitterly, "There's nothing there for me."

"All right, Rory. Captain Fallon and I will leave before the end of the week. If there's anything you want . . ." Rory shook his head.

They were interrupted by the welcome sound of a bleating horn. It was coming from the small mail boat. All work came to a halt. Liam, Rory and the rest of the men rushed down to the dock to await its arrival.

The mail was passed out and Liam received two letters from Kathleen. Rory glanced at the envelopes and, recognizing the handwriting, commented, "You're certainly doing a lot of corresponding with that little girl."

"That little girl is growing up fast."

"I never noticed."

"You never really looked. You always had an eye on quantity, not quality. Here, do you want to read one of them?"

"No. You can tell me the news later. I'm going to head back to the mill and see to things."

Liam angrily kicked at one of the pilings. "Damn it, that Sophie is still on his mind!"

The Alhambra was packed to capacity every single night. Sophie, manipulating her talent, looks and conspicuous advertising, had become the most popular personality on the Barbary Coast. Flying in front of the saloon was a giant canvas poster of Sophie seductively posed in a clinging costume. The poster had been reproduced on handbills and passed out in the mining camps. Larger versions were sold at the Alhambra for ten dollars each, a forerunner of the modern pin-up.

Sophie, now making money faster than she ever thought possible, continued to live at the United States Hotel. But with a difference! She had rented a small separate room next to her suite for Betzy, making it more convenient for her to entertain admirers.

She totally enjoyed her success. The men still flocked to see her. But now they kept a respectful distance because she was *somebody*. She also enjoyed her financial situation. Now she collected seven bags of gold dust each night, as well as the nuggets and coins tossed by enthusiastic audiences. After each show Betzy dutifully gathered them up. The following day they were taken to the bank and turned into golden double eagles, then stored in the hollow posts of her giant brass bed. Even gifts of jewelry, clothing, and objects of art were taken back to the dealers for a cash return. Sophie *never* intended to be poor again.

Each night was much like every other. Sophie performed three shows. In between she would mingle with the customers, making them feel welcome and giving them the impression that she was personally happy they were there to see her. Sophie wanted to insure her popularity among the patrons of the Alhambra. More entertainers were arriving daily in San Francisco, and the Barbary Coast establishments were vainly searching for someone who could compete with Sophie's charms.

One evening before the last show, Sophie forsook her rounds and instead seated herself at the far end of the bar. She was tired. Her feet hurt and she was looking forward to a long, hot bath before climbing into bed. More than that, she was bored. It had been a long time since she had met a man who had garnered her interest for more than a quick night of lovemaking.

She waved to Luke, who immediately lowered his eyes. "Luke, I'd like a drink."

"The usual, Sophie?"

"No, I'm bored with champagne. The funny thing is that now that I can afford it, I find that I never really liked it. I suppose that happens with lots of things. No, I'll have a whiskey please. With water on the side."

"Coming right up."

Sophie watched Luke as he dug through the whiskey bottles to select the best that the Alhambra had to

offer. How totally different he had become! In New
York his personality and drive were winning. Now,
wasted and apathetic, he was clearly marked as a loser.
What had happened to change him?

Luke set the whiskey and water in front of Sophie.
She downed a third of the whiskey and took a long
swallow of cloudy water. She caught Luke looking at
her. He immediately averted his eyes. "You don't
approve of me, do you, Luke?"

"That's not for me to say, Sophie."

"Luke, tell me honestly. You don't like what I'm
doing."

Luke picked up a glass and pretended to polish it. "I
like some of the things you do, Sophie. I like you on the
stage. Hell, watching you high-kicking around your
mama's barroom, I never thought you'd get as good as
you are." He grinned in remembrance. "I still can see
you sitting on top of that colored man's piano. What
was his name?"

"Stash."

"Oh, yes, Stash. And you singing your heart out. I
taught you the words to a couple of those songs. Do
you remember?"

"I remember," replied Sophie, tracing the rim of her
shot glass with a finger.

"They were pretty sassy. I recollect your Mama was
good and mad at me. I argued that you probably didn't
know what the words meant anyway. But, hell, you
probably knew all along."

"I knew," replied Sophie drinking another third of
the whiskey. "I guess I always knew."

"What was the one I liked the most? Let me see."
Luke closed his eyes and rubbed his temples with his
knuckles as he often did when he was trying to
remember something long lost among his drug-induced
dreams. "I—I—can't . . ."

"Did it go something like this?" asked Sophie. She
began singing in a low crooning voice:

"I'm just a home grown rose,
Grown, oh so tired, of my pose,
I'd like to be plucked from the vine,
But I warn you sucker,
Before you pucker . . .
Lips that touch liquor will never touch mine!"

Luke smiled and that smile softened the hard lines in his face, making him look almost as young as he did the day Sophie had fallen in love with him.

"That's it! You remembered! Do you remember all the words?"

"I'll try to recall them." Sophie, happy with Luke's pleasure, fought her way through two more choruses. "I'll tell you what, Luke. If my boys know the tune, I'll slip it into the next show . . . just for you."

"That would be wonderful, Sophie," he averted his eyes from hers again. "Would you like another drink?"

The liquor had made Sophie feel very bold. Before she could stop herself, she asked a question that had been on her lips for so many weeks. "Luke, how come it is you never . . . well." She wet her lips and plowed on. "Asked to see me home?" Luke looked agonized as a jolt of pain shot through his body. "Luke, what is it?" asked Sophie with concern.

"You've no right to ask me that question, Sophie."

Sophie's nostrils flared. "I have every right. We were lovers once. You left me to find something out here. What exactly did you find that was so much more important than me . . . then or now?"

Luke looked anxiously over his shoulder, hoping that someone wanted a drink, but the other two bartenders were taking care of customers in need. Sophie slid her hand over Luke's, which was clutching the edge of the bar.

"Luke, what's the matter with you? Are you ill?"

Luke leaned on the bar bringing his face close to Sophie's. "Yes, Sophie," he hissed. "I'm ill. Don't I look it? I used to be good-looking or at least the ladies thought so."

"You're still good-looking," began Sophie lamely.

"Bull shit! Do you know what hell it is to work in this place? There are mirrors everywhere—behind the bar, on the posts, on the walls, even in the goddamned toilets. You see, I don't like to look into mirrors anymore, Sophie. I don't like what I see." His voice became anguished. "You're a mirror too, Sophie. Your eyes see what I once saw." His eyes blurred with tears. Sophie hadn't expected this. She had expected tales of unsuccessful gold digs, of lost silver mines that remained lost, but not this.

"Luke, if you're sick, you ought to see a doctor. If it's money that's stopping you, I have plenty, more than enough. I'd be glad . . ."

"I've seen doctors, Sophie. A lot of them. There's—there's nothing they can do except keep me doped up."

"Drugs? You take drugs, Luke?"

"Surely you must have noticed that I don't drink, Sophie. And yet I stagger all the time. I don't touch a drop of alcohol, yet I always seem to be suffering from a hangover and the shakes. What in the hell do you think I'm taking, cocoa? I take opium."

"Why, Luke?" cried Sophie. "That's not a cure."

Luke laughed. It was a hollow sound from an empty vessel. "No, it's not a cure, Sophie. There's no cure for what I've got. The drugs are just a way out and faster than the disease itself."

Sophie grabbed at Luke's arm. Her fingertips became entangled in the garter that held up his sleeves. The elastic snapped and they both laughed at the welcome interruption.

"Luke, what have you got?" Sophie asked breathing hard. "Tell me, please. Tell *me*."

Luke swallowed and kept looking at Sophie's empty shot glass as he spoke the dreaded word. "Syphilis!"

Sophie involuntarily drew back. Luke smiled ironically. It was the expected reaction.

"But, but, there's no cure?"

"Syphilis isn't curable," replied Luke. "And I'm already in the . . ." he paused to recall the words, "tertiary stage."

Sophie shook her head and grabbed Luke's hand. "You mean you're going to die?"

"If I'm lucky. I might live ten years, but I'm already hoping I don't. Of course, as the doctors told me, I can never marry, and cannot cavort with any woman lest I contaminate her as well."

Sophie looked at him desperately. "Is there nothing that can be done? Can't you go some place, some place more civilized than San Francisco? Back to New York or Boston or Philadelphia? Luke, I've got the money."

Luke looked into Sophie's eyes. They were sad, full of concern. He was sorry he had hurt her. "Dear, sweet, Sophie. I'm sorry I told you. I'm sorry you're back into my life."

"Luke, *don't!* I'm sorry, so sorry. But at the same time I'm proud that you thought enough of me to tell me this. No one should have to keep such a dreadful secret all to themselves. I'm here when you need me and *please* need me, Luke. I'm not brave and I'm not as strong as I'd like to think I am, but I want to be your friend."

"I don't want to burden you, Sophie. I don't want you to worry about me."

"How can I worry about the inevitable, Luke? Just let me care a little. I've no one in this world to care about except Betzy and I'm awfully tired of myself."

"I'll see you home tonight after the show," smiled Luke as he poured Sophie another shot of whiskey. "Just don't get drunk on me. I've always had difficulty dealing with . . ." he caught himself and was about to apologize when Sophie said. "You made Mama very happy, Luke. And then you made me very happy. I think it's time I paid some of that happiness back."

Sophie felt someone touch her shoulder. She turned

around. It was Jack. "Sophie, you haven't forgotten about your third show?"

"Oh, no, of course I haven't, Jack. I'm sorry. I'll be on stage before you know it." She slid off the bar stool saying, "Watch me tonight, Luke, really watch me."

"I will, Sophie, I will."

Jack eyed Luke suspiciously. "Just what was going on between you two?"

"Oh, nothing," Luke replied enigmatically. "Sophie and I just found out that we knew someone in common back in New York City."

Five minutes later the red velvet curtain was raised and the patrons of the Alhambra began cheering and stomping their feet in anticipation. Sophie strutted out to center stage and the thrown hats caused the chandeliers to tinkle like toasted champagne glasses on New Year's Eve. She held up her hands for quiet and the crowd immediately obeyed her. "I'd like to sing a very old and *very* naughty song to you." There were several yelps and one poor fellow fell out of his chair. "This song was taught to me by a dear friend who had a unique talent for living his life to the fullest. I'd like to think that he still does." Sophie began singing in an energetic voice:

> *"I'm just a home grown rose,*
> *Grown, oh so tired, of my pose . . ."*

Jack looked oddly at Luke and shook his head. Why in the hell was his bartender blubbering over a bawdy song?

Chapter 13

Liam scanned the waterfront notice board outside the San Francisco Harbor Office. The board was littered with scraps of paper.

Barber in dyre need of a position. See Lewis Hardee on Fork Street.

Lessons given in the use of all musical instruments. Professor Terrance Stanislas, #27 Bay Street.

Shipboard work wanted—will do anything in exchange for passage back to (bless 'em both) New York or Boston—Boley Johnston, Union Street, third tent on the right.

Chinese cooks and laundrymen. Low weekly rates or by the month. See Mr. Bagley, Office, 2nd Floor of Kingman's Bar, Market Street.

Lost. A brand new wife, come all the way from
Baldymore, by the name of Mary Beth, about 5′ 3″
tall, skinny with a hurtful face. I don't want her
back. This here note's just to let her know that.
Elias Jennelfain.

Liam was just about to give up when a stray wind
slapped a wrinkled brown paper. The noise drew
his attention to the bottom of the board and he
read:

Experienced logger. Bull whacker, high climber,
highballer, bucker, peeler, faller. There be nothing I cannot do with a tree. See Wick Skansen,
staying at the Hacienda, off Market Street, leave
message if not there.

Liam drew out a stubby pencil and quickly copied the
ad on the back of the envelope that contained Kathleen's latest letter. Then he walked several blocks to a
waterfront tavern rudely called Neptune's Canker and
joined Captain Fallon.

"Any luck?" asked the captain.

"We've got one prospect," said Liam, seating himself. He read the pertinent items aloud.

"Skansen, eh? Name's Scandinavian. Maybe Swed-
ish. Probably was born in a tree top. Sounds good,
Liam."

"After we have a bite to eat, I'll look him up." Liam
called to the waiter for a beer. "How did you do,
Josh?"

"Hell, every day I feel more like a logger than a
ship's captain. There's machinery to be had, all right,
but the price is very dear."

"We'll have to pay it. And did you have our men post
the notices?"

"That I did. Let me tell you, Liam. You need forty
men and you're going to get four hundred makin'
application. Not enough gold to go around."

"With a lot of men to choose from, we ought to get some with experience."

"I wouldn't count on that, Liam. Most of these boys are from the East and the South. But if you get yourself a good highballer, he'll throw 'em into shape."

"I hope this is our man." Liam tapped the envelope in his breast pocket.

Sophie had her own carriage now. It was a smart barouche—a four-wheeled conveyance with a seat outside for the driver and seats inside for two couples facing one another, and with a calash top over the backseat. She had also purchased a pair of high-stepping roans to pull it.

The gleaming black and gilt vehicle pulled into the alleyway behind the Alhambra. Luke, wearing a smart blue gray uniform that Sophie had a tailor make for him, eased the horses and the carriage into the allotted space.

Ever since the night Luke saw Sophie home, they had become close friends. And Luke had become a wage-earning protector. She paid him the same amount he had been earning at the Alhambra as a bartender. Luke loved doing things for Sophie and it gave his life purpose. Now she could feel safe to go shopping, sightseeing or pleasure riding. Luke was taking less of the drug now, just enough to ease the pain but not enough to deaden his senses. Despite his illness, his renewed zest for life made him look years younger. Sophie discovered that Luke had a talent for building and painting, and she put him to work backstage at the Alhambra constructing props, set pieces and scenery for her shows.

Their relationship had only one drawback. Jack Baxter was jealous of Luke. He had wanted Sophie from the very beginning. Jack knew of Luke's disease, and realized that they were not going to bed together. Still, they shared an intimacy and a friendship that he coveted.

Luke hopped down and opened the door for Sophie and Betzy. He grabbed Sophie around the waist and swung her over a mud-filled ditch.

"Mercy!" squealed Sophie. "Why, Luke, I believe you're getting stronger every day!"

Luke beamed and turned to Betzy. "Now you, Betzy."

"Oh no, yo' don't. When I gets so old I can't jump across a mudhole, I want yo' to start pickin' flowers!"

Laughing, they entered the back door and encountered a scowling Jack. "What's so funny, Sophie? You're almost fifteen minutes late!"

"I'm sorry, Jack. The sudden rain delayed us. Market Street was so thick with mud that Luke didn't want to chance it with the new carriage, so we came the long way around."

"Why didn't Luke just carry you both on his shoulders?" suggested Jack sarcastically.

Sophie's good mood was not darkened. "Why, we never thought of that, Jack!" she said in mock astonishment. "Luke could probably have carried the horses and the barouche, too. Come, Betzy, help me get dressed. We don't want to keep the customers waiting a minute longer."

Sophie and Betzy hurried toward the dressing room. Jack glowered at Luke, who was still smiling from Sophie's banter. "You're her driver. I don't see why the hell you can't get her here on time."

"Next time we'll start out earlier, Jack."

But Jack was not to be placated. "See that you do. I'm not paying good money for an undependable entertainer."

Luke's expression changed. "That's a rotten thing to say, Jack. Why, Sophie's as dependable as the moonlight. She's always here, always gives three good performances and is still the biggest draw on the Barbary Coast. There's no one who can touch her for looks or talent."

"Well, I don't know about that," replied Jack,

lighting a thick cigar. "The El Dorado has a brand new act they're trying out tonight—a Parisienne chanteuse, no less."

"What's that?" asked Luke. "Sounds like something bad to eat."

"It's a French singer. And they've been doing a lot of advertising, imitating us." He handed Luke a handbill of a well endowed woman with flowing black hair and enormous sunflower eyes. The copy read "Beautiful Paulette from Paris Appearing Each and Every Night at the El Dorado."

Jack said stiffly, "I thought I'd go over there and see what she's like."

"She won't be as good as Sophie," responded Luke.

"We'll see!" He headed toward the door.

It was a petty threat and its significance wasn't lost on Luke. "Sophie's mother was French!" he shouted after Jack. Then he angrily tore the handbill into small pieces and threw them out the door.

Jack attempted to slip into the El Dorado unnoticed by its owner, a great hulk of a man named Willie Potamkin. But Willie, fleshy and florid, spotted Jack and called to him in his booming baritone.

"Fast Jack Baxter! Well, fancy you turnin' up for an openin' night at the El Dorado!" His grin revealed large and ill-fitting false teeth. He made his way through the crowd—the biggest he had had since Sophie had started at the Alhambra—and slapped Jack heartily on the back. "Curiosity got the best of you, eh? Well, my lad, ain't nothin' here you ain't seen before."

"What do you mean by that?" asked Jack. "Isn't your French chanteuse opening tonight?"

"She sure is an' look at the crowd! Maybe, just maybe, the Barbary Coast is gettin' tired of blonds."

"This Pauline will have to be pretty damn good to beat Sophie."

"Paulette," corrected Willie. "Find yourself a seat, Jack, an' tell the waiter that anythin' you want is on the house."

"If it's all the same to you, Willie, I'd just as soon pay," replied Jack and disappeared into the throng.

Willie shrugged his shoulders, caught the eye of the music conductor and whispered, "Is she ready yet? The boys is gettin' a little anxious."

The conductor jumped at Willie's question. "Why, er, yes, Mademoiselle Paulette is just about ready."

"Well, you tell her to get a move on!"

One of the men yelled good-naturedly from the bar, "Hey, Willie. When's this French chantoosie gonna get her bottom on the stage?"

"Any minute now, Abe." Willie announced to all within earshot.

Jack positioned himself against a post and tried to be inconspicuous. It was no use. The miners knew him on a first name basis. On seeing him, many called out greetings. He answered them glibly, trying very hard not to appear worried.

Feigning indifference, Jack focused on the bevy of nude paintings lining the walls of the El Dorado. They were crude and boring. Each was a nude of an overripe woman. Only the poses varied, leaning against a marble pillar, draped across a velvet couch, bathing in a pond. Jack winced at Willie's taste.

The crowd at the El Dorado was grubbier and more boisterous than those of the Alhambra. Jack knew that he offered his customers some semblance of class, and to a degree they acted accordingly.

He caught the eye of a waiter and ordered a whiskey and milk, a drink that calmed his nervous stomach. The bartender took the order without batting an eye. He knew Jack's penchant for the unusual concoction. When he returned the waiter said, "Mr. Potamkin told me not to accept money."

"Then take this as a tip," replied Jack and pressed a five-dollar bill into the man's calloused hand. Jack sipped the drink and stared ahead. A mottled curtain of blue velvet, stained and paint spattered hid the stage. It was not nearly as big as the Alhambra's and didn't have a runway. On stage left was a hand-lettered sign propped up announcing "Paulette, the beautiful chanteuse from gay Paree." A three-piece band, consisting of piano, fiddle and banjo, played an up-tempo version of *"La Marseillaise."* When they finished, the customers applauded without enthusiasm. Without preamble, the curtain was lifted and Paulette appeared. Jack leaned forward and squinted as the orchestra began playing Paulette's opening song. The singer moved, none too gracefully, to the edge of the apron and began to sing off-key: *"You Can Call Me, Mam'zelle."*

It was the same tune as "Let Me Make You Cozy" except that the arrangement had been somewhat Frenchified. Jack, barely containing his laughter, pressed the rim of his glass against his lips to keep from grinning. Center stage, dressed in a badly made gown of red, white and blue satin, her hair dyed shoepolish black and wearing enough makeup to cover the ravages of drink, was Maggie O'Brien—"Paulette the French chanteuse." She sang the song in a thick French accent to render the lyrics unintelligible, and punctuated every pause with an "Ooh-la-la!"

She was pathetic, but the patrons were too drunk to care.

Jack watched Paulette perform her opening song. She forgot as many lyrics as she faked. He finished his drink and started toward the side door. He ran into Willie, who shrugged his shoulders. "What can I do? She's one of the few white women out here. Everybody's gotta make a livin'."

Jack grinned. "Tell her to paste the lyrics on the side of a bottle. That way she won't forget 'em. See you later, Willie. Anytime you want to see a real woman and a great performer, come over to the Alhambra and tell the waiter that I said 'its on the house.'"

Once outside, Jack shed his good humor. He had been hoping that Paulette was good. It would have given him something to hold over Sophie's head. He gingerly made his way across the muddy streets back to the Alhambra. He was in a bad mood, not only because of Maggie, but mostly because of Sophie. He had bided his time long enough. He wanted her and he was determined to have her.

When he reached the Alhambra, Sophie's first show was over. Frowning, he marched through the saloon. Owing to Willie's opening night, it was not as crowded as usual. Jack found fault with everything. He cursed the waiters, yelled at the bartenders and for good measure criticized the orchestra even though he hadn't heard their performance. He went directly to the bar and ordered another drink. "Damn women anyway!"

He scowled at Sophie, who was holding court with a group of successful miners at the far end of the bar. She was laughing and flirting outrageously. Jack was seething with anger and envy and loss.

He withdrew his pocket watch. It was well past the time when Sophie should have started her second show. That added fuel to his fury. Carrying a half-finished drink, he marched down the bar. He reached the fringe of the crowd, caught Sophie's eye, held up his pocket watch and began swinging it back and forth. Sophie started to frown but caught herself. She quickly rearranged her face into a pouting expression and said, "I'm sorry to break up our fascinating discussion, gentlemen, but it's time for me to go to work." She smiled charmingly at each of them. "I hope you all enjoy the show, *n'est pas?*"

Amid a shower of compliments, Sophie emerged from the circle and swept past Jack on her way to her dressing room. "Wait a minute," growled Jack. "I want to talk to you!"

Sophie, without giving the slightest indication she had heard, continued on her way. Jack started to follow, but was stopped by several eager customers who required greeting.

Sophie slammed the door to her dressing room. The thud shook loose petals from the flowers in several vases. She was seething with anger, and the color rose in her cheeks. "That son of a bitch!" she sputtered and kicked off her shoes.

Betzy, who had been mending a gown for Sophie, looked up. "What wrong, Miz Sophie? Yo' had another run-in with dat Mr. Fast Jack?"

"Yesssss!" Sophie screamed. "Jesus God in heaven he gets to me!" She flopped into a chair and kicked her feet against the carpet.

Sophie's dressing room had been newly decorated at her insistence and at Jack's expense. The walls and ceiling were painted a muted shade of pink, and the woodwork was stained a rich shade of mahogany. An Oriental carpet in shades of rose covered the floor. The furniture was bleached birch and appeared white. The upholstery was a deep ruby-red velvet. The walls were hung with gilt-edged frames containing photographs of Sophie, each tinted to make them lifelike. The room was cluttered with vases of flowers from well-wishers, usually red roses in various stages of life. There was a free-standing three-panel mirror and a large ornate armoire.

Dutifully Betzy gathered Sophie's shoes, then began sweeping up the fallen rose petals.

Jack burst into the dressing room. Sophie looked up sharply. Betzy, sensing an argument, excused herself and went to the stage wings. Jack waited until Betzy had closed the door. Then he shouted, "Don't you ever walk away from me when I'm talking to you!"

Sophie narrowed her eyes and replied slowly and evenly. "How dare you embarrass me in front of my friends! You don't have to remind me of my show times."

"You arrived fifteen minutes late and . . ."

"So what? I wasn't aware that I was a toy doll."

Despite his anger, Jack grinned. "Perhaps not a toy, but you're a doll, all right."

Ignoring his flattery, Sophie began pacing the floor. "And how did you enjoy the French chantoosie?" Jack raised his eyebrows in surprise. "I know all about your sneaking over there. I could have saved you the trouble. Maggie O'Brien's just as bad as ever, isn't she? Despite her dyed hair and atrocious French accent."

"How did you . . ."

"I have my ways," replied Sophie blithely.

"So why didn't you tell me? You let me go over there and make a fool of myself."

"Well, if you're stupid enough to think that anybody's going to be better than I am, then you deserve to be made a fool."

Jack sat down. The evening hadn't gone as he had wanted. "Why do we always end up arguing, Sophie?"

"You pester me, Jack. You're always acting like I'm not doing my job or something. You're *always* on my back."

"I've done what I could for you. I increased your salary, had your dressing room redecorated, paid for a whole slew of new costumes . . ."

"Am I supposed to feel grateful?" Sophie snapped. "I'm the biggest draw on the coast. You, yourself, said that business had increased at least thirty percent since I've been singing here and if you had more space it would increase even more than that. God knows you've got them jammed in tighter than peas in a pod."

"True enough," Jack admitted. "It's just that I . . ." He gestured helplessly with his hands.

"I know what your problem is, Jack. And it's not my problem."

"Why won't you ever let me see you home, Sophie?" Jack asked plaintively.

Sophie sighed. "You never give up, do you, Jack? They shouldn't call you Fast Jack. Slow Jack would be more suitable! *Ma cher,* I don't let you 'see me home,' as you so delicately put it, for an enormously important reason." She faced him. "I am simply not attracted to you." Jack returned her gaze with a mixture of surprise and anger. Sophie quickly amended. "You're a very good-looking man, Jack. Perhaps too good looking for my tastes. It's just that. . . . Well, my mother explained it once. You either have a fever for someone or you don't. I'm sorry, but I don't have a fever for you."

"You seem to have plenty of 'fever' for everybody else," replied Jack sarcastically.

Sophie stood up. "You'll have to excuse me, Jack. I must change for the second show." She threw open the doors of the armoire and selected a gown of eggplant purple.

Jack jumped up and rushed to Sophie. He tore the dress from her hands and threw it on the floor. Then he roughly grabbed her arms and pulled her close to him.

"Don't Jack!" Sophie pleaded.

He kissed her hard. His mouth was hot and demanding. Sophie wrenched herself away. His strength and intensity frightened her. He clamped his mouth over hers again and tried to force his tongue between her clenched lips. Sophie pulled her lips away from his. "Stop it, Jack!"

He relaxed his grip for a second. Sophie broke free and began to run for the door. Jack lunged after her and grabbed the back of her dress, ripping it apart. He locked one arm around her throat, forcing her mouth shut so that she couldn't scream. The other arm pinned her body to his. Savagely he bent her to the floor and threw his weight on top of her. Then he locked one arm across her chest and clawed at her gown. The material gave way and her breasts were exposed. He shoved himself against her and ran one hand up between her legs. His weight forced her legs apart. Grinding his hips against hers, he pressed his erection against her soft flesh. Still holding her tightly with one hand, he kissed her mouth, forcing back her screams. And with his other hand he began to fumble at his trousers. Sophie pulled her arm free and began beating at him with her fists. She bit down on his lower lip, and her mouth became filled with the salty taste of his blood.

The door to the dressing room suddenly burst open. Luke, who had been alerted by Betzy's premonitions of trouble, rushed inside. He grabbed Jack by the collar of his jacket and in an amazing feat of strength lifted him straight in the air. Luke slammed him against the armoire and banged the back of his head against the hard wood until Jack slipped into semiconsciousness. Then Luke turned to Sophie. "Are you all right?" he asked with urgency.

"I'm . . . I'm fine." Sophie groaned. He helped her to her feet and Sophie attempted to hide her naked breasts with her arms.

"Here," said Luke handing her one of her many robes. "Put it on. The dress is ruined anyway."

Jack groaned. "What in the hell do you think you're doing . . . ?"

"Just stay where you are, Jack," Luke warned.

Jack didn't move. He rubbed his throbbing head with the palm of his hand. "I'm going crazy," he mumbled. "I'm not in charge anymore. I'm just a . . ."

"Get him out of here, Luke!" said Sophie. Luke picked Jack up and held him in midair so that his feet dangled like those of a marionette. "I don't give a shit whether you own the place or not," Luke growled. "From now on Sophie's dressing room is off limits to you. And if you ever touch her again, *I'll kill you!* Do you understand me?"

He pushed Jack through the door. After he had slammed it shut, Luke asked, "Did he hurt you, Sophie?"

"No. Just a few bruises. He's been drinking. I guess he needed the alcohol to get his courage up."

"The son of a bitch!"

"It won't happen again. I'm sure of that."

"Maybe you ought to quit, Sophie. Any of the other places would be glad to hire you for as much if not more money."

"Other than having to deal with Fast Jack Baxter, I'm quite satisfied with the Alhambra," Sophie stubbornly insisted. "My dressing room has just been decorated and the Alhambra is the nicest place on the coast. I don't think he'll bother me anymore."

Luke took Sophie's hands in his. "Your lip's bleeding, Sophie."

"No it isn't. It's *his* blood."

"Are you able to perform?"

"I'd better be," she grinned. "I imagine the place is packed to the rafters. All those men who were disappointed by the El Dorado's new chantoosie will be coming back to see Sophie. And," she added with determination, "Sophie's ready for them!"

Liam, wearing high boots, waded through the mud floe that was Market Street. He trudged past wagons and carriages stuck in the mire. San Francisco depressed Liam. Everyone seemed to be caught by the irresistible pull of gold. His own ambitions were meticulously planned and bound to succeed. He was, he felt, in direct contrast to the inhabitants of the boomtown. The ghost fleet of abandoned ships, the half-built houses, the ravaged fields all gave testimony to the sordid desire for gold! Gold!! *Gold!!!*

According to the San Francisco newspaper each day spawned an average of thirty new houses, two murders and one fire. Its young, heavily armed and largely male population drank at more than five hundred bars and gambled at more than one thousand gaming houses. Nothing was cheap in the city . . . except life. Eggs went for six dollars a dozen, and bread was two dollars a loaf. Landlords collected outrageous rents for canvas shanties, cabins, hulls of abandoned ships and rooms in tinderbox houses. Vigilantes looking for trouble roamed the streets and found it. Men accused of crimes were lynched without trial. Dozens of other criminals were flogged. The vigilantes succeeded, in a sense, by generally frightening the city's roisterers into a more acceptable behavior.

Liam stopped to recheck the address. He passed a printing house, a general store, a liquor store and a string of saloons, all doing booming business. At the corner he turned down a poorly lit side street. Liam instinctively gripped the handle of the pistol tucked into his waistband. A drunk lay on a bed of mud. A prostitute dug through the man's pockets.

"You!" Liam barked. "Get away from there!" The prostitute rose quickly, caught sight of Liam's pistol and, cursing, scurried back down the alleyway toward Market Street.

Liam shook the drunk but he would not come to, so Liam proceeded. The Hacienda Hotel loomed before him. It was a two-story building of raw wood. Attached to either side were tents that served as the bar and dining room. He climbed the steps to the elevated porch and removed mud from his boots on a boot scraper before entering.

The room had been sectioned off. The small space that remained contained a desk for registering and two hard benches, both occupied by sleeping forms. Liam scowled and stepped to the desk. He waited a moment, then rang the bell. The sleeping forms grumbled beneath their tattered blankets, shifted their weight and returned to their rhythmic snoring.

A squat man, as wide as he was tall, parted the curtains behind the desk and asked in a ragged voice, "Yeah? What you want? We ain't got no more space." He indicated the sleeping men on the benches. "We all sold out."

"I'm not looking for a place to sleep," replied Liam tersely. "I'm looking for a man named Wick Skansen."

The man scratched the back of his large head and thought. "Skansen, Skansen. Oh, yeah, that's the Scandie. Second floor. Turn left, all the way to the end. Room is on the right."

"Thank you," Liam muttered and strode up the narrow stairway.

"I'll watch for you to come down," the man yelled after him.

The stairs creaked and the hallway smelled of mud, manure and urine. Liam stopped on the first floor landing and caught his breath. The air was rank with odors of unwashed bodies, vomit and unemptied slop jars. He covered the bottom part of his face with a handkerchief and proceeded quickly up the next flight. He walked down a narrow hall, barely wide enough for another man to pass, and rapped upon a paper-thin door. "Ya, hey!" Liam waited for the owner of the voice to open the door. When he didn't, he opened it himself.

Wick Skansen, all six feet two inches of him, was stretched out on a narrow cot. His giant bare feet dangled over the side. As he read the latest issue of the *Police Gazette*, he flexed and unflexed his toes.

Liam cleared his throat loudly, and Wick dropped the magazine to the floor. He was a ruggedly handsome man with a mane of wheat-colored hair, a bull neck and a dazzling smile that revealed even white teeth. He was smiling now. "What you want with Skansen?" His voice was guarded but amiable.

Liam uncomfortably shifted his weight. The sheer size of the man made him uncomfortable. "I saw your advertisement. Are you still seeking work in a logging camp?"

Wick became more interested. He swung his feet around, planted them on the floor and stood up. His bulk filled the small room. "I am."

Liam looked around for someplace to sit. There was nothing but the bed. "Could we go somewhere and talk? This isn't exactly conducive to a comfortable business conversation."

"I put on boots," responded Wick. "And we go talk."

Liam eyed the rippling muscles of the Swede's brawny arms. He looked like he could pull a tree out by its roots. Wick tucked his plaid shirt into his pants and replaced the suspenders over his shoulders. "Ready," he announced and gently eased Liam out the door with a ham-sized hand.

Once outside the hotel, Liam breathed a sigh of relief. He felt less hemmed in by the man's size and was able to relax within his presence. "Where would be a good place for us have our talk?" asked Liam, aware that most of the saloons were noisy, boisterous places.

The large man replied, "We talk while we walk. That way we get business taken care, then we have drink."

Liam appreciated the Swede's down-to-business attitude. Most men he had hired would have been more interested in the liquor than the job.

Wick gave Liam a brief background. He was born into a family of loggers in Sweden. He had worked in Canada and California. He seemed to know everything there was to know about logging. Liam was satisfied and, in turn, told him about the Connemara Mill Company. He described the land, the timber and his plans for the future. They agreed upon a wage and shook hands in the middle of the street. They had inadvertently walked toward the Barbary Coast. Liam asked Wick if he could buy him a drink to celebrate the hiring.

"Ya, Mr. O'Sullivan. Now is the time for drinking."

Wick was the first to see the canvas poster hanging from the Alhambra and was immediately intrigued by Sophie's abundant charms. "We go there," said Wick pointing to the poster. Liam looked up and blinked his eyes in disbelief. The poster now read, "The Alhambra proudly presents the toast of the Barbary Coast, Miss Sophie Parmalee."

"What you bet, she don't look half that good."

"Oh, but she does," grunted Liam. "She does!"

Liam was reluctant to see Sophie again, but even more reluctant to disappoint his new highballer. And his curiosity was aroused. After all, the saloon looked large. It was highly unlikely that Sophie would see him.

They were stopped at the entrance by three busy black boys all under the age of ten, employing rough brushes to clean mud from the customers' boots.

"Do all the saloons on the coast do this?" Liam asked one of the boys.

"Oh, no, sir," the young man replied. "We does it at Miz Sophie's request. She don't like to get her fancy shoes all messed up from other people's mud." Liam could not help grinning. He flipped the boys a tip, and the men entered the Alhambra.

The saloon was packed with miners, gamblers and con men, all of whom had two things in common: their greed and their desire for Sophie Parmalee. Liam stopped a waiter. "Is Miss Parmalee going to perform tonight?"

"Yes, sir. The second show's a little late, but it's coming up."

Liam slipped the waiter a folded bill and asked, "Can you find us a table, but not next to the stage?"

"Well, I think I can do that, mister. Just give me a couple of minutes."

The waiter soon returned and informed them that a table was waiting. He led them through the rambunctious crowd to a small table at the end of the runway. Liam, not realizing the purpose of the runway, said the table would do nicely. He ordered an Irish whiskey, and Wick ordered a pitcher of beer. When the drinks arrived the two men clinked glasses in a mutual toast. "You say you going to hire forty men?" asked Wick, wiping the foam from his upper lip.

"That's right. At least."

"I would like to be in on hiring."

"That's agreeable."

"I can tell you by a look whether a man can be logger."

"It would certainly save us time and grief," Liam agreed.

Several of the customers began shouting for Sophie. Others joined in and the demand became deafening.

Sophie had covered her bruised arms with makeup. Unhappy with the result, she called to Betzy. "Betzy, bring me a pair of gloves. Something that will go with this gown."

"Are yo' sho' yo' all right, Miz Sophie?"

"Yes," echoed Luke. "Maybe you ought to cancel the show, Sophie."

"*No!*" Sophie was adamant. She threw up her arms and said, "Listen to that. They're calling for *me!* They don't want to see *anybody* else. *Nothing* can stop me from going on. Certainly not a few bruises and a rough flirtation from Mr. Fast Jack Baxter. No, Betzy, not the blue gloves, God damn it! Bring me the lavender ones."

The orchestra began to play, and the music replaced the shouts of the men. Liam found himself unexpectedly nervous at the prospect of seeing Sophie again. He ordered another drink and was relieved when the waiter delivered it to him before Sophie came on stage.

"I want to see this Sophie a long time," said Wick. "Her picture all over town. Some pretty woman!"

Sophie marched onstage, acknowledged her audience and before they could start screaming again launched into her song. Liam was astonished, not only by her beauty, which had become more sophisticated since her days on the *Connemara,* but also by her stage presence. He stiffened as he saw her step onto the runway. He realized with horror that she was going to be passing within a few feet of the table.

Sophie saw Liam as soon as she stepped onto the runway. She was astonished but didn't bat an eye or miss a note. Her heart leapt as she thought to herself. *He's come to see me. He's finally come to me!* As she approached the end of the runway, she saw him turn his chair so that his back was to her.

That bastard!

Then her eyes fell upon Liam's companion, a tall, big Swede who was grinning at her like a child staring through a window filled with Christmas candy. Even though blonds were not her style, Sophie was impressed by the handsome giant. And let Liam O'Sullivan cringe while she had fun with his companion.

Sophie did something she never did during a performance. When she was next to Wick and Liam's table, she stepped off the runway and sang her seductive lyrics directly to Wick.

*"I don't live as far as Italy's Rome . . .
or Alaska's Nome.
It's just a block or two away,
I'd love to walk with you today,
Say how'd'ya like to see me home?"*

Wick was transfixed. Never had he seen such a beautiful and sensual young woman. *And she was paying attention to him!* Sophie finished the chorus, ruffled Wick's hair, rolled her eyes and ad-libbed to the audience. "Ohhhhh, I wonder if he's tall all over!" The audience guffawed, and Wick's face turned the color of a ripe strawberry.

When Sophie's act was over, she rushed backstage and hurriedly changed into a sedate gown of white satin embroidered with tiny violets. She put on white gloves and touched up her makeup.

Betzy watched out of the corner of her eye and finally asked, "What yo' doin', Miz Sophie?"

"I thought I'd go mix with some of the customers. It's good business."

"Uh, huh. An' I saw who yo' plannin' on mixin' with," replied Betzy, who had seen only the young Swede. A view of Liam had been obstructed by the orchestra. "Dat yeller-haired man awful young fo' yo' taste."

"Don't tell me what my taste is," Sophie snapped. "If they're old enough to look, they're old enough to play. By the way, I didn't see Jack out there. Did he go home, I hope?"

"Oh, no. He lurkin' about," replied Betzy.

"Then I intend to show him and a few other people that I get what I want!"

Sophie twirled around in front of the three-panel mirror. "Hmmmm, I think I look a bit *too* sedate. And I certainly don't want to disappoint my admirers."

She undid the top buttons of her dress until the full swell of her breasts were visible. Then she took the bright purple boa and wrapped it around her shoulders. "There, that's better." She wet her lips and swept through the door.

As Sophie walked down the steps leading from backstage, she was stopped by Jack. "Sophie, I'm sorry, I . . ."

"I don't bruise that easily, Jack. Stand back and watch."

He stepped back to let her pass. Sophie went directly to Liam and Wick's table. "Why, Mr. O'Sullivan, how delightful to find that you're a member of my audience."

Liam's face darkened. "I happened here quite by accident, Miss Parmalee."

Sophie was unruffled and replied graciously to Liam's curt remark. "It was a happy accident for me, Mr. O'Sullivan." She turned to Wick. Remembering his manners, he quickly stood up and almost knocked over the table in the process. "I am Sophie Parmalee," she said grandly and extended her gloved hand. Wick stared at it for a moment before roughly shaking it. "Wick Skansen, Miss . . . I think you sing most beautiful."

"Enchanté," responded Sophie warmly.

"You want to get off feet?" asked Wick.

"Yes I would. How gallant." When Wick went to get a chair for Sophie, she turned to Liam. "How's your charming young friend, Mr. Fitzpatrick?"

"Getting richer by the day," replied Liam smoothly.

Sophie's smile froze. "Really?"

Liam didn't elaborate. He realized with some surprise that he enjoyed baiting Sophie.

Wick slammed down the chair and Sophie seated herself. "You drink?"

"Often," Sophie laughed. "Oh, you mean tonight? Yes, I'll have—" she was about to say whiskey and stopped herself, "champagne." Liam called to the waiter and ordered for Sophie and another round for himself and Wick.

"The French stuff!" Sophie called out after the waiter. Then she turned to Wick. "My mother was French, you know."

Wick looked perplexed. "I didn't know your mother," he responded quietly, as if Sophie were accusing him of something. Sophie laughed and patted the back of his huge hand.

"That's all right, Mr. Skansen. I didn't know yours either."

Liam stood at the entrance to the Alhambra. He knew that he was more than a bit drunk, and decided that it would be wise to engage a carriage back to the *Connemara*. He walked unsteadily to the edge of the verandah. Before he had even raised his hand, a two-seater had appeared. He stumbled inside and collapsed on the black leather seat. "Take me to the waterfront," he instructed the driver.

"Are you sure, mister?" the driver asked. "They's lots of better spots for a gentleman like you."

"What do you mean?" asked Liam thickly.

"There are places on Telegraph Hill for a gentleman with taste . . . and money," the driver went on. "Those waterfront taverns are nothin' but trouble and the girls down there, well, it wouldn't surprise me if . . ."

"I'm not looking for a girl," interrupted Liam. "I just want to go back to my ship."

"Well, pardon me, governor. You sure looked like you were lookin' for a girl."

The carriage began to move. Liam closed the windows against the cold and huddled in a corner.

The driver was right. He was looking for a girl. *Damn it, I don't want a whore. I've heard enough about whores to last a lifetime.* Liam shuddered as he recalled Rory's sordid tale of his three-day excursion into the underworld of San Francisco—the plush parlors of Telegraph Hill as well as the despicable cribs.

Liam reached his cabin, lit a kerosene lamp and sat down at his desk. He pushed his business papers aside, dipped pen in ink and, finding a relatively clean sheet of paper, feverishly began to write.

"My dear Kathleen,

This letter and its contents will no doubt come as a surprise to you. I apologize in advance for its brash tone for, as you know, I'm not a brash man. But changing times and spiraling events call for the immediacy of action. As I told you, Rory and I have established a mill on Puget Sound and now we own a large—larger than you can imagine—tract of land.

I'm in San Francisco now. We're going to be hiring more than forty new workers and, under the conditions of our business, our tract of land will double, even triple. You are now sixteen and a young woman. I'm sure that you've grown lovelier with each passing month. Could it be otherwise? You know, of course, that I've always been very fond of you and of your family. And I sincerely hope the feelings are returned. I should be writing your parents, but I know that you will read this letter to them and although the presentation may be somewhat unusual, I hope that they will understand.

Kathleen, would you consider becoming my wife? I will not expect an immediate answer. All I ask is your consideration. I am not a difficult man. I am, perhaps, set in my ways, but I assure both you and your parents that I would do everything in my power to keep you safe and make you happy. The prospects for the mill are enormous and although we are presently living in what most would call a wilderness, more people will come and a community will follow. You would appreciate the beautiful country and the mild winters. If you accept, I would see to it that a proper community is established with schools, a Catholic church and all things necessary to a proper way of life."

Liam reread his words and scowled. He felt his words were clumsy, bereft of feeling. How could he possibly hope to impress a beautiful young girl, secure her as his wife? Young girls wanted to hear words of romance. His words read like a letter of business. Liam continued the letter hoping to better express his emotions.

"I would deem it an honor if you would accept my proposal, Kathleen. I know that I'm asking a lot. It would mean leaving your family and Belfast. The trip to Puget Sound would be arduous at the least—a journey that you would, perhaps, be unwilling to undertake. But if you do accept, I will love you and honor you with every fiber of my being and count myself the most fortunate of men."

Liam blushed at his final words. Before he could change his mind, he quickly added his salutation and signature, folded the letter and addressed an envelope and sealed it. It was important that he post the letter that night. He felt if he waited until morning to come, he might change his mind and not send the letter at all.

The post office, a small building of board and canvas, was open twenty-four hours a day. The man on duty informed Liam that the letter would be sent by the Panama route and would probably be received by the party in Maine around Christmas.

The time element frustrated Liam. Christmas was a long time off, and by the time he received Kathleen's reply it would be spring. He made his way slowly back to the ship. The pungent air cleared his head. He tried not to think about the consequences of his letter. For all he knew, Kathleen might already be bespoken or even married. Perhaps the letter had been a mistake. He was, after all, an older man. But that aside, he argued with himself, his prospects were tremendous and his love for Kathleen was true.

A prostitute stepped out of the shadows, smiled at Liam and insinuatingly rolled her hips. "Want to heat up a cold night, mister? I've got the furnace if you've got the fuel!"

Liam winced. In the harsh light of the streetlamp she was a horror. Her mottled skin was unsuccessfully covered by thick white makeup. Her eyes were large, glazed and rimmed with red. Her hair was a tangled mass of dubiously colored black curls and her dress was garish—red, white and blue satin. She lunged toward Liam. Her breath was foul with alcohol. "Come on, mister. Let's pick up a quart of somethin' warming and go back to your room. I'll make it worth your time."

Liam shook himself free and hurried on his way. He was still breathing hard when he reached his cabin. He lay down on the bunk. His fingers touched the cross around his neck. Kathleen's image came to him and with it the obliteration of all the ugliness he had seen that evening. Liam smiled to himself. He had done the right thing in proposing marriage to Kathleen.

Chapter 14

The three Negro boys who scraped the boots of the Alhambra patrons slept huddled together in a corner just inside the door. They slept lightly, brushes clenched in their tiny hands, ready to spring awake if necessary.

It was well past two in the morning, and many of the patrons had relinquished the comforts of the Alhambra to find excitement in less austere surroundings. The orchestra played a listless medley for the hangers-on. The bartenders treated themselves to drinks. The waiters, anxious to get to bed, cleared the tables of glasses.

Sophie and Wick were so immersed in one another that they were completely unaware of the closing activities. Sophie was pleased with herself. She had achieved what she had set out to do. After the third show, Liam had left the Alhambra slightly drunk and in a state of controlled anger. And, of course, Wick had remained to be with her. Sophie sipped her champagne and asked Wick, "What will you be doing exactly in the great Northwest, Mr. Skansen?"

"I'm a highballer, Ma'am."

Sophie grinned. "And what, sir, is a highballer?"

"The boss man at logging camp."

"I see. Tell me more. I've always been divinely interested in logs."

Wick, his wit sharpened by alcohol, was quick to pick up her meaning. "I leave at the end of the week, Miss Sophie."

"Oh, really? Then we must enjoy our brief time together, mustn't we? Perhaps you'd escort me back to my hotel? It's not safe for a woman alone on the streets of San Francisco."

"I like!" replied Wick fervently.

"I'll get my wrap now," replied Sophie. She blew him a kiss and sashayed backstage. She stopped by the bar and instructed the bartender to give Wick whatever he wanted. "He's been drinking beer, Miss Sophie," replied the new bartender.

"Well, if it's beer he wants, give him beer."

Jack watched Sophie's antics with irritation. He turned his attention toward the gaming tables, checking the Faro and Black Jack dealers and the roulette wheel—the first one in San Francisco. Then he got deeply involved in a game of Faro with some men who chided him into playing, saying that he never bet his own money. Jack played for over an hour and didn't notice when Sophie left, taking with her a sack of nuggets, Betzy and Wick Skansen.

Jack questioned the waiter, who informed him that Sophie had gone with the big blond man. Jack ordered a bottle of whiskey and went back to the game. He proceeded to get drunk and lost most of the night's profits.

The manager of the United States Hotel treated Sophie like royalty. He met her in the lobby and if he didn't approve of the gangly Swede accompanying her, he gave no indication of it. Sophie ordered a bottle of the best champagne to be sent up to the room along with a cold pitcher of beer for Wick.

After seeing to Sophie's needs, Betzy retired to her own room and left the young people alone together. A waiter arrived with the drinks and Sophie generously tipped him. She excused herself to change from her performing clothes. Wick poured himself a glass of beer and settled into the largest armchair in the room. He liked to be in women's rooms. He liked the aroma and the touches of femininity that made them so different from a man's quarters. A silk stocking hastily removed by Sophie lay half-hidden under the couch. A length of red ribbon dangled from the arm of the lamp. In a corner of the room was a large pink feather from one of Sophie's shedding boas.

Sophie removed her heavy stage makeup and dabbed a touch of rouge on her lips and cheeks. She stripped, corsets and all, and splashed herself with heady perfume. Then she selected the sheerest dressing gown. Mauve silk, it clung tenaciously to the curves of her body. Satisfied that she looked properly alluring, she slipped back into the sitting room.

Wick almost choked on his beer when he saw her. Sophie smiled, seated herself on the edge of the armchair next to him and let him pour her a glass of champagne. She was pleased with her companion. Although she hadn't managed to seduce Liam, she took some satisfaction in finding his friend appealing. And Wick was appealing. True, he could do nothing but make her happy for a night. But there had been so many fat, middle-aged men to whom she had to be courteous because of her position at the Alhambra. And although she readily accepted presents from them, they got nothing more from her than a fleeting kiss or a brief touch of her thigh.

Sophie kicked off her slippers and curled her toes in the soft carpet. She sipped the champagne and became aware of how nervous she was making Wick. She felt the heat of his body and his muscular hardness. She set down her glass and began running her fingers through his sun-streaked hair. "How long before you leave with Mr. O'Sullivan?" Sophie asked softly.

"We go at end of week."

"Then we'll have to make the most of our time together."

She took his hand in hers, brought him to his feet, then led him into the bedroom. In the dim light they took off their clothes and stared at each other with a sense of urgent wonder. Sophie stepped closer to Wick and reached out to brush the perfection of his muscular flesh. Wick moaned at her touch. Like primitive dancers moving to a slow but insistent rhythm they came together. At the moment their bodies fully touched, Wick swept Sophie up in his powerful arms and carried her to the bed.

His lips traced the curve of her throat down to the hard tips of her breasts. He kissed each one in turn and continued moving his head downward. He paused at the tiny pink well that was her navel. He covered her taut stomach with a dozen gentle bites. Then downward until his eyelashes fluttered against the soft flesh of her inner thighs. Then his lips touched the center of her body and Sophie moaned with an impatient pleasure. "Now, Wick," Sophie pleaded. "Please now!"

Wick raised himself and Sophie's hands clasped his buttocks, drawing him between her legs, and with sweet whispered commands urged him into her. He slipped his hands beneath her and brought her body up to meet his.

It was an explosion, for they were two stars coming together and colliding.

Wick stayed at Sophie's suite at the hotel. Each morning sharply at eight he would meet Liam and Captain Fallon at the dock, and the three men would select equipment, order supplies and interview the scores of men who had applied for work at the logging camp. At the end of the third day, Liam was beginning to worry they weren't going to fill their quota of men. Wick had rejected a good many who Liam felt could have done the job. When he expressed his feelings to the Swede, Wick replied, "Beg your pardon, Mr. O'Sullivan, it not size alone. Good logger has to be swift, move quick, think quick. Do not worry. We will find enough men. And if we do not fill quota is better to take the right men."

"All right, Wick. I'll leave it to you. I've not had experience with trees of this size before."

"I will do my job good, Mr. O'Sullivan."

Liam wondered if Wick was still seeing Sophie. Noting the contented expression on the great Swede's face every morning they met, he assumed he was. He wondered if her name would ever come up between Wick and Rory, and he hoped that it would not.

Wick spent every evening at the Alhambra drinking beer and watching Sophie perform. Later they returned to the hotel where they made passionate love until the early hours of the morning. Friday, the day the *Connemara* was to leave, came all too quickly for Sophie and Wick. Wearing a hooded cloak to go unrecognized, Sophie accompanied Wick to the dock. It was an icy morning, and their breaths hung in the air like puffs of smoke. As they reached the harbor the sun was just breaking through the morning mist. Seagulls noisily ordered their breakfast, then dove to the surface of the water to see if their wishes had been fulfilled.

Sophie elected not to leave the carriage. She had no desire to see the *Connemara* again. She forced aside stray guilt concerning the harsh ending with Rory. And she did not want Liam to see her with Wick. The Swede had proved to be the most vivacious of lovers, imaginative and tireless. But he was just a lover. He could never be a friend or a husband. Sophie silently compared the men whose lives were logging. Wick, Rory, Liam. . . .

Wick snuggled his face close to Sophie's. "I be back every six or eight week," he murmured.

Sophie kissed him quickly, then smiled as she heard Captain Fallon's gruff voice shouting orders for the sailing. "You'd better be going, *mon cher*. Captain Fallon doesn't like to be kept waiting."

"How do you know Captain Fallon?" asked Wick.

"It's a long story," replied Sophie stroking his cheek. "I'll tell you all about it when you return to me."

Sophie sat in the carriage and watched the hulking Scandinavian as he boarded the ship. As Liam stepped into view, she caught her breath. She thought he was more handsome than ever. "Someday," she vowed to herself, "I'll make that man want me."

She instructed Luke to take her back to the hotel, closed her eyes and indulged herself in the fantasy that she had come to the dock to see Liam off. She parted her lips and breathed his name, *Liam,* and immediately the image of his dark brooding good looks rushed at her. If only he had been more civil to her at the Alhambra. If she hadn't been so intent upon displaying her power over other men when he was the only one she wanted, *if only* . . .

Sophie's reverie was interrupted by the clanging of the great city bell, a signal that another fire had broken out. Sophie shuddered and hoped that it was burning far from the hotel.

Kathleen stoked the fire in the great iron stove and checked the spice cookies she was baking for the neighborhood children. Dressed as witches, goblins and ghosts, they would be appearing at the back door that Halloween evening. Winter had arrived in Belfast. Silent and deadly, it had crept into the small community bringing a fine snow that covered the countryside in shimmering white brilliance.

Although the kitchen was warm and cozy, Kathleen shivered every time she looked through the kitchen window. She was watching for her father and brothers from the mill. Ordinarily she wasn't so attentive to their comings and goings, but they had informed her at breakfast they had a surprise for her that evening. She wondered what on earth it could be.

While the cookies were baking Kathleen prepared colcannon, a traditional Irish dish consisting of cabbage, mashed potatoes, parsnips and chopped onion. One's fortune depended upon what was found in the served portion. A ring, key, penny, or button respectively meant the diner could expect marriage, a journey, wealth or bachelorhood. It was a dish that Kathleen's late grandmother had entertained the Mulvany clan with Halloween after Halloween. In anticipation of something nice happening to her, Kathleen decided to prepare it that night to accompany the venison roast.

After mixing the colcannon, Kathleen checked the cookies once again. They were done. She moved the roast to the center of the oven and added more wood to the fire.

Delia Mulvany entered the kitchen, followed by a gust of wind and a swirl of snow. She removed her coat and eyed the colcannon waiting to be heated in the oven. "Eh, and what's all this foolishness? Colcannon, is it?"

"I thought it might be nice," replied Kathleen easily. "It *is* Halloween and Grandma Mulvany always made it."

"Silly old woman," grunted Delia. Kathleen ignored her mother and began setting the table.

"You'd better set another place," said Delia with a crooked smile.

"Oh, and why is that?" asked Kathleen. "I didn't know we were having company."

"Well, we are. Your father and brothers are bringin' home the new mill hand, young Ian Dowling." The Dowlings had just settled in Belfast. Kathleen had not met Ian.

"Is he my surprise?" asked Kathleen.

"The only surprise in this house is that you're sixteen and have chosen to turn your back on all the fine young men in Belfast."

Kathleen slammed the dishes on the table. "How dare father or any of you play matchmaker for me! I'll not have it!"

"Ian's a fine lad," remarked Delia without enthusiasm.

"Fine lad or not, I won't be made a fool. I won't be at dinner. You can serve it!"

"Nay, I'll not serve the dinner, my girl. That's your job. And it wouldn't hurt you to be nice to the young man. From what Mary Murphy tells me, he's a fine lookin' lad."

"Then let Mary Murphy entertain him!"

Delia stuck the tip of a finger into a warm cookie. "Cookies?" she questioned.

"What do they look like? I made them for the neighbor children. They'll be stopping by later."

"More foolishness."

Kathleen lifted her head from the table and looked directly into her mother's eyes. Evenly punctuating each word she said, "I hope I never become like you, Mama. To you everything is foolishness, everything that's pretty or bright or gay or surprising. You're older in spirit than anyone I know, even Papa. And I pity you because you enjoy so little in life that you might as well be dead."

Delia's eyes grew wide with outrage. "How dare you speak to me like that, wishing me dead!"

"I didn't say that, Mama."

"Yes you did. I heard it with my own ears."

"Mama, I'm sorry. I didn't mean that. Really I didn't."

"You're a fine one to talk about enjoyin' life. You've done nothin' but mope around the house since Liam and Rory left. Well, my girl, they're gone and Ian Dowling is here. And if you'll take my advice, you'll make the most of it before you end up a spinster like your crazy Aunt Sheelagh!"

Delia stomped into the parlor to observe her evening ritual of Bible reading until dinnertime.

Kathleen was exasperated. She was fighting with her mother more and more. And now her father and brothers were going to embarrass her by dragging home a suitor. Was her mother right? Was she really moping around after something that would never happen? She received a letter from Liam almost weekly . . . but not a word from Rory. But that was like Rory. He wasn't the type to write letters. As glad as she was to receive Liam's letters, something had disturbed her about the tone of the most recent ones. Liam had been writing to her like a suitor. Of course, that was it. Why hadn't she realized it before? *Exactly like a suitor.*

Kathleen basted the roast and thought about this revelation. Liam was handsome, of course, but so quiet, retiring. Not at all like Rory who pressed his good looks on the world. Tall, gentle and always endearing, Liam had always seemed like a proper older brother. Still he was the one who was writing to her.

Ian Dowling turned out to be an attractive, painfully shy young man who was immediately smitten with Kathleen. Despite herself, Kathleen could not help but like Ian and she was attentive to him. As she expected, her father and brothers misread her hospitality and began giving one another nudges and sly glances. When the time came for everyone to partake of the colcannon, Delia grandly announced that she would dish it up. Since a bottle of whiskey had been served with dinner, Kathleen's brothers and father were in rare moods. They jokingly poked the concoction with their forks, searching for the object that would predict their fortunes.

"I found a penny!" cried Kieran. "I'm gonna be rich! I'm gonna be rich!"

"An' I got a button!" announced Desmond, the

girl-hating fourteen-year-old. "Hurray! I won't have to get married!"

"And what did you get, my daughter?" asked Seamus, his face flushed crimson from the whiskey.

Kathleen triumphantly held up the ring for all to see. "I'm going to be married," she announced.

All heads turned to Ian who stammered. "I, too, have a ring."

Rory took an immediate dislike to Wick. He instinctively sensed that the tall, handsome Swede was his competitor, not only in appearance and strength but also in running the mill. Liam noted Rory's antagonism and decided it would be best to keep them working in separate parts of the forest.

Thirty-seven new men had been hired and each, by prearrangement, claimed a tract of land already staked out by Rory. For their percentage they signed their claim over to the Connemara Mill Company, bringing the total acreage to 8,320 square miles. Twelve Chinese men had been hired at low salaries to work the kitchens. Liam hated to take advantage of the coolie labor, but there weren't many white men who would work as cooks. The Chinese were not allowed to make a land claim, and that further irritated Liam.

The mill had been running smoothly during Liam's absence. Stacks of board piled as high as the mill itself were in abundance. A good many of the boards would be used to build cabins for the new laborers. They were put to work and by Christmas they were comfortably housed in warm cabins. There was to be a party at the Company House. The men had cut a fir tree and had decorated it with paper stars and photographs of loved ones.

Rory, already feeling the effects of several mugs of Christmas cheer, knocked on the door to Liam's room and stuck his head inside. "Liam, aren't you coming to the party?"

"Oh, yes," replied Liam absently. "I'd forgotten about it." He closed a book of figures and looked up at Rory. His voice grew in excitement as he talked. "Rory, do you realize with the addition of the new labor and new equipment, we have doubled our production. By February I expect we'll redouble it and before long we're going to have to build a second mill to handle our demands. I was talking to Josh. It looks like we're going to have to buy another ship to transport the lumber to San Francisco."

"What's wrong with the *Connemara?*"

"Nothing. But while it's on its way we can be filling up another one so that we've got two in transit at the same time."

"Well, that's real nice," grinned Rory. "But hell, Liam, it's Christmas Eve. Let's go have a couple of drinks with the boys."

"It looks like you've already started."

"Then you'll have to catch up with me. Come on, let's go."

When Rory and Liam entered the Company House everyone was in a holiday mood. Rory had provided a generous supply of drink. There were several musicians among the merrymakers. The men had built a roaring fire in the stone fireplace, and the entire room was filled with the scent of burning pine. Liam held up his hands and warmly shouted. "Merry Christmas, everyone." The men began cheering and hugging one another. A young man with a beautiful tenor voice began singing and they all joined in. Their voices blended and drifted across the bay and up the mountains.

"Silent night, holy night,
All is calm, all is bright . . ."

A party of Dwamish Indians, riding across the mountainside, paused on their journey and looked down the canyon at the encampment. They cocked their heads to one side and listened to the strange caroling as the sounds were carried up the valley on the back of the wind.

It was a dismal wintry morning between Christmas and New Year's. The bare trees cast dark shadows against the white snow. The air was sharp with the promise of more snow and the tang of wood burning in each and every fireplace.

Kathleen, returning from early morning mass, listened to the crunch of her footsteps on the frozen ground. She thought it was the saddest sound in the world—lone footsteps on the snow. She stopped on the hillside overlooking the mill and the bay. At one time the mill had been her private playground, but now that Rory and Liam were gone, she hardly ever went there. A sharp wind from the ocean spun her around. She hurried home, anxious to be in the warm comfort of her own kitchen. As soon as she entered the kitchen, she replaced her boots with a pair of fur-lined slippers and continued her daily chores.

Her mother, who was suffering from a cold, called from the parlor. "Kathleen, is that you?"

"Yes."

"Be a good girl and make me a cup of hot tea, would you?"

"I've already put the teapot on."

"There's a good girl," Delia sniffed.

The tea kettle began to whistle mournfully. Kathleen prepared the tea and carried the tray in to her mother, quilt-wrapped and huddled in a rocking chair next to the fireplace. She set the tea down and started back to the kitchen. "Oh, Kathleen, I forgot to tell you," said Delia begrudgingly. "The postman brought a letter for you."

"A letter? Where is it?"

"On the mantelpiece."

Delia watched her daughter rush to the fireplace, smile when she saw the handwriting on the envelope and anxiously tear it open. Kathleen sat down on the footstool next to the dancing flames and began to read. Her eyes widened in surprise as she read Liam's letter of proposal. Then she threw back her head and began to laugh. It was a bright, tinkling joyful sound.

Delia frowned. "What on earth is the matter with you, girl?" Kathleen jumped up and began to dance around the room. "Have you lost your senses then? What is it, Kathleen?"

Kathleen gaily waved the letter in front of her mother's nose and announced, "Mama, I'm going to see the elephant!"

Chapter 15

Liam received Kathleen's affirmative answer to his proposal of marriage in late January. Kathleen should arrive sometime in early April. He was ecstatic and made plans to build a house for his future wife. But Port Gamble was not the place to do it. With the great success of the Connemara Mill Company, Port Gamble became a mecca of free enterprise. The men who worked at the mill had to be fed, clothed and entertained. A group of buildings sprang up just outside the boundary of the mill land. They were crammed into a clearing deep in the shadows of the timber. Front Street, just a simple swathe through the forest, sported a notorious collection of bars and bawdy houses. There, fast-talking card sharks and bevies of soiled doves eagerly relieved the loggers of their weekly pay.

A logger's playtime was as dangerous as his worktime. It usually consisted of roughhousing, drinking, gambling and womanizing. Not all the establishments that sprang up on Front Street were of a dubious nature, though. There were also laundries, dry goods stores, a dentist and a lady barber.

Liam made an attempt to close down what he considered the "dens of iniquity," but the loggers rebelled and threatened to strike. Rory reasoned with Liam, explaining that the men needed their pleasures to keep them from leaving Port Gamble. Liam finally relented. The gaming tables and the soiled doves stayed, and so did the men.

Liam, realizing he could not change the loggers' ways, selected a site across the Bay. The infant town of Seattle would be a fine place to build a new home for his new bride.

Rory, upon seeing the building plans, asked Liam, "Why are you building such a great house? Is Kathleen bringing her family?"

"Of course not, Rory. I'm building it for our family. What's the good of all this profit if we don't have any sons to carry on our names?"

"You're the one that's getting married, not me."

"Well, you could use the calming influence of a good woman."

Rory grinned broadly and ran his hands through his auburn hair. "I'll settle for a bad one."

"I suppose you go to those establishments on Front Street," remarked Liam stiffly.

"From time to time. I'm not looking for a wife, Liam," Rory said in some exasperation. "Can't you get that into your head?"

"But a wife would . . ."

"God damn it, Liam!" Rory exploded. "You're the family man, not I. Look, I'm sure Kathleen will make you a wonderful wife, and you know I wish you both every happiness. Now why can't you wish me the same? You'll have your bride and I'll have my whores."

Liam put his hand on Rory's shoulder. "I can't believe that the life you're leading is making you happy."

"It's my life, isn't it?" Rory turned and walked out of the office, slamming the door behind him.

Liam, no longer able to concentrate on the house plans, rolled up the drawings and set them aside. He put on his jacket made from the fur of timber wolves by the local Indians, then stepped out into the fresh, biting air with no particular direction in mind.

Liam found himself heading toward Front Street. It was late afternoon, and the merchants were getting ready for another evening of activity. The Irishman cursed himself anew for not claiming the tract of land on which Front Street had sprung up, but the trees there had been scrubby and twisted from the sharp winds that blew harshly down the shallow valley. Well, it was too late now. Perhaps Rory was right. The loggers would stay only if they had their diversions. It didn't matter whether he approved or not, as long as the mill continued to increase its profits. Liam realized that the entertainment centers would last as long as the timber abounded and the customers remained. He believed that would be forever. For as they felled each tree, striplings were planted in their place. Liam smiled as he imagined his great grandchildren felling the same trees that he, himself, had planted.

Liam stood in front of the office of Dr. Painless Packer, who ran a thriving tooth-pulling parlor. In an open doorway Dr. Packer demonstrated his professional touch on a shill. The man was dressed as a logger and his job was to look happy in the dentist's chair. It was a device designed to disarm the timorous. Next to Painless Packer was a barbershop designated by a section of tree trunk painted in red and white stripes. The barber was a woman and called herself Madame Sevilla. She was a hefty creature with broad shoulders and an eager face. Madame Sevilla saw Liam approach and, thinking that he might be one of the loggers, sauntered out onto the porch of her establishment, shears in hand. She worked them back and forth, clipping the air, and called out pleasantly. "Shave an' a haircut, good-lookin'? I got the latest French scents for men which will make the gals howl like timber wolves in heat." Liam grinned.

"Not today." he replied brightly. He liked this robust woman. She had learned her trade from her husband, a small dapper man, who had died shortly after they arrived in Port Gamble. Madame had chosen to stay on and had prospered. He shook his head and continued down Front Street. Sidestepping a deep crevice of mud, he stepped onto the makeshift collection of boards that was a sidewalk.

A tattoo parlor that Liam hadn't noticed before opened recently. Garish designs neatly painted on boards hung from the eaves. Designs that could be reproduced on a logger's tough hide included a wiggling mermaid, a ferocious sea serpent, a bleeding heart with or without a dagger, a giant eye with a jewel-like teardrop in the corner. To Liam's surprise, there was even a design for the Connemara Mill Company: three furry pine cones surrounding intricate letters of the company name. Liam's first reaction was mild outrage, then amusement. Finally pride crept in. He played with the idea of getting such a tatoo himself and wondered how Kathleen would react to it.

He looked up. The bright blue vista was framed by the tops of the great trees beyond Front Street. Liam closed his eyes and thanked his God, who resided somewhere in that vast blue and cloudless sky. Kathleen was coming. That was all he could think about. That's all that mattered. And her forthcoming arrival eclipsed his thoughts of business. *Kathleen was coming.* He repeated the words over and over like a prayer—a prayer that was going to come true.

There was a shooting gallery and a clothing store that specialized in "Sunday suits," usually of the vibrant purplish hue favored by most of the loggers. Next to the clothing store was a photographer's salon, also new to Front Street. Liam went inside. After all, if he was going to get married, he would want to have pictures taken. The photographer, an officious little man with a brisk manner and a waxed mustache, hurried forward to greet Liam. "A picture, good sir? I specialize in the finest of portraits and you have a variety of backgrounds to choose from. A waterfall perhaps? No? Something more exotic?"

"I'm not here to get my picture taken today," replied Liam quickly. "I am going to be married sometime in April and . . ." His eyes scanned the photographs lining the wall of the tiny shop. "I see you are competent. Perhaps you would consider being in attendance?"

"That could be arranged, Mr.—?"

"O'Sullivan, Liam O'Sullivan."

The photographer's eyes filled with something akin to terror. Evidently he had heard of Liam's attempts to close down Front Street. "Ah—ah—you're Mr. O'Sullivan who owns the mill?"

"Along with my partner, Rory Fitzpatrick."

"I can assure you, good sir, that I do not in any way overcharge or cheat your men. Additionally, I do not take what is casually called 'art photographs.' No matter how much I am offered."

Liam smiled thinly. "No, I'm sure you don't. I'll let you know the date of the wedding." He nodded his head and started toward the open door.

"I also do hand tinting!" the photographer called after him.

Liam walked on. The legitimate establishments gradually gave way to the pleasure palaces. The first of such places was called the Workingman's Club. The dingy frame structure was moderately decorated by ill-fitting windows positioned along the street side. Liam curiously peered over the swinging doors leading to the main room and was slightly dazzled by the interior. A polished mahogany bar ran the full length of the hall and was stocked with every kind of spirits. Behind the bar hung a tapestry-sized oil painting of voluptuous pink nudes who were being mildly harassed by the legions of Rome. At the far end was a small stage where an entertainer was practicing. She was a fleshy young girl, not yet out of her teens, wearing a suit of pink tights. Nearby a pianist was struggling to accompany her. The girl was inexperienced, her voice strident and off-key and her grammar atrocious. Liam mused how well Sophie Parmalee would do in Port Gamble. Still, the young and pretty woman would be very popular among the lumberjacks.

He continued on past saloons and gaming houses. The gaming houses had mezzanines featuring cozy, curtained booths where the logger could do his dining, drinking and lovemaking in private. The girls who worked the mezzanines were independent. They were not on the house payroll, and it was a strict rule that none of the girls could set foot on the main floor.

One saloon advertised free lunch. Liam realized he was hungry. The saloon was Toby's, named after the man who owned it. Several waiters were arranging the free lunch on the bar. The platters overflowed with juicy roast ox, sliced sausage, stacks of bread, blocks of Scandinavian cheeses and small barrels of herring in brine. The condiment for this generous repast was homemade mustard, spicy and burning hot, residing in quart jars at three-foot intervals along the bar. Liam leaned on the bar. The bartender looked up, looked at his watch and looked up again. "You're through early, ain't you, jack? It ain't no holiday an' I know that Skinflint O'Sullivan don't let his men out early."

Liam winced at this nickname. He had heard it bantered about several times, but always behind his back. "I'd like an Irish whiskey, please."

"Comin' right up." The bartender set a shot glass and the bottle down in front of Liam. He downed the shot and the bartender poured him another. "I think I'll try a bit of your free lunch."

"Go ahead, jack. It's on the house."

"It's not jack. It's . . . Skinflint O'Sullivan!"

The bartender became flustered. "I—I'm sorry, sir . . ."

"It doesn't matter," Liam grinned. "I've heard it before. Since you know my name, you might tell me yours."

"I'm Toby Dolby, sir. I own the joint."

"Well, we have that much in common," Liam laughed as he speared a slice of roast ox.

As Liam ate his lunch, he had several more shots of whiskey and chatted with Toby.

"Yeah," Toby was saying, "We was really goin' through some skittery turns when you was tryin' to get us closed down."

"Well, Toby, I had my reasons. But looking back now I don't think they were very good ones," said Liam as he bit into a herring.

"It's too bad you didn't own this land, Mr. O'Sullivan. You could be clearin' a profit off that, too."

"We're doing all right at the mill."

"So I hear."

"Tell me, Toby, why do the men call me 'Skinflint?' I pay them fair wages."

"It ain't that, Mr. O'Sullivan. I guess it's just some of your personal habits. Your savin' ways. Like straightenin' the nails, for instance."

"What's so peculiar about saving?"

"Nothin'," laughed Toby. "But it ain't so usual 'round here. Why, many a fool lumberjack spends his whole winter's work by noon his first day in town! But that's why you own the mill, Mr. O'Sullivan, an' they work for you."

"Why, I never thought of it in that way before," said Liam. "It sort of eases the sting, if you know what I mean."

"Another whiskey?"

"No, I think not. I'd better be getting back to my work. It's been a pleasure talking to you."

"You stop in anytime, Mr. O'Sullivan."

As Liam left Toby's he heard the company bell signal the end of the workday. At the clanging a dozen or so soiled doves stuck their heads out their windows and beamed with anticipation. As the lumberjacks' day ended, theirs would begin. They saw Liam and began calling out good-natured invitations.

"Hey, love, want a little appetizer before supper?"

"Hello, handsome, look this way!"

"Tired of fellin' trees, honey? Why don'cha fell me?"

Liam wished he had taken another route back to his office. Worried that he might be seen by some of the men who worked for him, Liam ducked down the narrow strip between the last two whorehouses. He was about to make a dash for the trees when a young girl caught his eye. She was kneeling on the back porch dumping a pan of dirty water into the gulley which ran alongside the house. She looked up and shyly smiled at him. She was Chinese and heartbreakingly lovely. Her hair was glossy, black and worn in a single braid. Her childlike face was a perfect oval. As Liam moved toward her, he saw that it was marred by harsh makeup. He was astounded. Surely the child couldn't be working there? The girl lowered her eyes and, using a rag, began wiping the pan.

A gruff voice shouted through the back door. "Ain't you finished yet?" The door opened, and a tall, bearded man appeared. He roughly grabbed the girl by the arm and yanked her to her feet. "What's takin' you so long?" The man noticed Liam standing in the shadows and scowled. Then he turned to the young Chinese girl, drew back his hand and slapped her hard on both cheeks. The sharp sounds echoed like gunshots. "I told you no solicitin' outside the house!" He drew back to hit her again.

"*Stop it!*" screamed Liam. He rushed up the back steps and grabbed the man's arm.

He turned on Liam, his face glowering. "Who in the hell do you think . . ."

Liam slammed him against the wall and snarled. "Don't move, don't say anything."

The man was frightened of the power in Liam's voice and stood still, barely breathing.

"Are you hurt?" Liam asked the girl. She shook her head even though there were tears in her eyes and angry marks on her cheeks. "What is this girl doing working here?" Liam shouted over his shoulder. "She's too young to be in a place like this!"

"Oh, she's not exactly workin' here," the man stammered. "She's not one of the girls."

"Then who is she?" Liam demanded.

"She belongs to me," replied the man gaining more confidence. "She's an indentured servant."

"Indentured—to you?" Liam was incredulous. "For how long?"

"Three years."

"You have the papers that can prove this?" The man nodded his head. "Then I want to see them."

"Who are you?"

"Some call me 'Skinflint O'Sullivan.' I own the mill."

The man's jaw dropped. "They're inside, if you'll come with me . . . Mr. O'Sullivan, sir."

Her name was Pink Jade and she was fourteen or fifteen years of age. A year earlier her Cantonese parents had been beaten to death by a mob in San Francisco who hated the foreign laborers usurping their work prospects. Pink Jade was then illegally sold as an indentured servant by an evil uncle. She was bought by a man named Jabe Torrance who ran a house of prostitution near the Barbary Coast. Torrance was an inveterate gambler and lost his stable of girls in a card game. Rather than forfeit his livelihood, Torrance fled San Francisco with the ten whores and settled in Port Gamble's Front Street on Puget Sound. Pink Jade was the youngest female in Torrance's house. She was technically a virgin, but had been trained as a "warm-up girl" before the men fornicated with the older women.

Liam scanned the note of indenture. Realizing that it was an illegal document, he nonetheless offered to reimburse Torrance the three hundred dollars he had paid for Pink Jade. Noting that Liam was doing his best to restrain his temper, Torrance wisely did not ask for a profit. He readily accepted Liam's note, which would by payable at the mill office.

"You know, Torrance," said Liam flatly. "I wasn't able to close down Front Street, but I am able to command a certain amount of law and order. If I ever find you are trafficking in girls this young again, I'll see that you are on the next boat south. Now have the girl gather her things and explain to her that she's coming to live with me as a servant, nothing more. That she is no longer indentured and that she will be paid wages for her work."

"Why don't you tell her?" grunted Torrance. "She understands English!"

Liam explained to the young girl as simply as possible what had taken place. Pink Jade was overwhelmed. She believed Liam's words. for she instinctively felt that Liam was a kind man and would not mistreat her. She happily gathered up her meager possessions, packed them into a straw suitcase and left the house without looking back.

Liam took Pink Jade back to his cabin. She would stay in a small room off the kitchen until the house in Seattle was completed. Rory no longer lived with Liam, but had rented a room on Front Street to get away from Liam's watchful eye. Pink Jade was grateful for her new home. She proved to be a willing worker and kept the cabin scrupulously clean. Her cooking was an uneasy mixture of American and Cantonese flavorings. But she soon learned how to make a proper pot of coffee and how to prepare a New England breakfast.

Rory was amused by Liam's acquisition and teased him about it. "And how's your little Oriental sugar wafer today, Liam?" he asked his friend one morning in the office.

"Huh, what? You mean Pink Jade? If you mean Pink Jade, say so. That's her name."

"Is she taking good care of you?"

"She's excellent around the house," replied Liam stiffly. "But I do wish she'd stop putting soy sauce in the stew."

"Soy sauce in the stew!" Rory repeated with a lascivious grin. "And what do you think Kathleen is going to say about this pretty young thing living in your house?"

"What do you mean, Rory? I got Pink Jade to help Kathleen run the house when she gets here."

Rory could see that his friend was sincere and completely ignorant of the rumors about him and Pink Jade. "I suppose you realize that most people think you're sleeping with Pink Jade," remarked Rory.

Liam's eyes glinted with anger. He looked up from his books and replied sharply. "I don't give a damn what people believe! My God, Rory, she's just a child!"

"She's almost as old as your intended bride, and it's common knowledge you bought her at a whorehouse."

Liam pressed down on his pencil so hard that the lead broke. He snapped the pencil in two, threw it aside and exploded. "Get this straight, Rory! There's nothing between Pink Jade and me. You take that news and jam it down your cronies' throats. I don't want to hear any vulgar talk concerning the two of us. And I certainly don't want any rumors circulating when Kathleen gets here."

Rory, who hadn't expected such a display of anger, said quietly. "I'll see to it, Liam," and quickly changed the subject. "Have you heard from Kathleen? She's on her way, isn't she?"

"Yes. I received a letter only yesterday. She was scheduled to depart from New York by railroad on January 23rd."

"That sounds a hell of a lot easier than coming around the Horn."

"The railroad will only take her to Kansas. She'll have to travel by overland stagecoach the rest of the way to San Francisco and we'll meet her there."

"Jesus. That's going to be one, long, bumpy ride." He paused at the door. "She must love you a hell of a lot, Liam, to come all that distance."

Liam reached for another pencil and, instead of adding up his rows of figures, wrote Kathleen's name across the ledger. "I wonder," he whispered.

Chapter 16

Kathleen had decided to take the perilous Overland Trail to Puget Sound. It would mean four months of traveling time, but at least she would not have to endure the fearsome ocean. Her family, who had reluctantly given their consent to the marriage, were both tearful and joyful for Kathleen's going.

Kathleen, yearning for adventure, saw Liam's proposal as an escape from that stifling pattern of life in Belfast, Maine. She convinced herself that her attraction to Rory was merely a childish impertinence. By the time Kathleen reached New York, she sincerely believed she could love Liam as a wife should.

The trip from New York to Kansas lasted only a week, but it was most uncomfortable, particularly going across Missouri. Due to heavy rains, the rails rose and fell, first to one side, then to the other. Kathleen spent one night picking up and restacking luggage, which kept falling from the rack above her head. After the fourth try she gave it up and left them on the floor. It seemed like every part of her body was bruised. One passenger claimed the injuries were minor compared to the ones she might endure traveling by stagecoach. Kathleen sighed in resignation and settled for a sleepless night.

On January 30, the Erie Railroad pulled into Atchison, Kansas. Kathleen, exhausted, felt as if she had been traveling for months. She brushed the dust from the traveling suit she had made for herself—dark purple wool. Then she put on her cloak, adjusted her hat and peered at her reflection in the window. She looked weary, but so did the other travelers. Kathleen stretched her aching body as she alighted from the train, then searched for a porter to take care of her luggage.

A Negro porter carried her bags to a waiting carriage. She directed the driver to the Atchison Hotel. She planned to spend a few days recuperating before embarking on the stagecoach ride across the Great Plains. She looked out the window at the drab countryside with disinterest. The sky was shrouded by a chilling gray mist that seemed to infect everything it touched. Buildings, vegetation and people looked gray. Lord, would she ever see summer again?

Kathleen reached the hotel and found she was too tired to be shocked by the prices. A bellboy took her directly to her room, which as requested, had a private bath. She immediately called for hot water to fill the copper tub, and then surveyed the room. She decided not to unpack everything, since the clothes would get wrinkled again. Steam drifting out of the bathroom beckoned her like a welcoming hand. Kathleen went inside, tested the water. It was good and hot as she liked it. Then she stepped into the tub, slowly easing her aching body into the warming depths of the water. She leaned back against the tub and allowed herself the luxury of a deep satisfying sigh. Despite her exhaustion she was glad to be there and not in Belfast, Maine.

Her parents hadn't wanted to give consent to Liam's long-distance proposal. They cautioned about the dangers of the trip, the hardships of life in the Pacific Northwest and the recklessness of marrying a man she really didn't know. Those were the reasons they put forth, but Seamus Mulvany didn't want to lose his daughter to another man. Kathleen was the one who kept the home running. Without Kathleen he would lose the comforts of her homemaking. Delia didn't want Kathleen to leave either. She had no intention of giving up her barnyard and gardening activities for the kitchen.

Kathleen listened to none of their arguments. Instead she consulted Father McClafferty. He took the young girl into the rectory and, after offering a cup of tea, gave his advice. "It's not your parents' opinions that bother me, Kathleen, for I know you, you're a strong girl. You've made up your mind to go and go you will. There's something else."

"What is it, Father?"

"You seem to forget my child that I'm your confessor."

Kathleen stared at her teacup. "I haven't forgotten, Father."

"You're planning to travel all across country to marry a man you don't love."

"But I can love him, Father," Kathleen replied fervently. "I know I can. And I'll make him a good wife, I swear I will."

"I've no doubt you mean that, my daughter. But what about your affection for Rory Fitzpatrick?"

"That was a long time ago, Father. It was just a childhood infatuation. I'm grown up now."

"I wonder," replied the kindly priest.

Kathleen picked up the natural sponge and the cake of scented soap she had brought with her and began to wash herself. Her breasts tingled as she ran the rough sponge across them, her nipples hardened involuntarily. Kathleen let the sponge drop to the water and cupped her breasts in her hands. They were high and the skin as white and smooth as a gardenia petal. They had grown so in the past year! She wondered if Rory would like them. *No!* Not Rory, Liam. She knitted her brows together and bit down on her lower lip. "I won't think about Rory. *I won't.* It's Liam I'm going to marry, and I'll be a good and loving wife to him. I won't be cold like Mama. I'll make my husband happy."

Husband. The word seemed so foreign. Her mother had never used it for Seamus. She always called him Mr. Mulvany or simply Pa.

"Husband," Kathleen crooned over and over. It was the sweetest word she had ever heard, even sweeter than the name Rory.

She had no misgivings now, no thoughts of turning back. She recalled the trip from Belfast to New York aboard a ship that was near the end of its seaworthy days. Time and time again she wanted to order the captain to turn back. Kathleen was terrified of the sea and had been ever since the age of five when her parents had brought her across the Atlantic from Ireland. But the trip to New York had been a smooth one. She hadn't even gotten seasick, and yet Kathleen stayed sequestered in the cabin for the entire trip.

Kathleen had no trouble leaving her father, mother and four brothers. She would have loved them greatly, if only they had allowed her to. Her only regret was that she would never again see Father McClafferty. He had offered, as none of her family had, to accompany her on the ship to New York. But Kathleen would not allow the frail priest to make such a strenuous journey.

On the morning of the departure he had told her. "Cling to God's Good Grace, Kathleen. And remember, your heart is takin' a journey, too. Keep it well and keep it wise. But do not follow your heart, let it follow you."

Kathleen slept sixteen hours straight, then got up and checked on her passage at the Pikes Peak Express Company. It would take twelve days of dusty jolting travel to reach Denver.

The coach was painted bright red and was attached to four fine Kentucky Mules. It was driven by two well paid, experienced and fearless men who called themselves Tack and Leon. Kathleen, trying to stay aloof from her traveling companions, concentrated on only one thought—reaching San Francisco and Liam.

The coach wound across limestone hills heading southwest toward Fort Riley, which would be their first stop. Kathleen had never been so shaken in her entire life. The coach seemed to ride over every stray rock.

Their next stop was Fort Dodge. After a night of well-earned rest for the passengers, the drivers and the mules, they veered northwest along the Arkansas River toward Bent's Fork. The terrain became more rugged. A crusty old man who ferried them across a wide stream cautioned that the trail ahead was hardly fit for travel. A broken axle and several detours slowed down their progress. A band of Arapaho Indians trailed seven or eight miles behind the coach and caused a good bit of worry and consternation among the passengers. Then, as suddenly as they had appeared, the Indians disappeared into the hills. The drivers uncocked their Springfields and breathed easy once again.

Bent's Fork was built on the north side of the Arkansas River. At one time it had flown the only American flag west of the Missouri. It was a large structure surrounded by solid adobe walls, four feet thick and fourteen feet high. The upper portion was loopholed for defenders' rifles. The only entrance was a square tunnel large enough for a prairie schooner to pass through. That entrance was closed at either end by a huge plank door reinforced with heavy sheet iron. On either side of the door were windows where Indians could come to trade without being admitted into the main fort itself. They were safe enough at Bent's Fort. But after that, what, Kathleen wondered?

They were admitted into the great courtyard at the center of the fort. Surrounding the courtyard were living quarters, kitchens, arsenal, workshops and storage rooms for the trappers. The warehouses could hold up to a two-year supply of provisions and trade goods. Most of the inhabitants of the fort rushed out to greet the travelers, eager for news. The entire group was invited to dinner that evening with Captain Becknell, commander of the fort.

Communal washhouses, one for men and one for women, were discreetly located at opposite ends of the compound. The passengers agreed that they could all do with a thorough bath. Later that evening, freshly bathed and dressed in their best, they arrived at Captain Becknell's compound promptly at seven. The captain was a stately gentleman in his late fifties. He was gracious to his guests and particularly attentive to Kathleen. His disappointment was obvious when he found out that she was traveling to the coast to meet her husband-to-be. An Arapaho Indian girl, acting as a maid, served the delicious dinner: roast venison, stewed vegetables, spiced crab apples and corn pudding. After dinner the captain took the passengers to the Community House where a frontier dance was in progress. A rustic band was playing "Skip to My Lou" and the captain asked Kathleen to dance.

She held out her hand, he took it and led her out onto the floor. "May I say," said the captain in a voice mellowed by corn whiskey, "that your husband is a very lucky man."

"Thank you, Captain Becknell," replied Kathleen, "but I think I'm the lucky one."

"You mentioned he ran a logging camp?"

"That's right. In Puget Sound. That's in Oregon Territory."

"Yes, I know," smiled the captain.

He gripped her waist tightly and swung her around the floor, holding her close. He inhaled the sensual fragrance of her freshly washed hair. He desired her. He had known that from the first moment he had seen her, but what her feelings were toward him, he could not tell. If only the coach weren't leaving in the morning. If only he had more time with her . . . perhaps he could persuade her to stay. The band switched to a sprightly Virginia Reel, and the couples began spinning around the floor whooping with enthusiasm. Even though Kathleen was familiar with the dance, she told the captain she did not know it. She wanted to discourage his interest in her.

"You'll have to excuse me, Captain. I'm extremely weary and would like to retire."

The captain gallantly replied. "I understand perfectly, Kathleen. The honor of dancing with the most beautiful woman at the fort was an experience I shall not soon forget."

On the trail to Pikes Peak the stagecoach joined a wagon train bound for Fort Laramie. Everybody felt safer. Particularly since there were tales of skirmishes with renegade Arapaho Indians.

The countryside was dotted with small settlements started by disillusioned gold seekers. The "ex-Pike Peakers" were a dejected and impoverished lot. Kathleen wondered if they had "seen the elephant" and then lost it. One of the stops was a small settlement named Wildcat. Because of a flash storm Wildcat was impassable. The wagon train and the stagecoach were held up until the streams had lowered and could be forded.

They made camp on a muddy plain just outside of Wildcat. Branches were cut and placed beneath the wagon wheels so that they would not sink too deeply into the mire. Baskets of pebbles and gravel were gathered, which would insure friction for the wheels when the time came to move. They were delayed nearly a week before the warming sun dried the mud, the stream lowered and the currents were stilled enough to cross. Using the United States military route, they crossed the stream near Wildcat. Its trail wound several miles over rugged thin-soiled limestone hills, then dropped down into a prairie bottom on which they continued southwest to the Republican River. There were limestone bluffs on either side. Kathleen thought they looked like great starched napkins.

At the river they had to wait their turn to take a rope ferry across. There were a number of wagons waiting, all loaded with families going West. There was also a giant herd of cattle being taken to Laramie. The cattlemen had exhausted their patience trying to swim the cattle across, and it was decided that the rope ferry would be employed for the cattle as well as the wagons. It was a long arduous process transporting the cattle across the Republican.

It took twenty-eight hours of waiting time before the stagecoach crossed the Republican River. They continued keeping to the narrow belts of timber along the Republican and the Smokey Hill rivers. Then they entered what seemed to be a boundless sea of waving grass. For ten miles onward there was no sight of a house or even a person.

The scenery flattened out and the limestone rocks suddenly changed to a decaying red sandstone. The soil was sandy and the trail treacherous. Deep trenches worn by rain caused more than one wagon to lose a wheel or break an axle. The face of the country became slightly rolling, and the caravan crossed many streams on their way south toward Sullivan's Fork. A herd of buffalo was seen grazing in the distance. There were perhaps a hundred in all. One of the settlers, anxious to try a buffalo steak, fired into the herd. They lifted their heads and were quiet for a moment.

"*Son of a bitch!*" cursed Leon.

"That's got 'em all right," groaned Tack.

The herd began to stampede and headed directly

toward the caravan of wagons. Their hooves beating on the dry prairie ground sounded like the roll of distant thunder, and that thunder was coming nearer and nearer.

The women and children in the wagon train began screaming. The buffalo were no more than fifty yards away. Shoulder to shoulder, the herd came closer, a tidal wave of brown.

Leon snapped the whip on the backsides of the mules, urging them on. Tack began firing, first with a rifle and, as the buffalo neared, with his pistol, aiming at the rapidly moving edge of the herd. The shots felled several buffalo. Frightened by the sound, the herd began to veer left. Tack could see that they weren't going to change course fast enough to avoid collision with the stagecoach. Leon saw it, too. He jumped off the seat and landed on the back of one of the mules, then proceeded to cut them free. Tack yelled at the petrified passengers, "Get out! Jump!"

But it was too late. The herd crashed into the wagon directly behind the stagecoach and carried it along with them until the wagon wheels caught on a rock and was toppled to its side. Some buffalo jumped over but others ran directly into it, shattering the wood and ripping the canvas like it was a child's toy.

Kathleen and the other passengers were thrown to the floor of the stagecoach. The butting heads and shoulders of the buffalo banged against the side of the coach, turning it completely around. For a moment the stagecoach teetered on its wheels and was about to topple. But, mercifully, the last of the buffalo passed and the wagon righted itself. Kathleen peered out the coach window, straining to see through the swirling clouds of dust. She heard Tack call, "It's all right! They've passed!"

When the dust cleared away, the desolate family who had owned the shattered wagon began to search through the debris for their possessions. The wagon master reassigned the family members to other wagons, and it was understood that everyone in the wagon train would contribute food and clothing for their welfare.

The stagecoach was not damaged. The mules were rehitched, and it was decided to make camp. To relieve the tension of the day and also to take advantage of the slaughtered buffalo, the wagon master decreed that they have a buffalo roast. The buffalo were butchered, pits were dug and spits were set up. Kathleen joined the other women helping prepare and serve the food. The men, using loose planking taken from the sides of the wagons, made an improvised dance floor. Those that could play a musical instrument gathered together and began to play. The settlers and the passengers soon enjoyed high spirits.

Darkness closed in with a cold searching wind that chilled the merrymakers. Kathleen excused herself to collect her heavy wool cloak. The sharp breeze billowed her skirts and her breath turned to vapor. She reached the stagecoach and, as she reached for the door handle, a sharp whispering sound shot past her cheek. She turned her head and found herself staring at a quivering arrow not more than three inches away from her face. Kathleen was petrified. She opened her mouth to scream, but the scream was caught in her throat. She stared into the vast darkness, listening to the night sounds and fighting for control. Terror shocked and numbed her mind. Suddenly the clouds parted to unveil a full moon. She could see glistening bodies watching her from the bramble bushes. The strains of "Oh Susannah" filled the air. Kathleen had the sudden mad desire to laugh.

The door to the stagecoach opened. In one swift movement Kathleen was inside. She reached through the trapdoor to the area just beneath the driver's seat. An arrow whizzed through the open window of the stagecoach and out the other side. Her fingers frantically grappled for what she hoped she'd find. Then she touched it. The butt of Tack's pistol. She only hoped that he'd reloaded it after the buffalo stampede. There was a noise outside the window. She looked up. A Comanche brave was attempting to climb inside. Holding the pistol with both hands, she closed her eyes and pulled the trigger. There was a gigantic explosion. Kathleen felt a mist cover her hands and face. When she saw that it was the Indian's blood, she heard herself screaming.

Alerted by Kathleen's cries, the men rushed to the wagons and began firing at the band of Indians. Those who weren't killed or wounded ran whooping into the underbrush and disappeared into the dark thicket beyond.

When the count was taken, five Indians were dead and one was mortally wounded. Also dead was the stagecoach driver—the man known only as Leon.

"Don't worry, ladies and gentlemen," Tack announced to the stunned passengers. "I'll get us to San Francisco, all right."

Leon was buried the next morning. The grave was dug near the campsite. Because of the rains, the open pit quickly filled with water. His canvas-wrapped body had to be weighed down with stones. The grave was filled and marked with a wooden tombstone. "Here lies Leon. Killed by a Comanche arrow. He was a good man."

The next hundred miles were grueling. The rains continued intermittently. Wood had become scarce and what was available was too wet for burning. Each creek had to be crossed carefully, for they were sweeping torrents of danger. The Indians were easily in evidence. Bands of Arapaho, Cheyenne, Kiowa and Sioux would venture near the wagon train, their curiosity stronger than their fear. Trades were made and sentimental personal objects were given up for food. Kathleen was struck by what she called the "sullen, depressed countenances" of the Indians. For the first time she realized what the coming of the white man meant to them—a loss of position, hunting grounds and a way of life.

At last they reached Denver, a growing town of impressive proportions. Other than New York, it was the largest city in the United States that Kathleen had seen. It was a gold-crazy town because of the great diggings fifty miles due west in the glens of the Rocky Mountains. Boisterous and brawling, Denver hadn't settled down since the gold had been discovered. The caravan, not allowed on the main streets of Denver, was relegated to the outskirts.

After a night of rest they started across the Kansas Territory. It was a rugged path and the threat of danger was ever present. They traveled several miles along the crest of a mountain, then descended sharply to a ravine that led into a narrow valley fed by a clear creek. A wilderness of mountains rose around them. Some of them were thinly grassed between widely scattered trees, but others were generously timbered with yellow pine. They filled their barrels with the pure water that bubbled in the various brooks. The air was clear and bracing. Elk, blacktail deer and mountain sheep were plentiful.

At Fort Laramie the stagecoach parted from the wagon train. The new trail over the Rocky Mountains was the most difficult they had yet encountered. The soil was a sandy clay and lacked support from underlying rock ridges. The stagecoach reached South Pass and an elevation of nearly eight thousand feet above sea level. The winds were brutal and constant.

A day later they approached Big Sandy River, which wound through a deep narrow valley. There were three rope ferries to choose from. Tack bargained with each of the ferrymen and settled on the one who offered the lowest fee. After crossing the river, they began to see signs of civilization. There were more people on the trail. Settlers from nearby communities all headed for Salt Lake City. They passed scores of rotting ox chains, which had been thrown away by California emigrants to lighten the loads of their famished, failing cattle. Twenty miles later they reached Salt Lake City. It was a pleasant sight to the weary, dusty travelers whose bodies ached from a thousand miles of jolts and jounces.

The passengers put up at the Salt Lake City Hotel. The prospect of spending twelve hours at the hotel, sleeping on real beds and bathing in tubs thrilled each of them. Tack helped Kathleen carry her bags to her room. "Better get in a good sleep, Miss Mulvany. Salt Lake City is the last bit of civilization we encounter before we hit California."

"Are we that near?" cried Kathleen.

"That near and that far. We still have to cross the Sierra Nevada, and I'd like to say that's going to be a lark."

At early dawn they were in motion again and had seventy-five miles of rugged mountain road ahead before they reached Carson Pass. They encountered a trail eaten into the side of the mountain, with a precipice of five to fifteen hundred feet on one side and with a steep eminence on the other. They moved slowly along the shelf. There was hardly a place where two wagons could pass. It was on that narrow pass that the passengers realized how skillful Tack was.

They reached the south fork of the American River, and the road descended steadily on a beautifully inclined ridge. Tack stopped the coach abruptly, throwing the passengers into a tangled heap upon the floor.

"What—what's happened?"

"Are we falling over?"

"No," cautioned Kathleen. "We've stopped."

Just then Tack threw open the doors of the stagecoach. "Ladies and gentlemen," he announced with a broad grin. "We are now in California!"

Chapter 17

The glittering April sun dried the muddy streets of San Francisco to a fine reddish brown dust. Following Tack's advice, Kathleen shut the coach windows and closed the curtains so she would not have to breathe the choking air. He also advised her that the sight of a beautiful white woman was liable to throw the women-hungry miners into convulsions. But Kathleen was curious. She had read so many fascinating stories about the city. She parted the curtains an inch and peered out.

Kathleen was impressed by the swarms of milling people, particularly the Chinese. She thought there was a certain charm in their smooth yellow skins, almond-shaped eyes and straight black hair worn in chignons, braids or pigtails. By contrast, the white men frightened her. They looked fierce, unkempt and there was something more . . . a disquieting expression in their faces. Their eyes never rested but continually searched for something.

The coach turned down another street and Kathleen gasped. Between two wooden structures was a ship! Was she seeing things? She opened the curtain a bit more and started. It *was* a ship—a cargo vessel named *Niantic* had been grounded because of a land fill. A roof had been built over the deck and a larger sign erected: Store Ship—Washing Done Here. San Francisco is a strange city, Kathleen thought.

The stagecoach rode by a section recently destroyed by fire. Several buildings had been burned to the ground, and new ones were being built. Scores of devastating fires kept the tinderbox city in a constant state of renewal and dizzying change.

Soon Kathleen felt the coach come to a stop. Tack opened the door. "Dust is plentier than pleasure, Miss Mulvany, and here in San Francisco pleasure is more plentiful than virtue. Still and all, it's better than the last time I was here. I swear the streets were rivers of mud!"

"Is this the hotel, Tack?" asked Kathleen, somewhat disappointed. She expected to find in a city of San Francisco's reputation a more lavish hotel.

"Yes, ma'am. This is it. The best hotel in town."

"I'll be with you in a moment, Tack." Kathleen took a small mirror out of her purse and examined her reflection. "Well," she laughed, "I could look a good deal worse."

As Kathleen swept into the lobby of the hotel, she passed Sophie and Betzy on their way to the jewelers. Sophie stared openly at the beautiful young woman. "She's lovely," she whispered to Betzy in admiration.

"She sho' is dat," agreed Betzy. "An' she a lady, too!"

Sophie scowled. "Humph! I wonder what a lady is doing here in San Francisco?"

While Kathleen waited her turn at the desk, she noticed the two women. She had never seen a woman wearing so much makeup! Nevertheless she thought Sophie was breathtaking. Kathleen smiled and nodded.

Sophie smiled in return, and then she and Betzy disappeared through the front door.

"May I help you, miss?" asked the desk clerk.

"Yes. I'm Kathleen Mulvany. I understand that rooms have been held for me."

The desk clerk smiled. "Ah yes, Miss Mulvany. We've been expecting you for some time."

"Is anybody waiting for me?" Kathleen asked anxiously.

He glanced down at his ledger. "Why, yes there is. A Mr. Fitzpatrick. He's been here for several days. He's in room 327 just down the hall from you."

"Rory? Here?" Kathleen was incredulous.

"Shall I have a bellboy take your bags up to your room?"

"Yes! Ohhh, yes! And thank you."

Kathleen climbed the steps two at a time behind the uniformed bellboy. She could hardly believe her ears. Rory was here waiting for her. It could mean only one thing. Somehow the mistake had been realized. Liam, knowing that she really loved Rory, had stepped aside and had sent him to San Francisco in his place. Her heart leaped in her chest. Rory was going to be her husband! The man she had loved for so many years— Rory, the rogue with the blazing hair, the infectious grin and the teasing manner.

Kathleen barely noticed her room. After the bellboy had gone, she rushed into the bathroom and hurriedly began repairing her appearance. She pinched her cheeks until they hurt, and brushed the dust from her hair until it shone like polished ebony.

Running down the hall to Rory's room, Kathleen trembled with emotion. She had to stop and compose herself before knocking on the door. She leaned against the wall and willed herself to be calm. She pressed her fist against the door, but her quaking hand rapped involuntarily against the hard wood.

"Who is it?" It was Rory's voice. Kathleen opened her mouth to respond, but the words wouldn't come.

"Come in!"

She frowned. Rory's words were slurred. He had been drinking. Well, once they were married . . . she would see that he drank less. She sucked in her breath, turned the knob and stepped inside.

Rory was still in bed and he was not alone.

Kathleen flinched as if someone had struck her. They were both naked. The girl was young and arrogant. She bolted to a sitting position. Her hair was dirty blond, the color of tarnished brass. Rory, not fully awake and partly drunk, looked from one woman to the other. Then realization changed his expression from surprise to embarrassment. "Sweet Jesus in heaven, Kathleen!"

Kathleen turned her burning face from the scene. "I'll be waiting in my room," she said stiffly and quickly left.

Rory turned to the whore. "You got to get out of here!"

"Who was that?" she demanded.

"My partner's bride-to-be. Come on, hurry it up." Rory, who had searched San Francisco for a woman who vaguely resembled Sophie, now winced at the sight of the woman struggling out of bed. In the cruel light of day he saw no resemblance at all.

Kathleen leaned against the closed door of her room and fought for control. The scene she had just witnessed recalled in perfect clarity that cold winter night in Belfast—Rory's cabin and him bathing with Mary McGrath. Now all the pain rushed back. That and the knowledge of her own foolishness. Of course, there had been no changing of minds. Rory had been sent by Liam to meet her. How typical of Liam! How unromantic! Fighting back tears of disillusionment, Kathleen began removing her dusty suit. Damn Rory for making her still care. She didn't know her feelings had remained so strong. Well, let him have his whores. If he preferred them to her, he was welcome to them. She wanted more out of life than a philandering husband. She would learn to love Liam. *She had to*. She had promised Father McClafferty and she had promised God.

After opening a wrong bag, Kathleen found the one containing the garnet satin dressing gown she had made for her trousseau. She removed more hairpins from her hair, and it framed her face like a veil. Then she sat in the armchair and waited for Rory. For the first time in her life, Kathleen wished she had a brandy.

The expected knock came at the door, quiet, apologetic, almost indiscernable. "Come in, Rory."

Rory stepped inside. The rigors of his stay in San Francisco showed on his face. His eyes were red-rimmed and puffy, his skin pale and blotchy. His manner was nervous and startled.

"Come in and shut the door."

Eyes lowered, he entered. "I didn't expect you so soon," he muttered.

"That was obvious."

"And I didn't recognize you."

"I gathered that." Kathleen got up from the chair and held out her hand.

Rory eyed it dubiously. "You're not mad at me?"

Kathleen smiled. "I was, but I'm afraid I'd forgotten your reputation. Besides it wasn't the first time I'd . . ." She caught herself, "But you haven't told me how I look!" She whirled around. "I'm all grown up."

"Yes, you are!" said Rory with admiration. Suddenly he hugged Kathleen and swung her around. "Liam doesn't know how lucky he is."

"Thank you. But why isn't Liam here?"

"He was for the first week of April. You see we had to do it in shifts because of the mill. He would have been here again on Friday."

Some of Kathleen's anger at Liam's absence drained away. "When will we leave?"

"Anytime you're ready, Kathleen. We have two ships now. The *Connemara* and," he smiled, "the *Kathleen*. She's new and very pretty, like yourself. Liam said to buy you whatever you need." Rory grinned. "He's a little freer with the profits since you said 'yes.'"

"I don't need any clothes. I made quite a few things before I left home."

"You two will get along, all right. But you might as well spend the money. You've got it coming to you. Once Liam's married he can claim another one hundred sixty acres of land."

"That's not why he's marrying me?" asked Kathleen.

"You know it isn't," Rory replied gently.

"Yes, I know."

"How was your trip . . . tiring?"

Kathleen threw back her head and laughed. "Well, not if you discount rainstorms, broken wheels, renegade Indians and a buffalo stampede."

"Really? A buffalo stampede? Tell me about it."

"Why don't we discuss this over lunch. I'm starved and you look like you could use something to eat."

"All right. I'll give you a chance to get dressed." He touched her cheek and said softly. "I'm glad you're here." Kathleen started to answer when Rory added, "And I know Liam will be, too!"

The *Kathleen*, a sturdy sloop, was quickly swept up the coast by a favorable wind and a steady current. Urged by Rory, Kathleen stood on the deck of her namesake and watched as the ship entered the Strait of Juan de Fuca and sailed into Puget Sound. The clement weather, the pure waters, and the great trees enthralled her. "They're so tall, Rory. They actually seem to bring the heavens closer."

"There are the mills," Rory pointed out as they neared Port Gamble.

"You have two now?"

"And we've started construction on a third."

"I'm very impressed."

"We're going to stop here and pick up Liam before proceeding to Seattle."

As the ship nosed its way into dock, Kathleen saw a

figure running toward the dock. "There's Liam! It is, isn't it? Oh yes, it is, *it is!*"

As Liam ran toward the dock, a dozen crooked nails rattled in his pocket. The gangplank had barely been lowered into place when Liam dashed up the length of it. "Kathleen," he stammered, unable to believe the gracious change in her appearance.

"Liam!" exclaimed Kathleen. She rushed toward him and clasped his hands. "How good to see you, and you're looking so robust." *He's far better looking than I remember. He seems taller and stronger.*

"And you, Kathleen, you're looking . . . quite . . . fit." *How is it possible for her to be even more beautiful than I remember?*

"Dear Liam," Kathleen smiled. "You haven't changed after all." She demurely allowed Liam to escort her onto the ship soon bound for Seattle.

The mill equipment and camp supplies were quickly unloaded by a group of loggers who could not keep from gaping at Kathleen. Wick Skansen, prodding a yoke of oxen dragging a string of logs onto the skid road, caught sight of Kathleen standing next to Liam on deck. The husky Swede forsook the oxen, sidled up to Rory and patted him on the shoulder. Rory shrank from the man's touch. "What is it, Skansen?" he asked roughly.

"The boss's bride?" Wick asked. Unabashed admiration made his face glow like a morning sun.

"That she is," Rory's reply was tense. He shot the Swede a scathing glance. Wick shrugged his shoulders and went back to his work.

When the ship docked in Seattle a carriage was waiting to take Liam and Kathleen to their new home.

"You'll be driving yourself to the Great House?" asked one of the workers who sometimes doubled as a driver.

"Yes, Pete," replied Liam. "You stay with the ship."

"Great House?" queried Kathleen.

Liam smiled self-consciously. "That's what everyone calls the home I've built for you, Kathleen."

After having his men load Kathleen's luggage, Liam helped her into the two-seater and drove her through Seattle. It was a lonesome town—a handful of houses and a general store. But when Liam drove up the circular driveway toward the nearly finished home, she was astounded by its splendor. It was a two-story structure constructed of local timber and imported brick from San Francisco. Doric columns rose from the veranda and supported a balcony the length of the house. Groups of workmen toiled, painting the window frames, laying flagstone walks and planting shrubbery.

"Why, Liam!" Kathleen exclaimed. "It's magnificent! I see why it's called Great House. Are we really to live here? But why is it so large, Liam?"

"Well—I—I—never mind."

Kathleen replied shyly. "I, too, would like a large family."

She remained in the carriage admiring the house, while Liam greeted the workers. It was then she noticed a small round face pressed against the beveled window set into the front door. "Liam?" asked Kathleen quietly, "Who's that?"

"Oh, I forgot to tell you. That's Pink Jade. She's to be your housekeeper."

"My housekeeper? Liam, I don't know how to deal with a housekeeper. Besides she doesn't look any older than I am."

"She isn't, but she's quite capable and most willing to please."

As Liam and Kathleen ascended the stairs to the veranda, the door opened an inch at a time. Unable to contain herself any longer, Pink Jade ran out onto the veranda. She stopped short, caught her breath and cried, "Oh, Mr. Liam. Is this really Miss Kathleen?"

Kathleen was touched. "Yes, I am. And you're Pink Jade. I'm sure we're going to be great friends."

"Come," said Liam, "we'll take you on a tour of the

house. There's not a room that's finished and the furniture is still arriving, but I think it will prove to be comfortable enough." Kathleen looked at Liam questioningly. Reading her thoughts, he hurriedly added, "I've prepared a room for you to stay in until the—ah—wedding."

"When is the wedding to be, Liam?"

"I thought this Saturday."

"So soon?"

"You're not changing your mind, are you?"

"No, no. I just thought it might be pleasant to take the time to get to know my new house," she smiled at Pink Jade, "my new friend and . . ." turning to Liam she added, "for us to get reacquainted. We're not the same people we were. I believe we've both grown, and I think we owe it to ourselves to rediscover one another. I also need time to make my wedding gown."

"You didn't buy one in San Francisco?"

"Liam, San Francisco is hardly the city for a thriving bridal salon. I did find a bolt of white silk and a bit of lace."

"I can help," volunteered Pink Jade. "I sew."

"You see, Liam. Our wedding will take place before you know it!"

Alone in her room Kathleen knelt in prayer. She prayed for God to help her forget her attraction to Rory and to help her become the fine wife that Liam deserved to have. She prayed often over the following two weeks. When she felt she had sufficient strength, she announced that Saturday, April 28, would be the date of the wedding ceremony.

Each growing thing was touched with the fresh green of spring. The mills were quiet and the air held the hush of expectancy. Even the circling birds and the small forest creatures went about their business in pantomime, as if they were aware of the sanctity of the day and did not wish to intrude upon it.

The Church of Mary Star of the Sea stood on the

knoll of a hill less than one mile from the Great House. Enclosed on three sides by a forest of cedar, pine and spruce, the front overlooked Puget Sound and the islands and inlets beyond. The timber and flagstone building was still under construction. The floor had been laid and the walls stood sturdy. But stained glass windows were yet to be delivered. The roof, save for the beams, was uncompleted.

The interior of the church had been decorated with field daisies and rhododendron. Ropes of pine intertwined with more daisies, hung in festoons from the beams. Benches from the loggers' quarters served as pews. Nearly every logger from the mill was in attendance. The rest of the guests were townspeople from Port Gamble and Seattle, owners of legitimate businesses and a gathering of friendly Dwamish Indians.

The makeshift altar had been arrayed with lacy fern and lily of the valley. Standing behind the altar was Father Michael O'Reilly, a short, nervous man of twenty-four years. His hair was as red as a forest fire and his open friendly face was spattered with freckles. Even in his cassock he looked more like an altar boy than a priest.

A local choir gave a rustic rendition of Schubert's "Ave Maria." Liam appeared in a smart black suit. There was a muffled grunt of approval among the loggers. He eyed Pink Jade, who was sitting in the front pew, and smiled nervously. She returned his smile with such open happiness that Liam instantly relaxed. The assembly shifted in their seats and looked over their shoulders, not wanting to miss the first sight of the beautiful bride. Captain Fallon, dressed in a baggy blue suit, swung open the doors of the church. There, silhouetted against the mauve of the afternoon sky, were Rory and Kathleen.

Kathleen's wedding gown was of pure white silk. It had a high collar and bell sleeves and was trimmed at the neck, wrists and hem with delicate white lace. The skirt was made full by a bevy of crinolines and, out of deference to the rustic surroundings, just cleared the floor. Kathleen's hair was smoothly combed down from a center parting, turned over at the sides and pulled back to form part of a chignon. On her head she wore a small crown of lily of the valley from which flowed a white lace veil. She carried a simple bouquet of lily of the valley mixed with fern and dark green ribbons. Kathleen smiled as a signal to Rory. Starting on their right foot, each began the journey down the aisle.

When they reached the altar, Rory stepped aside and Liam took his place. Father O'Reilly began intoning the eternal words of the mass: *In nomine Patrii et Filii et Spiritus Sancti. Amen.*

The young couple exchanged vows beneath the outstretched limbs of the majestic trees outlined against the bright blue of the Northwest sky. The priest blessed the couple, and the local musicians struck up a Mendelssohn march. Liam could not believe that he was now married to the most beautiful young bride a man could imagine. His eyes were lit with emotion as he gently took Kathleen in his arms, and lifted her veil to kiss her.

The solemn mood was broken. The loggers let out a whoop, then pressed forward with hugs and kisses for the bride and shakes and slaps on the back for the groom. Rory and Captain Fallon stepped in to help shield the bride and then they escorted the newlyweds down the aisle. Carriages and wagons were waiting to take the wedding party and guests to a reception and feast beneath the great trees at the end of the timberland.

Front Street musicians strumming a hybrid harpguitar, banjo and fiddle filled the woods with music. They were seated on the edge of a giant tree stump, large enough to accommodate two sets of squaredancers. Tables laden with food were stretched out beneath canvas awnings, hung from the tree limbs in case of rain. Pits had been dug and oxen were roasting on spits.

Two audacious loggers appeared with a wagonload of uninvited guests. Wick Skansen and his burly sidekick Yester Day had not attended the wedding ceremony but had decided they would invite their own crowd to enjoy the feast and fun under the trees. Their companions were women, all employees of Front Street's notorious whorehouses. The soiled doves were all in a gay mood, dressed in their finest and most garish gowns. Pink satin clashed with orange taffeta. Electric blue and violent green side by side made a startling harmony. It caused Yester to remark that he was delivering a wagonload of broken rainbows. Girls sporting such nicknames as Hard Gertie, Soft Sarah, Lousey Lou and Nail-it Peg squealed and giggled their way out of the wagon.

Liam arrived with Kathleen, Rory and Pink Jade. When he saw the whores he turned on Rory in a fury. "What are *they* doing here?" he demanded between clenched teeth.

"Why, I don't know, Liam. I certainly didn't . . ."

"What is it, Liam?" asked Kathleen. Then she saw the girls. "Front Street?" she asked.

"Yes," Liam hissed.

"It looks like they've taken a lot of trouble getting ready for the celebration," said Kathleen, resting her hand on her husband's shoulder. "Liam, let them stay . . . please."

"Whatever you say, Kathleen. But . . ."

"Liam. I'm a grown woman, and now I'm a married one. They're here to share our happiness. Let's be generous."

The musicians began playing the sprightly strains of "Half-Pint Heaven." The loggers quickly gathered up the whores and carried them off to the makeshift dance floor.

Grinning, Wick Skansen walked toward the wedding party and extended a hand of congratulations to Liam. Liam introduced Kathleen to his highballer. "It's correct to ask the bride to dance?" asked Wick. Rory's face clouded. Kathleen, charmed by the Swede's clumsy manner, glanced at Liam in appeal.

"Of course," replied Liam.

"Oh, my bouquet!" cried Kathleen. "I neglected to throw it."

The music had stopped and the whores heard her words.

"Throw it here! Please!"

"I'm next, I'm next!"

"Throw it, Mrs. O'Sullivan!"

Kathleen gamely threw it toward the ladies of Front Street. Nail-it Peg caught the bouquet deftly. "Look out, boys!" she shrieked with unmitigated glee. "One of you's gonna make an honest woman of me!"

The loggers cheered as Wick lifted Kathleen up on the tree stump and they joined the others in a Virginia Reel.

Rory turned to Liam. "Now why did you let him dance with her?"

"Why not, Rory? Kathleen didn't mind."

"I don't like him."

"I'm well aware of that. I can't share your opinion. Besides that, he's a damn good worker."

"I'll concede that," replied Rory and marched off to the dance area. He claimed himself the prettiest dove, a buxom blond called Soft Sarah.

The music soared and the liquor flowed. By dusk nearly every logger was drunk. Fallers, peelers, buckers, choker setters, bull wackers, skid greasers, flume herders, chute flagmen, river pigs and bolt punchers, tired of dancing, had gathered at the edge of the water to show off for the beautiful bride in a variety of contests. There were tree climbings and log rollings and other feats of strength and endurance.

Rory, emboldened by drink, announced to everyone that he was going to ride the chute—a dangerous sport practiced among the loggers. The sport consisted of riding astride a sizable log as it hurtled downward in a water-filled chute called a flume. The flume worked by gravity; the logs plummeted down the precipitous mountainside at a dizzying speed and plunged into the sound below.

Rory walked up to Wick and cuffed him on the shoulder. "How about it, Skansen? Want to ride the chute?"

"Not me," replied the blond man. "I don't take chances like that."

"I didn't think you did," laughed Rory. "Only with women, eh?"

Before Wick could respond to Rory's insult, the Irishman had hopped onto the back of a speedy horse and was urging the animal up the side of the mountain.

Kathleen pleaded with Liam. "Don't let him do it, Liam! He's liable to get hurt! Please don't let him!"

"Since when have I been able to stop Rory from doing anything? Don't worry, dear. He's performed this little stunt many times before. He'll not be hurt."

The crowd gathered around the base of the flume. Loggers eased away the floating logs so that there would be no danger of Rory crashing into them. Rory reached the mountaintop. After putting on his caulking boots, he selected a log—straight and firm—to act as his transportation. Two loggers held the log in place while Rory climbed upon it. He dug his spiked boots into the bark deep enough to give himself a firm hold but not too deep to jump free if necessary. For the entire length of the chute he could see glowing kerosene lanterns lighting his way like giant fireflies. They were held by loggers about every ten feet along the run. At the bottom the lights were clustered together, as the crowd eagerly awaited his act of bravado.

"I'm ready!" he shouted. *"Let her go!"*

Rory began his descent. The log charged through the shallow water held by the flume, picked up speed to fifteen, twenty, twenty-five miles an hour. The wind raced through Rory's hair as he held his arms out to balance himself. Using his strong ankles, he rolled the log slightly from one side to another to keep himself vertical to the ground.

Thirty miles an hour, then thirty-five. The loggers cheered as he whizzed past them.

The doves and loggers at the bottom anxiously awaited their hero, but Kathleen could not watch. She buried her face against Liam's chest and murmured in a choked voice, "Tell me when he's safe."

A dangerous curve approached and Rory braced himself. He loosened the hold of his boots and, as the log slammed against the side of the chute, he had to employ some fast footwork to remain standing. The log continued bumping against the wooden trough as the curve got sharper. Rory, flailing his arms in the air, struggled to maintain his footing and balance.

"He's going over!" shouted one logger breathlessly.

"No, he's not!" Rory roared defiantly.

The sheer strength of Rory's legs held the log steady. The curve eased into a straight line again, and Rory remained standing. He was on the final leg of the run now—a sheer, straight drop down into the cool waters of the Sound. His speed increased by ten miles an hour. As the log and the Irishman careened toward the still waters, he loosened his foothold once again so that he would be able to jump free of the log.

There was a tremendous splash as the log broke the surface of the water. Rory jumped and his trembling body made an even bigger splash. He came up sputtering and grinning to the roar of approval. Kathleen, exuberant that Rory hadn't killed himself, rushed to the water's edge. Unmindful of her wedding gown, she waded several inches into the water to bestow a kiss upon him. The doves respectfully waited their turn and then lined up to congratulate their hero. Liam smiled benignly and slapped his young friend on the back. "You'd better change out of those clothes, Rory. Nighttime is coming on and I'm sure you're going to continue the party without us."

"That I am, Liam, my friend," he replied eyeing Soft Sarah, "that I am."

Liam turned to his wife. "I think it's time, my dear, for us to leave the party."

"So do I," Kathleen smiled in return. "Particularly if the games get any more rambunctious."

"I'll get the carriage."

Liam, Kathleen and Pink Jade left the wedding celebration quietly. The moon, thin and transparent as a communion wafer, lit their way. The Great House loomed ahead. Its appearance meant something different to each of them. Pink Jade was relieved to be back in the safety of her home. Liam was nervous. His experience with women was limited, and he wanted to be a loving husband to his wife. Kathleen didn't know what to expect. Her mother had always complained about her father's demands, but Kathleen knew in her heart that Liam was a kind and gentle man who would not hurt her. As she ascended the stairs to prepare for her wedding night, her promise to Father McClafferty echoed in her mind.

But I can love him, Father. I know I can. And I'll make him a good wife, I swear I will!

She must prove her words. She was now mistress of the Great House and was married to a wonderful man. And she wanted him, but not as much as she wanted his younger friend, Rory. After preparing for bed, Kathleen climbed into the great oak four-poster. She was angry with herself for still thinking about Rory. She closed her eyes and waited.

A few moments later Liam knocked at the door of the master bedroom. Kathleen licked her lips and calmly bade him enter. Liam was wearing a dressing gown of Prussian blue, which accentuated his blue eyes and was extremely flattering to his handsome body.

He extinguished the kerosene lamp and set it on a side table. Tentatively he approached the bed. He sat down next to her. "Kathleen," he said in a voice more appropriate for a confessional than a wedding night, "I am not an extremely experienced man in matters of lovemaking, but know that I love you with every fiber of my being and I will endeavor to please you."

Kathleen ran her fingers through her husband's hair. "You're no more nervous than I am, Liam. I love you and I trust you." She took his hand and held it to her breast. "I have promised myself and I have promised God that I will be a good wife to you, in all ways. In all ways and for always. Let us trust the love we have for each other and let us trust God, for there is nothing else."

BOOK THREE

BOOK THREE

Chapter 18

Winter came to the sound, once again bringing the lonely isolation. Loggers kept busy oiling and sharpening tools, playing cards, creating music, hunting and trapping till their restlessness forced them to propose, left and right, to every available female. Cookhouse ladies, soiled doves and squat Dwamish maidens were swept up. There were wedding celebrations practically every night. Those who preferred to go it alone continued to do so at Front Street. In that euphoria of drink and chance painted ladies still presented themselves to the loggers without benefit of clergy.

Liam was occupied with business much of the time. He and Rory were now in control of nearly a hundred thousand acres of timberland, ran four mills, employed over six hundred men and owned three ships. He brooded over the account books when he was not actually supervising his workers.

Kathleen became pregnant, the baby due sometime in May. She had kept her vow to make Liam a very happy man. Only one person knew of her secret desire for Rory, and that was young Father O'Reilly. Kathleen had found a friend in Pink Jade and had developed an intense passion for the plight of the Chinese. Sensing Pink Jade's loneliness, Kathleen urged Liam to hire more male Chinese workers.

Rory, bored with winter, whiskey and whores, became a frequent visitor to the Great House. He grew very fond of Kathleen, "Miss Kat," as he called her. Even though he teased her unmercifully, Kathleen enjoyed his raucous presence.

Liam reluctantly leaving his wife behind, set sail for San Francisco on the *Kathleen*. Rory was to have accompanied him, but a serious influenza had kept the young man in bed. Wick Skansen, eager to see Sophie again, took his place. Kathleen insisted that Rory be brought from his rooms on Front Street to the Great House where she and Pink Jade could care for him.

Liam thought of the hectic trip ahead. There would be selling the lumber, buying supplies and checking the progress of the new company office and lumberyard being built on the San Francisco waterfront. And, of course, purchasing Kathleen's long list of requests. Not that she was extravagant! But there were many things needed for their home and the coming child.

Sophie's immense popularity on the Barbary Coast instituted a new and extremely profitable policy, at the Alhambra. The tables next to the stage and runway could be purchased in advance at ridiculous prices by those who had the money to pay for them, the "nouveau riche" gentlemen of San Francisco who bought their respectability by the discovery of gold. But Sophie was no longer interested in marrying for wealth. She was acquiring that herself. Her values and her tastes had changed. She was bored. She often contemplated taking her savings and starting a business of her own. But not in San Francisco! The constant threat of fire brought back the nightmare of her mother's death.

As Sophie sang, her eyes scanned the audience looking for a temporary lover. There was no one who interested her. She sighed audibly and was startled when a note came out flat. Sophie quickly put her mind back to her song and continued down the runway. She reached the end and was about to turn, when she saw the Swede standing at the bar grinning at her. Wick Skansen was back in town!

She unhooked her garter and threw it at him. Wick caught it in midair and pressed it to his lips.

When her act was finished, Sophie hurried to her dressing room. Betzy and Luke entered carrying the unusually plentiful gold nuggets.

"We did real fine tonight, Miz Sophie," Betzy chortled. "Yo' think dat gold was still growin' on trees. I even had to get Mr. Luke to help me pick up dem sweet an' shiny things."

"It must be three, four hundred dollars worth," added Luke. "Are you about ready to leave, Sophie?"

"Oh, you two go on without me. Wick's in town. Did you see him? We'll have a drink together and probably go to that new restaurant Alfondos. I'll see you both tomorrow. Hmmmm?" She looked lovingly at both of them. "I'll be all right, really I will. Wick will see I get home safely." She tilted her head to one side and stared directly into Luke's eyes. They looked feverish. "Luke, are you all right?"

"Sure, I am, Sophie," he replied and looked away from her. "It's just that all these roses, they act up my hay fever."

"You're right. It does smell like a funeral parlor in here. Betzy, before you go, throw them out!"

"Suppose de gentlemens dat sent 'em come by later, Miz Sophie?"

"Well, leave a bunch of the damn things in one vase and put all the cards next to it. *Sacré bleu!* I'll shuffle the cards if I have to!"

Luke lay back on his unmade bed and waited for the morphine to take effect. He stretched out his arms and legs. His limbs ached from lack of circulation and his breath came in rasping wheezes. Little by little the pain went away and his breathing began to clear. His entire body became suffused with comforting warmth, which he knew would be with him an even shorter time than the last.

The dim kerosene light seemed to glow lighter and the bright colors of the wallpaper ran together, creating amorphous shapes and forms, soft and safe like the lining of a baby carriage. The room was large enough for a bed and a bureau. It was on the first floor back of the United States Hotel, obtained for Luke by Sophie who wanted him nearby. It had been originally intended as a servant's room.

Luke's breathing lost its ragged edge and his arms and legs ceased to feel as if they belonged to somebody else. His eyelids fluttered shut and the image of a young Sophie floated before him.

You needn't sleep on the bar, Luke. You can sleep in my room.

Smiling in remembrance, Luke gave himself up to Morpheus, the god of dreams and the namesake of his drug—his heaven and his hell.

Sophie gave the brocaded bell pull a yank, and a waiter appeared in a private dining room at Alfondos. "We've decided," she said brightly. "I'll have the oysters on the half shell and more champagne. Mr. Skansen will have a medium rare steak, fried potatoes on the side and a pitcher of your best beer. The oysters are fresh, aren't they?" Sophie demanded.

"Oh, yes, ma'am, they are," replied the nervous waiter, expecting the large Swede to go into a sudden rage and destroy the entire restaurant.

After the waiter had hurried away, Sophie asked Wick, "Well, what do you think of San Francisco's newest addition? I think it's very *tres chic.*"

"It's sort of cramped," replied Wick, looking around the heavily curtained room. "How come all these rich people don't want to eat together?"

Sophie laughed. "Wick, *mon cher,* this is the way it's done in *all* the better places! Tell me more about the Connemara Mill Company."

"It the biggest thing in timber I ever see. Going to make O'Sullivan and Fitzpatrick rich and I stick with them. I be rich, too."

"And what do the boys do for entertainment up there in the woods?"

"Well, there be Front Street."

"What's that? A ramshackle collection of whorehouses?" Wick nodded. "And what about this new town, the one where Mr. O'Sullivan built his Great House?"

"Seattle? There be nothing there."

"Nothing except money, that is. Ah," Sophie looked up brightly, "here's our supper."

Sophie scooped an oyster out of its shell, dipped it in sauce and contemplated it. Seattle might be a nice place to retire, she thought.

The *Kathleen* returned successfully to Puget Sound. Liam had concluded several lucrative business deals and had hired twelve young Chinese men to cook, launder and aid the loggers. Surely one of them would make a suitable husband for Pink Jade, thought Liam.

Kathleen was serving lunch to the recovering Rory when she heard the company bell signal that the ship had returned.

"I can finish myself," Rory smiled. "You go meet your lucky husband."

Kathleen rushed downstairs, smoothed her hair in the hall mirror and caught herself in silhouette. She was now five months pregnant and beginning to show. She put on her cloak and called to Pink Jade in the kitchen preparing vegetables for the evening meal. "Pink Jade, get a wrap. Let's go to the dock and meet the ship."

The Chinese girl appeared. "Are you sure you want me to come, Miss Kat?" She had picked up Rory's affectionate nickname for Kathleen. "Don't you want to be alone with Mr. Liam?"

"Don't be silly. We may have a surprise for you."

At dock, Liam descended the gangplank, leading a parade of Oriental men. Kathleen rushed into her husband's arms and kissed him warmly. "Oh, Liam," she whispered, "you brought them!"

Liam looked adoringly at his wife, "You're even more beautiful than when I married you, Kathleen."

Kathleen squeezed his hand and replied, "I have more reason to be."

They both turned to Pink Jade and noticed her staring at one young Chinese man in particular. The young man returned her stare shyly and smiled at Pink Jade. He was a good-looking youth, Kathleen thought, neater than the others. She took Liam aside and instructed him to have the youth sent to the house "where he's needed."

"All out for the woods!" came the familiar call that brought the loggers to work.

High in the woods at a felling site, a majestic tree was being attacked by a logging team with Wick as boss logger. The tree had been standing for centuries. The trunk soared two-hundred fifty feet, and at the base the bole swelled eight feet thick. The tree grew near the edge of a steep cliff and offered unsafe footing for the men who wielded the axes. A scaffold was built twelve feet high on the level side and thirty-five feet on the cliff side, so that the tree would be easier to fell. Wick wielded the first ax, striking his cut eighteen inches deep. From the wound gushed a fountain of pitch, barrel upon barrel of crude turpentine. It was impossible for the men to continue until the heavy flow ceased.

About midday they resumed chopping. After four hours of backbreaking labor, the tree was almost ready to come crashing down. Because of the precarious position of the tree and having to work on scaffolds, the men took shifts. Wick and his team were on a break. Wick had taken off his shirt and was amusing the men with tales of his latest Frisco trip and his woman.

Rory, making the rounds on horseback, stopped to observe the giant tree being felled. As Rory approached, he caught the end of Wick's impromptu speech.

". . . and after we have the champagne, she take me back to her hotel. Ya, the best one in Frisco, no fooling . . ."

Rory stopped abruptly and listened to Wick's words carried on the wind. The small hairs on his neck stood up. His spine crawled. He knew without hearing her name that Wick was talking about Sophie Parmalee.

". . . and then she undressed me until I all naked. And I stretch out on the bed."

"Then what?" cried one of the loggers breathlessly.

"Yeah, Wick. Tell us what happened next!"

The powerful Swede stretched his rippling muscles and ran one of his great hands over his formidable crotch. "Ya, Sophie make me stand up straight like this here tree."

His audience began sniggling and one of them yelled. "Show us the picture, Swede!"

"Again?" grinned Wick enjoying his position. He reached into the back pocket of his trousers and pulled out the popular poster of Sophie, folded and refolded like a treasure. Wick shook it and held it up. "This is Sophie, toast of the Barbary Coast!"

Suddenly the poster was snatched from Wick's high-held hands and torn in half. "You're a liar, Skansen!" roared Rory, his face a mask of rage.

"What you do that for?" demanded the Swede.

"*Liar!*"

Wick advanced toward Rory, "Give me picture!"

Rory balled up the torn poster and threw it on the ground. Wick let out a sound like a bull at slaughter, drew back his fist and punched Rory squarely on the jaw. Rory was propelled back and slammed against the scaffolding. The men working on the tree jumped to the ground. Dazed, Rory got to his feet and tore off his shirt. Then he dove at Wick, knocking him in the chest with his head. Wick fell backward, his breath forced from his lungs. Then the giant Swede was on his feet. The two men crouched and circled one another like jungle animals, their nostrils flaring and their eyes blazing. They moved closer to the scaffolding. Wick made a dive for Rory. The Irishman quickly brought his knee up, catching the highballer beneath the chin. Cursing, Wick floundered on the ground. Reaching out to right himself, his fingers fell upon the pickaroon, a sharp and pointed ax.

"HAH!" Wick grunted as he clasped the pickaroon in his huge fist and jumped up. He swung at his adversary. Rory jumped back just in time to miss the deadly spike, but the sound of the pickaroon hissing through its deadly arc made him realize that he would have to finish the fight he had started. He scrambled back toward the scaffolding, his eyes searching for a weapon. He saw another pickaroon above the first level of scaffolding. As he scrambled up the steps, Wick's weapon splintered the wood directly behind his foot.

Rory tripped on the top step and fell flat on the scaffolding, which heaved beneath the crashing weight of his body. Thrust into the trunk of the mighty tree not two feet in front of him was his weapon. Three tugs later the pickaroon pulled free and Rory turned to face his challenger.

The team of loggers saw the great tree beginning to shift its weight. They ran to the scaffolding shouting for the two men to stop their fight.

"They ain't gonna stop till one of them's dead!"

"I'm getting out of here. That goddamn thing's gonna go!"

"Somebody should call for O'Sullivan!"

Rory and Wick edged toward one another. They were ten paces apart now. They rushed toward each other at exactly the same moment. The pickaroons crossed. A flow of awareness came with that first contact. Both Wick and Rory realized they faced their equal.

"Sophie not like you?" grunted Wick through clenched teeth.

Rory's reaction was immediate. He attacked with a speed and ferocity that startled Wick. The Swede backed up defending himself, keeping the measure as wide as possible between them. He knew that the edge of the scaffolding must be dangerously near, but he must not look behind. His luck changed when Rory slipped on pitch and lost his balance. Wick dashed around the full circle of the scaffold, the planks trembling beneath his running feet. By the time Rory had regained his foothold, Wick was behind him.

Rory turned in time to see the pickaroon slice the air. Its point caught Rory across the shoulder, ripping into the flesh an inch deep. Rory stepped back, looked at the widening red line and flexed his arm. The muscle was unharmed.

Wick now began showing off, partly for his audience and partly to discourage his opponent. Speed was his tactic. And it seemed to the watching loggers that Wick was going to kill Rory.

Again their pickaroons became engaged. Wick made most of the lunges. Rory defended himself again and again, and succeeded in tiring Wick. He began to discover the Swede's sequence of movements. His shoulder throbbed, but that pain kept Rory alert.

There was a haughty expression on Wick's face that infuriated the Irishman. Rory lunged forward, their weapons locked at the center and pointed vertically up. For a moment they were perfectly still, their faces inches apart. Sweat poured into their eyes. They blinked rapidly, mutual hate spurring them on. It was then that Wick lifted his knee and hit Rory in the crotch. The Swede realized as the blow landed that at best it was only a partial success. Like most loggers,

Rory wore a hard leather pouch as a protective covering.

Rory gasped. His face twisted into a grimace of pain, which turned to horror as he looked down. The scaffolding and the giant fir had begun to tremble.

"It's going to go!" someone shouted.

It made no difference to the two men who were now committed to their dance of death. Wick, anxious to quit the scaffolding before the tree fell, flung his pickaroon at Rory. The tool flew through the air, spinning like a wagon wheel without a tire. Only by shifting his weight did Rory manage to miss the driving impact of the point. The pickaroon landed some twenty feet from the tree.

Rory gripped the handle of his pickaroon tightly, brought it up over his head and sent it flying. It whizzed through the air and pinned Wick's upper arm to the moving girth of the tree. The tree groaned and began to topple in the direction of the cliffside. The scaffolding was ripped apart, boards went flying and Rory was thrown to the ground. What remained of the base of the tree snapped. As if in slow motion, the great fir thundered down the cliffside, carrying Wick with it. The men ran to the edge of the cliff to see the great stalk of the tree as it plummeted into the sound. Wick, still attached to the tree, had been crushed.

Wick Skansen became the first resident of a new graveyard built next to Mary Star of the Sea Church. All the loggers gathered for the burial. Not one of them blamed Rory. They agreed that it was a fair fight, and although it was provoked by Rory, Wick had "dirtied it up." Everyone forgave Rory, except Liam. He was furious with his young partner for starting the fight, for causing Wick's death and because at the center of the fight was that "San Francisco tart." Rory had countered with a punch and told Liam that he wanted out of the business. Then Rory mounted his horse and spurred it toward Front Street, where he sought oblivion.

Father O'Reilly, whose religious experience had not yet included burying a man, was so unsettled that he began saying the marriage vows over Wick's grave. Kathleen moved next to the young priest, took his hand in hers and spoke for him. "Dear Father, hear us. We're burying our first and he won't be our last. We're all sad and nervous at the same time. Sad because the young man died in vain as a result of his own vanity. We're nervous because his death reminds us that our own deaths are imminent. Help us not to be frightened by the prospect of our own ends. For here in this wonderful country—Your country—we have a chance for a new and better life. We ask this in the name of the Father, the Son and the Holy Ghost. Amen."

Chapter 19

All spring rumors had been circulating that the hostile Indians, including the Yakimas and the Klikitats, were planning to reclaim the settlers' land by surprise massacres. Some settlers did not take the threat of Indian attack seriously. Liam thought otherwise. He had a business to protect, and now he had a home and a wife who was in her eighth month of pregnancy. Liam urged various settlers to take precautions. They listened to him; the Connemara Mill Company was the foundation on which Port Gamble and Seattle were built.

Liam formed a volunteer force to protect the settlement. Sentries stood watch at various posts throughout the day and night. Supplies were placed in the church, along with ammunition and other necessities in case of a long siege. Liam took a further precaution; he sent word of the impending uprising to San Francisco. The U.S. Navy responded by sending the *Decatur*, a sloop-of-war, to stand watch in the sound.

To announce its arrival, the *Decatur* fired off its big guns. The thunderous sound reverberated across the bays and islands and up the mountainsides. It was like a trumpet sound to the now wary settlers.

Pink Jade was fixing Kathleen's breakfast in the kitchen of the Great House. Her companion, the young Chinese man brought from San Francisco by Liam, was washing dishes. His name was Han Sung. After recovering from his early shyness, Han Sung made an able and willing worker in the household. He came to know and admire Pink Jade. She returned his affection. It was understood that, after the birth of Kathleen's child, Han Sung and Pink Jade would be married. "Is Miss Kat up yet?" asked Pink Jade. Her voice was light and musical.

"I do not think so. I heard Mr. Liam tell her to remain in bed. I believe she was ill during the night."

"That is so. Her time is very near and the rumors of Indian uprisings have upset her." A bell rang in the corner of the kitchen. "Oh, there she is. I'll take her up her breakfast."

Pink Jade was arranging Kathleen's tray when the knock came at the door. It was loud and urgent. She glanced uneasily at Han Sung. He motioned for her to stay and went to answer it. The back door was at the end of a row of pantries just beyond the kitchen.

Comeera, a Dwamish squaw who sold fresh fish and game to the O'Sullivan household, was crouched at the back door and kept glancing behind her.

When Han Sung saw the expression on Comeera's face, he knew that Liam's worst fears had been realized.

"The Yakimas, the Klikitats!" the woman panted. "They attack this morning!"

Pink Jade, overhearing the woman's words, set down the tray and quickly ran to the back staircase. She knew that Han Sung would be getting the wagon to take them to the church for that had been the plan.

Kathleen was sitting up in bed when Pink Jade burst into the room.

"What is it?" her words were clipped and her face was as pale as skimmed milk.

"Comeera has given us the warning. Quickly, Miss Kat, we must go to the church!"

Kathleen threw a cloak over her nightgown. Then she and Pink Jade hurried down the back stairs. The Chinese girl grabbed several biscuits and a small crock of milk.

Han Sung was waiting with the wagon. Not a particularly good choice, thought Kathleen, for it was open and they would be completely exposed on their way to the church.

Pink Jade helped Kathleen into the wagon. Han Sung cracked the whip and the wheels began to roll.

"Here," said Pink Jade, handing the biscuits and milk to Kathleen. "You need to eat something, Miss Kat." Kathleen absently began to nibble on a biscuit.

"It is too quiet," complained Han Sung. "It is not to my liking."

Kathleen tried to concentrate on the biscuit, but her mind would not let her forget the time she was attacked by marauding Comanches. She began to shake. Pink Jade placed an arm around her shoulder, saying softly. "We will be there soon."

No birds cried, no leaves stirred. The clouds seemed to be frozen in the sky. There was no sound except the steady clip-clop of hooves on the gravel path. Kathleen stared straight ahead. She knew that if she glanced toward the bushes and trees she would see Indians, whether they were there or not.

They met other alerted settlers along the way. Several of them hitched a ride. Many were carrying belongings and food. A tablecloth as a sack was testimony to their hasty departure. Around a turn in the road they saw Father O'Reilly hastening people inside the church. At the sight of Kathleen and the young Chinese couple, he wiped his brow in relief and signaled for the church bell to be rung. The clanging caused the rest of the townspeople to hurry to the church. One man became so rattled that he pulled on his wife's petticoat instead of his trousers.

The young priest had difficulty keeping fear out of his voice. "My dear Kathleen, I've been waiting for you to arrive before ringing the bell. Here let me help you." Before Father O'Reilly could put his arm around Kathleen's shoulders, a sudden pain made her wince and her knees went weak. Han Sung, quicker than the priest, caught Kathleen before she fell. She looked apologetically first at Han Sung and then Father O'Reilly before saying. "I'm sorry, but I believe I'm going into labor."

"Quick, Han Sung!" cried the priest. "We must get her inside and comfortable." They helped Kathleen down the side aisle of the church and through a door to the small rectory. She was put in the priest's own bed.

He ordered Pink Jade, "See if Hannah McCormack has come to the church. She's made claim to being a midwife. I'm afraid we're going to have to put Hannah to the test. Are you comfortable, Kathleen?" he asked.

"Yes, thank you, Father."

"Perhaps a cup of tea?"

"That would be lovely if it's no trouble."

"No, no, not at all. I'll brew up a batch for anyone who wants it. Of course, I don't have many cups. They'll have to drink it in shifts."

Kathleen smiled at the young priest. He was anxious to do anything to relieve his own nervous tension. "Perhaps Han Sung could help you," suggested Kathleen.

"I would be glad to, Miss Kat," responded the youth. "But will you . . ."

"I'll be fine, Han Sung, thank you."

After the men left, Kathleen made herself as comfortable as possible upon the priest's narrow bed. She could hear the settlers stirring in the church. They were frightened, too. She turned her thoughts to Liam. He would be safe at the Mill. She was glad he was there, but still wished he was with her. Kathleen touched her swollen stomach.

"Baby, your timing is bad."

It was May 3. She was three weeks early. A doctor engaged from San Francisco had not yet arrived at the sound. Another pain racked her body, and tiny beads of perspiration broke out on her forehead. Kathleen prayed the midwife was a good one.

When the marauding Indians were sighted, the captain of the *Decatur* sent over a hundred sailors ashore. They fired Howitzers into the woods hoping to scatter the Indians, but the Indians responded with muskets. The fight for Seattle was underway.

Surprised by the Indians' retaliation, the sailors left themselves open to fire. Several were quickly wounded. The sight of comrades' blood convinced the Americans that the Indians were serious about reclaiming their hunting grounds and would fight until death.

Cut off from the church by the hostile Indians and heavy fire, neither Liam nor Rory, who were now reconciled, were able to go to Kathleen. Liam's worries were increased because Kathleen was near her delivery time. The fight continued throughout the day. The *Decatur's* guns boomed out reassuring broadsides.

Hannah McCormack, the only midwife in the sound, was brought by Pink Jade to Kathleen's bedside. Mrs. McCormack, a great pudding of a woman with an air of brisk efficiency, went straight to matters.

"When did the pains start, Miss Kat?"

"Just as we were entering the church," replied Kathleen. "About ten-thirty this morning."

"And how often have they been comin' now, love?"

"About every hour and a half, two hours."

"That's good. You have some time left."

"Are they always this painful, Mrs. McCormack?"

"Hannah. Call me Hannah. This is your first, isn't it? I always say the first is the worst. Then it gets a lot easier."

"That's good," smiled Kathleen weakly. "Because my husband and I are planning a big family."

"Try to rest, Miss Kat."

"I will, Hannah . . . until the next one."

Some of the settlers began overflowing into the rectory. For the sake of privacy, Hannah instructed Han Sung to stretch ropes around the bed and then use extra bedcovers as draperies.

"What can I do, Mrs. McCormack?" asked Pink Jade.

"You can find me some clean sheets, dear. Make sure they're real clean. I don't care if Father O'Reilly is a priest, he's still a bachelor. I bring my own tools with me. We'll just need a clean pan for washin' the babe when the time comes and some boiling water to sterilize my cord cutters." Hannah patted the pocket of her voluminous skirt, which contained extra sharp shears used for the sole purpose of severing the umbilical cord. Several months earlier, Hannah had come to the sound with her logger husband Josiah McCormack. But so far there had been no births among the settlers. In her glory at last, Hannah bustled about the rectory issuing orders, uttering pronouncements. The women volunteered to help, but Hannah McCormack informed them that "too many cooks spoil the stew."

As the day wore on the unending gunfire served as a background for Kathleen's labor pains. Around evening a handful of Indians who slipped through the American lines approached the church. Seizing their chance, the painted braves rushed at the church doors carrying tree branches smeared with flaming pitch. They were spotted by the sailors as they started up the steps. The twilight was suddenly lit up as the Indians were riddled with bullets. They managed to throw the flaming bushes at the door. There they stuck and continued to burn.

The people inside the church were terrified. They had heard the shooting, and now smoke was pouring under the doors of the church. They believed that the Indians had surrounded the church and were intent on burning it to the ground. The men, their faces etched in horror, backed away from the smoking door. Several of the women grew hysterical and began screaming. Terrified children began to sob loudly.

Kathleen, who had been in a deep and fitful sleep, suddenly sat up. Tendrils of her hair were stuck to her face and her eyes were feverish. "What is it?" she cried hoarsely. "What's happening? Has Liam come?"

"Hush, Miss Kat," soothed Hannah, then whispered to the Chinese couple. "You stay with her. I'll see what's goin' on."

The midwife hurried into the church. The last rays of the sun filtered through the stained glass windows, staining each face in turn a different color of terror.

"What's going on?" she demanded.

Several people, kneeling in abject fright, stared at Hannah as if she were out of her mind. One of them pointed to the smoking doors and answered, but the words were garbled. Hannah rushed down a main aisle. She grabbed the priest, swung him around to face her. Father O'Reilly seemed to be catatonic. His face was drained of color and his eyes were wide and staring. Hannah's mind roared, *not the priest!* Without his guidance the people would give up.

Hannah dragged the priest into the darkened apse where the smoke was thickest. She seized him by the shoulders and roughly shook him. "Father O'Reilly, you're the priest! Lead the flock! *Lead the flock!*" The priest stared at her dumbly.

"What? What?" he muttered.

Years later Hannah still wondered how she dared do

what she did then. She slapped the priest hard across the face, and followed the slaps with several handfuls of cold water scooped from the font.

"Hannah, what's all this smoke?" he asked, as if seeing it for the first time.

"The damed Indians are tryin' to burn down the place, and we've got to stop them!" Hannah led the priest to the front doors where great black fingers of smoke were creeping over the sill.

"They've attached somethin' burning to the doors. Arrows probably," grunted Hannah. She had been through many Indian attacks. "Help me," she indicated the great wooden bar that held the doors fast.

They lifted the wooden bar from its fittings and set it near the base of the font. Hannah pushed open the doors, and an Indian fell inside. She started to scream, but seeing that the Indian was dead, pushed him aside. The pitch-smeared branches stuck against the doors were burning the wood. Hannah rushed to the font, which was backed by a semicircle of heavy purple velvet drapes. "Here, help me, Father," she called to the priest. The two of them yanked the draperies from their ceiling hooks, and attacked the burning doors, using them to smother the flames.

Several settlers, their fear dispelled by the sight of the priest and the midwife fighting the fire, rushed to their aid. The sailors saw what was taking place. One called out, "Not to worry, Father. We've dispatched the savages." When the priest saw the grinning Americans waving their rifles, his relief was consummate. He ran inside and loudly announced to the settlers that the fire and the Indians were under control, and that "God is in charge once again!"

Han Sung appeared from the rectory, his broad face wrinkled with concern. "What is it, Han Sung?" cried Hannah.

"I think Miss Kat's time has come!" As Hannah reached the bedroom door, she heard Kathleen howl in pain.

Pink Jade looked up, "The pains are coming every ten minutes now."

"Good, good," muttered Hannah. "Han Sung, go and get the water to boilin'. Hurry!" She glanced at Pink Jade. "Have you ever attended a birth before?" She shook her head. "Well, you might as well learn."

The midwife placed a pillow under the small of Kathleen's back. Then she positioned the young woman so that her bent legs were apart and her heels flat upon the mattress. "You just have some patience now, Miss Kat. It ain't gonna be long."

"Oh, God!" moaned Kathleen. "Please hurry it up."

"Can't hurry nature," replied Hannah gently.

Soon Hannah told Pink Jade to stand at the head of the bed and let Kathleen hold onto her arms. "It makes it easier if you're holdin' onto someone," pronounced Hannah. She examined Kathleen to make sure she was dilating properly. Satisfied that she was, Hannah began massaging Kathleen's swollen pelvis. Kathleen relaxed between contractions, and Hannah was able to thrust the tips of her fingers inside. "It's comin' out head-first!" she said joyfully.

She continued massaging Kathleen's passage, and slowly Kathleen opened up. Kathleen tossed her head from side to side flailing her wet hair across the sheets. She cried out with pain and fright and called out Liam's name. Suddenly a tiny head fringed with a fine mist of black hair began to appear. "It's comin'!" Hannah shouted and began encouraging the baby. "Hurry up, child! Come on, now. Hurry up. We all mighty anxious to see you."

When the baby had fully emerged, Hannah happily announced that it was a boy. She deftly cut the umbilical cord, tied a knot, then dipped the child into a waiting tub of water. The baby, surprised, began to cry. For Hannah that was a good sign. He was telling her that he was healthy.

Kathleen looked up with dazed hollow eyes. "Is it over, Hannah?"

"It's over, Miss Kat. And you just brought forth a big, beautiful boy." She wrapped the baby in a fresh sheet and placed it next to its mother. Kathleen raised herself on her elbow and stared in wonderment at her child. "He's beautiful, Hannah. Just beautiful. He was worth every bit of pain."

Pink Jade knelt beside the child. "He's going to be good looking, just like Mr. Liam," she said softly.

"Yes, he is," agreed Hannah.

"Oh, I wish Liam were here," sighed Kathleen. Then, exhausted from her ordeal, she fell into a deep sleep.

By midnight the Indians had suffered a significant number of casualties. The settlers and military had lost only two men. Their forces considerably diminished, the Indians made their retreat—forever relinquishing their hunting grounds to the white men.

The sailors began cheering. Their cheers were joined by those of the settlers, and the vibrant sound reached the confines of the church. Led by Father O'Reilly, everybody knelt to thank God for their deliverance. Then they stood, joined hands and sang a song of praise to the Almighty.

At last Liam was able to forsake his fighting post to hasten to the church. He panicked when he saw the burned doors, but was quickly informed by the sailor who was standing watch that no one had been harmed. Liam stepped inside and scanned the faces of the congregation. Father O'Reilly saw Liam and hurried through the crowd. "She's in the rectory, Liam. And God be praised, she's doing fine."

"Doing fine? My God, Father. Was she injured?"

Before the priest could answer, Liam dashed down the side aisle to the rectory door. He burst inside calling out his wife's name.

"I'm in here," cried Kathleen, who had regained some of her strength. Liam rushed to his wife's side, noting only that she was in bed and looked as if she had been through an ordeal.

"Kathleen, what is it?"

Kathleen looked toward the child cradled in her arms. "I'm afraid our little guest arrived early."

Liam looked down at his son and gasped with astonishment. "Is it all right?"

"It is a he, my dear. Our first born is a son."

"A son," repeated Liam. His eyes glistened with joyful tears.

Chapter 20

Sophie's fear of the rampant fires became a phobia. Every time she heard a fire bell she broke into a sweat and began to shake. Despite her anxieties, Sophie made plans for escape in the event of a widespread disaster. She purchased another set of horses and instructed Luke to have the coach hitched at all times. Not a bit of paper money was kept for more than a day. Every cent, every nugget, every bag of gold dust and every bauble was immediately converted into twenty-dollar gold eagles. The hollow posts of her brass bed were forsaken as a hiding place. Sophie wanted to leave the hotel at a moment's notice. She ordered special flameproof trunks of tin and brass. Sophie and Betzy working in secret, meticulously lined the trunks with an ornate wallpaper. Between the paper and the walls of the trunk, they neatly glued the double eagles in place.

Backstage at the Alhambra, Sophie grimly listened to the latest onslaught of fire bells. Her eyes were fixed and from time to time she shivered. Betzy, a good deal less pessimistic than her mistress, shook her head and said, "Goodness, Miz Sophie, yo' so all fuzzed up, dat yo' got me shakin' like a hand-me-down heart. Yo' gots to stick to yo' singin' an' jus' concentrate on makin' de money."

Sophie stood up and glared at her friend. "What the hell good will money be if we're all burned to a crisp!" She threw herself down on the chaise lounge and sobbed. "I want out of here! I'm tired of my heart stopping every time I hear the clang of those sons-of-bitchin' bells. *I'm tired of it!*"

"Miz Sophie, yo' gots to compose yo'self. Dose fire bells ain't nowhere near here."

Jack tapped on the dressing room door and, hoping to catch Sophie in some state of undress, entered without waiting for an invitation. "We've got a great crowd tonight, Sophie, a lot of swells from Nob Hill."

Sophie responded with an indelicate gesture.

The crowd at the Alhambra was particularly unruly that night. Twenty minutes before Sophie was to appear for the second show, they began chanting her name. Jack sent second-string performers to placate the audience, but they were not entertained. They had come to see Sophie and no one else. Sophie continued to be the biggest draw on the Barbary Coast. Jack was in constant fear of losing her, for no matter who Jack put in her place, the Alhambra would be doomed. He allowed the club to become so overcrowded that it was almost impossible for waiters to serve customers. Patrons stood on the bar, on the steps leading to the second floor, they crowded the balcony, dangled their legs through the railings. Luke expressed his fears about the overcrowding to Jack on many occasions. Jack shrugged him off, responding as usual, "There's more gold to be gotten from this saloon than from all the hills and rivers in California, and by God I'm going to get every last nugget!"

In the better saloons it was the custom to discourage the Negro trade. If a Negro came into a Barbary Coast establishment, he would be served one drink on the house, but that was all. He would then be told to leave. If the Negro persisted, he would be bodily thrown into the street.

That night Lemuel Johnson, freed by his dying master eight months earlier, arrived in San Francisco eager to strike it rich. He had no luck being hired at any of the gold digs. He knew full well that it was because he was a Negro. A sympathetic white man suggested Johnson try the Barbary Coast, where, in the lively atmosphere, he might encounter less prejudice and even make a connection for work. Johnson was fifty-four years old, but looked ten years younger. He was a large strapping man in perfect physical health because of a kind master through years of hard labor on a tobacco plantation. His owner had always given Johnson plenty to eat and good medical care. He had never suffered any mistreatment. He was a proud man and that pride was viewed as arrogance by hostile whites.

Dressed in his best Sunday suit the Negro wandered down the Barbary Coast, wondering which saloon might bring him luck. The Albambra looked prosperous and crowded. He entered. Johnson glanced with disinterest at the beautiful blond performer, then squeezed up to the bar and placed his coin on the shiny mahogany surface. "A whiskey, please, Mistuh."

The bartender, an incendiary southerner named Cory, looked up in horror as he recognized the speech of a black man. Without a word Cory slammed a whiskey down in front of the Negro, but would not take his coin.

Johnson downed his drink, placed another coin on the bar and called, "Mistuh, another—"

Cory spun around. "We don't serve *niggahs* here," he savored his flaunting tone. "And I don't let niggahs stand at my bar."

Johnson stood erect. "Mistah, I bin a free man too long to take yo' po' trash mouth."

Enraged, Cory jumped over the bar and gripped

Johnson around the neck. Johnson, struggling to free himself, fought back. The two men heaved and lunged and, locked together, fell on the sawdust-strewn floor. Patrons parted to give room and urged the fight on, taking bets. Cory was younger than Johnson, but not stronger.

Realizing the Negro was getting the best of him, the bartender pulled a knife from his boot. He lunged for Johnson and buried the blade in the black man's stomach, dragging it upward. A look of surprise covered Johnson's ashen face. He gasped and rolled back on the floor, crashing into a table and knocking over a lantern. Kerosene quickly ignited the dry sawdust. The stunned audience jostled each other to avoid the spreading flames. Waiters broke through the crowd and tried to stomp out the burning sawdust. Flying, burning sawdust inflamed nearby cotton drapes, which ignited the cotton batting decoration beneath the balconies. Within minutes the bar area of the Alhambra was a sheet of flames.

Miners and new gentry alike panicked. They surged against one another, fighting to get out.

Sophie, transfixed, stood on the stage in a paroxysm of fear. Jack fled to his office to empty his safe. Luke and Betzy rushed onstage. Betzy wrapped a cloak around her mistress's shoulders and cried, "Miz Sophie, come with us!" Sophie didn't move. Luke picked her up and Sophie was pulled from the hypnotic arms of the fire.

As Luke carried Sophie past her dressing room, she shouted. "Stop! Let me down, Luke!"

"Sophie!"

"Let me down! I have to get something! Betzy, Betzy, help me!"

Luke complied. Sophie and Betzy ran inside. Sophie called over her shoulder. "Luke, go get the carriage. Bring it to the back door." Sophie retrieved her jewel box from its hiding place inside the armoire. Then she and Betzy loaded themselves with as many armloads of expensive costumes as they could stuff into protective muslin bags. As they rushed toward the door, the clang of fire bells filled the night air. Sophie stopped and began shivering.

"Go on, Miz Sophie. We got to go on!"

Sophie took one step, then another. Then she began running. They hurried through the back door to Luke and the waiting carriage. Luke cracked the whip and they were off to the United States Hotel. At the corner, Betzy turned just in time to see the blaze shoot up the front of the Alhambra. The glass windows burst and shards flew in all directions. The flames crept up to the roof of the veranda, licking at the canvas poster of Sophie in all her glory. Sophie started to turn around, but Betzy stopped her. "Ain't no use in lookin' back, honey." She wrapped her great arm around Sophie's shoulder and shouted to Luke. "Mr. Luke, make dis here carriage fly!"

Luke skillfully managed the carriage and horses through the crowds. Some people were rushing from the fire, and others were rushing to see it. At the hotel Luke stood guard at the carriage. Betzy and two attendants went up to the rooms to collect the trunks. Sophie hurriedly paid her bill and informed the befuddled desk clerk that she was "checking out for good."

The attendants strapped the chests, four in all, to the back of the barouche. Sophie tipped them and commanded Luke, "All right, Luke. Now get us to the docks."

"But where we going, Miz Sophie?" asked Betzy.

"To Seattle!"

The conflagration roared through the Barbary Coast and the sprawl of jerry-built wood structures beyond, most of which were houses of prostitution. Exploding kegs of miners' blasting powder fed the fire. Bands of looters added to the terror of the blaze.

The whores and their customers scattered into the streets. Sophie stood up in the carriage and called to a fleeing prostitute. "Here! Come over here and get in the carriage!" The grateful woman did as Sophie bid. She was young and quite pretty, and told Sophie her name was "Li'l Jennie."

Betzy and Luke stared, flustered, at Sophie's humane act. Sophie continued standing in the carriage, hanging onto the calash top. Soon she cautioned Luke to slow down and signaled another woman fleeing the blaze. By the time Sophie was finished, she had selected five homeless prostitutes and had brought them all into the overcrowded carriage.

Betzy, as blunt as always, asked, "What fo' yo' pick up dese tarts?"

Sophie smiled broadly at the whores, perched along the edge of the calash like a row of brightly colored birds. "As I said before, Betzy, I'm *tired* of working!"

The bay, reflecting the burning city, was the color of blood. The dock was jammed with people hoping to save themselves from the encroaching flames. Many had brought their belongings. Like Sophie, they, too, wanted to leave San Francisco. But Sophie had the advantage. She had money.

Sophie pushed her way through the swarming mob, climbed a pyramid of unloaded crates and announced at the top of her voice, "I've got five thousand dollars! I've got five thousand dollars! *Five thousand dollars!*" The crowd of citizens and sailors grew quiet. "I've got five thousand dollars for passage for myself and my company of eight to Seattle! *Five thousand dollars!* Do I hear any takers?"

A short swarthy man inched his way through the throng. When he reached the base of the crates, he cried, "Hey, miss. I got a ship!"

Sophie looked down at him. He was a dirty man wearing a battered seaman's cap and a filthy white suit.

"Who are you and what kind of ship?" she demanded.

"I'm Captain Ned and it's a sailin' ship. Been usin' her for fishin'. Fish come to me easier than gold."

"Can your ship make it to Seattle?"

"In this weather? Of course it can, miss. An' let me tell you, you're not goin' to find any captain with no brigantine willin' to take you clear to Seattle for five thousand dollars. Why that's mule feed compared to what they make transportin' mine equipment."

Sophie held her hand out to the man. "Here, help me down. Now where is this ship? I want to see it."

"Follow me, miss."

They wove their way through the throng away from the wharf where the large ships were docked. Sophie noted with irony that the man's fishing ship was docked in front of the Connemara Mill Company's warehouse. The ship was in need of paint and patchwork, but it looked seaworthy to Sophie. Pretending she knew all about ships, she allowed the captain to take her aboard.

"Phew! It smells like rotten fish."

"Well, that's what I said it was, Miss—a fishin' ship. But she's sturdy even if she smells a bit." The captain leaned against the main mast and watched Sophie as she poked around the ship. Finally Sophie asked, "How soon can we leave?"

"We can leave anytime, miss. The way Frisco's burnin', I'd say the sooner the better."

"Fine. It's a bargain. I'll stay here. You go fetch my carriage."

"How will I know which one is yours, miss?"

"You can't miss it, Captain. It's full of girls."

A short time later the captain returned, riding next to Luke on the front of the carriage. Sophie took the girls aside and told them what she had in mind. Anxious to leave the fire-ridden city, they readily agreed to go with her. Then Sophie took care of her business with Captain Ned.

"Here's two thousand five hundred now, Captain. If you get us to Seattle in one piece, you'll get the rest."

"Fair enough, miss. You'll have to give me a little time to roust my crew. We weren't due to sail out till mornin'."

"Well, if you can't find them, hire others," ordered

Sophie. "I want to get out of here as quickly as possible."

An hour later the crew had been secured and the ship, the *Sea Witch*, was ready to sail. Luke took Sophie's hand. "Sophie, I know what you're planning to do and I won't be any part of it."

"Why, Luke, what do you mean?" she asked innocently.

"You're going to start a whorehouse up there in Seattle, aren't you?"

"Well, so what if I am? I'm not going to work in it. I'm sick to death of working."

Luke grew angry. "Sophie don't do this. You're only going up there because of that man, and he doesn't care one whit about you." He grabbed her shoulders. "You can't do this. You can't lower yourself. Why, you could marry the richest man in San Francisco and become a lady."

"What in the hell would I know about being a lady," retorted Sophie. "I just want some peace and I'm not going to find it here. I don't like San Francisco, Luke. It's not just the fires, but it's everything. It's all the failed dreams and all the shattered hopes. They're all around you. They're in the very air and they drag you down. I want to be where the air is clean and the people are bright and happy and have hopes for the future. And from what I've been told, that's Seattle."

"I'm not going, Sophie."

She realized he was serious. "You can't mean that, Luke. What would I do without you?"

He grinned crookedly. "Oh, you'll make out, Sophie. There'll be plenty of men ready and willing to act as your buffer against the world."

"Luke, if it's the whores, I'll get rid of them. My God, of course it's the whores, isn't it? That's how you got the disease."

Luke laughed. "It's not because of that. I wouldn't fool you, trying to be moral. It's not that at all, Sophie. Can't you see, I belong here. This land of ruined dreams—it's mine. I'm comfortable among my own kind. I'm at home in that stinking air of failure." He touched her on the cheek. "Besides, I haven't got much longer and I—I need to be here where I can get my drugs easily." Sophie sucked in her breath and her eyes began to sparkle with tears. "Yes, as you've probably guessed, I've been taking more of the stuff. I've had to. I'm—I'm not as strong as I pretend to be."

"But Luke, we can send to San Francisco for whatever you need. I'd gladly get it for you."

"I know you would, but I don't want you to see me when the end comes. Do you understand? It's not going to be pretty and you should only see pretty things."

"Oh, Luke," Sophie sobbed. "Please don't . . ."

Luke threw his arms around Sophie and held her tight. "Sophie, don't you know what you've given me these last few months? You've given me the love of a woman. Not the physical kind, but the kind I've needed—"

"Hold me, Luke," cried Sophie. "Hold me tight so that you'll remember me for always."

"Always isn't very long, Sophie. But I'll remember you, I promise. Nothing, not even the drugs could take that away from me."

With a muffled sob Luke broke away from Sophie. "I have to go now."

"Luke, let me give you some money, *please.*"

"I don't need any money, Sophie. And you've been mighty generous. I've been saving all along. But I'll tell you what you could do for me. Every once in a while when the barroom's quiet and when you think of it, sing my song for me. And I promise you, wherever I am, I'll hear you singing it." Luke smiled at Sophie a last time, then turned and rushed down the gangplank.

The sanguine moon appeared through scarves of motionless black clouds. It seemed to travel west, a solitary ship on an endless voyage. The wind, tainted with the odor of a burning city, came up and billowed the unfurled sails of the *Sea Witch*.

Captain Ned called to Sophie, "We've got to be goin', miss."

Sophie raised her head. "Yes, we're ready," she replied solemnly.

Captain Ned strode across the deck like a bantam rooster, squawking orders at his crew. In the distance more kegs of blasting powder exploded. The entire sky was lit up . . . a giant swirling sheet of red and black.

Betzy joined her mistress. Sophie looked up and breathed a sigh of relief. "This party has come to an end, Betzy." It was spoken like a prayer. Sophie dried her tears and turned her thoughts toward Seattle . . . and Liam O'Sullivan.

Chapter 21

Sophie told Betzy of her plans to open "an establishment" in Seattle. "Of course, I'll entertain once in a while, singing, that is. I'll let the others do the work while I make all the money."

Betzy was aghast. But now she understood why the five women were brought along.

Sophie had learned from Wick that there were about a hundred men to every girl at the sound. Sophie planned to make the most of her new doves' charms. Their names were colorful and obvious. Big Annie was a heavy, muscular woman with a deep throaty laugh. As strong as a man, she still could be coy when the occasion arose. Li'l Jennie was a four-foot-two bundle of femininity. Pert as a posy, she was the perfect miniature of a grown woman. Moonsweet was an almond-eyed Chinese girl with a veil of glistening black hair. She was very pretty and, as Sophie would find out later, a tireless worker. She wanted to save enough money to bring her family from China to America.

There was a sentimental slattern who cried easily and was aptly named Moist Meg. She was plain, but had a certain bruised charm. Sophie knew that many men found that appealing. The fifth dove was a plump woman whose pale, white flesh resembled risen dough. Her name was Georgette Lumpkin and she thoroughly loved her work.

"Perhaps I can lure Wick away from the logging business. He could act as our—our bouncer," Sophie continued.

Betzy grunted. "Mo' like a live-in stud if yo' asks me, Miz Sophie."

"Well, I didn't ask you and besides what harm could that do? You told me yourself you liked Wick."

"I like him once every six weeks," grunted Betzy. "An' so do yo'!"

Sophie laughed. "Come on, Betzy, we've got to get some sleep."

"I sho' don't know how we gonna sleep. Dis whole ship smell like one rotten mackerel!"

Upon their arrival in the sound, Sophie, Betzy and the whores gathered on deck. They inhaled the sweet morning air and "ooh-ed" and "ahh-ed" when they saw the majestic trees. Sophie, usually indifferent about nature, was thoroughly impressed by the setting. She was even more impressed as she counted the loggers' bunkhouses in the distance. Seattle, she knew, was going to be a paradise for women of any shape, size or sort.

A group of loggers, working near the Port Gamble docks spotted the women on deck of the *Sea Witch*, began jumping up and down and calling to them.

"Are we docking there?" asked Georgette Lumpkin hopefully.

"No," replied Sophie. "That's Port Gamble. It already has its fair share of . . . entertainers. No, ladies, Seattle's where we're headed. There we'll have *no* competition."

The doves groaned as the *Sea Witch* eased into dock at Seattle. "It sure is a dreary place," whined Li'l Jennie.

"Don't you worry none," bellowed Big Annie. "We'll liven it up!"

After the *Sea Witch* had docked, Sophie made arrangements with the captain so they could stay aboard until other living facilities could be obtained. Then she and Betzy went looking for property. Before the morning was out they had excellent luck. Hiram Gatling, who owned a sturdy house on a small tract of land on Mill Street, was looking for a buyer. Mill Street had once been the skid-road down which logs were slid to be taken to the sawmill. As the trees were depleted, the road was moved. Despite its given name, the loggers' name of Skid Road remained.

Gatling was an embittered man. Several months earlier in a card game he had gambled away his timberland to Rory. Not only was he anxious to leave Seattle, but he was looking for an opportunity to seek revenge upon the Connemara Mill Company. He took great delight in selling his poperty to Sophie, for he knew very well to what purpose she would put it.

Next day Sophie and her company moved into the house, and set about cleaning it up. It was a two-story building, but too small for Sophie's purposes. She hired a group of loggers who claimed to be carpenters to build a new wing that would contain bedrooms on the second floor and an immense parlor on the first. The parlor would be the saloon. Ignoring all usual thrift, Sophie ordered elaborate and expensive furnishings from San Francisco. She knew these would make her place *tres chic* and impress the loggers. Sophie intended to put the sleazy establishments of Front Street out of business.

Word reached Liam that a beautiful and ambitious young woman named Sophie Parmalee had come to Seattle and was ensconced on Skid Road. The Irishman was astounded. *Sophie Parmalee!* Summoning all his hypocritical outrage, Liam marched down to Skid Road to see if the rumors were true. Mill Street was a desolate area between the town of Seattle and the banks of the sound. There were only two houses on Skid Road. One was occupied by a pair of widows who shared frugal lives. There were no trees surrounding their small house, only unsightly stumps remained. As Liam neared the Gatling house, he saw a scene of intense activity. Ten men were constructing a new wing. Liam angrily realized that the carpenters were his own loggers, working in their spare time. They greeted him shyly, knowing that he did not approve of such a project.

Liam crossed the porch and knocked on the door. There was so much hammering that his knock could not be heard. He opened the door and stuck his head inside. "Hello! Hello in there!"

Betzy, in the parlor sewing new dresses for Sophie and the five doves, responded. "I'se comin'." When she saw Liam her face lit up. Then her smile quickly faded into an embarrassed grin. "Mr. Liam, we been expectin' yo'."

"How have you been, Betzy?"

"Lot better now. I sho' didn't like de trip up here, but anyhow we beats de fire."

"Fire?"

"Yes, sir, in Frisco. Look to me like it was gonna burn clear to de ground. We sho' got out in time."

"I'm happy that you did. Is Miss Parmalee available?"

"Yes, sir. She upstairs. I fetch her for yo'."

Liam seated himself in the parlor. The sparse furnishings had obviously been left by Gatling and were serviceable at best. But he was impressed by the cleanliness of the room. That had to be Sophie's doing, for Gatling was not any neater than he was pleasant.

Sophie was in the second-floor sitting room conducting, as she liked to put it, "a class to learn class." It was difficult teaching her five doves the rudiments of refinement as well as the rules of the house. They weren't a particularly intelligent or even attentive lot. And Sophie, to her exasperation, had to repeat herself many times.

". . . and I don't care how much a man has been drinking, I don't want any stealing here, do you understand? And as you know, I don't want you drinking anything stronger than wine or champagne."

"How about Sweet Charlottes, Miss Sophie?" asked Li'l Jennie.

"What in hell is a Sweet Charlotte?"

"It's a mixture of claret and raspberry syrup."

"Oh, I suppose that's all right," Sophie conceded. "As long as it doesn't break out your face. Speaking of faces, later I'm going to show you all how to make yourself up. *Quelle domage,* I've never seen that much paint put to so little effect!" Sophie paused for effect, giving her doves ample time to admire her own cosmetic expertise. Satisfied with their gushing compliments, she continued. "Let me see, where were we? Oh, yes. And no cigars, please. It's *tres* unladylike and does dreadful things to your breath. And I don't need to repeat my abhorrence of drugs! Do I?"

"Not even a little opium once in a while?" asked Moist Meg. "It sure helps me to sleep."

"You can have all the opium you like," answered Sophie sweetly. "But you'll be sleeping someplace else! Remember, girls, Front Street is not all that far away. If in any way you displease me, *or our customers,* that's where you'll end up. The Paradise is going to be one high class place, do you understand? No two-dollar drinks and no ten-dollar whores. It's going to be class and, *sacré blue,* you're going to be living proof that soiled doves can also fly."

"I like that," giggled Georgette.

Sophie looked at her sternly. "Now as for the men, I expect each of you to inspect the loggers' equipment to make sure he's clean. I don't want any diseases in this house, do you understand? If you have any problems with them, you come to me. I don't expect you to have to put up with any rough stuff. You're ladies. You don't have to do anything funny either. I'm going to hire us a big bouncer. I've got someone in mind. We're going to have a place that's genteel. *Comprendez vous?*"

"What?" grunted Big Annie.

"Do you understand?" explained Sophie.

The women nodded that they did. Betzy entered the sitting room. "Yo' got company, Miz Sophie." There was a warning note in her voice.

"Liam?" whispered Sophie.

"Ain't no one else."

"Girls, I'm going to be engaged for a short time, and I expect you to practice your flattery while I'm gone." She lowered her voice. "Betzy, would you mind staying up here and keeping an eye on them to make sure they follow my instructions. Besides, I want to see Mr. O'Sullivan alone."

Betzy looked at the quintet. "I think yo' wastin' yo' time, Miz Sophie. Don't seem to me like yo' gonna make no silk purses out of dese here sows."

"I'm not counting on silk, Betzy. Satin will do quite nicely, thank you."

Sophie rushed into her bedroom, arranged her curls, repaired her makeup and changed into a day dress of lemon yellow with a fitted bodice and a tiered skirt. A series of flounces edged the three-quarter length sleeves and was repeated on the skirt. Satisfied that she looked seductive as well as respectable, Sophie descended the staircase to the parlor below.

Liam got to his feet as Sophie swept into the room extending her hand. "Why, Mr. O'Sullivan. How nice to see you again."

Liam ignored her hand. "We can bypass the amenities, Miss Parmalee. I'm sure you've been expecting me. But things are different this time. You're on my ground now."

"Your ground? I was under the impression I owned the land on which you're standing," replied Sophie tartly.

Liam chose to ignore her statement. "What made you decide on Seattle, Miss Parmalee?"

"Please sit down, Mr. O'Sullivan." She sat facing him. "Tea?"

"This is not a social visit. Again I ask, why Seattle?"

"Why not?" she smiled. "I thought that rather than stay in San Francisco and be burned to a crisp, I would embark upon a new adventure. After hearing the many virtues of your fair town . . ."

"A new adventure! Opening a whorehouse!" Liam snorted. "I could use my influence to close you down, you know."

Sophie's eyes blazed. "How dare you! I'm not 'opening a whorehouse.' It's an exclusive and an expensive entertainment salon. Why, I intend to perform here myself."

"Upstairs or downstairs?"

Sophie looked Liam squarely in the eyes and said quietly. "It has always surprised me that you go out of your way to insult me. A man with your *supposed kindness* and *moral standards*."

"You're a fine one to bring up moral standards. No matter what you call it, it's still going to be an overpriced fancy house designed to bilk the loggers of their hard-earned money."

"Just listen to you. You—who makes, each and every man you hire sign over his claim so that you can continue to build your timber empire. I wouldn't call that moral."

Liam shot out of his chair and began pacing the floor. "And how do you think any of my men would do on their own? They'd come here, cut down the trees and not plant any new ones. They'd make a lot of money but they'd spend it all, probably in some place like yours. Then what? Then they'd leave and that would be that. Because of me, they have steady employment for as long as they live. And each man, besides his wages, receives a percentage of the profits. My men have pride in the Connemara Mill Company. They own a piece of it!" Liam stopped and bowed slightly toward Sophie. "But surely you know all that. I take it your source of information was Wick Skansen."

Once again Sophie became the coquette. "Well, I have been keeping company with Mr. Skansen."

"He's dead, you know." said Liam gruffly.

The color drained from Sophie's face. "What! What!"

Liam immediately regretted his bluntness. "I'm sorry, Miss Parmalee. I thought you knew. Nearly two months ago Wick was killed in a . . . logging accident."

Sophie covered her face with her hands. Liam reached out to comfort her but she pulled away. "You're really the bearer of good news, aren't you? First threats, now this."

"I'm sorry . . . I."

"Please go, Mr. O'Sullivan."

"I really do apologize. I didn't think. I'm always speaking first and thinking later. My wife scolds me all the time."

Sophie looked at him out of the corners of her eyes. "Your wife?" she whispered. "I didn't know you were married."

"Yes, last April." He added proudly, "We have a son . . . Michael Kevin. And we're expecting another in February."

Sophie got up from the couch, fighting back tears of disappointment. At the door she said, "Don't worry, Mr. O'Sullivan. I don't intend to corrupt your loggers. I've made my rules. No gambling, no heavy drinking, no drugs. I'll give them a fair shake for their dollar, that is, if you'll let me."

Liam sighed. "Go on with your entertainment center, Miss Parmalee. I'll not oppose it in any way. And again I apologize for being so tactless."

A sad smile appeared on Sophie's lips. "Your wife must be a very good woman to have softened you up."

Liam flushed. "Well, I'll bid you good day, Miss Parmalee."

"Not good luck?" Sophie asked hopefully.

"You'll make your own, Miss Parmalee. I suspect you always have."

On his way up Skid Road, Liam, exasperated, cocked his head to one side and looked at the sky and asked his Maker, "Now why did You see fit to make Sophie Parmalee my own personal nemesis?"

As soon as Liam was on his way, Sophie allowed herself the luxury of tears. She leaned against the front door and, crying bitterly, sank to her knees. Betzy, hearing her sobs from upstairs, hurried down to her mistress. "Miz Sophie, what de matter?"

Sophie's choked sobs turned to ironic laughter. "I guess—I've come here—for nothing." Then she thrust out her chin and dried her eyes on her sleeve. "Help me, Betzy. We've got things to do and money to make!"

Kathleen looked up from the stove as Liam entered the kitchen. "Liam, I didn't expect you home for lunch." Noting his stormy expression she asked, "What's the matter? Is something wrong at the mill?"

Liam kissed his wife warmly on the cheek. "No. Nothing's wrong at the mill, Kathleen. I hope you don't mind me coming home unexpectedly."

"No, of course not. Father O'Reilly's due for lunch and I know that he'll be pleased to find that you're here."

"How's Kevin? How's our son?" asked Liam going directly to the wicker basket near the window.

"He's better than any child has a right to be. Goodness, I don't remember my brothers being so little trouble."

Lovingly Liam gazed at his son. The child gurgled and grabbed his father's fingers. Nearly four months old, little Kevin had a full head of shiny black hair and a pair of extraordinary blue eyes. "Can I pick him up?" asked Liam.

"Why, of course. Don't worry, he's dry. I just changed him."

"As if a little water could come between us." Liam slipped his hand under the baby's body and lifted the infant to his shoulder. "He feels like he's gaining weight."

"Daily," laughed Kathleen. "He's going to be a fine, strapping lad."

"And come February, Kevin will be getting a little sister. . . ." Liam grinned. "If I can arrange another Indian uprising."

"That I can do without," replied Kathleen firmly.

Liam watched his wife as she stirred the pot upon the stove. "You shouldn't be doing that, my dear. You have Pink Jade and Han Sung. If you need any more servants, I'll get them."

"Oh, Liam, I like cooking and caring for the house. I'm afraid I'll never be a proper lady of the manor." She tasted her stew. "Besides, you like my cooking, don't deny it."

"That's true enough. By the way, where are our Chinese lovers?"

"Rory informed me that a shipment of furniture arrived yesterday. Things ordered for the spare rooms. I thought, since we don't really have any company yet, it would be nice to let them select what they like for their rooms."

Liam sighed with exasperation. "You spoil those two. You don't treat them like servants at all."

"Well, they aren't," replied Kathleen sharply. "How can you even say that? They couldn't be more devoted to us if they were our own family. I feel they are!"

"When is the wedding to take place?" asked Liam, attempting to placate his wife's sudden anger.

"You know as well as I. This Friday night."

"In the church?"

"That's why I'm having Father O'Reilly to lunch. I don't see why they can't be married in the church."

Liam put his son back in his basket. "They're not Catholic." he said simply.

"Oh, Liam, please. Not you, too. Stringent rules are not meant for out here. This is the wilderness. Rules have to bend to accomodate the needs of the people."

"Some of the men aren't going to like it. My dear Kathleen, there exists a good deal of hostility against the Orientals."

Kathleen lifted the pot of stew from the fire and set it on the side of the stove. "I'm aware of that, Liam."

"Then why force the issue?"

Kathleen crossed the floor, took her husband's hands in hers and looked into his eyes. "Because, Liam," she said softly, "it's the right thing to do."

"My sweet Kathleen," murmured Liam. He turned over her hands and kissed them. "I got more than I bargained for when I married you." He slipped his arms around her waist and drew her close.

"Liam," Kathleen protested. "The priest's due to arrive."

"Some rules are made to be bent, Kathleen. You said so yourself." He looked at her with a shining fervor.

They kissed tentatively at first and then with more passion. Kathleen had come to love Liam in every way.

A flustered Father O'Reilly, eyes lowered from Kathleen's and Liam's embrace, cleared his throat loudly. The couple broke apart. He apologized. "I knocked at the front door and when no one answered I tried the back."

"Oh, I'm sorry, Father," said Kathleen smoothly. "We didn't hear you. Lunch is almost ready. I hope you don't mind if I serve it here in the kitchen. There's just the three of us."

"Not at all, Kathleen O'Sullivan. Your kitchen is the nicest in all Seattle." The young priest, still blushing, took a seat at the round oak table. "And how are you, Liam?"

"Quite well, Father."

"And the babe?"

"Michael Kevin is almost too perfect," sang Kathleen. "He's sleeping in the basket if you wish to look at him."

"I do," nodded the priest eagerly. "I must make friends with the young scamp. He'll probably be running the mill one day when I'm old and doddering. I'd better get on the good side of him."

While the priest was playing with Kevin, Kathleen put Liam to work setting the table. She ladled the rich and hearty lamb stew into carved wooden bowls. "It's just plain fare," Kathleen apologized.

"Don't be modest," admonished the priest. "Miss Kat, your cooking is the best I've ever had and that includes my mother."

The guard at the Seattle warehouse was a short bandy-legged man who walked with a pronounced limp. "Tadpole" Kelly had formerly been a logger with the Connemara Mill Company. Good whiskey and bad judgment had caused Kelly accidentally to remove several toes from his right foot; it rendered him useless as a logger. Despite Liam's dislike for the untidy Irishman, he had offered him a job at the warehouse. Kelly took the job, but grouched constantly. The work went against his grain, his masculine self-image. And every day he griped that the job was "beneath a white man."

Kelly glowered at Han Sung and Pink Jade as they wandered through the warehouse, picking out furniture for the rooms they would share. Kelly sucked on his bad teeth, snorted and twitched and fumed. Free furniture for the heathen Chinks. It didn't make sense! What did he ever get for free? *Nothing,* that's what! He always had to work hard for every goddamned cent he made. Now here he was stuck working as a goddamned janitor in a frigging warehouse. Them chinks in there was picking out the best bed that could be had. Chinks was supposed to sleep on a mat on a floor, for Christ's sake, not in a white folks' bed.

Pink Jade and Han Sung were well aware of Kelly's feelings. Not wanting any further hostility, they were polite. Han Sung went up to Kelly, bowed and said, "We have made our selections, Mr. Kelly. Mr. O'Sullivan said that you would be kind enough to help me load our new furniture into the wagon we have waiting outside."

Kelly didn't bother suppressing a malicious grin. He sucked noisily on a tooth and spat out a glob of bloody spittle on the warehouse floor. "Now I don't doubt that Mr. O'Sullivan wanted me to help you load the wagon and I would, if I had time. But unfortunately, coolie, I just ain't got the time right now. I'm busy." Kelly leaned against a post and spat again.

Pink Jade touched her lover's arm. "It's all right, Han Sung. I am strong. I can help carry the furniture."

Han Sung swallowed his anger and nodded.

As they started back for the depths of the warehouse, Kelly gave Han Sung's queue a hard yank. "Just wanted to see if it was real, coolie."

Pink Jade placed a restraining hand on Han Sung's shoulder, and they continued about their business.

By late afternoon they had loaded almost every piece of furniture onto the wagon. The pieces would be more than adequate to fill the bathroom, the bedroom and the sitting room on the first floor of the Great House that were allotted to them by the O'Sullivans. The last piece to carry was the horsehair mattress, which had come all the way from St. Louis by way of San Francisco. It was a clumsy article, and the young people were having a difficult time getting it into the wagon. They stopped to rest, leaning the mattress against the wagonside.

At that moment the bull whacker Yester Day rode up to the warehouse. Since Wick's death, Yester saw Kelly more frequently. A generation or two back, they were distantly related. They came from Boston and rounded the Horn together on their way to San Francisco. Having no luck in the gold fields, they applied for work at the lumbercamp. Skansen would not have taken Kelly, but because the men were inseparable, he signed them both on.

"Hi yah, Tadpole," grinned Yester. "Hey, what's goin' on? Are the chinks goin' to open up a opium den?"

"Looks that way, Yester," spat Kelly.

Yester jumped from his horse and landed near the Chinese couple. "That so, coolie? You openin' up a opium den?"

Han Sung gritted his teeth but made no reply. Eyeing the mattress, Yester asked, "Or are you sellin' that little piece of lotus blossom to keep you supplied with dope dreams?"

Han Sung, his face contorted with fury, started for the larger logger, but Pink Jade grabbed him and held him fast. "Don't, don't, Han Sung. It doesn't matter. Come, let us load the mattress and go back to the Great House."

They started to pick up the mattress but Yester fell against it, forcing it out of their grip and onto the dusty ground. "Hmmmmm. Nice mattress. Hey, coolie, how about lettin' me have a little piece of that yellow blossom? I got money."

Han Sung could take no more. He dove at the bull wacker and began plummeting him with his fists. Yester, who was considerably larger than Han Sung gruffly pushed him away and began laughing. "How about that feisty little prick," he called to Kelly. "Hey, Kelly, I heard their manhood is all tied in with the length of their pigtails. I wonder how the wedding night would go if he didn't have no pigtail."

Kelly sniggered. "Heh, heh, heh. There's only one way to find out, Yester." He produced a knife from his boot and began flipping it from hand to grimy hand. "You hold him down, Yester, I'll clip him!"

Kelly's eyes twinkled, but there was no hint of humor or warmth. He advanced to the mattress oblivious to Pink Jade's pleadings. Yester, using the full weight of his body, had pinned Han Sung to the mattress.

"Please, don't do this thing!" cried Pink Jade. "Please, it will mean a loss of face!"

Yester laughed harshly. "Loss of face, my ass. Means a loss of a pigtail! " He wrapped his huge hand around Han Sung's throat and pulled the queue taut. "So what happens if we cut it off, lotus blossom? Does that mean he's not going to be able to get it up?"

Kelly knelt on the mattress, his eyes bulging with malice. "Let me do it," he breathed. "Let me cut off the pigtail."

"Be my guest," offered Yester.

Han Sung struggled but could not get out from under the burly bull wacker. Pink Jade jumped upon Kelly's back and began hitting him. The cocky Irishman threw her aside, knocking her into the dusty road. Pink Jade watched with horror as the knife severed her beloved's queue. Laughing Kelly tossed it at her. Then the two men set upon Han Sung, who was cursing them in Chinese, and began pounding his body with their fists.

Liam, riding toward the warehouse, saw the two men beating Han Sung. He dug his heels into his horse and spurred him on. "Here, here, what's going on?"

Pink Jade, cried, "Oh, Mr. Liam, please make them stop. *Please!*"

Kelly and Yester were so involved with their sport they didn't hear Liam approach. Liam jumped from his horse and rushed at them. He collared Kelly and threw him aside. He grabbed Yester's arms before he could punch the young Chinese any more. *"What in the hell do you think you're doing?"* he roared. The two men looked at one another nervously.

"Han Sung, are you all right?" Liam helped the Chinese man to his feet.

Pink Jade began daubing at his bleeding face with a

piece of cloth ripped from her shirt. "Mr. Liam, they made sport of us, then they cut off Han Sung's queue and beat him."

"You did nothing to provoke them?" asked Liam, knowing full well the answer.

"No, sir," stammered Han Sung. "Nothing."

Liam stood up. "The two of you are fired," he said harshly. "Go to the office and collect what's coming to you. And if you know what's good for you, you won't remain in the bay area, for I'll see that you get no work."

The men protested, but Liam was adamant. He turned to Han Sung. "Here, let me help you." He guided Han Sung into the wagon, loaded the mattress himself and, after hitching his horse to the wagon, drove the couple back to the Great House.

Chapter 22

On the morning of September 11, the day of the opening of the Paradise, Sophie and Betzy and the five doves stood on the dock anxiously awaiting the *Connemara*. Most of Sophie's furnishings had arrived, at least enough for her to open. They now waited for the piano. The doves, all "ladified," sported parasols, smart day dresses and new faces. They each still wore a good deal of makeup, but the cosmetics were skillfully employed to accentuate their good features.

"What are we gonna do if the pi-ano don't come?" whined Li'l Jennie in her posy voice.

"Then I shall simply be accompanied by the string instruments!" Sophie gestured broadly, calling the harp-guitar, banjo and fiddle to mind.

"It's just too excitin'! squealed Georgette, who at Sophie's insistence had lost ten pounds and had bleached her putty hair to a vibrant gold.

"Now calm down, Georgette," cautioned Sophie. "I don't want you to break out in hives again, *n'est pas?*"

"Maize oo-wee," chirped Georgette. She emulated Sophie in every way.

As the *Connemara* nosed its way into dock, the doves clapped and cheered. The sailors leaned over the side, shouting, "We're comin' to the openin'! We won't miss that!"

"Is the piano on board?" Sophie called out.

"That it is, Miss Sophie," boomed a voice. The captain, a handsome young Englishman, waved to Sophie.

Sophie sighed and remarked to Betzy. "I hope it's not too badly out of tune."

Just then a new cabriolet, a light-hooded one-horse carriage, two-seater, pulled into dock and claimed the sailors' attention. Han Sung was driving and seated next to him was Kathleen. She, too, was expecting a shipment from San Francisco—a baby crib of carved fruitwood ordered months earlier.

Kathleen wore a day dress of amethyst blue cotton trimmed with large mother-of-pearl buttons. The fashionably wide crinolined skirt concealed her five-month pregnancy. She saw the cluster of women standing on the dock and realized who they must be. Should she or should she not speak to the women? Feeling ill at ease, Kathleen decided to make the best of an awkward social situation. Liam would probably not approve but Kathleen could not find it in her heart to be rude. As she neared the group, she nodded and pleasantly offered greetings.

Then she saw Sophie and Betzy standing apart from the others. They were the same women she had seen in the hotel lobby in San Francisco! "Why, hello," smiled Kathleen. "I do believe I've seen you before." She offered her hand and Sophie took it. "I'm Kathleen O'Sullivan."

Sophie was stunned. She recalled the beautiful dark-haired young woman in the United States Hotel. And she had married Liam! Sophie's surprise vied with envy. This was Liam's wife, the mistress of his Great

House—beautiful, self-assured *and* a young woman of quality. Why did she have to be so nice?

"I'm Sophie Parmalee," Sophie said, regaining her composure. "And this is my companion, Betzy Bedamned."

"I'm so happy to meet you. Are you also expecting something to arrive?" So this was the infamous Sophie Parmalee who had led Rory such a merry chase. Kathleen could see why Rory was attracted to her. She was lovely under all that paint. And Kathleen was surprised to find that she liked Sophie.

"My piano," replied Sophie. "I'm opening my club tonight and I was afraid it wouldn't arrive in time. And you?"

"Nothing so exciting," replied Kathleen. "Just a crib for my baby."

"I would say that is just as exciting," smiled Sophie.

The piano and the crib were unloaded along with the other pieces of merchandise. Sophie and Kathleen promised to get together for tea.

As they peered through the lace curtains at the scene down the street, Emmy Serazin and Logene Banks were more titillated than frightened. "There must be four hundred men out there!" exclaimed Emmy, a wispy woman of fifty plus.

"Four hundred at least," agreed Logene, who was shaped somewhat like a lima bean. "Oh, I do wish we could go too, Emmy!"

"Logene, have you no shame? Why I wouldn't be caught dead in a place like that."

"Well *I* would," replied Logene wistfully. "I just wish I were younger, that's all."

"Logene Banks!" squealed Emmy. "You're a scandal to the jay birds!"

Sophie's Paradise was officially open. The bouncer, a hulk of a man named Royal Toomey, had to stand guard at the front door to keep the crowds from storming the house. The lines were three deep, stretched all the way down Skid Road to the widows' house. In the bright moonlight the Paradise resembled a chunk of ornate wedding cake. Turned wood pieces and brass knobs had been added to the eaves, the windows and the roof of the house. Everything was then painted white—a defiant gesture by Sophie, who reasoned rightly that white was linked with purity, highmindedness and class.

Lights from every window cast warm shadows upon the sparse but green lawn. The tree stumps had been replaced by small fir trees, which Sophie had the girls decorate in the manner of Christmas trees. Each of her doves had developed a craft, which kept them busy during the long hours of waiting peculiar to their profession. Their hand-wrought ornaments—corn husk dolls, crocheted doilies, strings of shell beads, decoupaged boxes and macraméd tassels were like bright signs of welcome.

Inside, the Paradise was crowded with raucous laughter, clinking glasses and honky-tonk music. The first floor swarmed with customers. Two bartenders were so busy filling drinks that a Chinese waiter had to man the cash register and make change. The waiters, Chinese imported from San Francisco, were dressed in black silk coolie costumes trimmed with red frogs and braiding. Their queues swung back and forth as they hustled through the rooms. Sophie was well aware of the prejudice about the Chinese—especially the working Chinese. But with a bouncer like Royal Toomey, nearly seven feet tall and almost half as wide, she didn't worry about the customers harassing her waiters, her girls or herself.

The elaborate rooms had been lavishly decorated. Red was the predominate color. The chandeliers were brass and the round globes were etched with ornate designs. The windows were hung with heavy velvet curtains and cut-glass beads. The rough-hewn plank flooring was left uncovered. A carpet or a parquet floor would be quickly ruined by the loggers' caulking boots. Thin stalks of incense burned from hidden nooks and crannies. The aroma of musk and jasmine masked the sweat and heightened the senses.

Sophie's Paradise featured the five doves. Under her tutelage, they were quite different from the whores of Front Street. Sophie arranged the doves on a button-upholstered circular sofa, five tufted seats, one for each one. Betzy had taken great pains designing a hairstyle that would suit their individual faces. Under Sophie's guidance their makeup was expert. Gowns, which the doves had made themselves under Sophie's direction and Betzy's assistance, were extraordinary and in the latest fashion. Monochromatic and unlike the clashing, glaring colors employed by the competition, the colors were selected to flatter each individual woman's figure and complexion.

Sophie, seeing the finished product, had laughed good-naturedly and called them "my flower garden of earthly delights. My ready-to-be-plucked flowers!"

Big Annie was dressed in a voluminous gown of royal purple—an iris. Li'l Jennie wore sunshiny shades of yellow—a daffodil. Moonsweet was arrayed in a scarlet gown that deftly employed Victorian lines and Oriental trim—a poppy. Moist Meg was swashed in orange water-marked taffeta—a zinnia. And Georgette looked like a million blossoms in frothy pink chiffon—a peony.

Sophie's "garden" sat demurely on the round sofa, exchanging compliments with the loggers and accepting light drinks. The loggers, impressed and impassioned, kept a continual circle around the sofa, hoping to cajole one of the girls upstairs.

Sophie's rule was, "no upstairs business on opening night and that goes for *everyone!* If you start off by hopping right into bed with them, they'll treat you like whores. Let them come and look and lust, then go to their bunks and dream and ponder. They'll come back and they'll be more anxious than ever to spend their money!"

Sophie managed the evening like a society hostess. Nothing ruffled her. Sophie eclipsed everyone, as she knew, in her resplendent gown of white lace. Its three-tiered scalloped skirt edged with teardrop crystals, short puffed sleeves and high wide collar made her the bride of the festivities. Her complexion was vibrant and her eyes glowed with good health She was gracious to each and every logger, for they were her future.

A waiter brought a message to Sophie. Royal wanted to see her on the porch. Sophie excused herself and approached the bouncer. "What is it, Royal?"

"Just look at all those men. Nobody's leavin', and they're gettin' mighty anxious. I don't know how I'm going to hold 'em back, Miss Sophie."

The young woman gasped at the sight of all the men anxiously waiting to enter the Paradise. "I have an idea, Royal. I'm not sure if it's against the law or not, but I can't see any other way out. Have the bartenders set up a bar out here in the yard. The musicians can move the piano onto the porch. Have the waiters bring out as many lamps as possible. *I'm* going to entertain them!"

"Are you sure that's wise, Miss Sophie?" asked Royal, awkward in a situation he couldn't understand.

Sophie, standing on her tiptoes affectionately, touched Royal's shoulder. "Of course, Royal. You worry too much. But that's all right. It makes you look all the more menacing. Keep it up."

Sophie's wishes were quickly fulfilled. The five "flowers" arranged themselves on the porch. Sophie called for attention and quiet. "Gentlemen," she began, "I'm completely overwhelmed by your touching response to the opening of the Paradise. I'm Sophie Parmalee and I would like you to meet my girls."

As she named them, each girl stood and curtsied gracefully amid the cheers and whistles of the rambunctious loggers. "As you can see, our club is not going to hold all of you. But not to disappoint you, we've brought the entertainment outside!"

The musical accompaniment began the opening strains of Sophie's song. With one deft motion Sophie parted the tiers of her dress and revealed her shapely legs, encased in white stockings inset with lace over each thigh. The loggers' shouts of joy echoed and reechoed throughout the woods, finally reaching the Great House.

Kathleen, crocheting in the parlor of her home, turned to Liam at his desk, who was concluding the accounts of the day. "What, in Heaven's name, is that noise?"

Liam looked up from his books and said bitterly. "The Paradise is officially open."

"Oh," replied Kathleen and went back to her work. She lifted her head and suddenly asked. "You don't like her, do you, Liam?"

"Who?"

"Sophie Parmalee."

He swallowed hard. "No, I don't."

"I found her to be a charming young woman."

"When were you speaking to her?"

"Today at the dock. I was picking up the crib and she was awaiting the delivery of her piano." Then she added, "I've asked her to tea."

"Are you out of your mind, Kathleen? Having that kind of woman in our house?"

"I wasn't aware that you've placed restrictions on who I entertained."

"Well, I haven't," conceded Liam. "It's just that . . ."

"You don't like her. Good heavens, Liam. Rory's a grown man. He had an affair with Sophie and it didn't work out. That's not enough reason to carry a grudge."

"She made him very unhappy."

"I've come to the conclusion that no woman could make Rory happy. You know I'm very fond of Rory, but he's not exactly a pillar of the community, is he?"

Liam smiled. "You've made your point, my dear. Of

course, have anyone you like to tea. I was being priggish."

Kathleen relinquished her chair. "Oh, no you weren't, darling. You were being a concerned friend and a thoughtful husband. . . ." She kissed him on the forehead.

Liam pressed his head against Kathleen's swollen stomach. "I can feel her stirring."

"Well, I hope it's a her. I'm afraid you're going to be terribly disappointed if Kevin doesn't get a little sister."

Sophie waited until the men had become quiet before starting her song. Then, strutting across the porch, she launched into her song.

> *The average girl of eighteen-fifty*
> *Wants to be what she ain't.*
> *I don't want men who are thrifty,*
> *So listen to my complaint.*
> *My prayers go unanswered.*
> *My pleas go unheeded.*
> *I want my gown to be velvet*
> *And my purse to be jewelled and beaded.*
> *Heaven Helps the Working Girl,*
> *and the Working Girl Helps Herself!*

A lazy wind picked up Sophie's throaty voice and carried it across the tops of the trees through the balmy night air.

A lone figure rode through the forest. At the sound of Sophie's voice, Rory reined his horse and listened, letting the sound caress him. Determined not to appear at Sophie's opening night, Rory had made the rounds of the bars on Front Street. Liquor had not brought relief, and the usual pleasant conversations with the whores had proved depressing. Rory reined again and headed toward the Paradise. He was going to see Sophie again, feel that sweet anxiety he had not experienced in over a year.

Rory reached the shelf of earth just above Skid Road. In the distance he could see Sophie cavorting on the porch. Her song reached him long after the words were belted. Rory lowered his head. He knew that he should not continue his journey, but he could not help himself. His horse carried him down and onward until he, too, joined Sophie's audience of admirers.

Rory dismounted. He eased his way through the mob to the outdoor bar, hoping to find drink that would ease his pain. Sophie entertained the loggers with two more songs and excused herself. She withdrew into the house.

Betzy was straightening up the saloon, emptying ashtrays and stacking glasses on the bar.

"Why don't you let the waiters do that, Betzy?" admonished Sophie.

"I jus' felt like keepin' busy, Miz Sophie."

"Quite a crowd! And they're running out of liquor."

"Lawd, I hopes we don't get dis many every night. I don't know how we gonna handle 'em all."

"If we have to, we'll expand. We've probably made enough money for that in just this one night."

"Yo' tired, honey?"

"Yes. There's so much involved in running your own place. It's not just being an entertainer. I'm finding that out soon enough."

"Yo' didn't see nobody yo' likes?" Betzy asked cautiously.

"I wasn't looking," replied Sophie. "Besides, they all look the same. Like grizzled bears. Still, Betzy, I never counted on not spending the night alone. If only—"

"De night not over yet," giggled Betzy.

One by one the girls returned. "They're all starting to go home," whined Li'l Jennie. "We sure could have made a lot of money tonight."

"They'll be back," reminded Sophie. "You wait and see. Why, you're liable to get bed sores."

Sophie ordered a strong whiskey from the bartender and carried the drink out onto the small back porch.

She observed the loggers making their way home to their bunks, drunk, happy and entertained if not sexually satisfied. She listened to the groups singing loudly and calling to one another as they made their way through the woods. Noticing the lights on in the widows' house, Sophie felt a pang of guilt. She decided that she would call upon them the next day and apologize for the disturbance.

Sophie leaned forward and peered around to see how many stragglers remained. The moon, pale and waxen, was riding low in the skies and cast a silvery light across the yard. A young man standing at the outdoor bar caught her eye. Silhouetted in the moonlight, he was tall, well-built and handsome.

"*Rory!*" His name slipped from her lips before she realized it.

Rory turned toward the voice and followed it. "Hello, Sophie," he said lamely. He looked, brightening, and remarked not unkindly, "Such a strong drink for such a lady."

Sophie was too tired for pretenses. "It's been a harrowing night, I had no idea that . . ."

"It's Saturday night. There's a lot of men up here and not a hell of a lot to do. You're going to make a lot of money, Sophie."

Sophie turned to Rory and looked directly into his eyes. They were troubled and sad, but still the lightest blue she had ever seen. "Rory, I don't want to spend the night alone."

The expression on his face didn't change, but the sadness left his eyes. In the pale light Sophie was excited by what remained—two burning fires of sensuality. "Neither do I," he replied simply.

Chapter 23

Pink Jade knocked lightly on the door to the morning room and entered. "I thought you might like a cup of tea, Miss Kat."

Kathleen looked up from her writing desk. "That's very thoughtful of you, Pink Jade. The morning sun has left us and it's grown cool in here."

"Do you wish for me to light a fire?"

"Oh, no, I won't be much longer. I just want to finish a letter to my parents." Kathleen smiled sadly. "It's such an effort really. I don't suppose I should admit it, but I don't care for them very much."

"There is nothing wrong in being truthful," replied Pink Jade. She set the tray down on Kathleen's rosewood writing desk and poured a cup of tea. Kathleen noted the two cups. "You'll join me?"

"Yes, Miss Kat. I'd like to." The Chinese woman sat down in a chair next to Kathleen's desk and poured her own tea.

"Is there something on your mind, Pink Jade?"

She lowered her lashes and replied quietly. "I am going to have a baby."

"Why, that's wonderful news!" cried Kathleen. "How long have you known?"

"Nearly a month."

"And you haven't told me?"

"I was afraid you and Mr. Liam might not like it."

"And why on earth not? I'm delighted and I know Liam will be the same."

"It will mean another mouth to feed."

"Don't be silly, Pink Jade. There's plenty. Lord in heaven, I never realized there was so much money in the world. But that's not the reason, is it?"

The young woman shook her head. "I—I want my baby to be an American."

"Why, it will be. It's going to be born here, isn't it?"

"But it will still be Chinese."

Kathleen took her friend's hand. "I know you've been mistreated, Pink Jade. I don't know why prejudice exists, but it does. But you'll never have to face it living here at the Great House, not you or Han Sung or your child. I promise you that. You're part of our family. I think of you as my sister. And with sisters, there's no difference in color."

"You'll pardon me, but Mr. Liam does not feel the same way."

"No, he doesn't," replied Kathleen honestly. "But be patient with him. He's a good man and would never wish your people harm."

"Thank you, Miss Kat," Pink Jade said gratefully, her black eyes glistened with gratitude.

"Speaking of children, how are my two?"

"Kevin is amusing himself in his new playpen and Brian sleeps."

"Good, let him. Heaven knows he does that little enough. I don't understand why he's so rambunctious—quite the opposite of Kevin. Must be his namesake."

"Brian?"

"Rory Brian. We had to call him Brian to avoid confusion. I should have known better than to name him after my husband's roguish partner."

"Mr. Liam wanted a girl so badly."

"Yes, he did. But he got over his disappointment. Besides," added Kathleen with a twinkle, "I've guaranteed that the next one shall be a girl." The demanding cry of a child echoed through the house. Kathleen sighed. "That'll be Brian."

"I'll see to him, Miss Kat."

"Thank you, Pink Jade. I'll be in shortly to feed him."

After Pink Jade had left, Kathleen read over the letter she had composed to her parents. It was brief and dispassionate.

March 7, 1852

"Dear Mama and Papa,

Our second child arrived on February 14th and you now have another grandson, Rory Brian O'Sullivan. I am told that in making his debut on St. Valentine's Day, he will possess a large heart and will be a humanitarian.

I'm glad to hear that you were able to acquire more acreage and that the mill is still serving you well. Liam and I are both pleased to hear that Donal is married. I don't recall the girl you named. Perhaps she is new to Belfast. Rory and Liam are both in good health. And although I fear they both work too hard, they do, thank God, seem to benefit from it. They both send you their regards. Did you receive the wedding portrait I sent you? You haven't mentioned it and it should have arrived by now. Next week I'm going to have a photographer take pictures of Kevin and, if we can keep him still, of Brian. I will send you copies of each so that despite my bragging you will know how handsome your grandsons are."

Kathleen couldn't think of anything else to say. She started to inform her parents of the forthcoming child of Pink Jade and Han Sung, but changed her mind. They surely would not understand her happiness concerning the birth of a Chinese child. She dipped the pen and added hastily:

"I fear I must end this letter short, for Brian is awake and demanding his lunch."

Your daughter,
Kathleen Mulvany O'Sullivan.

Kathleen folded the paper. Why did she feel such trepidation expressing happiness to her parents? "A duty letter," she muttered and hurriedly addressed an envelope. Brian was waiting for her to nurse him. That was a loving experience that even memories of her imperturbable parents could not belittle.

Sophie and Rory resumed their affair. Throughout the winter, spring and the welcome days of summer he was a constant visitor to the Paradise. He had all but moved from his rooms on Front Street, and most of his clothes and personal articles resided on the second floor of Sophie's house. Sophie, finally realizing that Liam would never want her, had settled for the man who truly did.

One mid-August morning Rory awoke and reached for Sophie. She wasn't beside him in the fourposter bed. He sat up and looked around the room. The clock on the mantelpiece told him that it was not yet seven. The door to the bathroom opened and Sophie emerged, her face as pale and translucent as morning mist.

"What's wrong, Sophie? Are you ill?"

She sat down on the edge of the bed, poured herself a glass of water from the pitcher on the nightstand and sipped it. Rory touched her forehead. It was oddly cold in contrast to the morning. "You look sick."

"Well, I am," she snapped. "I've been throwing up for the last half hour."

Rory quickly sat up and wrapped his arms around her shoulders. "Sophie, what is it? Did you eat something . . ."

She glared at him. "No, goddamn it! I'm pregnant!"

"You're going to have a baby?"

"I didn't say that. I said I was pregnant."

Rory scrambled from beneath the bedcovers. "I mean, how long? When? It's mine, isn't it?"

"Of course it's yours. I haven't been with anybody else since I came to Seattle." She smiled slightly. "You haven't given me a chance."

"*We're* having a baby?" he grinned.

"No, *I'm* having the baby, Rory. That's why I was so sick this morning."

"Why didn't you tell me before? How long has it been?"

"Two months. I didn't say anything because my times have always been a bit erratic."

Rory began counting on his fingers. "July, August, September, November . . ."

"You forgot October."

"October, December, January, February and March. It's going to come in March!"

Sophie looked peeved. "Rory, I can count."

Rory stood to his full height in the middle of the bed. "You're going to have a baby in March!" he sang, jumping up and down.

"Rory, stop it. You're going to break the slats. Besides, I didn't say I was going to have it."

Rory knelt beside Sophie. "What do you mean?"

"There are ways," she replied as lightly as possible, "of getting rid of it."

"You're not serious. Sophie, you wouldn't?"

"Not here, I wouldn't. I'd probably have to go back to San Francisco."

"But why would you do that?" his voice was full of hurt.

"What else am I going to do?" replied Sophie bitterly. "Bounce around the stage looking like I swallowed a watermelon? Christ, it must be catching. Kathleen told me the other day that she was expecting another one."

"I know. Liam told me. Maybe they'll have a little girl this time. Which would you prefer, Sophie? A little boy or a little girl?"

"What I'd prefer is not being sick in the morning. Rory, I don't want a big belly. I—I—I'm scared." Suddenly she burst into tears.

Rory held her close and stroked her hair. "You don't have to be scared, Sophie. I'm here. I'll always be here, don't you know that?" Hearing his words made her cry all the harder. He rocked her back and forth. "I want you, Sophie. I always have and I always will." She started to respond. "No, don't say anything. Let me finish. I've never said the word love to you. I've always been afraid to. But I love you, Sophie. And now I love you all the more. Shhhh. Let me finish while my courage is running high. There's no reason why we shouldn't be married. I know you don't love me, but you like me. We have good times together. We rarely fight and we always have something to say to one another. I don't know what you're looking for, Sophie. But if it's a man, you'll not find any that loves you any more than I do or one who'll treat you better. You don't need to keep the Paradise open. You've made a lot of money. Besides, I'm rich, I guess. If it's money you want, I'll give you every cent I've got and every cent I'll ever get. Besides, we look good together, you've said so yourself. Can you imagine how beautiful our baby would be?" He wiped her eyes with his fingertips and kissed the tip of her nose. "The way I see it, Sophie, we owe it to the world to have this child."

Sophie managed an off-centered smile. "Maybe," she whispered in a small broken voice. "Maybe all this time, I've been looking for you."

Rory brushed Sophie's hair out of her eyes and took her face in his hands. "Marry me, Sophie. Because if I can't make you happy, then, by God, nobody can."

Sophie fluttered her eyelashes and replied coyly. "I might as well. I didn't have anything planned for the afternoon anyway."

While Sophie was bathing, Rory rode to the mill to make arrangements with the new foreman. Liam was in San Francisco and wouldn't be back for several more days. Instinctively he wanted to wait for Liam's approval, but upon reflection Rory knew that it would be better to go ahead with the marriage without any interference from his older friend. Rory was too happy to court Liam's disapproval.

Later he rode directly to the church and waited impatiently for Father O'Reilly to finish Mass. The priest was reluctant to perform the ceremony. "Rory, she's not even Catholic."

"She's not anything, damn it! What difference does that make? She'll be Catholic once we're married. You have to marry us, Father. We're going to have a baby."

The priest colored and chewed his lower lip while he contemplated the situation. "Will you be willing to baptize the infant and raise it as a Catholic?"

"Why, of course, Father O'Reilly."

"Rory, I can't say that I approve of this marriage."

"I'm not asking for your approval, Father. I'm asking for you to marry us."

"All right," the priest agreed at last. "Go fetch your bride."

"We'll be here within the hour," replied Rory and rushed from the rectory.

The priest sank into a chair and groaned in exasperation. "What else could I do, Lord? This is not Boston!"

When Rory arrived back at the Paradise, Sophie and Betzy were waiting for him. Sophie had dressed in a modest gown of light pink silk. Betzy, alternately laughing and crying, was hurriedly stitching up a veil. "I still don't believe it, Mr. Rory. I jus' can't believe it!"

"I don't either, Betzy. We've got to whisk her off to the church before she changes her mind."

"In dat case," replied Betzy getting up, "let's get dat carriage movin'. I finish dis here thing on de way!"

Rory met Liam at the dock. Liam was furious when he found out that Sophie and Rory had married. The two men argued and parted in bitterness. Kathleen had remained at home since it was Pink Jade's time of confinement. When Liam entered his home he found Kathleen and the priest having tea together.

"A fine thing," he snorted. "How could you do it, Father O'Reilly? Why that girl's nothing but a trollop!"

"Liam!" cried Kathleen. "That's not fair. I think she's going to be a good wife to Rory. She's closed down the Paradise and if that doesn't show she means to settle down, I don't know what does."

"What happened to all the whores?" grunted Liam, as he poured himself a whiskey.

"I've been kept quite busy weddin' them all," replied Father O'Reilly.

"Now you're marrying whores in the church, Father?" Liam said, turning on the priest.

"As soon as the doors of the Paradise were closed, the loggers made a beeline for the girls. Now they, too, are blushing brides."

"If you'll pardon me for saying so, Father O'Reilly, I find your levity a bit out of place," said Liam tersely.

"Well, whores or not, Liam, they're still God's people and, I might add, mine. And who's to say that they won't make those loggers fine wives. Certainly Mary Magdalene . . ."

"You may accept her into your flock, Father, but I will never accept Sophie into the family."

"Liam!" admonished Kathleen. "What a dreadful thing to say."

"I mean it. I won't acknowledge her. Why, I've treated Rory like a younger brother. If it hadn't been for me, we never would have come to the sound. I did it so that we could establish a dynasty of Fitzgeralds and O'Sullivans—people to be reckoned with and to be respected. And what does he do? He off and marries a tart."

Kathleen slammed down her teacup. "Liam, I will not listen to this for another second! I've met Sophie and I like her. I don't see why you bear her such hate. It's unnatural to be so unbending. Don't do this. Don't do it to Rory, don't do it to Sophie, don't do it to me. Most of all, don't do it to yourself. If you could hear the way you're going on. I'm ashamed for you."

"I can't help the way I feel," replied Liam sullenly.

"Oh, yes you can. You can start by ridding your heart of your dislike for this girl. What kind of family are we going to have if we're split apart like this? I don't care if I did promise to obey you. I do not intend to exclude Sophie and Rory from our lives." Kathleen's voice broke and tears came to her eyes. "I just can't understand how you can be so kind on one hand and so cruel on the other." She turned and fled from the room. Liam, embarrassed because of the priest's presence, turned to Father O'Reilly.

"I guess I'll never understand women, Father."

The priest looked at him sternly and replied. "Not until you understand yourself, son."

Hannah McCormack cracked the whip across the backs of her mules. "Giddayup, you lazy jackasses!" she urged them over the rough passage of Skid Road. She had been summoned to Sophie and Rory's home. Sophie was due to deliver her child. The young woman was having a great deal of sickness and pain during the months of her pregnancy.

The midwife had been kept very busy that winter and spring. She delivered a girl child, charmingly named Mai Mai, to the Chinese couple. And Miss Kat had given birth to yet another son, whom Kathleen had named Sean Patrick O'Sullivan. The doves were pregnant by their logger husbands, except for Li'l Jennie who claimed that "we're still tryin' mornin', noon and night and sometimes in between!"

Arriving at the former Paradise, Hannah lifted her girth out of the wagon seat and hurried across the frozen ground. The door was flung open even before she reached the porch by a very distraught Betzy. "Thank goodness yo' here, Miz Hannah. She havin' a hard time of it."

Sophie's labor lasted fourteen hours. It was more of a fight for life than a delivery. At last, Sophie, weakened by the long and hard convulsions, brought forth a tiny girl child. Sophie commenced to bleed profusely. After the child was pronounced healthy, Hannah and Betzy doggedly worked to stop Sophie's blood flow. The baby, washed and comfortable in a warm blanket, was forgotten for the moment. Hannah made Rory wait downstairs until the bleeding could be stopped, reasoning that there was no point in upsetting him any further. Then she sent Betzy on an errand. "Get me some cobwebs, Betzy! All you can find! And hurry!"

Betzy rushed to all unused parts of the house, and managed to return with both of her palms covered with the torn filmy substance. She and Hannah packed the gauzy webs in Sophie's passage. A short time later the bleeding miraculously stopped. The two women then washed Sophie and changed her nightgown.

Sophie pathetically asked, "Why are you keeping my child from me? It was born dead, wasn't it?"

"No, honey. It here," replied Betzy, handing Sophie the tiny baby girl.

"She's so little," said Sophie. "Is she all right?"

"She's fine," said Hannah. "It was you we were worried about." Hannah looked at Betzy. "Call for Mr. Rory now. I know he's anxious to see his wife and little girl."

Rory raced up the steps three at a time and hurried to Sophie's side, "Liam and Kathleen are going to be jealous," Sophie said managing a weak smile. "It's a little girl."

Rory kissed his wife and then took the child into his arms. "She's got blond hair," he exclaimed with delight.

"What yo' gonna call her, Miz Sophie?" asked Betzy.

Sophie lifted herself to her elbows and announced, "I'm going to call her Starlyn."

"That's pretty," commented Hannah. "I don't believe I've ever heard that name before."

"I made it up," replied Sophie smugly. "It sounds French, don't you think?"

Six weeks later when Sophie had sufficiently regained her strength, arrangements were made for Father O'Reilly to christen the child. Since their argument Rory and Liam had been barely civil to one another, and had only spoken in matters concerning business. Kathleen was determined that Liam was going to attend the baby's christening. On the eve of the event, after serving Liam his favorite dinner, Kathleen faced her husband in the parlor.

"Liam, I'm going to ask you one more time. Please come to the christening with me this evening."

"I thought we had that all settled, Kathleen."

"No, you had it all settled, I didn't. I'm going to be greatly disappointed in you if you don't come. Sophie almost died giving birth to Starlyn."

"A ridiculous name!" Liam muttered.

"I think it's lovely," countered Kathleen.

"Don't you think you should be staying at home taking care of your own children?"

"Pink Jade can see after the boys without any help from me. Now, Liam, I want you to stop all this bull-headed nonsense. It's long past time for you to make friends with Sophie. She's Rory's wife, the mother of his child." Liam, pretending to read his newspaper, didn't answer. Kathleen continued. "Rory sent for a doctor from San Francisco, you know, because Sophie hasn't been well since her delivery." Liam looked up. "She can't have any more babies, Liam. The doctor told her if there are any more children, it will surely kill her."

"I am sorry to hear that," said Liam sincerely.

Kathleen gently pulled the newspaper from her husband's hands. "Liam, if you don't go, you're going to do irreparable harm to your relationship with Rory. You may never again have a chance to put things right." Liam didn't reply. "I'm not going to ask you again. I'm going to go get ready now and if you decide not to go with me, I'll never mention it again. But know this, Liam. I'll *never* forgive you."

The small christening party was already gathered around the altar when the church doors opened. Father O'Reilly looked up and saw Kathleen enter. He frowned, for she appeared to be alone. Then Liam stepped inside. After crossing themselves, they hurried down the aisle hand in hand. They took their seats on the new wooden pews and listened to the now familiar ceremony. Out of the corner of his eye Liam caught Rory smiling at him in gratitude. That smile caused Liam to recall the events that had intertwined their lives. Leaving their families behind in Munster County, traveling across the Atlantic aboard the *Perseverence*, the early struggles in Belfast, Maine, the trip on the *Connemara* that took them to New York and introduced Sophie Parmalee into their lives, the treacherous voyage around the cape and their arrival in San

Francisco. And finally coming to the sound and discovering the magnificent forests which they had made their birthright.

"Look at them, Liam! They go right up to the sky. Why it looks like they're holding up the clouds."

"They do indeed. They're the very pillars of heaven themselves!"

Chapter 24

As the Connemara Mill Company continued to grow, so did Seattle. New and legitimate businesses appeared overnight and catered to the needs of the emerging community. A small theatre was built. There were two banks now and clothing stores, feed stores, a post office and even a Protestant church. Seattle was no longer considered a boomtown. People came and stayed, bringing their own sense of community.

Seattle's new ladies' shop was owned by Eula Lacey McVey, a tiny, fluttery hummingbird of a woman. Eula had emigrated from Boston to help fill the shortage of women in Seattle. She married a stalwart logger by the name of Jumbo McVey twenty-four hours after her arrival in Seattle. Unable to have children and discontent merely as a housewife, Eula had turned her energies and talents to her dress shop.

Eula was pleased that two of Seattle's leading citizens, Sophie Fitzgerald and Kathleen O'Sullivan, were among her enthusiastic customers. Kathleen, in particular, was a community leader, and her approval meant success for Eula. She watched anxiously as the two women tried on dresses that were to be fitted. She marveled at Kathleen's beauty and figure, particularly after having three children. And she was such a kind person . . . really, a thoughtful, caring woman. Eula didn't care much for Sophie. She felt that she was crass and flamboyant. She often thought what an odd combination the two woman made. Kathleen—dark and gentle, Sophie—blond and bold. Still, they seemed to be fast friends and got along famously.

"I don't know," complained Sophie. "I don't think the color is flattering to me." Sophie, who had never completely recovered her health since the birth of Starlyn, was pale. The apple green cloth reflected uneasily against her skin.

"I agree with you, Sophie," said Kathleen. "I think something in a deeper color. Perhaps the rose taffeta would be more flattering to your complexion."

Sophie frowned and gazed at her reflection in the mirror. "I do look pallid, don't I?" She pinched her cheeks and glanced uneasily at Kathleen. "I suppose you've guessed the reason for it?"

Kathleen's eyes darkened with concern. "You're pregnant again, aren't you, Sophie?" she said in a hushed voice.

"Yes."

"The doctor advised you . . ."

"I know what he advised, Kathleen. But Rory and I want another child so badly. And really, despite all my complaints, you know how delighted I am with Starlyn."

"She's an angel," Kathleen agreed. "I'm only envious of you having such a lovely little girl."

"I daresay she'll break hearts someday," Sophie smiled. "Did I tell you, she put together her first sentence?"

"Not really!"

"Yes. Rory's having a fit. He expected her to say

something like 'I love daddy so much!' but instead she . . ." Sophie began laughing. "Oh, I know it's silly, but she began singing 'Heaven Help the Working Girl' and strutting around the room like a real little performer." Kathleen looked perplexed. "It's a song I used to do in my act. 'Heaven Help the Working Girl and the Working Girl Helps Herself.'"

Kathleen giggled. "That's wonderful."

"She hasn't gotten through the full title yet, but when she does I'll start teaching her the other lyrics."

Kathleen touched Sophie's hand. "Oh, I am happy for you, Sophie. I didn't mean to sound like I was judging you. But we all are concerned, you know."

"I know," replied Sophie. "I don't believe Rory's told Liam yet. He didn't want to worry him."

"Poor Liam. He worries about all of us, doesn't he?"

"I never thought we'd become friends. I don't think he still quite approves of me but . . ."

"That's all part of Liam's personality," reflected Kathleen. "He doesn't entirely approve of me either. He's always muttering about that 'independent woman he married.'"

"Dear Liam," said Sophie. "We're all products of our own fantasies, I think. Only Liam sees each of us as we really are." She glanced at her reflection in the mirror once more. "I think I will try the rose."

While Sophie was changing dresses, Kathleen chatted with Eula. "I'm going to need new suits of clothing for the boys, Eula. Something very durable. Goodness, how they wear out their clothes."

"How are the little darlin's?" asked the dressmaker who was most taken by Kevin, Brian and Sean.

"Into everything, I'm afraid. Sean's just about managing to walk, which means that I or Pink Jade must keep a constant vigil."

"It must be wonderful," remarked Eula wistfully. "A house full of children. And, of course, there's Pink Jade's little girl."

"Mai Mai. She's a beauty! Oh, she's charmed Kevin, all right. They've already decided they're going to be married when they grow up."

Eula frowned and said quickly. "Oh, I think it's wonderful, Miss Kat, how you don't seem to have any prejudice about anyone or anything."

Kathleen was somewhat taken aback. "How could I?" she replied swiftly. "Han Sung and Pink Jade are part of our family. Sometimes I feel that Mai Mai is my very own."

"And I'm sure Pink Jade feels the same about your boys," said Eula, hoping to placate the riled Kathleen.

To Eula's relief Sophie emerged from the dressing room wearing the rose taffeta gown. "I don't know," Sophie muttered. "It's tight around the waist now and in a few months it'll only have to be let out."

"The color is terribly flattering to you, Sophie," Kathleen ventured.

"I suppose I ought to get it. Rory enjoys it when I spend his money. I need something to wear to your tea party and it'll mean one less thing Betzy has to make for me. God knows, she has her hands full with Starlyn."

"Betzy's a wonder," chimed Kathleen. "I don't know how you'd get along without her."

"I don't know either, Kat. I'm not much at running a house. My cooking is enough to gag a horse and dust makes me sneeze." She whirled around in the dress. "Don't you think it needs a little . . . something? Perhaps some lace, or beads!"

Eula blanched and Kathleen quickly came to the dressmaker's aid. "Oh, I don't think so, Sophie," she said smoothly. "It might destroy the nice line of the gown."

Sophie scowled. "Well, maybe I'll wear my pink boa just to make it a little *tres chic.*" Eula looked like she was about to faint. "I'll take it, Mrs. McVey. Do you want to do the fitting now? I'll need it by next week."

"That would be fine, Mrs. Fitzgerald."

Sophie turned to Kathleen. "Aren't you going to get a new dress for your own party, Kathleen?"

"Oh, I don't think so. I thought I just might make over my lavender bombazine."

"The wife of the richest man in town!" grinned Sophie. "And she's making over dresses?"

"Well, I want to keep him that way, don't I?" laughed Kathleen.

After the fitting, both women, bundled in beaver coats, climbed into Kathleen's cabriolet. Kathleen headed the horse back toward Skid Road and Sophie's home. Passersby nodded or called out greetings. It was obvious that Kathleen was the better liked of the two. Sophie didn't care. She was interested only in being accepted by those she loved, and that included her own family and the O'Sullivan household.

"I understand," began Kathleen, "that Mr. Malone is planning to initiate his theater opening with an opera."

Sophie made a face. "You mean one of those long things they sing and everybody dies?"

"Yes," Kathleen blithely continued. "He was telling me that he had been in contact with the San Francisco Opera Company and they're considering sending up 'La Traviata'?"

"What's that all about?" asked Sophie with feigned interest.

Kathleen turned down Skid Road. "It's about a courtesan dying of consumption."

"Well, I don't want to see that," grunted Sophie. "I like happy things. Did I ever sing you that song Luke taught me?"

"Luke, your—ah—first lover?"

"Yes."

"I don't believe you did."

Sophie, uninhibited as always, began singing in a vibrant voice, "I'm just a homegrown rose, grown, oh so tired, of my pose . . ."

By the time they reached the ornate house on Skid Road, Kathleen and Sophie collapsed in a fit of giggles.

"That's marvelous!" cried Kathleen. "You must teach that one to Starlyn when she gets a bit older."

"Rory would kill me," laughed Sophie. "He hasn't given up on making me respectable."

"Oh, I think Rory loves you exactly as you are, Sophie. And so do I. Don't ever change."

Sophie was touched, for Kathleen was the only person in Seattle whose opinion really counted with her. "Won't you come in and warm yourself with a cup of tea, Kat? I'll add a little dollop of something to ward off the chill."

"I don't think I will today. Thank you, Sophie. I'm anxious to get back to the Great House." She bit down on her lower lip. "I always feel so self-conscious calling it that. But it's habit. Brian still has a cold and sometimes he won't let Pink Jade give him his medicine. He waits for me."

"Then you best get back. We'll be seeing each other Saturday for supper."

"Till then. And my best to Rory."

Betzy met Sophie at the door and helped her with her packages. "Did yo' an' Miz Kat have a nice time, Miz Sophie?"

"*Extraordinaire!* Where's Starlyn? Is she up from her nap?"

"She up, all right, an' prancin' around like a trooper," Betzy chuckled.

Hearing her mother's voice, Starlyn bounced into the foyer. She was nearly three and an incredibly beautiful child. Her hair was even lighter than Sophie's and shimmered like incandescent moonbeams. Her eyes were also her mother's—huge and light green like the juice of fresh lime.

Starlyn curtsied extravagantly as Sophie had taught her to do and asked, "Where's Aunt Kat? I thought you were going to bring Aunt Kat?"

"She had to hurry back, Starlyn," said Sophie

kneeling in front of her little girl. "Brian's got a bad cold and she wants to take care of him."

"Brian's always got a bad cold," Starlyn snipped.

Sophie kissed Starlyn on the tip of her pert nose. "You mustn't be rude, darling." It was then Sophie noticed that Starlyn was wearing lip rouge. "Have you been into my makeup again?"

"Just a little, Mama."

"My goodness, you've got it all over your chin. Come, let's go upstairs. If you're going to paint your lips, then you let Mama show you how to do it properly."

Sophie took her daughter's hand and the two of them hurried up the stairs to experiment with cosmetics.

Betzy, beaming, watched them go. "Dat Miz Sophie sho' loves her baby." Then Betzy's face clouded with worry. Without being told, she knew Sophie was pregnant again.

As Sophie's delivery neared, everybody in the respective households held their breaths. The baby was due in late August. Rory had summoned a doctor from San Francisco. A prim man in his late thirties, Quentin Derringer was considered the finest doctor in San Francisco. His stay at the sound was costing Rory nearly three hundred dollars a week. Sophie still suffered frequent spells of illness and although her stomach was swollen to full capacity, she had lost more than twelve pounds. Hannah McCormack was also a frequent visitor to the Fitzpatrick household, and she would be there to assist Dr. Derringer when the time came. Hannah fretted over Sophie's frail constitution and appearance.

The sound had been bereft of rain for more than two months, and a fierce hot spell plagued the people of Seattle. The nights were uncomfortably sticky. Sophie's sleep was interrupted by feverish perspiration, and often she would have to change her nightgown four or five times during the night.

Rory felt guilty, for he knew Sophie was having the

)aby because he so desperately wanted a son. During
he terrible nights he stayed up bathing her brow with
lamp cloths and changing her nightgowns.

On the night of August 23, Rory was awakened by
he sound of his wife's ragged breathing. "Sophie,
Sophie darlin', what's the matter?"

"I can't seem to catch a breath of fresh air," she
gasped. "The air in here seems so stale. Are the
windows open?"

"Yes, darlin', they're open all the way. Why don't
you let me move the bed closer to the windows."

"Oh, I don't want to do that. We might disturb
Starlyn."

"Nothing disturbs that child," smiled Rory. "Here.
You just stay still and I'll pull your side of the bed closer
o the window." Rory, naked, climbed out of bed and
began to pull the four-poster across the floor. The
wooden posts made a dull sound as it slid easily across
he expensive but garish carpet. "There, is that bet-
er?"

"Yes," Sophie lied. "Much better."

"Would you like a glass of water?" asked Rory going
o the sideboard.

"Please. And let me put a little bit of whiskey in it,
Rory. It might help me sleep."

"The baby's going to be a drunk," he chided her.

"Dr. Derringer said it was quite all right," replied
Sophie.

Rory made the drink and brought it back to his wife.
"Perhaps we ought to have him take a look at you."

"Oh, no. Don't wake him up."

"Why not? Let him earn his money. God knows he's
costing us a lot."

"I'm sorry," Sophie pouted.

"Oh, no, no, no," said Rory quickly. "That doesn't
matter. You know it doesn't."

"I know," said Sophie sipping the drink. "You're a
far more generous man than any I've ever known."

"Why shouldn't I be?" replied Rory snuggling next

to his wife. "You've given me everything I ever wanted."

"Have I, darlin'? I'm hoping to be giving you a son."

Rory frowned. "Sophie, if I'd known it was going to be this difficult for you I wish I'd never had—We won't have any more," he promised fervently. "We'll give up having sex if we have to."

Sophie grinned. "Now that, my dear, would be the end of you."

"The end of *me?*"

"I don't mind admitting that I enjoy you, too. But I suppose that's a sin to say. Father O'Reilly would be most upset with me."

"Father O'Reilly!" Rory snorted. "He's a prude!"

"He's nothing compared to Dr. Derringer," whispered Sophie. "You should have seen his reaction when Betzy told him he was staying in the former room of a prostitute. I actually thought the man was going to have a conniption."

Rory ran his hands tenderly over his wife's stomach. "Has it kicked yet?"

"No, he's a quiet one, all right. Mercy, Starlyn practically danced."

Rory bent to kiss his wife's bare stomach. "I don't want to lose you, Sophie."

She ran her fingers through his mass of auburn hair. "That's silly talk, Rory. You're not going to lose me—ever."

Thunder rolled across the sound, bringing the blessed promise of rain. The mere hint of it lifted everyone's spirits. But the booming thunder frightened Sophie. She had had a particularly bad night.

"I declare," she told Betzy. "If I weren't supposed to be a lady, I'd strip myself naked and when it starts to rain just run up and down the street."

Betzy chuckled. "Dat would give dem widows somethin' to stare at. Dat fo' sho'."

The high temperature and low humidity had an

ominous and cumulative effect on the forests, sucking gallons of moisture out of the trees and the ground, leaving the forest floor dry and ready to burn. Heat lightning, vibrant and fierce, rended the darkened sky with jagged forked tongues. It struck a fir high on the mountain top. The tree ignited immediately.

The flames were fanned by a merciless wind that swept across mountains to the Pacific, starting a dozen more fires. Many fires spread through the treetops like red waves of breaking surf. The dry timber burned rapidly, as great arcs of light became jagged scythes of flame and ate into the wilderness. Billows of smoke rose and merged with the clouds leaving red and white tongues of fire racing across roads, wiping up streams and drinking up ponds. Roaring like tornadoes they marched forward, scorching everything in their paths. The woodland animals raced fanatically to clearings and lakes.

Liam and Rory organized loggers, farmers and shopkeepers to fight the flames. At Liam's suggestion they used explosives and blasted the deep ravine between the fire and Seattle in an effort to keep the blaze from reaching the settlement.

Sophie, crazed with fear, wandered through the house, clutching her stomach and crying in pain. Her fright was so great that she didn't realize her labor pains had begun. Dr. Derringer and Betzy managed to get her into bed. Sophie, crying with terror, buried her face in the pillows and tried to blot out the terrible red glow beyond.

The day became as dark as midnight as blankets of smoke blotted out the sun. Betzy brought her mistress a handkerchief soaked in cologne to help assuage the terrible odor of the burning vegetation. Betzy quickly moved about the room lighting kerosene lights to ward off the darkness of the day. She was thankful that Starlyn was staying at the O'Sullivan house.

The winds drove the fire away from Seattle, guiding it toward the mills at Port Gamble. Liam and Rory, anxious to save their lumber as well as the mills, oversaw construction on a deep trench, which separated the mills and the stacks of cut lumber from the encroaching flames. They worked alongside their men throughout the day and into the terrible red night trying to halt the giant wall of fire. But the fire was not stayed. Loggers had to abandon camp, farmers left their clearings and shopkeepers began emptying cash drawers.

By dawn half an inch of ash covered Seattle. The smoke grew thicker and the air hotter. Then suddenly the full force of the racing fire came down with a deafening whoosh. A stream of flame greedily fed itself and made its way toward Skid Road.

Blackened ashes like swarms of mosquitoes riddled the air. Sophie broke into terrible fits of coughing, adding to her already dangerous state. Dr. Derringer was worried. He feared that Sophie's condition was going to affect the child.

Hannah McCormack, cut off by flames, was unable to reach Sophie's house. Reluctantly she turned her mule-drawn wagon around, her lips rapidly moving in prayer for her dear friend.

Sophie, maddened with fear, had to be strapped into bed to keep from injuring herself. Betzy cried tears of heartbreak as she laced Sophie's pathetically thin ankles and wrists to the bedposts. Dr. Derringer gave her a dollop of laudanum, which helped quiet her. Betzy and the doctor attempted to keep the air as pure as possible by covering the windows in Sophie's bedroom with blankets and continually dousing them with water.

The baby began to arrive about midafternoon of the second day of the fire. Sophie, relaxed by the drug, bore it easily. Betzy started to cry with glee when she saw that it was a boy child, but something was wrong. The baby wasn't breathing. The doctor quickly severed the umbilical cord, and after tying the knot, frantically began working on the child. He laid it down on the dresser and rhythmically pressed its tiny chest with his fingertips, but to no avail.

He looked up at Betzy, remorse coloring his voice, and shook his head. "The baby is stillborn, Betzy. There's nothing that can be done."

Then they turned their attentions back to Sophie. She was hemorrhaging badly. Every device known to the young doctor was employed to stop the blood. But the flow steadily continued. He even allowed Betzy to employ cobwebs, but this time they did not stay the bleeding.

Sophie knew that she was going to die. She felt like she was rapidly being emptied of her life-giving fluid.

"Betzy," she asked weakly. "Do you think you could get through to the Great House?" Betzy, her eyes brimming with tears, nodded. "I've got to see Miss Kat before I die."

"Yo' wants me to fetch de priest?" Betzy asked in a broken voice.

Sophie's lips slowly formed her words. "No, not the priest, but Miss Kat, *please*. You must get Miss Kat. There's something I have to say to her."

"I brings her, Miz Sophie." said Betzy getting to her feet.

The men fighting the fire succeeded in keeping it from the mills, but word came that the shifting winds had carried the flames to the edge of Seattle. The men climbed into long boats and frantically began rowing across the red waters of the sound.

Kathleen held onto Sophie's hand and, tears streaming down her face, listened to the dying woman's confession.

Sophie held onto Kathleen's hand tightly. And when she was sure that the doctor and Betzy had left the room, she confessed her "sin" to her dear friend. She had always been in love with Liam. "But know this, Kat. I have learned to love Rory in my own way and we have had a good life together. I'm sorry to disappoint him. I'm afraid he'll never have the son he so wanted."

"Sophie, don't!" Kathleen cried. "You're not going to die, *you can't!* You simply can't!"

Sophie smiled weakly. "I can and I am. But I feel at peace with myself now. Thank you for coming, Kat. You've always been a comfort to me."

Sophie loosened her grip on Kathleen's hand and her fingers went limp. Her eyes fluttered closed and she uttered one last rasping breath.

"Sophie!" screamed Kathleen. "Oh, Sophie. Don't leave us!"

The doctor and Betzy rushed into the room. Kathleen looked up. "Sophie's not dead," she said in a flat, hollow voice. "She can't be."

The doctor listened for Sophie's heartbeat. He shook his head. Betzy fell to the floor and began wailing.

"Oh, my God in heaven," groaned Kathleen. "How do we tell Rory? *How?*

Betzy looked up sharply. "I gots to tell him, Miz Kat. I brung Miz Sophie into dis world. It my 'sponsibility. I gots to tell him."

Several hours later Rory reached his home. Betzy was waiting for him. He was covered with soot and was nearly as black as she. She took him by the shoulders and looked him squarely in the face. "Dey both dead, Mister Rory. Sophie an' yo' little baby boy." Rory's knees gave way and Betzy grabbed him around the waist. She pulled him to the stairs and sat holding him, rocking him back and forth like a child while he howled out his agony.

Following five days of inferno, the wind shifted and clouds rolled in bringing rain. The fires were driven back upon themselves, and one after the other they smothered. It was estimated that over fifty million board feet of timber had been burned. The human toll was put at thirty-five deaths, but nobody knew for sure how many men, women and children had died. During that dark time their ashes mingled with those of the cremated trees.

Rory was inconsolable. He was convinced Sophie's death was his fault. His grief changed him. He was no longer the boisterous, rowdy young man with the easy laugh. He kept to himself and brooded, leaving the running of the mill to Liam and the rearing of Starlyn to Kathleen. Try as they might, there was nothing the concerned couple could do to bring Rory out of his misery.

The camps were slowly rebuilt and millions of lumber feet were salvaged with great difficulty. As the great timber hardened, it resisted saws and axes as if it were petrified wood. The people who had fled the sound returned, and once again the mountainsides echoed with the shriek of the mill saws.

One evening late in October, Rory half drunk and mad with despair, wandered up into the mountains and encountered a newly built flume. Remembering a happier day when he had shown off, he climbed upon the trestle and, releasing the water and the logs, he took one last ride. When he reached the bottom of the run—a manmade lake—he was crushed by the churning logs. Rory's misery was at an end, and he joined his beloved Sophie in peace at last.

Kathleen, Betzy and Pink Jade became very close friends. They reveled in the delight of watching the children grow up in an atmosphere of love and wealth. Kevin, a strapping and headstrong young man, emulated his father and worked at the mill. He fell in love with Mai Mai. The girl had grown into a rare beauty and returned his love. The family defied convention, and the young couple was married by Father O'Reilly in the Catholic church. Brian fulfilled his promise of having been born on St. Valentine's Day. A quiet and serious youth, he took the world's troubles to heart. When he was of age, he traveled to a seminary in New Orleans to become a priest.

The fates of Sean and Starlyn were understood by anyone who knew and loved them. They were in love and always had been. Starlyn was now a lovely young woman whose coloring and countenance strongly resembled Sophie. Sean, dark and brooding, was the very image of Liam. They became bethrothed to one another, and waited until Brian was ordained so that he could return and perform the marriage ceremony.

Epilogue

In the spring of 1870, Sean and Starlyn were married at an outdoor ceremony in a cathedral of magnificent trees beneath the canopy of clouds. As Brian intoned the sacred words that would join them together as man and wife, a vagrant breeze swept through the tree tops and caused the leaves to shake and whisper. Kathleen looked up and listened. It seemed to her that the trees were telling the story of their interwoven lives, passing it on from one to another until the tale became an eternal narrative. She tilted her head to one side and eavesdropped. Had she been able to understand the language of the trees, she would have heard bits and pieces of dialogue—incomplete threads of the tapestry that was their lives. That tapestry was still being woven, the motif yet imcomplete.

"Here's a cross I made, Liam. I want you to have it to remember me by."

"Sophie Parmalee. It sounds like something sweet to spread on bread and eat."

"*Betzy, bedamned if yo' gonna take any mo' bad treatment!*"

"*You needn't sleep on the bar, Luke. You can sleep in my room.*"

"*They're the very pillars of heaven themselves!*"

"*My mother was French, you know.*"

"*Kathleen, would you consider becoming my wife? I will do everything in my power to keep you safe and make you happy.*"

"*Mama, I'm going to see the elephant!*"

"*But I can love him, Father. I know I can. And I'll make him a good wife, I swear I will!*"

"*And every once in a while when the barroom's quiet, and when you think of it, sing my song for me, and I promise you, wherever I am I'll hear you singing it.*"

"*I don't want to spend the night alone.*"

"*Neither do I.*"

Kathleen forced her attentions back to the wedding ceremony. Brian pronounced Sean and Starlyn man and wife. Kathleen was surprised to find that she had been crying. But her tears were tears of happiness. They were all joined together now . . . for eternity.

The pattern was complete.